Rachael Stewart adore[s] ... from heartwarmingly ro... She's been writing since ... paper—as the stacks of scrawled-on pages in her loft will attest to. A Welsh lass at heart, she now lives in Yorkshire, with her very own hero and three awesome kids—and if she's not tapping out a story, she's wrapped up in one or enjoying the great outdoors. Reach her on Facebook, X @rach_b52, or at rachaelstewartauthor.com.

After ten years as a television camerawoman, **Ella Hayes** started her own photography business so that she could work around the demands of her young family. As an award-winning wedding photographer, she's documented hundreds of love stories in beautiful locations, both at home and abroad. She lives in central Scotland with her husband and two grown-up sons. She loves reading, travelling with her camera, running and great coffee.

WHAT HAPPENS AT THE BEACH…

RACHAEL STEWART

DRIVING HER IMPOSSIBLE BILLIONAIRE

ELLA HAYES

MILLS & BOON

First published in Great Britain 2025
by Mills & Boon, an imprint of HarperCollins*Publishers* Ltd,
1 London Bridge Street, London, SE1 9GF

www.harpercollins.co.uk

HarperCollins*Publishers*, Macken House, 39/40 Mayor Street Upper, Dublin 1, D01 C9W8, Ireland

What Happens at the Beach… © 2025 Rachael Stewart

Driving Her Impossible Billionaire © 2025 Ella Hayes

ISBN: 978-0-263-39672-0

02/25

WHAT HAPPENS AT THE BEACH…

RACHAEL STEWART

MILLS & BOON

For Michelle Douglas, Amy Andrews
and Clare Connelly.

Thank you for providing a 24/7 Aussie Q&A hotline. :-)

Love ya, ladies!

xxx

CHAPTER ONE

FAE THOMPSON DROPPED her solitary bag on the footpath and stared up and up and up at the three-storey building before her.

No. Freaking. Way.

She'd known Sasha was rich. Her stepsister, her stepfather, her entire stepfamily were sickeningly, toe-curlingly, 'roll around in bed and get banknotes stuck where the sun don't shine' kind of rich, but this…

She plucked off her shades and immediately shoved them back on again. Gave a wince. Was it possible even the sun in Sydney outperformed the sun in Melbourne?

And now she was just being plain ridiculous. But while the ocean rolled with its ostentatious roar against the impressive rocks behind her, the looming structure ahead with its white walls and abundance of sea green glass had officially become offensive to her eyeballs. Never mind her sensitized ego, which had taken something of a reinvigorated poking since Sasha's Big White Wedding a week ago.

And yes, the day needed capitalizing.

Much like Sasha's Big White Bondi Beach House before her.

Bitter, much?

No, Fae wasn't. Not really.

Sasha deserved every bit of the happiness she had found in her BFF turned wife. Gabriella, aka Gigi. A stunning supermodel who had finally seen the light, or rather the love that had been right in front of her all along.

To know that her uberconfident stepsister had been in love with her best friend since forever and had been too scared to admit her feelings... To have sat back and watched Gigi repeatedly fall in and out of love with others and been there to pick up the pieces, time and time again... All the while, loving her unconditionally and wholeheartedly and unrequitedly.

Fae felt the goofy smile on her lips and swiftly batted it away.

Love. Who'd go there? Not Fae, that was for sure. All those tortured and wasted years pining for another... Now she shuddered, any remnants of the smile thankfully dislodged.

But her stepsister was in love. Gigi was in love. Her mother and her stepfather were *still* in love. After four years of marriage and six years together. And Fae had given *them* a year tops. What was the world coming to?

And now Fae was here. Her own life unrecognizable. Her home and livelihood back in Brunswick East reduced to rubble as rich-ass developers rolled in and tore down the bar she'd worked in with Mum since she was fifteen years old. Her home above it too!

Not that Mum cared; she'd moved on—six years ago to be exact. It was Fae who hadn't. Fae who, at twenty-four years of age, didn't know what to do with her life. What she wanted out of it. Where to live. What to be.

For the last couple of years, she'd filled her spare time protesting the redevelopment project. And when that had become futile, she'd put her efforts into ensuring those around her had been taken care of. Her regulars at the bar as well as her more vulnerable neighbours in need of a new home that they could still afford to rent. Because Brunny East was on the up and so were the rents, pushing out the old tenants and bringing in the new. Ones with bigger purses, flashier purses.

People like the Sashas of the world who could afford it. No thought given to those who had lived there all their lives and their ancestors before them.

As for the bar…it hadn't just been a place to enjoy a drink; it had been a place of respite for her regulars. She'd been there for them. A smile when they needed it. An ear when they wanted to talk. Quiet company when they didn't.

With it gone, where would they go? Were they as adrift as she suddenly felt?

'Can I help you?'

She started, blinking this way and that on the empty foot-path. 'Hello?'

'You've been stood there for all of five minutes,' the dis-embodied voice continued, Fae's hackles rising with every plummy beat. British. Pompous. Male. Joy of joys. She'd had her fill of those of late. 'I'm assuming you're lost and in need of assistance.'

She spied a camera protruding from the neighbouring prop-erty, its red light winking at her, and cocked a brow right at it. 'Or that I'm casing the joint?'

Because she knew exactly how she must look to someone of his breeding. She didn't need to *see* him to know his kind. The kind that were pushing her out of her own neighbour-hood back home. The kind that lived in houses like this. Right alongside Sasha. He was Sasha's kind…though to be fair, his property was quite different.

No less ostentatious but less blinding. A mix of wood and stone, softened with swaying palm fronds that peeked from a terrace overhead… She liked those, she begrudgingly ad-mitted.

His low rumble brought her appreciation up short. Was he *laughing* at her?

'That too,' he admitted.

Flicking her choppy bob back, she jutted her chin out. 'I'm fine as it happens.'

She dipped to grab her bag. It was time to move and make good on her promise to Sasha—and get out of *his* eyeline.

She was here to house-sit for six weeks while Sasha yachted it around the Caribbean on her honeymoon, *not* get into a showdown with the hoity-toity neighbours on day one.

'If you're sure,' came that low, self-assured English drawl.

'I'm always sure.'

Correction. She'd always been sure right up until the time Mum got hitched and then all her sureness flew out the window with her Mum's 'I do'. And how was that for weakness?

Hitching her life plan to her mother's and the four walls they lived in without even realizing it?

Kaboom!

'Suit yourself.'

'Too right I will,' she murmured under her breath, striding forth, head held high, even if her pride wasn't.

Because hell, she knew she'd played herself for a fool the last few years. But she was making amends. She was here to get her life back on track.

If only she could find the keys...and no, that wasn't some fancy way of referring to the keys for getting on the right track. Though it might as well have been. She really did mean the physical keys to the physical joint. Because she was getting hotter and redder and she swore he was still watching.

They had to be here somewhere... What was it with rich people and having to make everything so bloody perfect it couldn't—

Ah, there! A discreet doorbell, complete with camera and key safe, was tucked into the side wall of the double ground-floor garage.

Tugging her phone from her pocket, she dialled her step-sister as agreed.

'Fae-Fae!'

As with nails down a chalkboard, Fae's insides curled with her outsides—toes, fingers, even her tongue curled into the roof of her mouth. One day she'd get used to her stepsister's pet repetition of her name. One day. *Maybe.*

She forced a smile through gritted teeth. She wouldn't be surprised if Sasha was watching her through the camera right now. Watching her, assessing her, finding her lacking...

Not fair, Fae. Sasha has been nothing but adorable *to you!*

Perhaps the adorable bit was the problem.

Fae wasn't used to people treating her adorably and being genuine about it.

The bigger the purse, the greater the insincerity too.

And they didn't come much bigger than Sasha's.

'Hey Sash.'

'You made it then?'

'Yes, I've made it.'

Approximately fourteen hours and very little sleep later, not that she would admit to being grouchy because of it. She had after all refused to fly to Sydney, turning down her step-father's offer of the private jet to take the overnight bus, so it was her own fault her body felt folded in two still.

But then, she'd never flown anywhere, and she didn't plan to start now. She preferred to keep her two feet firmly on the ground, thank you very much.

'You get that, Fae-Fae?'

'Get what?'

'I didn't think so.'

Her stepsister's voice tinkled with loved-up cheer. Its default setting for the past year or so. Ever since Gigi had said, 'I love you too'.

'I swear you're only ever half with us...'

Fae bit back the retort *Says you!* and went with 'You were saying?'

'The code...'

This time Fae focused and breathed a sigh of relief when the thing slid open to unveil a key and what looked like an alarm fob. She took them out and closed it up again.

'I had a grocery shop delivered this morning with the things you listed...' Had the tinkle taken on a ring of distaste now? Fae bit back a grin. 'And Freya, the local dog walker, is returning Precious this evening, in time for her evening walk. So she'll be able to take both you and Precious down to the local park, show you around. It's timeshared so you can only use it—'

Fae huffed out a laugh. 'A dog sitter for the dog sitter? Really, Sash, you trust me *that* much?'

Because this was the real reason Sasha had asked her to travel almost a thousand kilometres north. It wasn't to make sure her precious abode was okay; it was to make sure her precious Precious was.

No pressure, Fae.

'It's not a question of trust, but as you said yourself, you've never owned a dog before and Precious is—'

'Precious, I know.'

She managed to suppress an eye roll as she headed for the house—not over her stepsister's love for her dog, but her lack of faith. Because she absolutely respected Sasha's love for her hound. She did... She just didn't quite get the obsessive worry. She was a dog. How hard could it be? Really?

The house, on the other hand...

'Tell me, is there a special way to open the gate or is it— Ah, never mind, I've worked it out.'

She spied an access reader to the right of the gate that came off the garage wall, the shape of which matched the key fob in her hand. She swiped it against the panel and hey presto, the gate popped ajar.

'You do remember you sent me a *looong* email with the dos

and the don'ts,' she said as she pushed on through the gate, making sure it closed behind her. 'Along with where I can take Precious and when, complete with map.'

'Yes, but—'

'A list of where to shop, where to eat, where to grab the best takeaway coffee.'

'Yes, but—'

'And you know you're supposed to be on your honeymoon forgetting about your life here for the time being...'

Though how anyone could forget about a place like this was beyond Fae's imagination. She walked up the steps that led to the first-floor terrace, her mouth hanging open as she drank it all in. From the architectural masterpiece that was Sasha's home to nature's paradise that stretched out before it. Nothing to hinder the incredible view of the ocean that had to be worth a fair sum alone...

'It's why you asked me to come, is it not?'

She was barely aware of asking the question as she reached the last step, her eyes bugging out over the white stone platform adorned with designer sun beds, tables, chairs, fancy topiary bushes... Jeez, the 'garden' was bigger than her entire apartment back in Brunny!

'Yes, you're right.'

'So will you trust me to do as you asked?'

She could imagine her stepsister's smooth complexion wrinkling up with worry. Not wanting to poke the bear but poking it all the same as she hesitated. Their sisterly bond still too fresh to test with the truth.

'I do trust you, Fae,' she said carefully. 'It's not that I don't.'

So, she wasn't on Fae-Fae terms now...*interesting*.

'But Precious has been my everything for the last five years. If anything were to happen to her... Well, she's my child really. I should have brought her with me, but—'

'But nothing!' Fae scratched away the sudden prickle in

her neck. 'Seriously, Sash, it's your honeymoon! Time for just the two of you. The *two* of *you*. Get it?'

Her mother certainly hadn't wanted to drag Fae along on *her* honeymoon travelling the world when she'd headed off four years ago. Not that Fae would have gone. Not in million years. But still...

'Besides, the last thing Precious is going to want to do is be cooped up on a yacht for over a month.'

Now she was just making stuff up because she had no clue what a fancy poodle would or wouldn't like to do, but it didn't *sound* like the sort of thing a dog would enjoy—did it?

'And you can't blame Gigi for wanting you to herself, not after the year you two have had to get to this point. You deserve it, Sash, you both do, so please, let me take care of Precious and your home, and you take care of your wife.'

'My...my wife...' She could hear the smile in her stepsister's voice once more, and this time she was glad of it. 'It still feels surreal, I have to pinch myself every morning—Ow! Gigi!'

'Did she just pinch some sense into you?'

There was a rustle down the line, a giggle, and was that a—*smooch*?

'Hey Fae, how are you?' came the other woman's distinctively Spanish lilt.

'Hey Gigi, I'm all good.' She smiled, realising she now had an ally. 'Or I would be if you can get Sash to chill the heck out. She might be in need of an intervention. Do you want to hang up and hide her phone somewhere?'

'Don't even think about it!'

'Too late, I am thinking, and I am all for freeing you from your technology, darling.'

'Gigi!'

'Fine, but if you still want to join me in that bath I just lovingly poured, you need to step away from the device.'

'Ladies!' Fae blurted, short of cutting the call herself. 'TMI!'

'Sorry, Fae,' Gigi cooed. 'I'm backing away…but you have five minutes, Sasha, darling. No more. No less. Bye, Fae.'

'See you, Gigi. And you'd best go too, Sash.' Thank heaven they weren't on a video call. Fae's cheeks were on fire. And it wasn't that she was a prude, but she didn't need to know what her stepsister and her new wife were about to get up to. She really didn't.

'I will. There's just one more thing…'

Fae hitched her bag higher on her shoulder and crossed the terrace on the hunt for the main door. At least this *was* obvious. The grand glass door screamed, *Main event this way…*

'Yes?'

'Some guy has just moved in next door and I don't know much about him but…'

'Which side?'

'Side?'

'To the left or the right if you're facing the house from the beach?'

She slotted the key into the lock and gave it a twist. It turned effortlessly—surprise, surprise. Nothing like the lock on her old flat, which took a special combination move and a hefty shove to budge. Oh, how she missed it though.

'The left.'

'You mean the Brit?'

'You've met him already?'

Fae paused, her ears pricking over Sasha's perturbed tone.

'*Met* isn't the word I would use—he saw me on the footpath and asked if I needed assistance.'

'Did he now? Well, I'd appreciate it if you gave him a wide berth. Or more specifically, that dog of his.'

'He has a dog?'

'A great big hound of a dog who pounced on my poor Precious like she was a piece of meat.'

Oh, dear. The horror in Sasha's voice was enough to make Fae grimace. As for avoiding a repeat of the encounter, that suited Fae just fine. She had no intention of going anywhere near the guy.

'We'll steer clear, don't you worry.'

'Thank you! I've put her schedule on the fridge, so it'll be easy for you to keep abreast of everything. Food. Timings. Walks. The works. But any problems, you call me, anytime, day or night.'

'No worries, Sash. You relax and— *Holy guacamole!*'

Fae froze just inside the entrance.

'What's wrong?'

Her bag fell to her feet with a thud. A cloud of dust lifting with it. *Her* dust. *Her* dirt. Never Sasha's. Because, my God, this place was pristine. Posh *and* pristine.

She wasn't sure why she was so stunned. She'd *seen* the outside so she should have *expected* the inside. And it *was* Sasha all over.

But expecting it and seeing it were two different things.

From the golden herringbone floor to the white walls, to the mix of glass, soft wood and duck-egg-blue accents, the place was a coastal dream. The glass to the front framed the terrace with its panoramic view of the ocean, the glass to the rear framed the pool—the *pool!* Way bigger than she'd imagined and surrounded by a garden with space to dine at one end and sunbathe at the other.

And above her, a central atrium style ceiling bathed the entire space in light.

'Fae? What's happened? Where are you?'

She rubbed her sweaty palm against her torn denim shorts, not daring to touch a thing for fear of spreading her muck further, or worse breaking something…which again was ridiculous. She was living here for six weeks. She could hardly keep her hands to herself.

'You didn't tell me your house belonged on *Grand Designs*, Sash.'

'Is that a compliment?'

'It's a "this place is something else" comment.'

And Fae had never felt more out of place.

Or she had, a long, long time ago…

'It's home.'

'Home. Right.'

Something Fae no longer knew much about.

'I hope you'll like it there.'

'Sure.'

'You will enjoy yourself, won't you? You can help yourself to anything. Use whichever of the spare bedrooms you're most comfortable in. But the one next to mine has the best view of the beach and since you'll probably find Precious sleeping in mine, it might help her settle to know that you're next door.'

'I'll bear that in mind.'

'And thanks, Fae-Fae, really truly. This means so much to me. And Gigi. And Precious. We love you.'

She gave a choked laugh. For a girl who'd grown up wishing for a family, for siblings, for a father to consider her worth knowing…now she found herself floundering in the face of it.

'No worries. Now go.' She pulled a face—*hardly warm and sisterly, Fae*—and with a meek smile Sasha couldn't even see, she added, 'Enjoy that bath.'

'I will, just…send me updates, okay.'

'So long as you promise not to obsess over them, and only because Precious is your baby.'

'Thanks, Fae.'

'And I'll guard her with my life—no big grey heffa will get within sniffing distance of her. Not on my watch!'

Her sister giggled, just as Fae had hoped, breaking the tension she had unwittingly put there with her inability to respond like any normal sister would. 'Speak soon.'

And then she hung up, clutching her phone to her chest that still felt too tight to breathe. She understood it. The tension. The awkwardness.

She didn't trust the affection. She couldn't count on it. Her father had taught her that from day dot. There were no guarantees when it came to love.

Don't demand it, don't expect it, don't *anything* it, and then you can't get hurt.

Period.

It wasn't in Rick Pennington's nature to be nosy.

In fact, it was in his nature to be the exact opposite.

If it wasn't his business to know, consider him well and truly out of it. He knew well enough what it was like to have people prying into the nitty-gritty of your life. Sharing it as gossip for a laugh or their own social advancement or a pretty penny with the press.

His childhood sweetheart—ex-fiancée, for his sins—had shared her own stories over the years, the odd tale cropping up even now a decade down the line.

Maybe he ought to take it as a compliment that Zara still thought him worthy of comment. Though any hope she harboured of a reconciliation had sailed the day she'd walked with the threat of bankruptcy hanging over him and his family.

A poor reputation she could handle, a lack of Louboutins not so much.

And he was done living his life under some kind of a microscope. Part of the reason he was glad he'd upped and left London to make a home for himself here, on the other side of the world, where the anonymity was as surprising as it was blissful.

He also had the beach on his doorstep. The sun, sea and

surf all at his disposal. Features his property agent had leaned into when closing the deal months ago. But the truth was he hadn't needed the hard sell. He'd been ready to sign on the dotted line long before she'd even spoken. Ready to leave London behind. It's grey skies, boardrooms, even the rolling hills of the Pennington country estate too.

Though he'd stuck it out for Christmas. More to keep Mum happy, but now he was here, had been for two months, and he was all about finding a new way of living...of laughing.

Because, to use his assistant's words, 'Lord Pennington does not laugh. Not ever.'

It was a simple statement made to a simple passing remark, and to this day Rick couldn't shake it. Because his assistant, Geoffrey, was right. At the age of thirty-one, he'd lost the ability to find the joy in anything. The excitement. The thrill.

Idly he stroked at the stubble along his jaw.

He wasn't missing his daily shave, or the regular trip to the barbers as he put less effort into looking so clean-cut. But he *did* miss the fire pumping through his veins. He couldn't remember the last time he'd felt anything close to a spark. There was the exhilarating hit of a workout in the gym or a hard run. The rush of a successful takeover bid. The unbridled joy he found when his charity that specialized in rare disease research made a groundbreaking discovery that could change lives, save lives even.

But the joy in the everyday, the ordinary...things that should make your mouth twitch up more than once on a regular basis...

With every social function, every date, every family engagement since his assistant had made their candid observation, it had become more and more obvious they were right.

Though seconds ago, when a certain pink-haired pixie had the gumption to outright suggest she was casing the joint next door... *Oh, yes*, something had definitely come alive inside. A sure sign he wasn't completely dead after all.

And though it hadn't been an all-out gut-rumbling laugh, it had been something.

Which was probably the reason she had him feeling all sorts of curious about her now.

That and the fact she looked about as out of place as he was... Two months in and he still felt like a guest within his own home. Like he'd soon be packing up and flying back out.

A nudge to his knee accompanied a low whine and he looked away from the security footage to take in his Great Dane's doleful look. 'Don't worry, Ralph, I'm not bailing. Not yet anyway.'

Those sad brown eyes blinked up at him, looking far too wise for almost a year on this earth, and he lowered his hand to scratch behind his dog's ear. That earned him another whine. He checked the clock. 'It can't be that time already?'

Though in Ralph's world, it seemed like every hour of the day demanded a whine of some sort. Each indicating something else on his very full rota of eat, sleep, walk, repeat... and he was doing his best to ensure Rick kept to the same.

Just as Rick's sister had hoped when she'd suggested he get a dog. Her answer to Geoffrey's comment when Rick had raised it over whisky one evening. He'd looked at her like she was mad. But then she'd calmly explained, it was something else to think about that wasn't work. Something that depended on him for food and exercise and couldn't be ignored.

'Unlike a woman,' she'd teased.

Because, of course, a man accused of lacking a sense of humour had to be a workaholic, and was therefore in need of something that would force him to find a life outside of work.

And she was right about one thing: it couldn't be a woman. He wasn't interested in a relationship. And flings served a purpose to a point. But he'd cleared up enough of his late father's messes to find them oddly disquieting, let alone satisfying or fun.

So a dog it was.

And his sister had been right to tell him to get Ralph. The Great Dane had brought him balance and many an unexpected benefit.

Had Ralph gifted him a new way of life though…?

'What do you reckon, Ralph? Is this living?'

Ralph lifted his head off his knee, where it had happily settled with his petting, and gave a 'Ruff!'

'I thought so. Come on then…' He got to his feet and Ralph eagerly followed suit. 'A run and then dinner.'

Though as he exited his gate, he found himself pondering Ms Pixie once more. Who was she? What was her connection to the sun-kissed blonde who owned the place? They certainly didn't *look* alike.

He'd only had the 'pleasure' of meeting his neighbour once. And yes, the encounter really did need quotation marks. Not that he could blame the statuesque blonde who had taken one look at Ralph eyeing up her poodle like one might their next meal and swiftly cut their conversation short. Informing him that she wouldn't be around for the next few weeks, that her sister was house-sitting and that she'd swing by on her return and, 'ta-ta', dialling up her passing jog into an all-out sprint.

He'd have to teach Ralph some table manners if he ever hoped to get acquainted with his new neighbours.

But then who was to say that people got to know their neighbours in this part of the world? What did he truly know of Australian living other than what he'd seen on the TV as a kid? What did people say about the Aussies—friendly, right? Always willing to throw another shrimp on the barbie…?

Though the blonde hadn't seemed the type. To barbecue or to welcome him in.

Then again, Ralph had seen to that.

As for Ms Pixie, who had disappeared inside the blonde's pad, she seemed more cool chip-on-her-shoulder than warm cheer…and was *she* the blonde's sister? Really? She looked nothing like her. Dressed nothing like her. As for *their* first impression…

'Maybe you can win her over better than my voice did, Ralph.'

CHAPTER TWO

'I CAN STICK around a bit. I don't have another job to go to this evening…'

The glossy brunette eyed Fae's clenched fist around the lead and Fae slackened her grip with a forced grin. 'I've got this. You can go, Mikaela.'

Because the last thing Fae wanted was to be babysat by a girl who looked all of fifteen. Though she had to be at least eighteen for Sasha to have entrusted Precious to her care for the last few days. And she didn't have a mucky scuff or a hair out of place…neither did Precious.

How was that even possible?

She frowned down at the dog whose slender snout was stuck so far north it reached as high as her waist.

Did this dog even poo?

'Well, if you're sure. Here's her treats and poo bags…'

And there was her answer. How lovely. She took them with a strained smile. Now that was *one* job she wasn't looking forward to. But snuggles on the sofa might be kind of nice. To have some company again…

'Let me at least walk you back to the house.'

Fae's gaze shot up, cheeks burning. Did Mikaela really think her *that* incapable?

The house was almost within sight, a mere kilometre back up the winding coastal path…she couldn't get lost and more importantly, she couldn't lose Precious. They were attached. Where Fae went, Precious went. Easy.

Though since Fae had been the one pulling a face at the poo bag dispenser—a fetching pink with its designer branding liberally on display—she couldn't blame Mikaela for continuing to fret.

'Perhaps you ought to attach that to the lead so you don't forget it, here like this...'

She manhandled the dispenser out of Fae's grasp and used the gold lobster clasp to hook it onto the matching pink lead that she'd hung around her neck earlier. Because apparently, *this* lead was for confined quarters, aka looking good in the city. The retractable lead that Precious was currently attached to was much better for the dog-friendly beaches, parks and open coastal paths—go figure.

'There. Better. You don't want to leave home without them, else you'll be fined.'

'Fined, right. Of course.'

Two leads. Poo bags. Treats.

What could possibly go wrong?

Precious chose that moment to raise a sardonic brow beneath her perfect white bouffant. A hairdo that would require daily brushing. All by yours truly.

'Dogs don't have brows, right?' Fae murmured, without breaking eye contact with the haughty pooch.

'Oh, they do!' Mikaela cooed, clasping her hands beneath her chin. 'Not like us humans, of course, but they reckon it's all because of our domestication of the species. It's just another wonder of evolution!'

'A wonder indeed,' Fae muttered, under no illusion that she was being assessed and found wanting, never mind communicated with.

And there she'd been worrying about the house and fitting into it...not the company pushing her out of it.

'Yeah.' Mikaela hunkered down in front of Precious, gaining the poodle's attention and a tail wag to boot. 'It's where dogs and wolves differ... *You* clever creatures have developed muscles in your inner eyebrows to communicate with us, haven't you, beautiful?'

Fae watched as she gave Precious a kiss to the tip of her nose—*not* something Fae was about to repeat in a hurry. Did she not *see* where those things went?

And then Mikaela was back on her feet, quizzical expression returning with her gaze. 'Are you *sure* I can't walk you back?'

'I have your number,' Fae was quick to assure her, *both* human brows raised to discourage further objection. *See, I can work them too, Precious.* 'I'll call if I—*we* need anything.'

'Day or night?'

'Absolutely.'

Over Fae's dead body was she going to ring. How hard could it be? Seriously.

She'd dealt with drunken strangers. Out-of-control hen parties. Over familiar men and women with hands travelling where they shouldn't. All in a night's work at the bar. She could cope with one high maintenance pooch almost half her size at the beach.

Though to be fair, Precious standing on her hind legs would come close to her height...with her impressive hair, probably outreach her too.

'Okay, then, I'll catch you later. Bye, Precious. Bye, Fae. Lovely to meet you!'

'And you.'

'And don't forget to stick to the off-leash hours at the park... the rest of the time.'

She gestured with her hand around her neck and Fae started—harsh!

She means 'collar and lead' not 'choke and hold', doofus!

'Got it.'

She saluted and with one last look of blatant hesitation, Mikaela jogged off into the sunset, glossy ponytail swinging, and Precious strode forward, determined to follow.

'Oh, no, you don't.' Fae tugged her back, correctly deploying the control button on the retractable lead—*Well, look at you go, a natural in the making.* 'It's home time for us.'

She started off in the other direction, happy to have done something right, only to find herself being jerked back by the unmovable four-legged mountain that was Precious.

'Come on, this way.' She gave a gentle tug on the lead but Precious was going nowhere. How could a dog with such skinny legs and tiny feet be so strong? Or should that be headstrong? *Surely* she didn't need to deploy treats already?

Though if it meant an easy life...

She opened the bag and was about to extract a 'tasty' morsel when suddenly Precious took flight, sprinting and barking and sending the treats spilling onto the footpath. Dogs came racing for a scrap, seagulls too, but Precious was off, Fae with her as she struggled to shorten the retractable lead and gain any traction in her thongs.

'No! No, no, you don't!' she hollered, trying to haul the pooch back. *'Precious! Sit! Stop! Heel!'*

They were causing a scene. *She* was causing a scene. She scraped her hair out of her eyes. Tried to right her sunnies that almost hit the deck. Wished she'd worn her running gear because at least *then* she'd look like she was supposed to be running. Instead her thongs were slapping the footpath machine gun style and drawing every eye in the vicinity along with a fair amount of sniggers too. And no wonder. She'd be laughing too!

Who was supposed to be walking who?

And then the view up ahead changed. Mikaela and her swinging ponytail were obscured by a half-naked bronzed god running towards her. A giant four-legged hound running with him, ears flapping, tongue out…

What *was* that? A grey version of Scooby-Doo? It was speeding up too! The attached bronzed god with it.

She'd never seen a man like him. Not in real life. And now she was running and gawping and the scene had shifted into slow-mo. His hair undulated with his stride. Dark and almost to his shoulder, with highlights from the sun or the salon— who knew, who cared, because *man*, he was half-naked!

A grey T was hooked into the waistband of his black shorts where he'd also secured the lead for his dog. Daring, but practical since it freed him to run.

And those arms, *that* torso, all those exposed muscles unhindered and rippling as he came towards her. Body slick, either by sea or sweat. Again, who knew—who cared! He was glorious. In all his laid-back, surfer-like glory.

And then his eyes met hers…at least she thought they had… He was wearing shades that hid his gaze, but she *sensed* his attention, the connection, the sizzle… Her heart joined the drum of her thongs and Precious gave a bark. *Hell.* Fae wanted to bark. *Woof* indeed.

Bronzed god frowned. Grey Scooby-Doo barked. The barks became a repeated yap back and forth and before Fae knew it, everything changed.

They were no longer running. Mikaela had been forgotten. Precious had applied the brakes and some kind of doggy tango was under way. Their leads became entwined and she was propelled forth by a hot furry body, into a hot bronzed body! Chest to chest! The leads wrapped around their legs and tightened as the dogs chased one another around and around in a frenzied yapping, sniffing, excited-to-get-acquainted fest—and, *really*, was there any way to get out of this with her dignity intact?

Sunglasses askew. Hair in eyes. One palm pressed to one

very slick pec. The other fisted around the lead so tight that her knuckles flashed white. She opened her mouth and inhaled summer. Sun and coconuts. How could he even *smell* delicious?

And none of this was helping. She went to speak but nothing would come. Probably because her breasts were pushed so far into her ribs it was impossible to make a sound.

Your breasts? You're kidding, right? Nothing to do with your wildly beating heart trying to climb up out of your throat now that you're squished against Adonis himself.

'I'm so sorry!' she blurted.

He lifted his sunglasses to unveil eyes so blue she was bedazzled anew and, *oh, my days*, never in her life had she used such a girly phrase as *bedazzled*. What was happening to her?

Bondi Beach had a *lot* to answer for. As did Precious.

'You know they have a button to stop the lead from extending quite so much.'

That *voice*...

Like an ice bucket, she was doused. Chilled to the bone as recognition coursed through her.

'It's you!' she declared, a very different kind of heat rushing to fill her cheeks as she struggled against the restraints, desperate to get away.

Though if she wasn't careful, she was going to land on her arse because her legs were well and truly locked against his. As was his arm around her waist.

He gave a lopsided grin that reignited a mutinous spark deep within her. *He is* not *charming, Fae. He* is *one of* them.

Not only that, he was Sasha's neighbour, which meant that grey hound... *Oh, God.* She shoved her glasses up as she glanced down at Scooby-Doo, now with its nose right up Precious's—

Crap!

'Precious!'

'I prefer the name Rick, but—'

'Can you get your dog out of my dog's butt?'

He blinked, brows raising as he followed her pointed stare.

'If I may be so bold, he's saying hello and returning the greeting yours delivered not seconds before when—'

'I don't care if it's tit for tat, can you just do it!'

Before my sister somehow learns of this and declares me a failure on the spot!

His eyes were back on her. She didn't need to look to know it. Could feel his burning blues penetrating her wild mop and she wasn't *going* to look because she also knew her cheeks were flaming, her freckles ablaze and damn if her tiny button nose would be too!

'Very well. Ralph. Sit.'

The dog made a noise akin to a grumble but promptly plonked his butt to the concrete.

'Happy?'

No, she was *not* happy. Because she looked like a prize idiot. And they were still pressed together like a strung-up duo of meat for roasting. Not that she needed to see an oven with the heat she was giving off.

And it was all her fault for not taking control of Precious sooner.

So perhaps you ought to quit giving him the evils and show a little gratitude...

So much for Ralph's first impression going down better. Ms Pixie looked about ready to burn his four-legged pal to the ground. Or…maybe not as slowly she lifted her chin, her gaze with it.

Those hazel eyes *seemed* to ease…or was that the effect of the setting sun, softening her depths from their aggressive fire to molten gold?

Had he ever seen eyes quite like those before?

The kind you could truly lose yourself in…

And what dreamlike sequence are you getting lost in now?

He reared back—well, as much as one could rear back when still chained to another's tiny frame. And she *was* tiny.

Now that they were this close, and he wasn't viewing her through a lens, he could appreciate just how small. Her smile only just reached his pecs…if that thin-lipped, upturned quiver was indeed a *smile*?

His own mouth twitched to life with his gut. Though he daren't laugh. Her knee was too well positioned for him to chance any humour just yet.

'Thank you.'

As far as thank-yous went that had to be one of the most forced he'd ever heard. It reminded him of his sister, Kate, when she'd been fifteen and forced to thank Great-Aunt Lottie for the 'fetching' dress she'd been gifted for Christmas and made to wear for the family New Year dinner. Though his knitted sweater hadn't been much fun either.

'You're welcome.' Meanwhile *her* dog was having a good old rummage at ground level now that Ralph had planted his obedient behind. 'Would you like to tell yours to do the same?'

Her cheeks flushed a delightful shade of pink again as she dipped her head to give a hissed *'Precious, sit.'*

Her nose ring sparkled up at him, a delicate hoop with a stud flower. He liked it. A lot.

Almost as much as he was enjoying this hilarious little exchange as Precious refused to take a blind bit of notice. Ms Pixie did a little jig against him, gesturing at the dog like it would somehow listen if she tried to act out the command… while still attached to him.

'Precious! Down! No, not down, I mean up, the other way. No, not that way, this way…'

Oh, this kept getting better and better. If they stayed like this long enough it wouldn't just be him laughing; it would be every man and his dog stopping to cast an amused glance their way.

'Come. Here!' She upped her wriggling. 'Look! For *goodness*' sake! Could you just…?'

And now she was directing her ire at him.

'Could I?'

He cocked a brow and wide hazel eyes pleaded up at him. 'The leads?'

He looked down at their tightly bound bodies. His half-naked, hers not quite but very much trapped against his, and if he could have managed it, would have slapped himself upside the head. What was he doing? Or not, rather!

She may have got the hump from the off, but he should have seen her extracted from his nakedness immediately. He blamed her pluckiness. Her eyes. Her hair. That nose ring… *all* the distracting qualities. But really it was down to him.

And he, a supposed nobleman by birth, a man of gentle breeding… If his mother could see him now… Granny even! He moved before his blush could consume him.

'Let me see…' He took in the state of both leads, tried not to notice the way her lightweight vest and cropped shorts left little to the imagination. 'I suggest we move like so…'

He threw himself into the tangled puzzle that they made rather than his tangled thoughts, guiding her this way and that. Much to the amusement of their dogs, who tried to join in one too many times.

When finally they were free he locked her lead for her and handed it back.

'You want me to show you how to do that so it—'

'I know how to, thank you.' She snatched it to her chest, the cool chip fully reinstated to his dismay.

And there was that blush again. Delightful, though she probably wouldn't agree. She cleared her throat, forked her hair, which left it in more disarray than before, and still he found himself smiling. *Oh, Geoffrey, if only you were here now.*

'Come on, Precious, time to go.' And she was off, so fast it took him a second to hurry after her.

'Wait, you can't—'

She halted, one offensive brow cocking. 'Can't?'

'You're just going to go, no names being exchanged, no pleasantries?'

'No *pleasantries*?' she spluttered over a laugh as Precious yanked forward, trying to edge closer to Ralph. 'Could you be any more British?'

'I'd rather think I was just being polite.'

'Precious!' She hauled the sniffing poodle to her side. *'Will* you just *stop* with the whole butt sniffing.'

'You know if you let them get it out of their system they will.'

'Right. Sure. And in the meantime…'

'In the meantime, we can at least exchange names?'

'Names? Why?'

That spark in his gut was back, his mouth curving up and if he wasn't careful, the laugh was going to out itself and she wouldn't understand that it was a long-awaited occurrence. And once out, it likely wouldn't stop.

And then he'd probably look a tad demented too.

Which would really build on the whole splendid first impression…

'Because it's what people do…?'

'When they expect to see one another again, yes.'

'And we don't?'

She mumbled something under her breath that sounded an awful lot like 'Not if I can help it.'

'What was that?'

Her eyes flared, the betraying colour in her cheeks deepening. 'Nothing.'

'I could have sworn you said—'

'It's Fae.'

He smiled. A name at last. 'Now was that really so hard?'

'You have no idea,' she mumbled, giving the impression he wasn't supposed to hear that either.

'Fae…' Could there be a more perfect name for her?

'Without the *y*,' she swiftly added, and there was the defensiveness again. The fierceness too. So much so it had Ralph's ears pricking. Even Precious stopped with her sniffing to cock her head in their direction with a whine.

'Duly noted. I'm Rick.'

He held out his hand, determined to rescue the situation for the sake of his gentlemanly reputation. Not for his ego, though that was taking a severe bashing the longer this went on. The bashing becoming a full-on trample as his hand hovered in midair for a second too long and he wondered whether she was going to ignore it entirely.

But eventually, she surprised him by giving it a swift shake.

He grinned. 'It's a pleasure to meet you, Fae.'

She gave him something of a smile in return. 'I'd say it's a pleasure to meet you too, but I don't make a habit of lying.'

'Ouch.' He choked on a laugh. A laugh that morphed into an all-out rolling chuckle and as expected, she stared at him like he was mad. But man, it felt good. So good to let it out.

It also felt good to have someone be so frank, so brutally honest…

He'd never met anyone like her. Even back in the day when his family's name had been mud, people would sooner whisper behind his back than be outright rude to his face. Even Zara.

Call him a sucker for punishment, a fool, but he liked it— he liked her.

'Shall we walk?'

Her eyes bugged. *'Walk?'*

'You look like you're heading my way? Back to the house?

I assume as you were there earlier, you're looking after the place while the owner is away…which is why I also thought names might be useful. You know, in case you need to borrow a cup of sugar or…' *And now you're just making this up as you go along! Afraid she'll race off if you let her get a word in?*

So sue me, he mentally countered.

She shook her head and started to walk, and he fell into step beside her. Not that he had much choice as Ralph and Precious took it as a sign to stride ahead together and his waist was very much connected to the former.

'Sugar not your thing? Let me guess, you're sweet enough already?'

She gave a disparaging laugh and inside he cringed.

'I can't believe I just said that.'

'That makes two of us.'

What was wrong with him? And why did he care so much whether she wanted to walk with him or not?

He lowered his shades back into position and studied her out of the corner of his eye.

And what weird attraction was this? To be drawn to someone who openly disliked you in return? And why was it so funny?

'Stop it.'

'Stop what?'

'Stop looking at me like that.'

'I'm just trying to suss you out. If you prefer, I could take my lead from Precious…'

Her mouth pursed to the side but he was pretty sure she was holding back a laugh. A *genuine* laugh. 'If you value what's in your boxers, I wouldn't even joke about it.'

'Fair enough. I don't think I've ever had someone take such an instant dislike to me before. It's lucky I have such a thick skin.'

'Don't take it to heart. I'm like this around your kind all the time. Even with Sasha.'

'Sasha?'

'Your neighbour. She's my stepsister.'

'Ah, the blonde.'

Of all the things to say, that was *not* it as she snapped her gaze away and lowered her shades.

'The blonde! Of course that's all you see when you look at her.'

'Wait, no, of course, not. It was just a way to differentiate her from you and—'

Her brows were lifting higher and higher with his rambling explanation, her mouth forming a tight pink line.

'You're right, I'm sorry, I'm sure I could have come up with a better way to describe her.' Not that anything was coming to mind right this second because he was flustered. And he was never flustered. He didn't know how to *deal* with flustered.

And it wasn't like he'd been crushing on her sister. Not in the way he'd been… He cleared his throat.

'Look, what I'm trying to say is that you're very much chalk and cheese.'

'Because that sounds so much better?'

'Why do you see that as a negative?'

'Because if you hadn't noticed my stepsister is stunning in every way.'

'And you think that in turn means you are not?'

Her dark brows hit the sky again.

'Well?' he pressed, daring her to answer him.

Instead, she turned away and for a moment he thought she was done with the conversation but then she surprised him with a shrug. 'She is classically beautiful. She walks down the street and heads turn. It's just the way it is. I don't envy that attention.'

'But you envy her something?'

She didn't respond.

He'd tell her she was equally beautiful, more so in his eyes if she thought she'd hear it, but something told him she wouldn't. In fact, something told him she'd take it in entirely the wrong way, so he kept his mouth shut and spoke on something he knew enough about to write a book.

'I'd much rather get to know the person beneath the glossy outer shell...'

'Yeah, right,' she scoffed, 'I bet you say that to all the girls.'

'I'm serious.'

She flicked him a look. 'Show me a camera roll of your ex-girlfriends and I might choose to believe you.'

He gave a laugh that sounded more like a strangled cat as he realized she wasn't joking. 'You're serious?'

'Too right I am.'

Well, that wasn't going to work. Too short. Too condemning.

Especially if he was to show her Zara. Then she'd think him the opposite—anti blondes because of her. The ex-fiancée. The one that got away. Which of course he wasn't. Not in the slightest.

Zara had taught him a valuable life lesson. To trust no one. Not even those you think you know.

Hell, he'd known her his entire life. She'd been as close as family to him. But then his father had been the same. Worse even. Corrupt. Unfaithful. A drunk and a liar.

'Okay, that look tells me all I need to know.'

'No, wait.' He hurried after her as she picked up her pace once more. 'You've got it wrong.'

'Really?' She didn't look at him as she said it.

'Why does it feel like we got off on the wrong foot?'

'Perhaps because we did.'

'What I don't understand is why.'

She fell silent though the air remained charged with his

question. The dogs on the other hand were merrily walking together in front. Noses occasionally nudging, content in one another's world.

'Look, Rick,' she said eventually, flicking him a look behind her shades—and what he would have given to see her eyes, to get a glimpse of her true thoughts...or not, as the words that came next felt awfully false: 'You seem like a really *nice* guy and all that. But I seriously doubt we have much in common and I'm here for a few weeks, looking after Sasha's place and this one... And I just want to do what I promised her without any trouble.'

She paused as they reached the gate to her home and she gave him what could only be described as a weak smile. Was she suggesting that he and Ralph were trouble?

'I take it that's a no to me inviting you round for a spot of shrimp on the barbie then?'

She pursed her lips and her shoulders trembled. Was that another trapped laugh?

'There are so many things I want to say to that invitation...'

'A yes would be great.'

'I can't. I'm sorry. But thank you. Come on Precious, bedtime.'

And with that she disappeared inside, a reluctant Precious trailing behind.

Ralph gave a whine and pulled on the lead to go after them.

'I know the feeling, Ralph.'

Odd, but true.

Though she was living here for a while. Did she honestly think she could avoid him for that entire time?

They *were* neighbours. And though Rick wasn't nosy, he was persistent. When he wanted something, he was known for getting it.

And what he wanted right now was to understand his new

neighbour better. Her obvious aversion to him right up there with the rest...

First his neighbour and now Fae. Though his neighbour's disinterest had been of the 'polite but too busy to stop' kind. Fae's was something else.

Even now he could feel his lips quirking, his gut sparking to life. He shouldn't *like* it. Only he did.

And he wasn't about to question it because he was trying to be a new man. A man who put living in the moment first. And maybe, just occasionally, acted on something simply because it felt good.

'Come on, Ralph, tomorrow is another day. We can try and impress them then.'

Ralph grumbled and Rick chuckled. 'My sentiments exactly.'

CHAPTER THREE

FAE SNUGGLED DOWN deeper into the billowy softness all around—money certainly bought a different level of comfort. And she ignored the judgemental niggle as she basked in it a little while longer. Unwilling to wake up.

Her dream was too much fun. *He* was too fun. The Brit with the cheeky grin. Eyes that sparkled with mischief as he leaned that little bit closer. His mouth so near she could almost taste it. His nose nudged against hers. Damp. Insistent. He growled.

He—*growled*!

She shot up, eyes wide, and Precious reared up with a whine.

'Jesus, Precious!'

She clutched her chest as the dog snorted and came back down to earth, her front paws narrowly missing Fae's thigh and bringing her nose to nose. Beady eye to beady eye.

'It's too early for that look, Precious.' Fae turned to take in the view of the ocean and the sun already high in the sky, the number of people already out enjoying the day. 'Or maybe not.'

It had to be close to midday. Had she really been asleep that long? No wonder Precious looked about ready to eat her alive. She had to be starving…*and* desperate to get out.

Day two and Fae had failed. Again.

She threw off the sheets, Precious inadvertently with them,

and winced. 'Sorry, darl.' She gave the poodle a clumsy pat as she got to her feet. 'Let's get you out. Then I can mentally berate myself.'

Raking a hand through her crazy mop, she jogged from the room and down the stairs. Throwing open the sliding doors to the enclosed lawn to the rear, she let Precious out while she went about preparing her breakfast as per the schedule that had been stuck to the fridge door. She took a second to ponder the effort it had taken to draw it up. It was like the email only bigger and brighter and broken down by day.

Mealtimes—what she ate and when. Walk schedule—where and when. Toilet habits, brushing schedule… And right there in big bold letters across the bottom: 'AVOID THE GIANT GREY DOG NEXT DOOR!'

Fae grimaced. She'd be insulted if she hadn't already failed multiple times over.

The pad of feet behind her announced the return of Precious, and she plucked the bowl of meat and veg off the side and placed it in the fancy gold stand beside her. Took up the water bowl next to it and filled it while Precious tucked in.

'At least you're not complaining,' she murmured, placing the water down too and turning her attention to coffee.

She wasn't a huge breakfast fan, but coffee, yes. *Always* coffee. And since her head threatened to return to the dream she had been indulging in, she threw her focus into her sister's barista machine. Because she was a pro at making coffee, not so much making light with dreams she really shouldn't be entertaining.

Coffee downed, Precious fed and watered, they set off for their morning walk, albeit almost lunch walk now. They had gone three strides when Precious promptly halted, sitting herself down on the concrete.

'What's up?' Fae frowned at her. 'I know we can't go to the park until this evening now, but surely a walk along the path is better than no walk at all...' Then she looked to the sky. 'And what am I even doing talking to a dog?'

'Worried she'll talk back?'

She jumped and turned in one movement.

'Rick!'

He grinned that same grin from her dream. 'Having fun?'

'Fun?'

She looked from him to Precious, who hadn't budged an inch. Though the dog did lean in to give him a sniff and he gave her an affectionate stroke, adjusting the paper bag he carried into his other arm and away from the nose that reached ever closer... Sausages, perhaps? Bacon?

And no, Fae did not observe that big strong hand issuing the caress and wish it upon her own skin. Not for a moment. Though the Fae from her dream...

'Does it really look like I'm having fun?' she blurted.

'It looks like you're trying to move a mountain.'

Twice in two days...was this going to be her life every day for the next six weeks? Trying to move the unmoveable?

'We're late getting out.'

'I'd say she's going to cook going out at this time.'

'It's hardly that hot.'

'She's a dog with fur. And you've got to think about her paws on the hot pavement.'

Fae looked down and frowned. Surely it was her butt that was taking most of the heat right now. But her paws...*oh no!* 'I should have thought.'

'They don't sweat either, except through their paws, which is hardly ideal so perhaps she's trying to tell you something.'

She palmed her forehead and closed her eyes, took a swift breath. Precious would just have to go without her morning walk.

You had one job, Fae! One job!

And she couldn't even get that right.

'Hey, it's okay, you know, she'll survive.'

Her eyes snapped to his, expecting to find him laughing at her but he wasn't. His eyes were full of compassion, warm and dizzying with it. Looking ever more blue against his tan and the blue of his T, too.

He really didn't look like an arse.

He just sounded like one.

And that wasn't fair.

She knew it. Even as she thought it.

She knew nothing about him. And instead of giving him a chance, she'd lumped him in with all the rest…all the wealthy men and women over the years who had made her life a misery, her father first and foremost.

'But if it really bothers you that much, I have an idea…'

'You do?'

'Do you fancy getting wet?'

She frowned. 'Do I…?'

'Well, not you so much as…' He looked to Precious, who had got to her feet, her nose edging ever closer to the paper bag in his arms, which he lifted again as Fae shortened the retractable lead. She wasn't falling foul of that again. Whatever he had in there, Precious wanted and likely shouldn't get. Her morning walk, on the other hand…

'If it means this one gets her exercise, I'm all for it.'

'Great. It's a ten-minute drive. Just let me swap this bag for Ralph and grab the keys.'

'Wait, what?'

'Rose Bay is a few miles away. It's a twenty-four-hour dog-friendly beach. Perfect for this time of day. They can roam off the lead and use the water to keep cool.'

'You're going to come too?'

'Unless you want me to give you directions and you can see yourself there?'

'I don't have a car.'

'Then it's settled, I'll take you. It's really no bother. We were at a loose end today anyway.'

'I...'

You what? You really want to say no and sound ever more ungrateful?

'That's very kind. Thank you.'

But what about her promise to Sasha?

And which one, exactly?

Making sure Precious got her exercise. Or making sure that Precious didn't get set upon by 'the giant grey dog next door'?

Rock and *hard place* sprang to mind.

'Do you want to go pack her a water bottle and anything you need too, meet you back here in ten?'

'Sure.' She gave a tight smile. Because *of course* she knew what she was doing. *Not.*

He clearly did though. And she needed some of that dog owner wit right now.

Only some?

She looked down to find Precious cocking that brow beneath the white bouffant that didn't look quite so perfect today— *Oh, God*, she hadn't brushed her yet either.

And what was the pooch—telepathic?

'Okay, Precious, I could do with plenty. Now let's go get packed before your dainty paws fry, or that stubborn butt of yours...'

Rick reversed his van out of the garage to find Fae waiting on the roadside. Precious sat at her heels. Amazing how a dog could appear haughty without doing much at all.

He pulled to a stop, hopped out and slid open the rear door.

Ralph came forward immediately.

'You stay there.' He encouraged him back. 'You've got a friend joining you.'

Or not, it would seem, since neither Precious nor Fae had moved from their spot.

He frowned. 'What is it?'

She lifted her shades into her hair as she looked from the classic camper to him and back again, honeyed gaze sparkling in the midday sun. '*This* is your van?'

'Is there a problem?'

'*These* are your wheels?'

'How many other ways do you want to ask the same question?'

Her mouth quirked to one side—an *almost* smile. 'I *never* would have had you pegged as a man for the van life.'

He eyed his most recent acquisition with folded arms. It's grey-and-white paint job might be muted but it screamed fun all the way. 'What are you trying to say?'

'I... You... Well...'

He cocked a brow as he looked back at her. 'Well what?'

She coloured and dropped her shades. 'Okay, got it wrong. You *look* the kind. You just don't *sound* the kind.'

She had a point, sort of, because up until three months ago he wouldn't have been.

'Do you want to know the truth?'

'Always.'

'I haven't tried Wanda out in earnest yet, but I—'

'*Wait.* You called her Wanda?'

He angled his head, not sure whether to be coy about it or own his momentary return to Marvel fandom days. 'I did. You have to name your van. It's a thing.'

'*I* know it's a thing. I just wasn't so sure *you* would.'

'Because of how I sound?'

'And you went for a classic too?' she said, smoothly avoiding his question.

'If you're going to try it, you've got to do it properly.'

'Define your view of *properly* because I would have

thought for someone like you that would mean a fully working toilet, shower, kitchen, air con...'

He started to chuckle. 'Okay. It definitely has the air con,
a sink, something of a shower and even a portable loo, which
I would show you but that feels like it oversteps first-date
territory.'

She stiffened and he moved on swiftly. 'I did consider
something a little more, shall we say refined, but when I saw
this on the forecourt, I figured why spend more than I needed.
And Ralph liked it. Didn't you, Ralph?'

Ralph gave an obedient woof, to which Precious responded
in kind. 'Seems Precious likes it too.'

'What about you?'

She grinned, giving him all the approval he needed. 'You're
full of surprises, Rick.'

'Good surprises?'

'What do you think?'

And with that she stepped forward, coming to an abrupt
halt when her phone started to ring and she pulled it from the
pocket of her denim shorts—a size too big, he'd say, from the
way they hung so low. But who was he to judge, and besides,
on her they worked, in a laid-back 'I don't care' kind of a
way. The kind of way he was trying to get to grips with himself. Her grey vest top was the same. Hanging loose, showing off her midriff and the straps of a pale pink bra or was
that a bikini?

She grimaced at the screen and cut the call, pulling him
up sharp.

'What is it?' Or perhaps the more pertinent question should
have been who?

'Nothing.'

'Do you want to call them back? We can wait...'

'No, it's fine.'

'Sure?'

'Absolutely.'

Ralph poked his head out of the van, and she bit her lip. Hesitated. 'Do you think Precious can come up front with me?'

He looked at Ralph. The front was usually his boy's designated spot, but since they were taking passengers he'd figured dogs in the back, humans in the front. But to stick Ralph in the back on his own hardly seemed fair.

'I'm not sure whether Precious is a nervous passenger so I'd best ride with her,' she explained, wrapping the lead around her hands and giving off *all* the nervous vibes herself. 'Perhaps if we swap with Ralph and I'll sit in the back with her.'

That sounded better, but...was it more about putting distance between them now?

'If you're sure?'

'Positive.'

They swapped places, Fae getting into the back with Precious while he settled Ralph into the front. The task took a lot more effort than it should have since his boy was far too interested in following the female contingent into the rear.

'Yeah, yeah, I know, mate, I'm with you. But you'll have plenty of time to get reacquainted at the beach,' he assured him, clipping his harness to the seat belt before settling himself into the driver's seat. 'You ladies all set?' he added loud enough for them to hear.

He checked them out in the rearview mirror and bit back a laugh. Perhaps the whole nervous-passenger thing hadn't been a lie either because if Precious sat any closer to Fae, she'd be on her.

'We're good,' Fae mumbled into a mound of white fur, pressing Precious away to offer a smile of sorts. 'You can drive.'

'Excellent.'

He pulled out onto the road and set his playlist going—a chill-out mix from the noughties. 'This okay for you?'

'Mm-hmm.'

He checked her face, what he could see of it with Precious still doing her best to suffocate her. She appeared to be watching the world go by. Though he sensed she was deep in thought. For someone who was probably midtwenties tops, the crease between her brows seemed etched in. Like she carried the weight of the world on her shoulders day in, day out...

'So, where do you live when you're not house-sitting for your sister?'

'*Step*sister.'

'Sorry.' So that was a touchy subject—there was a story there, if he ever got to know her well enough to learn it. 'Stepsister.'

'It was always just me and Mum growing up,' she offered by way of explanation. 'No family but us.'

'And where was that?'

'Melbourne. That's where I've just come from, Brunswick East.'

'I've never been. I've been to Melbourne a couple of times, but not Brunswick East. What's it like?'

'I loved it.'

'Loved?'

She met his gaze in the rearview mirror and immediately looked away again. Did she fear giving too much away? Coming across as vulnerable not her bag? What was it with the whole tough exterior? Did it make her all soft on the inside? He'd like to think so...

And why, exactly?

He'd clearly been in his own company far too long...

'You don't have to tell us if you don't want to, but we make good listeners, don't we, Ralph.'

Ralph gave a whine and he reached out to stroke his head.

'It's not been the same since the rich-ass developers rolled in and tore down the strip…'

He recognized that edge to her voice. The bitterness. It wasn't too dissimilar to how she'd spoken to him. Did she see him as one of them? A 'rich-ass' developer? All because of how he sounded?

'I'm sorry to hear that.'

'Are you?' she bit out before pressing her lips together, her eyes once more flicking to his in the mirror. 'Sorry, it's… it's a little raw, that's all. They've taken my job, my home…' She shrugged and Precious harrumphed at being displaced. 'Sorry, darl.'

She hooked her arm beneath the poodle's neck and gave her a scratch. 'I'm trying to find my feet again but it's hard when everything you've known is no longer the same.'

He gave a grim smile. 'I hear you.'

'Do you?'

He could hear the doubt in her voice. She didn't think he could possibly understand and yet he did because he'd been there. He'd almost lost both his home and his family as he knew it, his job too. A decade ago now, but the fight to keep it would stay with him until the day he died. It was likely the reason he'd lost the thrill in the very thing he'd fought to get back—his life.

He loosened his grip around the unforgiving wood of the classic steering wheel. 'Been there and bought the T-shirt. If you want to talk about it, consider me well versed and willing to listen.'

'Really?' The crease between her brows deepened with her surprise. 'Is that why you're here? Making a new life on the other side of the world? You lost your job and your home back in England?'

'I almost did once.'

Now she was interested.

'I managed to save the family home and the family business, eventually. But for a long time I wasn't sure I'd be able to. I lived with that risk hanging over me and my family for many years.'

'You were lucky you had the opportunity to save them.'

'Lucky?' *Lucky* wasn't the word he would use. Not when he'd been labelled an outcast. His father's behaviour had cast a shadow over everything he did. Banks turned him away left, right and centre. Investors wouldn't trust him. Supposed friends wouldn't. No, he hadn't been lucky. Not by a long shot.

'Well, you kept them, didn't you? Me, on the other hand... I fought to keep the bar. I fought to keep the flat. I fought to keep a safe space for the customers who've been coming to me for almost a decade but would anyone listen? Not the banks. Not the council. No one. Because I am a no one. And the people I'm worried about, they're nobodies. They don't have the money that talks. I don't have the money that makes people listen. So we just slip under the radar.'

And now he understood. The chip on the shoulder. The attitude he'd been getting from day one. The reason she wanted nothing to do with him...perhaps even the envy she'd been throwing at her sister too. Because it hadn't been about her stepsister's classic good looks or where she lived; it had been about her wealth. The wealth that made people stand up and take note.

'I see.'

'And now you sound just like them again.'

'Huh?'

'The bank. The council. Those with the money *and* the influence. I tried to plead with them all. And they all said, "I see." And "I'm sorry." Right before telling me they couldn't help. That it was best for the area and therefore best for the people in the long term for the redevelopment to continue. Even my stepfather when I went to him as a last resort. He had the contacts, the lawyers, he could have made a difference, but he chose not to. They even convinced Mickey in the end.'

'Mickey?'

'My boss, the guy who owned the bar. Though neither of us had a choice in the end. The bar, my flat, we were in the minority, the building was going.'

'Is it possible that they're right?' he dared to say.

'Why don't you ask the people who have lived in the area all their lives and now can't afford the rent on the pokiest of flats? And those who are lucky enough to keep a roof over their head, who will struggle to afford the kind of prices these developers seem to think they can charge in their hoity-toity wine bars and food joints? And don't get me started on the older generation whose kids and grandkids are being pushed out into the surrounding suburbs, because they can't afford to live close by. Leaving them alone in their later years. The number of customers I had swing by our bar towards the end bemoaning the situation… We all knew what was coming. I just never expected it to be so…final.' She gave a choked laugh. 'Stupid really, considering they were one and the same.'

'They?'

'My flat and the bar being in the same building. One bull-dozer. Job done. Once the developer had it in its sights, it was only a question of time.'

'How long did you have?'

'Not long enough.'

'They must have given you due notice…'

'Oh, yes, they served notice, all right, followed the letter of the law, dotted the i's and crossed the t's, but no amount of notice can prepare you for having to upend your life. Mickey was sorry, of course, but he had Bali and his sweet retirement in his sights, and I couldn't hold that against him.'

With each word her voice had thickened, catching on the last. So much emotion. All for the job she had lost, the home…

She was looking out the window, either to avoid Precious's fur or to avoid his eye, but he swore he could see tears.

'And what about your mum, where's she living?'

Her lashes flickered and her throat bobbed and there was the pain, the true pain. 'Wherever her dreams take her.'

Oh, God...

Her eyes shot to his in the mirror. Had he gasped?

'She's not *dying*!'

'Sorry, it's just...' He pulled the van to a stop at a red light and gave her reflection his full attention. 'When you said it like that, all weepy and wistful, I thought...'

'Yeah, well, no, that's not what I meant...' She swiped at her cheek—a stray tear, he'd bet. 'I meant she's off travelling the globe with Tim—my stepfather—who's made it his mission to ensure she follows her dreams and sees every location on her bucket list...a thousand times over if she so desires.'

Beneath the derogatory thrum and the roll of the eye, he could sense the appreciation, relief even... She was happy for her mum. Stepfather's obscene wealth aside, she was happy.

'Sounds fun.'

'Considering it was her lifelong dream to travel but she never thought she'd step foot out of Melbourne, it's more than just fun. And I'm happy that she's happy—that's all that matters. I'm *not* weepy.'

He opened his mouth to argue back but the words wouldn't come. Silenced by the emotion still shining in her eyes. The raw passion in her depths.

'I just...' She pressed her lips together, her nostrils flaring with her breath. 'I miss her.'

Her open confession reverberated through him and he turned in his seat, needing to look at her without the distance of the mirror. Even Ralph turned his head with a gruff rumble.

Her hazel eyes glistened and she gave the smallest of

smiles, the smallest of shrugs. 'Pathetic, right. A grown-ass woman and I miss my mum.'

'That's not pathetic, Fae.' He gritted his teeth, swallowed against the ache building in his chest. 'Far from it.'

The aura she had about her. The restless sense of being at sea. That permanent crease between her brows. It made so much sense now. He wished himself beside her, wished his arms around her so that he could somehow absorb some of it. Offer her warmth and comfort and companionship, even for a moment. Because he'd been there. Those days after he'd lost Zara, his friends, his father…

A horn sounded and his head shot up with a curse. He was supposed to be driving. Not acting as counsellor, getting lost in his passenger and his own past.

He twisted back around and checked the lights. Green. No surprise there.

Waving an apologetic hand out the window, he rejoined the traffic ahead. Waited for the mood within to calm before saying, 'So, your mum's off travelling the globe with her man, happy with her new lot in life. What about you? What's next for you?'

Nothing.

Had she even heard him?

He glanced at the mirror to find her idly stroking Precious, who had dropped into her lap, likely sensing the same as him. That need for companionship, for comfort…

He was convinced Ralph would've joined them too given a chance.

'Who knows,' she said after a long pause. 'I don't. It's why I'm here. Helping Sasha while I work out it out. Where I want to live. What I want to do. Who I want to be.'

'Sounds exciting,' he tried to inject enthusiasm into his voice, into the air that still felt laden with it all. Her past and his. An unknown future too.

'You think?' She choked on a laugh. 'Not terrifying?'

'Maybe you just need to look at it in a different light, see it as an opportunity for a fresh start.'

'A fresh start…'

And then she smiled at him in the rearview mirror, and it was like the sun coming out from behind the clouds, warming him through and almost making him miss the turning to the car park.

'Okay then, Mr Insightful, if you're so hot on hope for the future,' she said as he pulled into a space, 'why don't you tell me what you're doing here so far from home? You don't sound like you've been in Aus all that long, or does an accent like that just stick around like a bad smell?'

He yanked the handbrake up, wishing to park the conversation more than the van. But he'd asked for it—poking into her life, her family, her past—so he owed her a bit of his own. And as he glanced over his shoulder and saw the teasing sparkle chasing away the shadows in her eyes, he found he no longer cared. It was a price worth paying.

'How about we get this pair in the sea first, and then I'll tell you whatever you want to know.'

Up came one dark brow. '*Whatever* I want to know.'

'Why do I feel like I'm going to regret saying that?'

'Because if I were you, I would be.'

She was serious and yet he was chuckling.

What the hell was wrong with him?

CHAPTER FOUR

THIRTY MINUTES LATER, shoes in hand, they were strolling through the shallows while the dogs lived their best lives jumping through the waves. So many other dogs getting involved too that it had taken a good fifteen minutes for Fae to trust Precious off the lead and the other fifteen to relax enough to remember the drilling she'd wanted to give Rick.

She cast him a discreet look as he raked his windswept hair out of his face, his eyes hidden behind aviators that reflected the sun back at her.

'You ready for the third degree?'

His mouth twitched up. 'And there I was thinking you'd forgotten.'

'Nah. I'm like a dog with a bone, me.'

He chuckled. 'So, what do you want to know?'

'It might be quicker to ask, what *don't* I want to know?'

'How about, "Where shall I start" then?'

'Easy. What brought you to Australia?'

It did *seem* like an easy question—something he should have a ready answer for—though she'd sensed in the van that it wasn't. Not for him. And again now, as she freed him from her inquisitive gaze to take in the prancing dogs ahead, she could sense the tension in his six-foot-plus frame.

'It's quite a move from the UK,' she said into his silence.

'It is…'

Ralph raced up to them and dropped his soggy ball at their

feet. He gave an excited bark and backed up as Rick dipped to pick it up without breaking stride and threw it, releasing some of the tension with it.

'At the risk of sounding like a cliché, I fancied a bit of sun, sea and surf. And since I can work anywhere in the world so long as I have decent Wi-Fi, Australia fit the bill.'

So he did work; he wasn't here living off his parents' money or rather bumming off his parents' money. She knew well enough that places like Bondi Beach were teeming with such 'kids' who refused to grow up. She was glad he wasn't one of them.

'Sun, sea and surf. You can't get that in the UK?'

'Have you ever *been* to the UK?'

She laughed. 'I've never even been on an airplane.'

'What, like never?'

'All right, all right, keep your pants on. It's not that shocking. Plenty of people live their whole lives without flying anywhere.'

'Sorry, you're right. I just… I haven't met many people who haven't flown before.'

'Yeah well, enough trying to divert attention back onto me. This is about you.'

'I wasn't. Though you must know enough about the UK to know it's not known for the sun.'

'But you have coastal towns. I've seen them on the TV. And people surf over there. I met a guy in the bar just recently who said he learned in some place where the land ends.'

'You mean Land's End.'

'That's what I said.'

'No, that's what it's called. Land's End. It's in the south of England. A pretty place at the tip of the southwestern peninsula.'

'Well, whatever, it was there that he learned.'

'Yes, well, good for him. I'm not ashamed to admit that

I'm a fair-weather surfer and I prefer my sea a few degrees warmer than the biting temps of the Atlantic. And no matter how beautiful Land's End is when the sun is shining, it's too rare an occasion for me.'

'So you can't take the cold, fair enough.'

'You also drive on the right side of the road.'

She cocked her head. 'We drive on the left.'

He gave her a lopsided grin and damn if a sharp frisson of excitement didn't rush through her middle…

'That's what I said—the *correct* side.'

She laughed trying to quash the rush within her as she prodded him with her index finger. 'Funny!' Though the sound warbled out of her as her body reacted to the contact. A second at most where the tip of her finger pressed into the solid wall of his chest, and that was all it took for his heat to burn through her. For the hint of his strength to make her palm tingle with the desire to explore the rest of him. She curled her fingers into a fist, snatched it back. Not going to happen!

Just because he's not a beach bum, or a judgemental snob, it doesn't mean you can get the hots for him. You're here to get your life on track, not derail it with a holiday fling.

Especially with someone way out of your league. On a different life track entirely.

'Oh, the joy of the English language,' she said hurriedly, picking up her pace. 'With all its peculiarities and double entendres.'

'You see, that's another benefit.'

'What is?' Now she was confused. What had they been talking about? Oh, yes, Australia and why he'd chosen to buy a place here.

'Not having to learn another language.'

'I feel like this is all surface-level stuff.'

Her eyes tracked Precious in the sea as she waved her hand through the air under the pretence of waving off his reasoning when she was still trying to wave off the lingering effect of *him*.

'Surface level?'

'Sure.'

She tugged her phone from her pocket, took some snaps of Precious to send to Sasha later…along with the truth about their companions. She was sure once Sasha knew how adorable Ralph was—and how kind Rick was—her sister would be more than happy that they'd all become acquainted.

Fae could hope.

'Can't one move country for surface-level stuff?'

'Halfway across the world?'

She pocketed her phone and shoved her glasses into her hair, turned to walk backwards before him. Maintaining a safe distance, she brazenly studied him and the enigma he represented. The image didn't fit with the upper-crust accent, but it *did* fit with the surroundings. The van. The life he was now living. Very much so.

Was he working to fit in, or *was* this him?

Had she judged him wrong from the moment he had spoken?

You already know the answer to that.

But still, the accent… His life before he came here…it had to have been quite different, didn't it? She wanted to know, but did he want to tell her? She got the impression he was holding back on purpose. As was his right. His life was his own after all. But she had warned him there would be questions and he hadn't run the other way, so…

'You know if the wind changes, your face will get stuck like that.'

'I'm sorry?' she spluttered, tugging her hair out of her mouth as a well-timed gust caught it in its path.

'Your face. The wind.' He raised his hands, eyes and mouth aghast, tongue hanging out as he froze into position.

A giggle rose up within her. 'Jeez, don't do that again. You'll scare the dogs!'

'Got you to break out of it though, didn't I?' He gave her that panty-melting lopsided grin, normal charm service resuming, and she spun away before the heat reached the apex of her thighs, where it had threatened to head all day.

What *was* it about him?

He shouldn't be her type.

No, correction. To look at, he was. To listen to, he wasn't.

Maybe that's what she had to do. Listen, not look.

And encourage your prejudicial nuances…really?

'It did,' she conceded, eyes tracking the dogs once more… as they should be.

Responsible dog walker…go, me!

'So come on, there has to be more to it, surely? I know of people who upped and left the UK for Australia to follow their careers, their family, a loved one… Is that what it was— did you meet a girl, fall in love…?' She waggled her brows.

'God, no.' This time his chuckle was tight, stilted. 'Only a fool would move for love.'

'Yet people do it all the time.' She folded her arms, pressed her lips together, thought of the people who had come to her bar to drown their sorrows after such extreme moves had gone disastrously wrong.

'Not you though?'

He could tell all that by her voice…

'No, not me.'

'Not a fan either?'

She flicked him a look. 'Of love?'

He nodded, the crease between his brows just visible behind his shades.

'Don't trust it. Don't want it. Don't believe in it. Actually…' She paused, thinking about it further with the recent developments in her life. 'That's not *quite* true.'

'No?'

'I believe it's possible for some people. Or at least, I hope it's possible.'

'Because of your mother?'

'Yes. And Sasha. She married her BFF last week. Who'd have thought it? Known each other for years and years then one day, poof! You see each other in a different light.'

He clenched his teeth together, glanced away.

'You okay?'

'Yeah. Just stood on a pebble.' He flicked his foot out, shook it off. 'So she's on her honeymoon then?'

'Yup. Yachting it around the Caribbean. And they seem happy. More than happy. And I want that for them. I really do.' Horrified at the wistful turn her voice had taken, she was quick to add, 'But I'm quite happy without it in my life, thank you very much.'

'You and me both.'

They shared a look, a smile of sorts, an understanding per-haps…or was that just the sun going to her head and the alien current that he had stirred up within her that she couldn't seem to shake? The idea that maybe she was missing out on some-thing. Something that he could perhaps deliver on…

And then what, Fae? Really?

'So not a girl—' she went back to flapping her hands about as though deliberating it '—and you've already said you can work anywhere. What about family? Where are they?'

Because she realized he hadn't mentioned them.

'They're back in the UK.'

'Mother, father, sisters, brothers…?'

'My father is dead and—'

She halted in her tracks, her feet sinking into the wet sand. 'I'm so sorry.'

But he was off, hardly breaking step or breath to say, 'It's fine. It was a decade ago and believe me, the world is a better place without him in it.'

She hurried to catch him up while she wrestled with this snippet. It sounded strange to hear him be so blasé about it. Unfeeling, even.

Maybe it was because he was so genial. And kind. And nice about…well, everything.

'I've shocked you?'

'No.' She blurted and bit her cheek at her blatant lie. 'I mean, yes, kind of…'

'Did you ever know your father?'

Doubly shocked as he turned the focus back on her, she floundered for a beat. She could fall back on the lie of her youth—tell him he was dead. It had served her well for a long time. But she wasn't the schoolgirl she'd once been, making excuses for the man who'd never been there because he'd been too busy with his other family. His real family. The ones that truly mattered to him.

'I knew *of* him,' she said carefully. 'And he didn't want to know me. That's all I needed to know.'

And now he was looking at her, his eyes probing behind the shades. So many questions were forming…so much rising up within her too that she'd kept buried for years.

'Why do you ask?' she countered.

'I guess because it was cruel of me to say such a thing when it might have been a trigger for you, a reminder of something tragic in your past.'

She shook her head. 'No, nothing tragic.'

Not for her at any rate. Her mother though—her heart had finally healed with Tim, but it had been a long and torturous road.

As for Fae, she'd learned that some mistakes were lifelong. Like her.

'So, what about your mum?' she said before the pain of it could take hold. 'What's she like?'

The warmth of his smile beat back the sudden chill trying to consume her.

'Ah, now in the mother stakes, I have been very lucky. She is the most loving, caring, endearing woman. Too much at times. Even now, with her living in the UK, thousands of miles away, she's doing her best to interfere in my life.'

'But let me guess, she's only doing it because she knows what's best for you.'

'You sound like we have that common too.'

'Oh, yes!'

'Because they love us dearly.'

'Very much so.'

Though her smile in return wavered as she realized that was how it *had* been. For years, her mother had been on at her. Overbearing, fussing…then she'd met Tim, and the reins had gradually slackened.

At first it had been a relief. Not to have to account for every minute of the day. To panic when she was late home and race back. Now she actually *missed* having someone to race back for.

And Fae couldn't help thinking that her mother's interference these days stemmed more from maternal guilt that she was no longer around. That she was off living her best life, while Fae was still living their old life…

Or not, now that the bar and the flat were out of the picture.

And all her mother's worries centred around the future and what Fae would do with it. Make of it. And heaven forbid, she would do it alone.

'Oh, God, I think it's happened!'

He looked at her in abject horror and she froze, the blood draining from her face. 'What? What's happened?'

'Your face, I think it's really stuck!'

'Rick!' She punched him this time, right in the bicep as

the blood returned to her cheeks in a rush. 'You scared the life out of me.'

'To be frank, you already looked like the life had been sucked out of you. Where'd you go?'

'I was thinking about overbearing mothers.'

'Yours is really that bad?'

'*Was* that bad. These days she's too busy living the life of Riley with Tim to worry about me in that way.' She winced. 'Actually, that's not quite fair. She does worry, just not about the same stuff. What used to be concern about the present has turned into worry about the future and who I plan to share it with.'

'Our mothers should share a pot of tea sometime. They'd get on like a house on fire.'

'Yours too?'

'My mother, my grandmother *and* my sister.'

She shuddered. '*All* the women.'

'And plenty enough women for one man, I can assure you.'

She leaned in with a raised brow. 'No brother to share the burden?'

'No, no brothers.'

'Then has your sister met her perfect match and set a fine example for you to now follow?'

'Not yet.' He frowned. 'But I have a feeling that call will come soon enough. She's determined to find herself a man worthy of the family name.'

'Won't she take the guy's name?'

'Absolutely not. She's determined to be the first of our line to break with tradition.'

The first of our line… He sounded so gentrified and she had to bite back a giggle.

'Well, I like her already.'

'I think you would, though woe betide the man she chooses, because he'll have me to answer to.'

'Woe betide indeed…' Now she giggled. She couldn't help it, but it was more in adoration of his fierce protectiveness than the fancy old English phrase. 'But for now you can count yourself apart and very lucky indeed because since Sasha got herself engaged and of course, with the wedding, all I've had is, "Just look at how happy she is, how settled… You could have all of that too if you simply opened your heart to it and found someone to share your life with".'

'Because it's so simple.'

'Precisely. You'd think my mother would be more concerned about where I'm going to live and work now the flat and bar are nothing more than rubble. But no, it's all about my love life and why I can't be more like Sasha.'

Didn't Mum realize how much it stung? How much it made her feel inadequate again? Just like her own father had done for all those years when he'd chosen her half siblings over her.

'But you like her? Your sister? Sorry. *Step*sister.'

She gave him a meek smile. 'Just sister's fine. In fact, if you ever speak to Sasha about me, she'll insist. It's only me that gets all weird about it.'

'Why is that?'

'It's a long story.'

'I've got time.'

'Well, I haven't got the words. Not right now.'

He studied her intently, demanding more, but she couldn't. Just couldn't. Those wounds were buried so deep it would take more than just a chill-out session in the sun to dredge them up. It would mean talking about Dad's second family. Her insecurities. Being classified as unwanted, the mistake, not good enough. A label she'd learned to live with, but to talk about it…

To air it with a guy who was so confident and sure, so good-looking, too… No, just no.

'If you ever change your mind…' He eased back and her

shoulders eased with him. 'Though it does sound like your mum's current priorities are a little off…'

'A *little*?'

'Okay, a lot. But I guess she thinks a partner will fill the hole that she left behind and has more chance of making you happy.'

'Yeah, well, I don't need a partner to make my life complete. To make me happy. Or heaven forbid, define me and the person I am now. What I need is a new home and a new career.'

'You'll hear no argument from me.'

She smiled at him. 'Thank you.'

'And frankly, I'm impressed.' He paused, making her stop too. 'Plenty of people in your position would have packed up and followed their mother. Taken the easy road and benefited from their stepfather's wealth. I assume they would have welcomed you with open arms.'

Her eyes widened. He *saw* that. She shrugged. 'That's her life, her love, her road. I need to find my own way.'

'And it's admirable.'

Her breath caught. The intensity in his voice, the closeness of those lips that had delivered such praise…

He lifted his aviators into his hair. 'You do know that, don't you, Fae?'

She licked her lips, struggling to find her voice amid the desire and emotion rising up her throat. 'I guess.'

Neither of them moved on. The sea breeze whipped her hair into her eyes but she found herself immobilized by him. His blazing blues dipped to her lips as his own slowly parted.

'You should more than guess.' He reached out to smooth her hair behind her ears. 'You should know it.'

The only thing she knew in that moment was that she wanted him to kiss her. Badly. But she wasn't about to tell him, was she?

Precious came bounding up, water spraying them head to toe and Fae leapt back with a squeal. What timing!

Precious dropped the ball at their feet and looked up at Rick. Barked. Fae gave a tight laugh.

'Do you think she's sexist and assumes you're a better thrower than me?' she said, avoiding his eye.

'You can have it if you want.'

'With all that slobber and sand?' She pulled a face. 'No, thanks! You've got it handled.'

He grinned and threw the ball far, watched as Ralph and Precious raced off to fetch it. 'So you think she's as caught up in looks as you?'

Heat bloomed in her cheeks as her gaze snapped to his. 'Who said I was caught up in your looks?'

'I didn't.' His grin twisted, curiosity turning into something deeper, something richer as she realized her mistake and all she had given away. 'I said "looks" in general. It was you who made it about me.'

He's got you there...

'You tricked me!'

'I don't believe I did.' Rick's pulse raced, hot with her unwitting confession... So she did fancy him...at least, that's what her response suggested.

'You know I was just starting to like you,' she muttered, doing everything to avoid his eye, even picking up the ball that Ralph returned before Rick could get to it and giving it an impressive throw. 'And then your ego had to step in like that.'

'*My* ego?'

'Yes!'

'I was merely pointing out your prejudicial tendencies so that we could—'

'Oh, no, you don't!' She speared him with her gaze. 'We were supposed to be talking about you, not me. Yet you seem to have a knack for turning the conversation back on me. Turning me into some kind of faulty slot machine!'

'A *faulty slot machine*? I'm not sure I follow.'

'The kind that loses all the money while you give it so little.'

He gave a slow nod. 'Right. I got you. I think.'

'That's just it, you do. Or at least, you know more about me than I do you.'

She wasn't wrong, not entirely; he *was* skilled at talking around his past and pushing the focus back onto others, gleaning what he could while giving little away.

'Isn't that the whole point of conversation though?' he hedged. 'To share information, a bit of to and fro?'

'In my experience, people tell me their stories and I do the listening, not the other way around.'

'Well, in my experience, I tell no one my stories because they end up front-page news.'

She huffed as she raced ahead, clearly eager to keep some distance between them. 'You're funny.'

Only he wasn't laughing, and she slowed her pace to look back at him.

'You *are* joking, right?'

It came out strained, her brows drawing together.

'Rick'

'I only wish I was.'

And he knew with absolute certainty that she wasn't going to like this. He'd only said what he had to distract her from her embarrassment. Now he was going to have to explain himself.

He cursed his big mouth, because he was sure they'd been getting somewhere. Somewhere good, a point where he sensed she was starting to like him.

And he *wanted* her to like him.

She opened her mouth and he shouted, 'Ralph!' to beckon his dog back from the outer reaches of the waves. Though Ralph wasn't all that far away. He just wanted his four-legged friend closer as he sensed the storm about to strike. 'Here, boy!'

Fae checked Precious too before her narrowed gaze returned to him. 'Rick?'

'No. Sadly, I'm not joking.'

'But why would the press be interested in you? What is it you do for them to want to know about it?'

'You know how the British tabloids are...' He tried to shrug it off.

'No, that's just it, I don't.'

Though she was probably coming up with a thousand scenarios now, each one worse than the last.

'Anything and everything is newsworthy when it comes to me and my family. Financial, charitable, royal or salacious, there's always an outlet for it.'

'Royal?' she squeaked.

He was surprised she hadn't focused on the salacious...not that there'd been an awful lot of that in recent years. None of it true at any rate.

'Rick?'

'I'm a Pennington, Fae.'

Like that's going to explain anything to her!

Her frown deepened, her glossy pink mouth forming a full-on pout, and he adored her for it. 'A *what*?'

'A Pennington.' He stood taller, shoulders back—an affliction of his youth. 'Lord Cedric Alexander Pennington, if one wants to be exact about it.'

And now she wasn't pouting; she was pursing her lips around an eruption. Her cheeks were fit to burst, her eyes dancing bright.

'Not the reaction I was expecting,' he mused, his shoulders drooping as he ran a hand over his stubble. If she didn't breathe soon, he feared he'd have to pop her. 'Fae?'

'Cedric?' she blurted.

'Yes.' And damn, if he was starting to feel a little affronted. 'But my friends call me Rick.'

'Good job too.'

'Is it really so funny?'

'I've never met a Cedric before.'

'And *that's* what you're taking issue with…not the title?'

'Holy sh—' She gave a cough-cum-choke. 'A lord! You're *really* a lord!'

'All right, all right, keep your knickers on.'

'You don't get to say that to me.' She shook her head, almost dislodging her glasses from her pale pink hair as she stared up at him.

'You said it to me earlier.'

'About flying in an airplane! This is totally different.'

'How is it different?'

'Because this *is* shocking!'

'It really isn't.'

'It so is!'

'It's so not.'

'It so is!'

He had the insane idea of kissing her to end the ricocheting and promptly quashed it.

'You're not winding me up, are you?'

'Sadly not.'

'So you're as posh as they come? Like a lord of a manor with land and a lady and stuff?'

'I have an estate back in England if that's what you mean. But no Lady Pennington other than my mother, who still holds that title.'

'So when you said about your sister earlier being the first of your line, you really did mean a *line* line?'

'You make it sound like a washing line.'

She laughed, shook her head. But at least she looked more amused than horrified.

'Look, Fae, I'm still the same guy who brought you here in Wanda.' He stopped walking and held his palms out, pleading with her to see he meant every word. 'The same guy with dreams of trading the concrete jungle for the open road for a month or two or three. Who wants to master the surfboard and learn to chill. And not take himself so seriously. I haven't changed because of who I know, who my parents are or who I am on paper.'

'Right.' She choked on a laugh and continued walking. 'Just a guy.'

'Fae!'

He had to fight the urge to make her stop as he caught her up. Worse still, he had to fight the urge to make her stop so that he could kiss her deeply because he had a feeling it would dislodge every misconception she had and make her think only of the connection he swore was there, burning just beneath the surface.

'I really am just a guy.'

'This is crazy,' she murmured.

'Is it though?'

'Yes!'

'Why?'

'Because…because I don't hang around with people who have titles and know the king!'

'I didn't say I know the king.'

'You know what I mean.'

'I do. And I hate to break this to you, Fae, but you do now. You. Me.' He twirled a finger to encapsulate what they were doing. 'Hanging out, but if you're having a rubbish time, I can take you back right now.'

She stopped. He stopped. And they stared at one another. For a long moment the world seemed to fall away, all he saw was her…those vibrant eyes, the quick-fire lips, the sparkly little nose ring and pixie-like hair.

Maybe it was because she was so different. So very different to all the women in his acquaintance…

'Is it really so bad?'

'Is what so bad?' Her voice had softened, taken on a husky edge, much like his own.

'Hanging out with a lord?'

'Is that your ego asking?'

'Does it really matter?'

'I guess not.'

'You guess not, it doesn't matter? Or you guess not, it's not so bad?'

'I'll leave you to work it out.'

He chuckled. 'You're really hard work—you know that, right?'

She tilted her head, her golden eyes sparkling in their intensity as they remained locked with his own. 'Is that why you're looking at me like that?'

'Like what?'

'All goofy and if you really must know, like Ralph. All you need to do is let your tongue hang out again and you'll have mastered it.'

'Wow...' he drawled, palms itching to reach for her, his body warming with the desire to lean that bit closer.

'Well, you asked.'

'And you didn't feel the need to sugar-coat it?'

'I never sugar-coat anything.'

Something else he liked about her. He'd had enough sugar-coating of the truth in recent years, when the money had started rolling back in and the women had come flocking, Zara included. Then there were the prospective business partners and employees keen to impress.

'Jeez! No need to scowl about it.' And then she reached up on tiptoes, palms hooked on his shoulders as her mouth drew level with his and she blew a gust of air over his face.

'What are you *doing*?' He laughed and choked at the same time, surprise and desire a heated rush within as he gripped her by the hips. He wasn't sure if he was trying to steady her or himself.

'I was seeing if your face would stay like it.'

He chuckled harder, tighter, stared into her eyes, which were almost level with his as he held her there. Her denim shorts and bare skin warm in his palms. Tantalizingly soft. 'But for the record, I wasn't scowling at you. I was admiring you all over again.'

'You were?' He felt a tremor run through her, the vibration feeding into him.

He nodded. 'Promise me something, Fae.'

She licked her lips, the hint of tongue adding fuel to the fire building within him.

'I'm not sure you've earned a promise from me yet.'

He smiled, because of course she wouldn't just hand one over…this was Fae.

'But I'll consider it…if you tell me what it is.'

'Okay.' His chest warmed, liking this offer and liking her even more for it. 'Don't ever change. Not for anyone or anything.'

He didn't think she was capable of surprising him any further. He was wrong. First, she gave him tears, the corners of her eyes glistening and sending his gut rolling with guilt. And then she kissed him.

Not the mindless, illicit kind he'd been toying with but equally heart-stopping as she swept her lips against his cheek and whispered beside his ear. 'Now *that* I can do. Thank you.'

She dropped back, escaping his hold, and he was too stunned to do anything but let her go. 'What for?'

She grinned wide and wiped her face clear of the emotion that had been there seconds before. No more tears. Though there had been. He was sure of it.

'Just thank you. Now shall we…?'

She started to head away from him, but he caught her hand

in his and tugged her back. She came willingly, so willingly that her body was pressed up against his in a beat, and rather than let her go, he held her as he pressed, 'Then what was with the tears?'

'I was being silly.'

'I thought you didn't sugar-coat stuff.'

'That's not sugar-coating—that's being honest.'

'There's nothing silly about the kind of pain that causes you to cry.'

'Who said I was in pain?'

He frowned.

'You made me happy, Rick.' She held his gaze as she said it and he knew she spoke the truth. 'Granted, it was for a moment because if you knew me for longer than twenty-four hours, I'm sure my lack of sugar-coating would start to grate and you'd beg me to take my promise back, but—'

'No buts, Fae. I meant what I said.'

'Uh-huh, so you say.'

'I do say.'

'Uh-huh.'

'Less of the hesitant *uh-huh* and more of the definite *mm-hmm*, okay.'

'Mm-hmm.'

'Mm-hmm!'

And they really had to stop making that sound because each time they did it their chests vibrated against one another, provoking one another's nerve endings, stimulating one another's— He cursed and she giggled, which was even worse.

It really was time to get out of the sun.

'Though I am thinking we should head back. Even with the sea, the sun can be a bit much for them…and for us.'

Because of course it was the sun's fault his libido was threatening to take over.

'You're right.' She grimaced. 'I have a feeling I already look like a lobster.'

A very hot, very appealing, very kissable lobster if there ever was such a thing.

'Rick?' she said when neither of them moved.

'Yes?'

'We have an audience.'

She gestured with her eyes to hip level and he looked down. Sure enough, two dogs sat panting up at them. A sure sign they were hot and thirsty and ready to bail on the beach. Either that or they were curious to see what happened next.

And they weren't alone in that thought...

'Beer back at mine?'

But it was one thing to acknowledge he was attracted to her and her to him. Another to act on it knowing there could be no future in it. But agreeing there was no future and *then* acting on it... Now therein lay a future of enticing possibility.

She nipped her lip, the sparkle in her eyes deepening. 'What you're really desperate to ask us round for is that barbie...'

'How did you guess?'

'I can read you like an open book.'

God, he hoped not.

'In that case, fancy some shrimp?'

This time she pulled out of his embrace to stroke Precious's damp curls back from her eyes. 'What do you say, darl? You up for some?'

Precious gave a resounding bark.

'I think that's a yes.'

And damn if he didn't fist pump the air like a teen.

Oh, if Geoffrey or Kate could see him now. They'd either be overjoyed or deeply disturbed. Probably a little bit of both. Much like Rick himself...

CHAPTER FIVE

WATCHING RICK COOK was a thrill.

Watching him eat finger-licking food, more thrilling still.

And now that they were fed, watered, dogs included, they were enjoying the late-afternoon sun in his equally thrilling rear garden. She'd thought Sasha's pool terrace had been a delight, but it had nothing on this.

Black lava stone and vibrant green plants created a mini-oasis that if she hadn't seen it with her own eyes, she wouldn't have thought it could exist here in Bondi.

She particularly adored the waterfall-fed pool, easy on both the eye and ear. Its shape was perfect for swimming lengths, while just around the corner, set back and surrounded by paradise, was a hot tub crying out to be used.

'You have Bali in your backyard.'

He chuckled as he handed her a fresh coldie.

'I can't take credit for any of it,' he said as he reclined on the low-slung seat beside her—though it was more king-size cabana than seat. But thinking of it as a seat was far safer.

And it was entirely the dogs' fault they'd ended up here as their furry counterparts had taken up the entirety of the corner sofa arrangement across the way.

'It was like this when I bought it and I have no desire to change it.'

She smiled into his eyes. 'Why would you when it's perfect just the way it is?'

Her innards winced. Did it *have* to sound like she was talking about him and his face? Which incidentally *was* perfect. From his captivating gaze to his chiselled jawline, to his strong nose and supremely kissable lips—

Jeez, don't look at his lips!

She lifted the bottle to her own and promptly gulped. Though maybe she should stop with the drink. Sun and alcohol, never a good mix when her body was all too willing to get drunk on him.

'I'm glad you like it.'

Oh, she did…she liked it all. The garden. The house. *Him.* A little *too* much. Especially when she was so out of her depth. He was out of her depth—*league.* Especially when he said things like 'Don't ever change. Not for anyone or anything.'

Such words were dangerous. They could go to your head. Make you *feel* good enough, special enough. After a lifetime of feeling the total opposite.

'Though that frown says something's not quite up to muster.'

Yes, her. She couldn't help the thought as her eyes snapped to his. 'Not at all, it really is lovely.'

'Liar. I saw that look, so out with it. I promise not to be offended.'

She cursed her wandering mind and smiled to reassure him, losing herself in the blue of his eyes that looked ever more vibrant in the shade provided by the drapes of the cabana.

She should move. They were too close like this. Their bodies stretched out beside one another. Elbows planted into the cushioned haven as they faced one another.

Well, you could return to the table, her common sense suggested, and she looked to the sensible spot now like some kind of sanctuary.

Was it too late to shift position? Would he think her weird? She could blame it on her…*what*, exactly? A dodgy hip? Yeah, right!

'Is it the beer?' He followed her line of sight, spying the wine he'd left on ice. 'Would you prefer to move on to wine?'

She gave a tight laugh. 'No, the beer is fine. Seriously, Rick, I'm fine.'

So, start acting like it again before the poor man regrets inviting you over.

'Thank you for taking us out today and for dinner. I'll have to return the favour and have you over to Sasha's, but I warn you, I'm not much of a cook.'

'No?'

She shook her head. 'I'm ashamed to say that Mum always took care of the cooking, while I was always picking up extra shifts in the bar to help out with the finances. After she left, I guess I carried that on. I'd rather be in a bar full of people…'

'Than an empty flat?'

'Exactly. And the one benefit to working in a bar is you get free tucker!' She tried to inject some enthusiasm into her voice, which had started to sound far too hollow.

'Sounds super healthy.'

She laughed. 'It may be the reason I have something of an unhealthy addiction to a schnitty.'

'To a *what*?' he spluttered, mid-swig of his beer.

'By the look on your face, I'm guessing they're very much an Aussie thing. Though technically I think they're a German thing. Not that I would know much of foreign cuisine, not having flown an' all,' she teased.

'Well, I've never come across a *schnitty* in my life, and I have travelled. But I guess I've never eaten in a place that serves up schnitties.'

'Schnitties!' She erupted as she repeated his plummy pronunciation. It might be grammatically correct but it sounded hilarious coming from him. 'Probably best you leave it that way if you want to keep that figure of yours.'

'I'm sure there are worse things to be addicted to. They

don't seem to have done you much harm.' His words brought her laughter up short, the heat in his eyes as they dipped over her all the more so, and she swallowed the sudden tightness in her chest—a tightness and a heat and an inordinate desire to lean that little bit closer.

'Bob rationed me,' she blurted.

'Bob?'

'The chef.'

'Did he now?' He didn't look like he believed her. No, he looked very much like he knew she was trying to change the subject up and put out the fire that had lit between them.

She nodded anyway. 'He absolutely did. No more than once a week.'

'You really miss it, don't you?'

She swallowed the sudden lump in her throat. 'Yes.'

'Please tell me that passion isn't all about the schnitties.'

She gave a tight giggle—it was about so much in that moment. The past, the present, the confusing race of her thoughts in his presence. The fire that she desperately wanted to act on but feared more than anything.

It wasn't like she knew what she was doing either. Her experience was limited to a silly crush in high school and the odd fumble after hours in the bar.

She'd never had the time for a real relationship. Nor the inclination.

And at least with him, she was guaranteed *all* the sparks before they both moved on with their lives if this heat was anything to go by.

Though who was to say it wasn't all in *her* head, *her* body, an entirely one-sided desire. Because *look* at him—he was all godlike and she was…well, she was simply her. Ordinary.

She wasn't Sasha. She didn't turn heads. She was a nobody.

'Oh, my God, it really is all about the schnitties. I'm going to have to try one.'

'What, no!' She covered her mouth, more to hide her all-consuming blush than her beer spray as she choked on a true belly-rousing laugh. 'It's not about a good schnitty. Though once you try one of Bob's chicken schnitzels—that's what they are, you know, tenderized chicken that's been crumbed, fried and loaded up—even you would struggle not to miss it.'

He smacked his lips. 'Yum.'

'Are you mocking me and my addiction?'

'I wouldn't dare.'

His eyes danced and her fingers itched to reach out and give him a shove but—been there, got the T... Fireworks!

'I'll just have to take your word for it.'

'And you know what my word is worth.'

'I do.'

He smiled at her, the meaning in that one look causing the lump in her throat to return as she attempted a smile back. And she'd thought touching him was dangerous!

Supping her beer, she looked away before she said something—*did* something stupid. She focused on the conversation they'd been having, on what she truly did miss about her days in the bar.

'But as much as I loved the food, and Bob—Bob was fun, when he wasn't losing his cool over something in that special way that chefs do—it's the customers I really miss. Yes, the money from the extra shifts came in handy but I actually loved being there, around the people. Bringing out a smile when they'd had a day from hell. Coaching them through whatever mess life had thrown at them. Just being there and feeling like I was helping in some way, sharing their load, making a difference.'

'Have you thought about turning that into a career?'

'Which bit?'

'The talking, the being there for people? Getting paid to be a professional ear?'

She cocked a brow at him. 'A professional ear?'

'You could be a counsellor? A therapist? A life coach?'

'A life coach?' She choked. 'Look at me—what do I know about life and how to live it? I can't even get mine right.'

'But you've just told me about all those customers you think you've helped over the years by being there, or am I mistaken?'

'No, but…'

'And I get the impression you've lived through a lot in your— How old are you?'

She felt her cheeks warm. Not through shame so much as something else…something she couldn't quite put her finger on. 'Twenty-four.'

He nodded. 'Twenty-four years. I think you have a lot to give. And if that's where your passion lies, listening to others, helping them, then you shouldn't reject it out of hand.'

Why did it feel like he was lifting her up? Sitting her upon a pedestal. Encouraging her to be loud and proud of what she had achieved, rather than have her slinking away with embarrassment over what she hadn't.

'I don't know.'

'You should think about it.'

She lowered her lashes, picked at the label on her beer bottle as she considered all he had put to her. All she had admitted voluntarily and meant every word of, and how he had turned that back around and spun it in such a way as to make it into something positive, something she could use to build on. Progress with. Make a future out of.

Something that wasn't just a continuation of the old. But something new. Something exciting. Something that could help people and help herself too. A true career, a true passion, a life that was of her own making too.

'I will. Thank you.'

Because she would. Now that he had sown the seed. Because he wasn't wrong. And people went back to college at all ages. She could work and study part-time, get the necessary qualifications if that's what she wanted to do. It was an option she'd never considered before but he was right; it played to her natural talents and her passion.

He'd known her all of twenty-four hours and had figured that out.

Mind. Blown.

Bzzz... Bzzz... Bzzz...

Her blown mind snapped back together as her phone started to travel across the side table with an incoming call. She reached out to grab it. Sasha. She cursed. She'd forgotten to send her the update she'd promised.

'Everything okay?'

'Sorry, do you mind if I just...?' She gestured to the phone as the call cut off. 'It's Sasha checking in.'

'Wow, it must be the crack of dawn for her.'

'Told you, Precious is her everything. Well, her everything plus her wife.'

'Of course. You go ahead.'

Hearing her name, Precious had lifted her head and was now yawning wide as she watched them. Fae typed a quick message to Sasha, filling her in on their trip to the beach. She paused. She wanted to tell her about Rick and Ralph. But that would require a longer explanation and, in all honesty, a face-to-face chat too.

She added a quick Video chat in morn? This eve for you. And dropped in a photo of Precious on the beach, careful to make sure it only showed her furry pooch enjoying the waves.

Sasha's response was immediate and effusive, full of gushing emojis.

Perfect! Call me when you're up, we'll be around! Speak soon! Love to you and P xxx

She dropped the phone back down and Precious, sensing she wasn't about to be called upon to perform, stood, circled and flopped back down. Positioning herself that little bit closer to Ralph, who opened one eye to greet her and promptly closed it again with a satisfied grunt.

Fae smiled softly. They were so comfortable with one another and as she took in the slightly dishevelled pooch, Fae realized she too felt a little more comfortable with her. Perhaps because Precious *looked* more mongrel than pedigree hound, much like Fae herself.

And there she went being ridiculous again.

'What was that sigh about?'

'You'll think me ridiculous.'

'Try me.'

'If I tell you, you can never tell Sasha.'

'Ha, I don't think you ever need to worry about what I will or won't say in front of Sasha.'

'Really? Why's that?'

'I don't think your sister will stay in my orbit long enough to tell her anything.'

She bit her lip and looked away. Supped her beer. Oh, dear. Just how rude had Sasha been to him when they'd met? Was she *that* worried about Ralph around Precious? And if she was, what did that mean for their convo come morning?

But they were so happy together. Ralph and Precious, she meant. Perfect in fact.

So where was the harm? Truly.

'What did Sash say to you?'

'She said very little and moved very fast. Impressive really.' He grinned. 'It seems both you *and* your sister are ones for acting on first impressions and for whatever reason, I failed to pass the test.'

Her shame was written in her eyes, but she refused to look away. She had to own this for her sister as well as herself.

'Sasha's very protective of Precious. If she gave you the impression she wanted to steer clear of you, I'm sorry, but it was more about concern over her dog than anything else.'

'Concern?' He frowned. 'What did she think was going to happen?'

Her cheeks bloomed and his brows disappeared into his hairline. 'Oh, right. I see.'

He cleared his throat, his gaze drifting to the dogs safely and very innocently asleep across the way.

'In that case, consider me and Ralph very much told on that score. I'll bear it in mind when I next see her. As for what you were thinking about…?'

Oh, God, her?

She was thinking all manner of things, none of which she should be thinking but all of which she wanted. One straight after another.

'Me?' she gulped.

'The thought that triggered the sigh? The thing I can't tell Sasha.'

'Oh, right…yeah, that.'

Her blush deepened as she looked to the dogs too, reminding herself of where her head had been before everything else had taken over.

'Is it awful that I kind of like her like this?' She nodded to Precious. 'I haven't brushed her down properly yet so she's kind of scrappy. Less polished. I almost don't want to brush her down tonight and have her looking so perfect again.'

He huffed into his beer as he took a swig.

'You think she looks more like your dog.'

'More like she's on my level, yes.'

'Have you considered that maybe you put too much stock in appearances?'

Had she? Only her entire life.

But what else did she have to go on when she'd been pushed

out, singled out, victimized because of her own apparent short-comings?

'Perhaps that's easy for you to say when you come from a titled family with land, status and wealth. You didn't have to worry about appearances because you already had what everyone else wanted.'

'Until I didn't.'

And just like that the sizzle and the fun, the joy of the day, got taken out by the dark cloud that came over him.

She shivered as she lowered her beer bottle to the bed. 'Sorry, Rick, I didn't mean...'

'You did.'

'I just...'

'You felt overexposed, and wished to expose me too.'

And what could she say to that, when he was right? He knew her better than she knew herself at times. And that terrified her as much as it lured her in.

CHAPTER SIX

'Man, you really are insightful—you know that, don't you?'

Surprise broke through the tension that had clawed its way through every limb. A compliment was the last thing he'd expected. More defensiveness. More retaliation, yes. But a compliment…?

'Growing up in a house predominantly filled with women can do that to you.'

He'd also found his grandmother to be more emotionally intelligent than most. Whether it was through her own loss of his grandfather at a young age or living through her son's self-destruction, the woman had lived and learned and knew a lot about life. She was always willing to lend an ear or offer up advice. Though there were times when he chose not to listen…like when she jumped on the marriage bandwagon.

So I wonder what she'd make of this cosy scene right now?

He cleared his throat and thoughts in one. 'And you were the woman who likened herself to a faulty slot machine earlier today, so it was hardly a leap.'

'I did, didn't I?' She gave a small smile. 'You really do listen, don't you?'

'Always.'

And still the scales were tipped in his favour. No wonder she was on the defensive. She studied his face a moment longer and then she lowered her lashes, rolled away.

'Maybe it's time Precious and I made a move, it's—'

'It was my sister who insisted I get Ralph,' he interjected, ready to give her more. To make it fair. To make her stay...

And what was he being so cagey about anyway. It was simply the truth. He was a grumpy old bastard and he was doing his best not to be. 'Apparently I needed to get a life and she thought getting a dog would aid that.'

She dropped back, her gaze lighting up as it reconnected with his. 'Get a life? How so?'

'Settle in and I'll tell you.'

She leaned back into the cushions, her appreciative smile worth every uneasy beat of his pulse.

'Up until very recently my life revolved around work. I don't just mean Monday to Friday, daylight hours, I mean every waking moment. I was in a road traffic accident a couple of years back and while they were trying to run their tests, I kept demanding my phone be returned to me so that I could call Geoffrey—'

'Geoffrey?'

'My personal assistant. Not my mother or my sister. My PA. And not because I wanted to get word out that I was okay but because I had meetings to reschedule, emails to respond to, things that needed to be actioned that couldn't wait, not to my mind. They finally relented when they realized my heart was suffering more through lack of connection to the world than the injuries I'd sustained.'

'That's...'

'Sad, I know.'

'I was going to say *concerning*, but I guess *sad* is a good word too.'

He lowered his beer bottle to the bed and ran a hand across his neck recalling the many things he'd said and done over the years that, looking back, made him grimace now.

'You know, there's always that person at a social event—a christening, a wedding, something special where everyone's wrapped up in the emotion of it and then a phone goes off...'

'Let me guess, you?'

'I'd make a quick exit. Try and be as inconspicuous as possible, but by then it's too late, the damage is done. That's if I got to the event at all. Most of the time, I'd make my excuses up front and send a gift in my place. Though you have to understand, I don't owe these people anything. I don't have friends anymore as such. What friends I had when I was younger, I lost a decade ago, when my family became social outcasts for a spell.'

Her eyes widened. 'You were…*cast out*?'

'Oh, yes. And since then I haven't had the time or the desire to form new friendships, real friendships.'

'So that's what you meant just now…' She hesitated, her cheeks warming. 'When you said you didn't always have what everyone else wanted?'

'Yes.'

'What…what happened?'

'My father.'

He got the impression she already knew that much. She barely blinked, holding his gaze, the warmth and trust in her eyes urging him on. Making him feel secure enough to recall those days and a time before…

'When I was a kid, he was my idol. I wanted to be him in every way. People loved him, or so I thought. He was always the centre of attention, everyone wanted to be in his circle, in *our* circle… He was forever throwing his money about— fast cars, yachts, lavish parties and hotels—there seemed to be this never-ending supply of cash and while others piled on for the ride he saw no need for restraint.'

He supped at his beer, willing it to wash away the bitter taste.

'I was thirteen when I found him with a half-naked woman in his study, coke lined up on his desk. He tried to tell me it was some prank, but I was young, not stupid.'

She paled, her eyes awash with his pain. 'You must have been crushed.'

'Inside, I was crushed. But outside, everything was so normal. Mum was normal. My sister was normal. Gran and the rest the world, all normal. Oblivious to anything out of the ordinary. So I just thought maybe it's a blip. Some random act that I had the misfortune of witnessing. Not the prank Dad tried to dismiss it as, but a one-off. And I was away so much at boarding school that I could push it to the back of my mind, almost forget it had ever happened.

'And I was happy. I'd found my place amongst my peers, discovered a passion for mathematics and I was doing well. Kate was a year older than me and had never left home. In hindsight, I don't think the money had been there for both of us to go to boarding school and being the boy, and the heir, I was the one to invest in—she was not. A joke really since she was the one who lived in Dad's shadow, who by the age of eighteen could run that estate with her hands tied behind her back and her eyes closed...'

He took another drink, raked a hand through his hair.

'I figured, so long as things were okay at home, things *had* to be okay, right. Call it naivety. Childish hope. Selfish ignorance.'

'I think you're being a bit hard on yourself. You were thirteen, Rick. You did nothing wrong.'

'I was blinkered. So determined to make my own fortune in this world, to build on the Pennington name rather than take the title and the wealth that had been handed down the generations.' He gave a scoff as he realised how stupid that had been. 'But there was barely anything aside from the land left, and even that he'd started to mortgage off piece by piece. If he'd lived...'

He shook his head, not wanting to put words to the fact that his father's untimely death had saved them from total ruin.

'It turned out, it wasn't all roses at home. That Kate knew and had been protecting me, not wanting to taint my view of

Dad. Mum the same. All of us protecting the other. Even poor Gran. The only person unconcerned with protecting anyone was Dad. The only person he wanted to protect was himself, and when he couldn't do that anymore, when his actions could no longer be hidden and people started to turn their backs on him, he took his own life.'

He'd never said it out loud before. And to say it now… It hung in the air between them. Raw. Unfiltered. And finally, out there.

'Rick, I'm so sorry.' She covered her mouth, eyes glistening up at him. 'I… I can't even begin to imagine how that must have been for you. For your family.'

He took a breath, his brows lifting with surprise, a strange sense of release flowing through him. 'And I've never said that to anyone before, but it felt good just to be free of it.'

'I'm sorry I've made you relive it.'

'You haven't, you've helped me get it off my chest. Admit it to myself, I guess. The truth is, we don't know if it was intentional or accidental. He was an addict, Fae. Drink. Drugs. Sex. Gambling. You name it. He never knew when enough was enough. If only I'd taken that episode in his study at face value, I could have…'

'Could have what? You were a child—what could you have possibly done differently?'

'I don't know. Called him out for a liar, told him to get help. Told my mother. Not left my sister to live through it alone. The things she must have witnessed, the things she had to endure…'

'She could have told you.'

'She was too busy protecting me from the truth.'

'And you her. You talk about admiration for what I did but look at you. I had no choice in what I did, not really. I kind of fell into the role I played for others behind the bar. Whereas you, you had plenty of choice and yet you chose the tougher route. You chose to study hard and find a way of making your own money, rather than take what you thought was coming to you by birth and bumming off it like a thousand others would.'

'Let me guess, another of the thoughts you had about me when we met?'

She didn't need to say it; the pink in her cheeks said it for her. And one day he'd make her explain herself and her prejudice but right now it was his turn because...*slot machine*.

'Places like this are full of people like that,' she said softly, though he sensed the guilt she felt in admitting it.

'And money attracts money.'

'Yes.'

'And I have no interest in those that want to come flocking, Fae.'

'Because they are the same as those that desert you when you have none?'

'Exactly.'

'Did they really do that? Your friends?'

It was more than just his friends; it was Zara. But he saw no need to taint such a perfect evening with mention of his ex-fiancée. His father was enough.

'It started with whispers behind my back, but eventually people started to take a wide berth in public, make excuses not to meet up. Eventually I stopped giving them the opportunity to cut me out and cut them out instead. That was when Dad was around, and when he was gone, well, my priorities shifted. I didn't have time to socialize, or to care what they thought. They didn't matter. My family and saving the estate did.'

'But knowing you like I do, I can't imagine how your friends could do that. They must have known you were hurting.'

'I had the odd friend return following Dad's funeral only to find a story printed in the tabloids soon after. I learned my lesson there.'

She cursed.

'My sentiments exactly.'

'How on earth did you get through it?'

'I had my family and they can be quite fierce. My mother never shed a tear. Not in front of me at any rate. I warrant it was a relief for her, to no longer have to turn a blind eye to Dad's behaviour.'

'And your sister?'

'In the early days, my sister spent all her time out on the land. With the gamekeeper and in the stables. Anything to avoid being in the house. Now she runs that land far better than any man, me included.'

'And your grandmother, is she your father's mother or...?'

He nodded. 'Though I think she felt she'd lost her son years before to all his vices and now we're all that's left. We're everything to her...so long as we're okay, society can take a running jump.'

'Good woman.'

'She is that. And all three of them would like you.'

She ducked her head, all coy and sweet and ever more impish. Lighting the flames within him in a beat. He'd never met a woman capable of sparking such need, a need from what had been such misery...it was, as Gran would say, remarkable.

'Still, your friends should have had your back too.'

'Says the woman who's obsessed with a world where image is everything.'

Her eyes met his, big and round. 'Well, isn't it? Look at how they treated you.'

'They were under pressure from their parents and their peers. Their relationships were being tested, and their futures were being put in jeopardy merely by association to us.'

'Are you making excuses for them now?'

'No, I'm explaining why I moved on without looking back and why I don't regret cutting ties now. I didn't have the time for it anyway. By that point, everything was in jeopardy. The estate, the funds, Dad was spiralling…and then he was gone. I was fresh out of uni, but time wasn't on my side. I needed to make money and fast.'

'You didn't have time to grieve.'

He lowered his gaze as her question struck a very deep nerve, the pain too raw to breathe. He took a second to recover, another to find his voice again.

'I guess a part of me grieved the loss of him that night in his study, so when he died, it was strange. But I didn't have time to wallow in it, no. My sister struggled enough for the two of us and I had to stay strong for her. While my mother and my grandmother faced up to the social backlash, I did what I could to rebuild our financial stability. And it wasn't just the dodgy business decisions but the family estate. What good is a title when the land that came with it has to be sold off bit by bit, though Kate came into her own then?'

'You must have been younger than me.'

'I was twenty-two, Kate twenty-three. And we had three decades of underhand dealings and mismanagement of funds to undo. It took a long time to get people to trust us again let alone deal with us. So forgive my lack of best mates and personality if you will, but *that* is the true reason I am in Australia, Fae. And the reason my dear sister insisted I get Ralph. To get a life. Happy?'

She cupped his cheek, stealing his breath with the surprising touch and the look in her eye.

'I am sorry for everything you've been through, Rick, but I am happy that it brought you here.'

To her.

Is that what she wasn't saying? Is that what her eyes were telling him? And if so, what did that mean?

Slowly she lowered her hand to take up her bottle and he wondered if it was more for distraction, a way to pause the connection thrumming between them. The heat that was building rather than ebbing with the coolness of the night.

'Though I think the more important question is, are *you* happy?' she said softly. 'Has it worked, this extended holiday?'

'This isn't a holiday for me, Fae.'

She studied him, her lips curving around the bottle once more. She took a sip before asking, 'How can it not be? Don't lords have to return to get married and make babies and pass on their beloved titles?'

His mouth twisted to the side. 'Normally they do, yes.'

'Normally?'

'But you see, my sister loves that land and the estate, and with my blessing she runs it now and she runs it well. I'm hoping that given enough time, everyone else will see what I see.'

'And what's that?'

'That the marriage, the babies, the title, they are all my sister's dream, not mine.'

'Are you serious?'

'Why not? I told you I have no interest in love and that includes marriage and children.'

He had once and look where it had landed him. Only a fool would go there again.

'But the title?'

'What about it?'

'Are you saying you're going to pass it on to her? Is that even possible? I thought you old-fashioned English types were all about male descendants…'

'She's older than me. If she'd been born a boy, we wouldn't even be having this discussion.'

'Yes but…are you giving it up because you don't want the wife and the children or because you don't want the title?'

'Does it matter?'

She stared at him. 'I guess not.'

'And she's the one at home running the estate while I'm here heading up an investment arm. Yes, my work helps fund what is essentially a never-ending money pit. The estate is vast and old and no matter how much we try to make the land self-sufficient, those bills get bigger year on year, but *she* is the true lady of the manor and she deserves that title.'

'Have you told her this?'

'Repeatedly.'

His smile turned inward as he thought of the numerous conversations-cum-arguments over the years but he knew in his gut this was the right thing to do.

'And she's happy?'

'I think she'll believe it when she sees it.'

'And your mother, your grandmother?'

'We'll cross that bridge when the time comes. I think my mother will understand, my grandmother less so. But she will come around when she realizes I'm not trying to escape, that it's not through a lack of love for the land or my heritage, but a need to experience what else the world has to offer, to play to my strengths and let Kate play to hers.'

She shook her head. 'Are you sure you left because you wanted to and not because you thought your sister wanted it for herself?'

He gave a soft chuckle. 'Do I look like that much of a push-over?'

She studied him intently, her eyes glimmering in the soft glow from the lights that had switched on at dusk. 'No, that's just it, you don't.'

'So are you ready to admit it?'

'Admit what?'

'That I'm not the egotistical Mr Darcy you had me pegged as?'

'I already know that.'

'Are you sure about that?'

She wet her lips, nodded. 'A hundred percent.'

He searched her gaze, feeling her sincerity and wanting to act on what he saw looking back at him but knowing he couldn't. He didn't want to risk what they'd found. This ease of friendship. Something he hadn't had in so long and hadn't known he'd been missing. Until now.

He smiled. Swallowed. Dragged his eyes away to take in the dogs in the distance. To Precious and her fur, which although rinsed of the sea and sand, definitely needed the brush she had so far forgone.

'I've got to admit though…' He cleared his throat, aware of how gruff he sounded. 'It's good to know that your prejudice extends to the four-legged variety too.'

'Rick!' She shoved him.

'What? You just admitted that you—'

'I know and I'm not proud of it!'

'No, being proud *and* prejudiced would be a step too far.'

'Rick!' She moved so quick he was on his back in a heartbeat, her body pinning him down. It took them both by surprise, judging by the way she froze, her mouth mere inches from his own. 'I could…'

'You could what?' He raised a brow, his body twitching to life below the waist, his pulse racing with what she was about to say—about to *do*.

'I…' She swallowed, eyes dipping to his lips. 'You really are quite maddening, you know.'

'I think it's you who is quite maddening.'

She gave a low growl, shook her head and pushed away. Disappointment washed over him as she scurried back to sit at the foot of the bed.

'I am sorry for how I was when we met. For how I am. It's not your fault.'

'I know that,' he teased as he propped himself up on his elbows, trying to lighten the sudden tension in the air. 'I just wasn't so sure *you* knew that.'

She gave him a wry smile over her shoulder. 'And it's not even about how you look because when I first saw you…' Her blush returned tenfold, and his body fired with it. 'It's your voice. Stupid, I know! And if I'm honest, I still can't match the voice with the image.'

She waved a hand in his direction, and damn, if her coyness didn't make him want her more.

'That's because it's all part and parcel of my lifestyle change.'

He pushed himself up to sit beside her. Keen to calm his body as much as his mind, which were both getting far too out of hand.

'I'm having something of an image overhaul. The hair, the stubble...' He stroked at his chin. 'My mother's not a fan. My grandmother, however, she's surprisingly supportive of the longer hair. Apparently there's something quite regency about it.'

'Regency?' She choked on her beer. 'Okay, I think I'm going off it all of a sudden.'

'Ah, so you liked it then.'

She stiffened and coloured in one. 'I didn't say that.'

'To use your words, you thought you were going off it, which suggests you were once on it.' He nudged her knee with his and hell, he wanted to turn into her. Wanted to roll her onto her back as she had done him, sweep her hair from her eyes and kiss the lips that she had just nervously wet, again.

'Yeah, well, don't let it go to your head.'

'I wouldn't dream of it.' Though it was soaring straight there, along with a rush of blood south...

'And I *am* sorry you know.'

Her repeated apology surprised him, and he shrugged it off, his head not quite as engaged as it should be. 'You make too many assumptions, but then I've been burned, I've lived and learned and—'

'Don't do that,' she blurted, his ill-considered response hitting a nerve. 'Don't belittle me because I'm younger than you.'

'I'm not. That came out badly and I'm sorry. What I mean is it's what we go through that makes us who we are.'

'Yeah, well take my word for it, it's what I've been through that's made me who *I* am. And I don't want to ruin this perfect day and evening by dredging up more of my imperfect past.'

Which is what he'd suspected all along. Maybe he'd hoped to coax out some of that past by saying what he'd said but there were better ways to go about it. And he'd blown it because he'd failed to think before speaking. A trait he thought he possessed in spades.

Maybe she was right about his ego after all. Her words had inflated it so much, there'd been no room for thought.

'Another night then?'

Because he for one wanted there to be another and another...

She gave him a smile that was worth a thousand more and hope rose within him.

'Sure. I'll see if I can get Bob to send me his schnitty recipe and have you over to Sasha's.'

'Now there's an offer I can't refuse.'

'You say that now. Just wait until you try my cooking.'

She could serve him charcoal on a plate and he had a feeling he'd go back for more.

So long as he didn't depend on that plate always being there, it was okay.

Because only a fool depended on another always being there.

And he wasn't that kind of fool.

Not anymore.

His father, his friends, Zara...they'd taught him that in spades.

'Consider me warned and still willing, Fae.'

'A week Friday then? Gives me time to practice in the kitchen.'

'Friday. Great.'

'A *week* next Friday.'

'That too.'

CHAPTER SEVEN

FAE ROSE WITH the sun the next morning, keen to ensure that Precious was preened and looking her best for their call with Sasha and ready for a walk straight after. *Before* it got too hot this time.

She set the laptop down on the coffee table in the front room, the perfect height for Sasha to see them both, and dialled.

'Fae-Fae!' Sasha's gloriously tanned face filled the screen, her blue eyes sparkling, golden hair billowing in the breeze as she wrapped a kimono around her bikini-clad body. 'Precious, my darling!'

Precious barked back, her tail wagging.

'Hey Sash, you look as fabulous as ever. The Caribbean clearly suits you or is that more the honeymoon?'

The familiar wriggle made itself known deep within Fae's gut, but this time it was different. Stronger.

And Fae hated that she felt it. She was happy for Sasha. Truly overjoyed for her—

Doesn't stop you being jealous, though.

But she didn't want what Sasha had with Gigi, so why was it getting worse?

'It is magical out here. The sea, the sky, the sand...'

Fae widened her grin as she wrapped her arm around Precious, bringing the pooch closer as Sasha gave a blissful sigh.

'Even the sounds of nature on the breeze...just listen.'

Her stepsister looked over the top of her phone as she went quiet, letting the island do the talking for her...

To know that someone of Sasha's wealth still found beauty in such things, no matter how many times she must have visited the Caribbean, was heart-warming. But it also made Fae wonder if it had more to do with Gigi being with her this time. The company over the locale.

Sasha's sparkling gaze returned to the screen. 'So what about you two? That photo you sent this morning...' She pressed a hand to her chest. 'Utterly adorable! Was it fun, Precious, darling? It looked fun!'

'It really was. There's so much to do here—no wonder you love Bondi so much.'

'I told you it was a great place to live. A great place to come and visit too, but you kept making excuses.'

'I know, I know, consider me told. And we're having a great time, aren't we, Precious?'

Fae turned to the pooch, who had very happily planted a paw on her thigh, and smiled, surprising herself with just how much she meant what she said. To have gone from anxious houseguest and dog sitter to this in such a short space of time.

But she knew the reason why and it was time to fess up.

'It's such a relief to hear that. I must admit, I was a little worried.'

'You were?'

Of course she was! And you knew it too!

'It wasn't that I didn't trust you, you understand, Fae-Fae. More that Precious and I are rarely apart, and I wasn't sure how she'd react...and well, I really wanted you to relax and enjoy yourself and not see it as a chore. So, the idea that you're actually having fun together is more than I could have hoped.'

Fae gave an edgy smile. 'Well, it's good that you think so because—' she took a breath '—Precious and I have a confession to make.'

'You do?'

Fae looked at Precious, who looked at her and gave a little whimper as though she could sense the mounting stress this side of the call. 'It's gotta be done, darl.'

'What's gotta be done?'

Fae stared into Precious's doleful eyes and took another breath.

'Will one of you please tell me what's going on before my wild imagination has me breaking out in hives?'

'Ooh, wild imagination, sounds exciting!' The tanned, dark-haired goddess that was Gigi came up to the screen, earning another bark from Precious. 'The hives, less so.'

Fae scrunched up her face, gave a little wave. 'Hey, Gigi.'

But Sasha was looking less than thrilled. 'Apparently, these two have a confession to make.'

'Really?' Gigi kissed her wife and settled in beside her. 'I'm all ears for this.'

Perhaps Gigi's presence would ease the fireworks, Fae hoped while she led with 'About the grey giant next door...'

'What about him?'

'His name is Ralph and he's a Great Dane and he's really rather soft and sweet and Precious is quite taken with him and I know you said to keep her away from him but I... Well, he... Well, Precious... Well, we... Well, they... Well, we kind of went to the beach together.'

'Aw, Precious went on a date?' Gigi cooed.

'Gigi, how can you say that?' Sasha exclaimed. 'And Fae, how could you *do* that? I specifically asked you not to—'

'I know, I know, but I promise you there was no mounting of any kind!' Fae rushed to say, ignoring the unhelpful flashback of her mounting Rick as she pressed on. 'Well, not after the initial... Well no, there was some butt...' She cleared her throat, cheeks burning as Sasha's eyes widened. 'I mean, dogs say hello, right, suss each other out, all the sniffing and whatever, like they do, right, and we got past that. And then they were just sweet and happy and running about together. And I... I didn't see any harm.'

'You didn't see any *harm*?'

'Sasha, darling, cut her some slack.'

'But she promised!'

'I know I did, Sash, and I'm so sorry, it wasn't my intention, but Rick just turned up and—'

'Rick?'

Both Gigi and Sasha were looking at her now.

'Yes, Ralph's owner. He's really nice and thoughtful and if I'm honest, I was making a hash of things and he helped me out. Came to my rescue. He took us to the beach, told me what to watch out for, and we had so much fun. He made me laugh. A lot. And Precious really likes him.'

Now they were both staring at her like she'd sprouted three heads.

'She really likes Ralph too. Just to be clear. Likes them both.'

Nope. No change with the look.

'What? Why are you both looking at me like that?'

Gigi cleared her throat, looked to Sasha. 'See, darling, all is well. Precious is happy. Fae is happy. You can stop worrying.'

'You like him,' Sasha said. And it wasn't a question; it was a statement of fact.

'Well, yes. I just said that. He's nice.'

'No, you *like* like him.'

'What do you mean, I *like* like him? What are we—five?' Though she could feel the betraying colour creeping into her cheeks.

'I've never heard you gush about anyone like you just did him.'

The hairs on her neck prickled. If her heart had them, they'd be prickling too.

'So?'

'*So*, I think you have the hots for my neighbour.'

'No, I do not.' *Yes, you do*, came the inner voice. 'And even if I did, what does it matter?'

'It doesn't. I guess.'

Though it did. It mattered a lot. To Fae. To Sasha.

But at least it had distracted the latter from worrying about Precious and the company her precious Precious was keeping—so something good had come of it.

'Just…be careful, okay. He's not lived here that long. Who knows how long he's sticking around for or what his plans are. And isn't he older than you?'

She grimaced. 'Barely. He's early thirties tops.'

'Okay, he just seemed…' Sasha twirled her wedding ring around her finger, her face creased with concern. 'I don't know, worldly, I guess.'

'And I'm not?'

'What your sister means is, just be careful, kiddo. She's in protective-big-sister mode now.'

Kiddo, ugh!

Just because they were ten years her senior, did they have to make her feel *completely* inferior and incapable?

And as far as guarding her own heart went, she was more than capable; she'd been doing it for long enough.

Though having a big sister wanting to look out for her… not a stepsister, a *big* sister. She pressed her fist into her chest to dislodge the sudden wedge. That was huge, monumental, and damn if tears weren't about to sprout.

'Don't worry, Sash, I'm not going to jump into bed with your hot next-door neighbour if that's what you're worried about.'

'I wasn't suggesting you would.'

Fae raised a brow.

'But I invited you to stay so if anything were to happen and it went south—' her stepsister gave a hapless shrug '—I wouldn't forgive myself.'

Sash wasn't the only one.

'Like Gigi says, just be careful, Fae-Fae. Please. I love you.'

Sash might 'love' her, but 'Fae-Fae' couldn't help wondering, would her stepsister be worrying so much if she considered her one of them? Wealthy and worthy of someone like Rick's affections.

Fae was pretty sure she knew the answer.

'I best go if I'm to walk this one before it gets too hot. I'll drop you some more pics soon.'

'Fae—'

'Have a good one!'

She closed the laptop, sucking in a breath as she swiped at the unshed tears.

And then the regret set in with the quiet of the room. She hadn't returned her stepsister's love—her *sister's* love. Something that was long overdue.

Precious whined—the look of judgement making a return.

'I know, darl. I know. I'll message her now.'

Because Fae's insecurities were her own cross to bear; Sasha didn't deserve her hostility.

She snatched up her mobile and typed a quick message reminding Sasha that her honeymoon was supposed to be about her and *her* love life, not her sister's, who incidentally loved her too, and hit Send.

'Right! Walkies!'

She grabbed all the necessary paraphernalia—treats, poo bags, lead—and headed out. Quick to get away from next door, with Sasha's cautionary words hanging over, her own cautionary heart racing in her chest too.

She didn't like the sea of change within. It had been one thing to envy Sasha's life. To have been wanted and loved by *both* her parents from birth. Her confidence and her grace.

But to want love and marriage? To envy that?

That was new.

And that was terrifying.

And that was Rick.

She kept up a fair pace until she was a safe distance away. She wasn't breathing freely until she was free of a certain someone and then she slowed to take in the paradise that was Bondi Beach at sunrise. Picture perfect.

But no matter how beautiful it looked, it couldn't ease the anxious churn.

Sasha had been right to warn her. It was only what Fae should have been telling herself. But for some reason, hearing it from Sasha… Well, it sucked.

Because it meant there was something to it.

'And while I'm in this pickle, I'm best avoiding the jar, Precious.' The dog looked back at her, gave a whimper. 'And you can blame my mum for that crazy saying. It just means we're going to have to keep our distance if we know what's good for us.'

Another whimper.

'You saying my company isn't good enough for you?'

Oh, God, Fae, get a grip. Now you're putting words in a dog's mouth.

She hadn't put them in Sasha's though.

And her sister had totally agreed with her.

Hadn't she?

But she'd promised him dinner a week Friday; how was she going to get out of that?

'Fae! Hey, Fae! Wait up!'

Oh, God. Rick!

She kept on walking. Not so much pretending she hadn't heard as unable to respond. Not while her heart tried to beat its way out of her chest. But of course, Precious had no such issue. The pooch whipped around, sending Fae spinning on the spot, and she grabbed the railing before she face-planted.

And there she'd been thinking she'd done so well getting out without running into them.

Now what? She could hardly make a break for it.

Smile, play nice. Make your excuses. Say goodbye.

'Morning.' She gave a tight smile, wishing she'd worn her shades to hide behind.

He jogged with Ralph to catch them up, his grin as easy as his stride and setting her heart alight.

That's right, blame his tantalizing smile and not your body's impossible reaction.

She turned and walked, dragging Precious, who was far too interested in showering their new arrivals in kisses and paws.

'Up earlier today, I see,' Rick commented as he came up alongside her, eyes boring into her as she kept her own pinned on the scene ahead. The two dogs now walking side-by-side. The ocean rolling to their right, waves lapping against the shore as the early-morning joggers and walkers strolled along it. And that sunrise…it was to die for.

But nothing could beat the sight of him.

That's why she refused to look.

'Only a fool makes the same mistake twice.'

'Now that is a motto to live by.'

She made a non-committal sound as she tried to keep pace with Precious. The dog's stride lengthening in line with Ralph's and threatening to pull her arm out of its socket.

'Precious.' She pulled her back and the dog simply gave her that cocked brow and carried on regardless. 'Precious, *heel*.'

Rick made a noise akin to a stifled snort. 'Who's taking who for a walk?'

'Funny, very funny.'

Especially when it was *his* dog setting the pace.

'Just an observation.'

'Well, you know what you can do with your observations.'

'Stick them where the sun don't shine.'

She smiled serenely. 'Took the words right out of my mouth.'

'You just need to show her who's boss.'

'*Precious* is a spoilt pooch.'

He had the audacity to laugh. 'Precious is showing you who's boss when you should be showing her.'

She blew her hair out of her eyes as she puffed along. 'You're kidding, right?'

'Nope.'

'All right, Mr Know-It-All. Just how does one go about showing her that?'

'Take charge.'

'By…?'

'Stop walking.'

'Just stop?'

'Yup. You don't go anywhere until she starts to listen.'

'Then our walk will take all day.'

'Got some place else you need to be?'

'No, but you must have.'

And I really need my space from you, so…

'I'm not the one walking her.'

'That's very true, so why are you hanging out beside us?'

'Good question.'

'In that case, feel free to go about your day and we'll carry on with ours… Have a good one!'

And off she marched. Recalling the exact same farewell delivered to Sasha earlier and feeling the exact same pinch of regret as she realized she was yet again projecting and being unfair.

'But that's just it—it is a good one,' he said keeping pace with her. 'It's the perfect morning for these two to enjoy a run around Marks Park before off-leash hours end.'

'But…'

'But what?'

Yes, what exactly, Fae?

'Is it Sasha? Are you worried about them being together?'

She could lie and say yes. In fact, she could bend the truth and say yes. Use *them* in the all-encompassing sense.

'Look, Fae…' He raked a hand through his hair. 'I really enjoyed last night…'

Oh, God, she could hear the hesitancy in his voice, wondered where he was heading.

'Me too,' she said cautiously.

'But I sense something's shifted since then.'

'No— No shifting.'

Defensive much?

'Said the coins rolling through the slot machine…'

'Rick!'

'What?'

'You can't use my own analogy on me.'

'Why not when you're the one giving me the cold shoulder again this morning?'

'I am not. We're walking together, aren't we?'

They carried on in a strained silence, the dogs panting the only sound for several strides.

'Seriously, Fae, what's wrong?'

She turned and looked up at him, regretting it immediately. Luscious heat, as confusing as it was all-consuming, swamped her head to foot as the fluttering took off deep inside. She couldn't tell if it was nerves, desire or something more—but it was there, pumping through her blood stream, thick and fast, making it hard to breathe. To think straight.

He was *too* good-looking. *No one* should be this good-looking. And when he looked concerned like he did now, that charm was magnified. Because he cared what she thought, and that made her think wild thoughts. Crazy thoughts. Like maybe there could be something real here. Something with potential.

As if, Sasha's voice chimed with hers and a thousand others from her past. *He's miles above you on the social strato-sphere, in looks, in wealth, in everything that matters. He'd choose anyone but you. Don't be a fool.*

She'd risked an unattainable crush once and it had devastated her.

As a kid, she hadn't known any better.

As an adult, she had no excuse.

'Fae, please?' He started to reach out and she took his hand to stop him, lowered it away and released it before his heat could warm her any more.

'All is good, Rick. Marks Park will be good. Come on.' She dragged her eyes from his and as they walked, she focused on their stunning surroundings once more. The sunny affluence of the beachy neighbourhood. And felt a pang for home—the safety of her inner-city suburb. Because there she would be almost a thousand kilometres away from him. 'Though I'd quite happily take the Yarra River over this any day of the week.'

'Right, stop.'

She frowned at Precious, who was finally walking at a nice sedate pace. 'But she's walking fine now.'

'And you're not.'

'What?'

'I'm sure the Yarra River is spectacular enough and that Melbourne has plenty of other amazing attractions, but that's not why you said it.'

'And what's that got to do with me walking?'

'I want you to stop and look me in the eye and tell me *you* are fine, that *we* are fine.'

'Rick, come on, don't be so…'

He placed a gentle hand on her arm, forcing her to pause. 'I'm worried about you, Fae. You weren't like this when you left last night. Not even after I spoke without thinking, and if it's that coming back between us, please give me the opportunity to clear the air again.'

'Trust me, there really is no need…' Her words trailed away as she looked up into his distraught gaze. How could she let him take the heat for this when it was all in her?

All *down* to her.

She took a breath and let it out slow.

'It's not you, Rick, it's me.'

'Oh, God,' he choked out. 'That old chestnut.'

She laughed. He was right. It was such a cliché. And it was going to take more than that if he was to believe her. She was going to have to explain herself. Which she could do…minus her feelings for him.

'Yes. But it's true. And if you're serious about walking with us, I'll explain. Though I warn you, my past ain't pretty so you best buckle up.'

Because she certainly was.

CHAPTER EIGHT

HE SMILED DOWN at her, so much emotion rising up within him, but most of all—hope. Hope that he was close to understanding her. And what was truly going on between them.

'I think I buckled in the day I met you.'

'Oh, cheers.'

'You say that like you think it's an insult.'

'Well, isn't it?'

'Not at all. I think it's fair to say it's been something of a thrilling roller-coaster ride.'

With periodic whiplash, but he wouldn't mention that. Especially as he sensed he was *this* close to unearthing the root cause.

She gave him the side-eye. 'You act like you've known me forever.'

'In a strange way, it kind of feels that way.'

Because how had he trusted her with all that he had? Family secrets. Personal struggles. Things she could now sell to the press. Was he mad? Old news was still news with the power to hurt those that he cared about when given a fresh spin.

'Time clearly flies when you're stripping your soul bare,' she murmured.

Was she talking about him, or her?

In either case, he was just relieved that she was talking *to* him again.

'I guess it does. I meant what I said though—it felt good

to talk about the past with someone.' He was clinging to how it had felt the night before, how it *still* felt when he was in her company, when he let go of the doubts about trusting another with his past. 'Maybe it will help you too.'

'I very much doubt it but—' she gave him a conciliatory smile '—I'm willing to give it a go and I do owe you an explanation for being so…'

'Prickly,' he suggested.

She chuckled. 'I was going to say something far worse.'

She reached into the treat bag and gave one to Precious. Stalling or genuinely rewarding the poodle for walking nicely, he wasn't sure, but Ralph came looking for one too.

'Is it okay if he has one?'

'Of course.'

She gave Ralph a tickle and a treat, then dropped back to Rick's side. Took another moment before saying, 'I told you I knew of my father growing up…'

'You did.'

'Well, a lot of people know of my father. He's a highly sought-after surgeon who spends his days perfecting the image of the world's elite. Shocked?'

'That depends. Are you about to tell me that he knew of your existence too?'

'Oh, yes, he knew about me.' She leaned in, a wry smile on her lips. 'I was his dirty little secret. The product of an affair with his eighteen-year-old housemaid. Can you *imagine* how it would go down if the news got out? What it would do to his reputation? What it would do to his beautiful wife and his utterly divine daughters?'

He cursed.

'Precisely. So, he couldn't have that, could he? At first, he tried to insist my mother get an abortion and when she refused, he had her shipped off to the city. Set her up in a nice apartment, got her the best doctors, no expense spared. And then out I popped and from a distance he tried to control everything. Where she went, where she didn't, who she spoke to. His biggest fear was that the news would get out and his reputation would be ruined.'

'In this day and age, where affairs are ten a penny, I think it more likely he was worried about his wife and children.'

The flash of pain behind her eyes was unmissable. '*I'm* his child, too.'

'I'm sorry, I shouldn't have said that.'

'No, you're right to say it. I've had twenty-four years to get used to it—there's no need for you to apologize. He chose them. I was the mistake. The unwanted one.'

'Bloody hell, Fae, you can't see yourself like that because of his actions, because of how you were brought into this world—'

'Can't I?'

'But Fae…'

'Anyway, he insisted I was privately schooled,' she spoke over him. 'Liked to throw money at his problems. I think he was trying to assuage his guilt by making sure Mum and I never wanted for anything. Couldn't claim me, but he'd make damn sure he felt good about me any chance he got. Never spoke to me, never looked me in the face, never asked me what I wanted. And hell, I was miserable as sin at those schools. Singled out for being the weirdo who dressed differently, acted differently and, heaven forbid, had a cleaner for a mother.'

'But if your father was sending money, why couldn't you make yourself…you know…?'

'Fit in? Look the part?'

Her eyes were fire and ice, burning him to the ground.

'Because I *knew* I wasn't one of them. I didn't want his money to buy me the designer handbag that every girl was after. Or to splurge on shopping trips that were all about flexing your bank balance. Or to leave Mum for days at a time to go on the ridiculously expensive trips the school would put on. What I wanted was a father that would turn up to parents' evening or cheer me on at netball. What I wanted was a father who was there for me. What I wanted was a father who—'

She broke off. Not that she needed to finish, he was already there...

'You wanted a father that loved you.'

'Yes. I wanted a father that loved me like he clearly loved his other family.'

'You don't know what went on inside those four walls. You don't know what shape that love took.'

He doubted it was the rosy, idealistic picture she'd clearly built it up to be. Not with a man like that.

'He loved them over me. Protected them over me. Chose them over me.'

'Perhaps. But can't you see that it wasn't your fault? That it had nothing to do with who you are?'

'It doesn't matter. It's shaped who I've become and I'm sorry that you bore the brunt of it.'

'You just need to give people a chance before you go giving them this...'

He nudged her shoulder with his knuckles. 'Just because some of us are wealthy and *sound* it, it doesn't mean we're all jerks.'

She gave him a weak smile. 'I know and, believe me, I tried. Those days back in private school, I tried. I tried to get to know people, let them in, and it backfired. Spectacularly.'

She chewed her bottom lip and he fought the urge to tug the poor flesh free. To make her look at him as he told her in no uncertain terms how beautiful, how funny, how captivating she was. To encourage her to open up and trust him with it, as he had trusted her the night before.

'Oh, there was the silly stuff like getting your lunch stolen, or your clothes hidden after training. Getting picked for the team and no one throwing you the ball. Getting "bogan" stuck to your back and not realizing until you get home.'

'Bogan?'

'Not heard that one before, huh?'

He shook his head.

'Just putting me in my place, reminding me that I didn't belong. Once a westie, always a westie—I heard that a lot too. But having "bogan" stuck on my back and enduring a trail of smothered laughter all day, that was a real treat.'

He cursed, his stomach churning as she tried to make light of it.

'And then it all came to a head one day.'

'How so?'

Though he was pretty sure he didn't want to know.

'There was this guy, Jasper. *All* the girls loved Jasper.'

Not the lead-in he was expecting...or wanting.

'How old were you, just so I can get a handle on this tale?'

'Fourteen.'

No hesitation. The memory so sure in her mind, as was the damage to her soul.

He'd hoped the added detail would make him feel better. It didn't. A rush of protective heat overlaid the jealous burn, his fists clenching with his gut.

'And even though I was young, I should've known better because he was *way* out of my league. We're talking me here and him, way up there...' She flung her hand in the air. 'Good-looking. Clever. Funny.'

Her gaze flitted in his direction and away just as quickly. Whoa, what was that about?

'Pretty unbelievable, right? All the girls wanted to snog his face off, all the guys wanted to be his mate, and here he was showing an interest in me. Hanging around after class to wait for me. Wanting to carry my bag. Take me for pizza. Whatevs. At first, I was wary, couldn't believe he could possibly mean it. I told Mum about it and she was like, of course he likes you, you are beautiful and you are kind, and just as good as all those other girls. I should have known Mum would have her Mum spectacles on. But I lowered my guard, let him flatter me, and after a couple of weeks, I caved. Said yes to a date.'

She gave a mocking laugh, her cheeks colouring as she looked away.

'Turned out I was some dare. I sat in that corner booth like some loner until thirty minutes in I overheard the sniggering. Sure enough, there they were pressed up against the glass, pointing and staring. It was all I could do to pay for the single Coke I had sipped and walk out with my head held high. Mum was traumatized, of course, for convincing me to take a chance on him. And I tried not to cry, for her sake, told her I was fine. But then the bullying took on a whole new level, social media being the toxic hell that it is, and I couldn't hide that from her. They made memes about me, you know. This one British lad gave me a goatee and a bell with the tagline "Beware of Billy". That one confused the masses, and if you've got to explain it, it's no good, right?'

She gave another tight laugh but he wasn't laughing; he was mad. All over a ten-year-old twisted joke. So mad he couldn't speak through the sickness of it.

'You see, it's Neville No-Friends, or Nigel No-Mates, or a variation thereof, out here,' she was explaining, thinking *that* was what really got his goat. 'The pom called it wrong. But his blunder was nothing compared to mine, which could never be lived down. You can just imagine the kind of comments that were flying about. "Can you believe she thought he'd be into her? Has she not looked in the mirror lately? Where does she shop—Oxfam?" Why, yes, yes, I do—thank you very much. Not all of us feel the need to keep up with the Joneses or stay ahead of them more like.'

She was being fiery and flippant but beneath the effervescent energy lay the wound, open and bare. The wound that she wore like armour to protect her soul from more of the same.

'Kids are cruel, Fae.'

'They are. Though I think it destroyed Mum's faith in human nature even more than it did mine. She felt so guilty for talking me into trusting him and then took it out on my father. Which, if I'm honest, I was secretly pleased about. For years I'd begged to go to a normal school, to be among my true peers, and she'd always refused, telling me he could afford the best and that I therefore deserved the best. But there she was, on the phone with him, having this blazing row, standing my ground for me.'

'Good on her.'

'Though she took it one step further than that and stood her ground for herself too. Reclaimed her own life. Told him she was done living under his thumb. That we would choose where we lived and how we lived and if he didn't like it, he could lump it.'

'Wow, after all that time?'

'It was worth having my teenage heart crushed just for that.'

'Perhaps, but no one deserves what happened to you.'

'No, but it gave Mum the kick she needed to take control of her life. I was so proud of her in that moment. I wasn't supposed to be listening, but I did the whole glass-against-the wall trick. I grinned from ear to ear when she told him if he didn't want to take an active role in my life, then he got no say in how I lived it. I think there was a part of her that hoped telling him the story of what had happened at school and delivering the ultimatum would wake him up to his behaviour. Bring out the protective father and that he would lay claim to me. Come running, so to speak.

'Of course he didn't. His solution was another school, another relocation, just as secret, just as ignored. Mum refused and told him we were done. We were selling up, taking the proceeds from the sale and didn't want to hear from him again. She threatened him with going to the press if he didn't let us go quietly and that was that.'

'Sounds like he got off lightly.'

She shrugged. 'Mum took the money from the sale of our home and put it into the flat above the bar, then saved the rest. We got a job in the bar below and worked to support ourselves. We were free of him and his influence and we were happier, so much happier.'

'Good riddance to bad rubbish.'

'Something like that.'

They reached the park and he paused, looking for the right words to convey how he felt. 'I wish I'd been there all those years ago to defend you, to knock some sense into all those idiots at school.'

'You might have been one of them, Rick. After all, to use your words you hadn't been burned by then.'

'No, but I'd never be so cruel as to treat someone like that.'

'Who knows? We all behave differently depending on our surroundings and the company we keep.'

'And despite all of that you still turned out pretty amazing.'

She gave a surprised laugh, choked on it as she stared up at him, eyes glittering and bright. 'Have you forgotten why we're having this conversation?'

'No.'

'It's because I'm damaged, remember, and prejudiced against people like those who hurt me—wealthy people, like you.'

'Yes, but you still gave me a chance, so there's hope for you yet.'

She shook her head, bowed down to unhook Precious from her lead so that she could run off into the park. 'Maybe... Off you go, honey.'

She straightened, her eyes caught on Precious already racing away. But her hazel depths were distant and caught in the past. *God*, how he wanted to turn her into him, wrap his arms around her and kiss her until all he saw there was passion and warmth and—

His arm jolted to the left and his body went with it as a connected Ralph leapt after Precious.

'Rick!' Fae yelped as she grabbed him, just managing to stop him from hitting the deck as the Great Dane froze with a whine, his eyes and ears trained on a disappearing Precious.

Fae smothered a laugh. 'Now who's showing who who's boss?'

'I was distracted.'

'By…?'

A certain pair of hazel eyes and inviting pink lips and all the feelings you inspire in me that I'm struggling to keep a lid on.

And he wasn't about to admit to any of that.

He released Ralph from the lead and sent him off.

'Go find your girl, Ralph.' Then he added, remembering Sasha and her warnings, 'But behave.'

And maybe he should be telling himself the same, because the more he learned about Fae, the more he cared about her. And the more he cared, the more he wanted…

Taking her hand in his, he gave it a squeeze. 'Thank you for telling me, Fae.'

She looked at their entwined fingers, her own soft and then strong as she returned his grip and smiled. 'I've not scared you off then? You don't think I'm a pathetic loser with daddy issues?'

'No. I think… I think you're pretty amazing. You and your mother could have gone to the press, sold your story for the money. Hell, you could have ripped apart your father's family purely for revenge, but you're too kind and too good for that.'

She gave a huff. 'All right, all right, I don't think you need to go that far.'

She was blushing, struggling to take the compliment.

'Oh, but I do, because I don't think you hear it enough. Or accept it.'

'Yes, well, I'm still bitter and twisted and messed up, because I'm the one who struggled to adjust to Sasha and her father, struggled to welcome them in...'

'Because they're like the other family.'

'Yes. It was just Mum and me for my whole life. When my stepfather came along, with all that he had and his daughter...'

'You felt like he was taking your mother away, that she was choosing them over you like your father had?'

'Yes.' She said it so quietly, and this time he didn't hesitate as he pulled her into his arms.

'Stupid, right?' she blurted into his chest. 'I'm her blood and still...'

'It's not stupid, Fae. You can't help how you feel.'

They watched the dogs play together as he stroked her hair, and slowly he felt the tension ease from her body. He looked down as her scent lifted on the breeze, fresh and floral. Took in her choppy pink bob and remembered how confident—bristly but confident—she'd first appeared. Though he'd had his suspicions all along that she masked so much... and now he knew.

'Fae?' He hooked his finger beneath her chin, encouraged her to meet his eye. 'Don't dismiss your feelings as stupid. Own them so that you can deal with them and move on.'

She searched his gaze, her hazel depths ringed with gold from the morning sun. 'Spoken like a true tortured soul.'

'One who's doing his best to fix it.'

Seconds ticked by. The dogs raced around their legs, blissfully unaware of the charge building between their responsible adults. Or maybe they were aware and were sticking close, making sure they didn't step out of line. That they behaved.

But Rick had no desire to release her and as her palms slid up his front, the heat spread through his body like wildfire. Her eyes dipped to his lips as his did the same. Her mouth softly parted. It would be so easy to snatch the swiftest of kisses—

And ruin the emotional ground and trust you've built...?

'Ruff!' It was Ralph who came to his rescue. Followed by the same from Precious.

Fae inhaled softly as the lustful haze lifted. 'Please tell me that's a ball in your pocket?'

He choked on a laugh and broke away. 'Never leave home without one.'

Which was a little white lie but the air demanded it. And today he *did* have one. Thank heaven for furry friends.

He pulled the ball out and took her hand again. The move so natural he didn't question it. Though if he was to think about the number of times he'd held a woman's hand before, maybe he would have questioned it.

A lot.

CHAPTER NINE

'GAH!'

Fae shook off her hands, wishing she could shake off her nerves as easily.

Why had she agreed to this? Dinner at Sasha's!

Not only could she not cook but she had also invited Rick into Sasha's home, where there was no chaperone.

No one to stop things getting out of hand.

Nothing to stop the wild imaginings that had been building since the day they'd met.

It didn't matter that she knew they had no future together. That for all they had shared and grown closer, their futures weren't suddenly one and the same. But the connection—the sizzling chemistry between them—didn't care. *That* was building by the day.

And up until now they had succeeded in toeing the invisible line. Just.

They'd come close. At the beach. On his cabana. In the park. And every walk they'd taken together since.

For the past two weeks they'd managed to keep things perfectly platonic...*just*.

But now, tonight, the opportunity that would exist...

'Maybe we should dial your mum in, Precious?'

The pooch cocked her head at Fae, gave a yap.

'Yeah, my thoughts too.'

She tucked the front of her white vest top into her denim

shorts and caught her lip in her teeth. Maybe she should've made more of an effort. Worn a skirt or at least something more than her everyday attire.

And why, exactly? You're not out to impress him, remember? It's not a date.

She strode up to the bedroom mirror and leaned in. Her hair was too ruffled. Her cheeks too hot. Her eyes too bright. Her lips too pink from biting.

Who needs cosmetics when they have a Rick?

She spun away and paced, wishing she had something else to do. But the table was set outside in the shade beside the pool. The wine was on ice. A couple of beer bottles too. The chicken à la Bob and salad were prepped. The nibbles were out. She'd even cleared it all with Sasha so her sister wouldn't chew her ear off if she was to spy him on the door camera that evening.

So there was nothing left to do but—

Bzzz!

She leapt as the intercom on the gate went and Precious skittered down the stairs, her nose pressed up against the glass with a bark. Fae was slower to follow, her breaths shallow as she struggled to contain the nervous flutters.

'Show time.'

She pressed the button to release the gate and walked outside to greet them.

Ralph and Precious were already running circles on the front terrace as Rick came up the steps. Fae stalled, her breath disappearing with her footfall. He wore a dark T and ripped jeans. Sexy AF.

She cocked a brow at the torn denim; mocking him surely beat drooling over him.

'Part of your new image too?'

He chuckled—low and deep—and she curled her toes into the stone floor, willing herself not to react but reacting all the same.

'They're also cooler too. Temperature-wise, I mean.'

'Right,' she drawled, turning away. 'You hungry? Because everything is pretty much good to go.'

'I'm always hungry.'

And even that simple statement had her pulse leaping and her body overheating. 'Follow me.'

She led him through to the rear patio and gestured to the table. 'Wine? Beer?'

'Wine sounds good. I brought some with me.'

Funny how she hadn't noticed the bottle before now. Not! She reached out to take it, careful to keep her distance. 'Thank you.'

She popped it in the ice bucket and removed the one she'd opened earlier, pouring them both a glass.

'Cheers,' she murmured, offering his out to him and taking a generous sip of her own.

Her heart was racing way too fast. How was she ever going to eat if she spent the entire evening like this? In some heightened state of overdrive. Too aware of everything, and every bit of him.

'Cheers.' He took a far more modest sip by comparison, and she could sense his eyes on her, curious, probing. 'Everything okay?'

'Yup.' She nodded enthusiastically, almost sloshing her wine. 'Just nervous about dinner. I told you, I'm not a great cook. Even *with* Bob's recipe.'

'Well, don't be. I can help you if you like.'

'Absolutely not!' His brow flicked up and she forced her voice to calm. 'It'll only make me more nervous if I have an audience in the kitchen.'

'Are you sure you're not more worried about having us over knowing how Sasha feels about...' He gestured to Ralph and Precious, who were now laid out on the grass together.

She gave a soft laugh. 'I've cleared it with Sasha—you don't need to worry.'

'That's good. I meant to—' His phone started to ring and he took it out of his pocket to cut the call. 'Sorry about that.'

'It's okay if you need to take it. I'm going to be a few minutes finishing off the chicken anyway.'

He grinned. 'You really don't want me coming anywhere near the kitchen, do you?'

She managed to return his grin. 'I really don't.'

Rick waited until Fae was out of earshot before taking a seat at the table and dialling his PA back. 'What is it, Geoffrey?'

'The fund-raising gala is two weeks today, sir. This is our attendee catch-up call. You know that call we have *every* year, on this day, to review the list of confirmed attendees and take any necessary action. It's in your diary.'

His PA sounded bemused and Rick couldn't blame him.

It wasn't so much that the annual charity gala had slipped his mind…though the call certainly had. It was more that he'd been living in a bubble since Fae had come along and he was less aware of time passing.

In fact, he didn't care for time passing. He'd only come to care for her. He went to bed thinking of her. Woke up thinking of her. Spent every moment without her thinking of when he'd next see her. And when he was with her, the world seemed to revolve around her. She was Technicolor. And everything else was monochrome. Save for Ralph, of course. But then he was a great big grey lump…and he loved Ralph.

He didn't love Fae.

He couldn't love Fae.

It had been a fortnight. Not long enough for real feelings. But he couldn't deny that he felt something…something quite deep. And never before had he been so caught up in another.

'Sir?'

'Sorry, Geoffrey.' He raked a hand through his hair, his thoughts as shocking as the sudden rush of realization that was now working its way through him. He had feelings for Fae. 'Wow, that's come around quick.'

And he meant it in more ways than one.

'Well, don't forget you have your final fitting on Monday.'

He had forgotten, and now that he was thinking about it…

'You know, I reckon I'm going to lose the dicky bow.'

'I beg your pardon, sir.'

'The invites don't specify black tie, do they?'

'No, but you always—'

'Good. This year, I feel like being different.'

'You do?'

'Yes, Geoffrey. I do.'

'Wonderful!' If it was ever possible to *hear* someone smile… 'I'll give Alberto a heads-up. He should be with you around ten.'

'Excellent.'

'Now on to the gala…'

Geoffrey took him through the esteemed guest list, running off the big names that had confirmed and those that needed an extra nudge from Rick. There was always the odd personal call that needed to be made at this late stage. A bit of schmoozing from Rick to get people to remember their manners and RSVP. It was the reason they always scheduled a two-week countdown catch-up. To finalize the list and make those necessary calls.

It also gave them the opportunity to swap people in if need be. An empty seat wasn't just wasted headcount; it meant a potential hit to the fund-raising total.

'Which brings me to the last table. It's the Hamiltons.'

'Okay. How's it looking?'

'Well, you know Sir Hamilton always has to be seen as holding court, even at events hosted by others…'

Rick's mouth twitched. He couldn't care less so long as it meant the charity received the funds that it so desperately needed. They were labelled rare diseases for a reason and underfunded because of it.

'He hasn't confirmed every attendee on his table yet.'

'Hamilton's a law unto himself. Always has been.'

'Yes, well, he's fully paid up with extra thrown in on top.'

'Of course he is.' The gala always made a show of announcing the highest fund-raising table at the end of the night, and Sir Hamilton would be sure to earn himself a head start on that honour. It was why Rick made sure guests had the opportunity to do such a thing. And if one's ego was what drove them, then far be it from him to stand in their way when it helped so many in need. 'And so long as he fills all those seats on the night, I'm happy.'

'He's never failed to before.'

'Exactly.'

'However…'

And here it came, the real cause for his PA's concern. 'Out with it, Geoffrey.'

Though he could already guess. The issue wasn't so much Sir Hamilton as it was his daughter: Zara. His ex.

'There's talk that *she* might be in attendance this year. Simon from the *Daily Tattle* dropped an article earlier this week with some suggestive comment from Zara that you'd rekindled your relationship and that she was looking forward to a public outing very soon. He closed it off with mention of the charity gala.'

He cursed.

'Would you like me to ensure she's *not* on the list?'

'What, blacklist her? I've never blacklisted anyone, and I don't plan on starting now.'

'Some people deserve it.'

'I'm not playing schoolyard games.'

'You're right, of course. Going on previous performances such a move will only make her throw her toys out of the pram, and upsetting her father probably isn't the way to go, but—'

'It's fine, Geoffrey. We're both adults. We can be civil.'

'*You* can be, yes, but that woman…' He could hear his assistant's shudder all the way down the line.

'Behave, Geoffrey.'

'Yes, sir.'

Rick's attention shifted as Fae appeared from the house with two plates. He smiled as he took her in. She was so very different to Zara. Her elfin features inspired all manner of *feelings* inside him as she smiled back, nervously ducking her head as she slid the dish before him.

Oh, he felt things all right. Lots of things. It's what he did about them now, that's what he needed to work out.

'I'll leave her on the list, but—'

'Sorry, Geoffrey, I need to go. I trust you have it all in hand, but if you need anything further for the gala, drop me an email and I'll pick it up in the morning.'

'Will do, sir. But before you go, there's just one more thing…'

'Yes?'

'There's also a rumour that Simon is making plans to head to Sydney…'

'Because of what she said?'

'I think there's more to it than that. He's been to the estate, hounding Kate.'

He stiffened. 'When?'

'Yesterday. Don't worry, he was thrown off the grounds fairly promptly.'

'Kate hasn't said anything to me.'

'She's had her hands full with that equestrian rehab centre she wants to—'

'She's not still trying to make a go of that.'

'She is and you'd do well to encourage it. You know she has had a lot of interest from—'

'Do I need to remind you whose PA you are, Geoffrey?'

'No. Sorry, sir.'

He blew out a breath, a niggle of guilt setting in. Hell, maybe Geoffrey was right. He'd been allowed to branch off, indulge his love of maths, make money from his passion. Who was to say Kate couldn't find a way of making her side passion into a money-spinner too?

And even if it didn't make money, if it helped her four-legged friends like his charity helped so many faceless people...

He could just imagine what Fae would say if she could hear both sides of this conversation. She'd call him out for being a pig-headed hypocrite. And she'd be right.

'No apology necessary, Geoffrey, I was an arse.'

'You *were*?'

He caught Fae's eye, the sparkling laughter there too. 'I was.'

And imagined a similar sparkle and look of shock on his PA's face too and had to bite back a laugh. 'Now what was he doing at the estate?'

'I think the man is trying to write some anniversary article.'

'Anniversary of what?'

Silence.

'Geoff—?'

'It'll be ten years next month, sir.'

'Ten...' His father's death. 'Who would want to read about that?'

'I imagine it would be quite the puff piece with all you and your sister have achieved. Not what you would want to read though. And certainly not by his hand.'

No. Absolutely not. None of them would.

'I thought you'd want to know, sir.'

He schooled his features, refusing to let the storm reach Fae across the table. 'You were right to tell me.'

'I thought it best to let you know just in case he turns up in Sydney.'

'Consider me told. And well done on that guest list. Hopefully this means we're on track to smash last year's gala total.'

'We're all working hard to see it happen. The prizes that have been secured for the sealed auction are particularly appealing. The ones you secured personally will raise a hefty sum and the raffle tickets are already selling like hot cakes.'

'Good, good... See it carries on and I'll see you at the gala in two weeks.'

'You will. Oh, and, sir? I know you said you weren't going to bring a date, but on the off chance Zara does turn up, it might work in your favour and cease the speculation if you reconsidered? You might need the protection.'

He huffed. 'Goodbye, Geoffrey.'

He cut the call with a shake of his head, eager to push all mention of Simon, his father and Zara from his mind and enjoy the moment and his much more pleasing company.

'A gala?' Fae said from across the table. 'That sounds... fancy.'

'This looks—' he eyed the dish of cheese-and-tomato-smothered crispy chicken with fries '—fancy.'

She laughed and he felt the remaining tension ease from his body.

'It looks the very opposite of fancy, but I'll take it. Help yourself to salad.'

He did as she suggested.

'So, what's this gala?'

'It's just a posh name for a party where we raise some much-needed money for the charity that I run.'

'The charity that you *run*?' She choked on some wine, her eyes narrowing. 'You never mentioned a charity.'

'It never came up.'

'But we've talked about so much…'

'And I never saw the need to drop it into conversation.'

'Never saw the need…' She was shaking her head. 'But what does it do?'

'It specializes in rare disease research. We have a centre here in Sydney. It was actually one of the reasons I relocated here.'

'Why didn't you say that when I asked you about your move?'

He didn't answer. He didn't need to.

'You thought I'd take it as you boasting?'

'There was a chance you would, yes.'

'But, Rick…'

'But what? There are plenty of bad people in this world who invest in charities, *create* charities for spurious reasons, Fae. I didn't want you to lump me in with them and give you another reason to doubt me. Especially since all it took in the beginning was my voice.'

She bit her lip. 'Will you ever let me forget it?'

'I'm sorry. I didn't bring that up to upset you, more to explain why I didn't tell you about it in the first place. It wasn't the most important thing to know about me.'

'No, then what is?'

He gave a lopsided smile. 'Probably that I'm lactose intolerant.'

She looked at the abundant cheese layer he'd been about to tuck into and recoiled. 'Rick, are you—'

'I'm kidding!'

'That's *not* funny.'

'And yet you're grinning, which hopefully means you're no

longer worrying about your cooking and are actually going to eat and enjoy it with me.'

'Either that or I'm going to stick my fork in you—I haven't quite decided which.'

'Fighting talk. I like it.'

She shook her head, her eyes dazzling in their intensity. 'I almost wish I had burnt it now so I could watch you eat every last morsel.'

'How did you know I was brought up in a household that insisted on a clear plate?'

'A wild guess.'

He chuckled. 'Got any more wild guesses in there that you'd like authenticating?'

'None that are safe for the dinner table.' She coloured as soon as she said it, her gaze falling to her plate as she blurted, 'And on that note, let's eat.'

Why did he get the impression he'd just got a glimpse of the confident, flirtatious Fae he might have seen more of in her Melbourne bar? The one at home among her peers. The one who had escaped the private school system imposed by her father and found her true home. The home she had since lost...

Was she finally truly at ease around him?

The idea had his grin building, his heart warming, his gut...

Well, his gut was doing pretty well until he got his mouth around his first forkful. At what point should he tell her that she may have used sugar instead of salt...or was a schnitty meant to be a sickly sweet, cheesy, crispy chicken strip?

It was certainly an acquired taste...quite different.

Much like his feelings.

'Is it okay?'

And *smile*. 'Mm-hmm!'

CHAPTER TEN

'OKAY, YOU CAN say it.'

Rick handed her the last of the bowls to load into the dishwasher. 'Say what?'

'It was awful.'

'It was not awful. I ate everything and went back for more.'

She sniggered, pressing the back of her hand to her lips. 'You did too.'

'And you didn't eat enough of it.'

'Because I'm telling you there was something wrong with it.' She set the dishwasher going and topped up their wine glasses, handing his back to him. 'I followed Bob's instructions right down to brining the chicken first and even made his parmi topping. It should have been perfect.'

She lifted her gaze to his, spied the amusement dancing in his depths, and realised two things: one, he *knew* what she'd done wrong, and two, he was *laughing* about it. Laughing at her.

She raised her glass ever so slowly above his head...

'Fae, what are you doing?'

'You have five seconds to tell me, or you'll be wearing this.'

'You wouldn't dare.'

'Wanna bet?'

'Sugar!'

'Now isn't the time for your plummy swear words, Rick.'

'No, *sugar* was the problem! I think you need to check your salt pot because whatever you were seasoning it with tasted an awful lot sweet and awful less savoury.'

She frowned. She couldn't have. Surely.

She crossed the kitchen and swapped her wine for the fancy glass jar adorned with a cluster of shells and stared at the *salt* inside.

'It has shells on! Shells mean sea and sea means salt. I know we're at the beach, but come on, who would put sugar in a jar that looks like *this*?'

He gave a hapless shrug. 'Sasha?'

Nooo. She popped the lid and dipped her pinkie inside. She knew before she sampled it, he was right.

'At least you weren't trying to ward off evil spirits with it.'

'Oh, my God!' She slapped the jar down. If only she'd found out before now, took sugar in her tea or coffee, cooked more... 'I can't believe you ate it all too.'

'A portion and a half. Taking one for the team.'

She spun to face him. 'You didn't have to do that.'

'It was actually okay, once you got accustomed to the flavour profile.'

'The *flavour profile*?'

Another shrug. 'Yeah, the sugar sort of worked with the tomatoes.'

'But not with the *cheese*!'

'I don't know, cheesecake is a thing and that's loaded with it. I reckon you should feed it back to Bob. It could be a new twist on an old classic for him.'

'The guy would think it sacrilege, defacing his recipe like that.'

'Ah well, a treat to save just for me then. And at least we don't need pudding now.'

She shook her head, still disbelieving of her own faux pas, but a smile building regardless. How could it not when faced with his good humour?

'Now, shall we enjoy the last of this wine inside or out?' he asked.

She looked to where the dogs were fast asleep on the rear terrace, but the front had the ocean and at this time of night she loved the sound of the waves breaking against the shore. You didn't need music when nature delivered on this level...

'How about we move to the front room. From the sofa we can keep one eye on them but slide the doors open to the view.'

'Sounds good to me.'

Just like everything else in Sasha's home, the sofa was the height of luxury. The plush duck-egg-blue cushions were soft enough to sleep on, and the L-shaped arrangement was designed to hug one corner of the room while making the most of the view.

She tied back the soft white drapes and slid open the doors. The sun was already low, its soft orange glow working its magic over everything it touched—Fae included. She breathed it in with a sigh. She would miss this when she left. The view. The sea. The...company.

'That was a sigh.'

She jumped. She hadn't noticed him come up behind her. Which wasn't like her. Normally she sensed him before she even saw him.

But then her mind had already been occupied by him...

'To be honest, I hadn't expected to like this place so much.' She wrapped an arm around her middle and sipped at her wine.

'Well, *to be honest*, Bondi looks good on you.'

Her lips quirked around the glass. 'Quite the smooth talker tonight, aren't you?'

'I'm serious, Fae. Your shoulders no longer sit all the way up here.' He brushed a finger along the underside of her ear—the briefest of touches, hardly there at all, but her breath caught. Her pulse charged with a thousand volts as her body pleaded for more. 'You're glowing too. Maybe it's living on the seafront. Getting out with Precious twice a day. Or—'

'Or maybe it's you.'

It came out in a rush and she clamped her mouth shut, her eyes too. How could she have just blurted it out like that? Confessed her deepest, darkest thoughts—fears even. 'Sorry that— I didn't mean— That's not...'

She fled across the room, placed her wine glass down on the coffee table with an unsteady clink.

'What I'm trying to say is...' She rounded on him, gripping her middle tight. 'We've had a lot of fun together. And you're right, being able to talk to someone about the past has been good.'

He stepped closer with every word she said. His expression unreadable but then she couldn't look him in the eye. She was too embarrassed. Too worried about what she would see. What he would see in return.

She flopped down on the sofa, grabbed her wine and took a much bigger gulp as he eased down beside her.

'It really has been good, and I'm glad you're happier, Fae.'

Did she *say* she was happier? She was confused. Scared.

'I wouldn't go that far, but I do feel like I know what I want from my future now.' *Kind of,* she thought, focusing on what she did know thanks to him and ignoring the uncertainties. Her confused feelings. Her fears. 'I want to help people in some way...granted I won't be able to do it on the same scale you do, *Mr Charity Owner.*'

He smiled. 'I wondered when you'd bring that back up.'

'I'm not saying it to rib you. I'm saying it because I'm... I'm impressed, Rick.'

Impressed and falling a little bit in love with you every day and I can't stop it.

'It's helped a lot of people and it will help a lot more. That's what matters.'

'Spoken like a true altruist.'

'Hardly.'

'No?'

He leaned forward to place his glass on the table and stayed hunched over. His eyes on his hands as he interlaced his fingers and rested his elbows on his knees.

'My grandfather died of a rare disease long before I was born. He left my grandmother broken-hearted and my father without a paternal role model. Who knows how different things might have been if his condition had been detected early and treated?'

And there he went, trying to save others from the same fate. An altruist through and through, even if he couldn't see it for himself.

'What did he have? Your grandfather?'

'Something known as Brugada syndrome.' He looked at her and she shook her head, she'd never heard of it.

'It stops the heart working as it should, causes sudden cardiac arrest. It affects more men than women, only five out of every ten thousand are estimated to be affected...'

'Is it hereditary?' She felt sick with the possibility, her hand reaching out to rest upon his thigh. 'Do you...?'

'No, as far as tests have shown, both my sister and I are free of the genetic mutation, though there's a chance it could skip a generation.'

'So your children...'

He nodded. 'For those nieces and nephews my sister's been promising, and our line that needs to continue, the Pennington Foundation exists.'

She considered him for a moment, cherishing the warmth of his body beneath her palm, unwilling to break away...not wanting to *ever* break away.

'Something tells me the foundation would exist regardless,

in some shape or form. Brugada syndrome or not, you would have invested your wealth into something that helped others.'

'You think so?'

'I know so.'

He covered her hand upon his thigh, his impassioned blue gaze penetrating hers. 'After knowing me for all of a fortnight?'

'Yes.'

'So not only are you admitting that I'm not an egotistical Mr Darcy, you're now saying that I have a giving heart, Fae?'

She swallowed, too choked up to speak.

'Fae, are you about to cry on me?'

'No.'

'Yes, you are.'

'I am not.'

'Then what is this?' He reached out and cupped her face, swiped his thumb across her cheekbone to sweep away the betraying tear.

He's got you there. Once again.

Only this time she didn't care because she was done letting her insecurities win out. She was going to throw caution to the wind and go after what she wanted…

Live for today and not tomorrow.

Right now.

Rick couldn't bear to see the torment in her face. Couldn't bear that he had put it there with talk of the disease that plagued his family. But to bring tears to her eyes…

'It really doesn't warrant this much emotion.'

She lowered her lashes, turned her face into his hand. 'Maybe not, but you do.'

Her lips brushed against the inside of his palm, the warmth of her breath too… Why did he get the impression she was telling him more? Like before, when she'd laid the blame for her 'glow' at his door.

'Fae, is this your roundabout way of telling me that you like me? And I mean more than in the "I don't hate you any-more" sense.'

'I'm saying…'

Her lashes lifted and he couldn't breathe for the heat in her gaze.

'I'd like you to kiss me,' she whispered. 'If it's something you want too.'

'Something that I want…?' Was she seriously questioning the possibility? 'Are you mad, I—'

She stiffened, eyes flaring, cheeks burning. One minute they were as close as they could be *without* kissing; the next she was soaring away. Taking his words as rejection. No!

He grabbed her wrist and tugged her back, claimed her gasp with his kiss.

And not just any kiss. He forked his fingers into the hair that had been driving him crazy from the second he'd laid eyes on her and plundered those lips that had done the exact same. He left her in no doubt that he wanted it. That he wanted to taste her, explore her, learn every part of her…

That was the kiss he gave her.

And it burned him to his very soul.

By the time he dragged his lips away to suck in a breath and tell her his truth, he was no longer sure who had needed it more, but he needed to do it again. And again. And again.

'You have no idea how long I've wanted to do that for,' he rasped against her lips, his forehead pressed to hers.

'Really?' She blinked up at him, dazed and flushed, her breaths coming in short, harried bursts.

'You better believe it.'

'I'm not sure…' She tugged on his bottom lip with her teeth

and his body pulsed. 'Maybe you should do it again just so I can be certain.'

He gave a low chuckle and swung her under him on the sofa. 'I've unleashed an animal.'

'I think it's the other way around.'

Then she kissed him as thoroughly as he had her. Her dainty tongue anything but dainty as it swept inside his mouth. Her hands too as they reached inside his T and raked along his back. The perfect pressure of her body as she wrapped her legs around him making him groan and buck against her.

God, how he wanted her.

'You smell of the sea and of the sun,' he said against her ear, his hand sweeping beneath her vest top and delighting in her silken skin.

She laughed softly. 'I bet you were good at poetry at school.'

'No.' He ran his palm along the underside of her breast, felt her skin prickling to greet his touch. 'Only math.'

'I don't believe *y*—'

She broke off on a cry as he stroked his thumb across the lace of her bra, catching her need-puckered nipple... *My God.* If she kept reacting like this, he had no chance of keeping his cool.

'The doors?' she panted, gifting them a panicked look.

'Don't worry, no one can see us up here.'

'But they can hear.'

'Not with the sound of the sea...so long as we time it right.'

He smothered her remaining concern with his kiss and the rock of his hips. It became something of a game. To tease each erogenous zone with the waves crashing on the shore... He felt like the animal he'd accused her of being. Feral. Wild. Impossible to contain.

She pulled her vest over her head, no coyness now as she pulled him back to her, her legs tight around his waist, the colour high in her cheeks and chest. The shortness to her breaths telling him how lost to their self-made waves she was.

Nature had never been more stunning.

'You are beautiful, Fae.'

She shook her head, her eyes tightly shut even as she whimpered and writhed against him.

'Don't shake your head at me.'

He leaned back, his eyes burning into her. How could she not see it?

The soft light of the room had turned her skin to gold, her rose-coloured nipples pressed eagerly through the white lace of her bra and her slender stomach dipped and flexed with every roll of her hips as she sought her release against him.

Hell, he'd never been more turned on, more hungry.

'Look at me when I tell you you are beautiful… *Please*, Fae.'

She opened her eyes. Honeyed rings, almost black, connected with his.

'I want to explore every inch of you, taste every inch of you, and worship you until you *tell me* how beautiful you are.'

Her mouth parted with a soft intake of breath.

'I don't say these words for the sake of saying them. I say it because it's true.' He buried his hand into her wild pink locks. 'I adore your hair. It was the first thing that drew me in on the camera. Then it was your eyes when I saw you in person. They're like liquid gold, enough to send a rich man mad.' He was only half teasing. 'And your nose, this piercing—' he kissed the tip '—so cute and sexy.'

She gave a lustful laugh.

'And these lips…' he traced them with the tip of his tongue, coaxing her mouth to part. 'They are entirely distracting.'

He dipped inside, the heat exploding within him as their kiss took over, their lower bodies melding together in a mindless rhythm that almost had him forgetting his purpose. But he wouldn't, he couldn't, she had to see him as he did.

He tore his mouth away, rasped along her jaw, 'And then there is your body...'

He kissed the skin beneath her ear, her throat...all the while attuned to her, every sound she made, every twitch of her body.

'Your skin is like silk...'

He followed the line of her bra with his lips, his tongue... treasured the way her breath hitched, her hands clawing at the fabric of the sofa.

'And your breasts are teasing me right now, begging me to...'

He surrounded one tantalizing nipple through the lace and her hands flung to his hair with a cry. He grazed it with his teeth, laved it with his tongue, fed her whimpers before moving onto the other. Alternating until she lost all patience with the rhythm of the sea and the tempo became her own.

'Please, Rick. Please.'

He rose up over her. 'I told you—you need to admit it.'

She dragged his T up and he threw it off, cherishing the way her eyes dipped and her mouth dropped open.

'*You're* the one who is beautiful.'

'Not what I asked for, Fae.'

She lowered her palms to his chest and his pecs flexed of their own accord.

'Then stop showing off.'

'I wasn't, that was all you.'

'So it's my fault?'

'Because my body thinks you are a goddess, Fae, like your namesake, a sweet little pixie goddess, and you've caught me up in your spirit and your spell.'

'A *pixie goddess*?' Her eyes sparkled as she gave a choked laugh. 'Okay, I'll take that. So long as you—' she took hold of his jeans and eased the button undone '—take me.'

Oh, Christ.

His hands soared to hers, halting their progress. He needed a moment. Two. One, to make this last, to make it as special for her as it was for him. And two, he had to be certain that *she* was certain. He couldn't risk regrets come morning.

'What's wrong?'

Yes, what are you doing? his body screamed while his groin strained against the zipper of his jeans. He closed his eyes. He couldn't look at her and maintain his good sense. But his head was full of her. So flushed and perfect, lips swollen, pupils pleading, white lace concealing very little…

'Rick…?'

'I want you, Fae. Badly. But I need to be sure… I don't want you to have any regrets.'

'I'm on the pill.' She pulled herself free of his grasp and rose up onto her knees to meet him. 'I'm safe and I'm always sensible.'

She thought he was referring to her past and the regrets of her own parents. Repeating *their* mistakes. And his eyes flared open.

'I meant regrets in terms of us crossing the line.'

'I've had enough regrets for this lifetime.' She eased his zipper down, her hand slipping inside his briefs as pleasure tore through him. 'I want to live for this moment and enjoy it.'

Now *that* he could do… *God, yes.*

CHAPTER ELEVEN

Faye woke to the smell of bacon, her body deliciously sore but her head deliciously light.

Because he was still here.

He hadn't made love to her, then taken flight.

He'd stayed. And by the scent on the air he was making breakfast!

She threw back the sheets and raced to the bathroom, freshened up, tugged on some PJs and hurried downstairs.

She found him in the kitchen wearing a different T and shorts. He must have nipped home. And he'd showered too.

Now she felt a mess by comparison and considered doing an about-turn when he looked up and caught her eye.

'Morning, sleepyhead.'

'Hi.' Her cheeks warmed as his eyes dipped over her, hot with appreciation and obliterating her uncertainty. She smiled, gesturing to the sizzling pan. 'You've been busy.'

'I didn't want to wake you. You looked like you needed the sleep.'

'Well, if someone will exhaust me with their nighttime antics…'

'You weren't complaining last night.'

He strode up to her and pulled her into his embrace, the easy contact along with the recalled pleasure of the night sending a shiver of anticipation running through her.

'For the record, I'm not complaining now either.'

'In that case…' And then he kissed her, deeply, his hands reaching down to her thighs and lifting them around him. 'I think I'd rather you than food, but one needs energy, and the dogs need their walk.'

'Can't we do it all?'

He chuckled. 'You really are an animal.'

'Takes one to know one.'

He gave her another toe-curling kiss then set her down. 'Come on…'

He led her outside where he'd already laid out juice and fruit. The dogs were happily curled up together in the same place they'd been the night before.

'It's like they haven't moved.'

He smiled. 'You'd think they'd known each other forever.'

'I know that feeling.'

It was out before she'd fully considered it, but as his eyes found hers, she realised she meant it. She did feel that way about him. And hadn't he said something similar too, the first time they'd gone to Marks Park…

'Why don't you take a seat and I'll bring out the rest.'

'I'm sure I'm supposed to be doing all of this,' she called after him, though she did as he suggested. Pouring herself some OJ, a wistful smile on her lips as she remembered the days when her mum used to do this for her. How strange it felt to have someone else do it for her now. To have *him* doing it. Strange but good. Too good.

A nervous wriggle tried to work its way in and she promptly quashed it with her OJ.

'Or are you scared about OD'ing on sugar again?' she teased as he stepped outside. Then she saw the plates, stacked high with waffles, bacon, eggs—*my God*, it looked good. *He* looked good.

'Maple syrup is on the table, so the sugar rush is yours for the taking. I'm sweet enough already.'

'That you are,' she laughed out, though she meant every word of that too.

He set the plates down and pulled his seat alongside her, his smile...his smile made her do a double take. It was edged with *nerves*?

She lowered the fork she'd only just picked up. Rick didn't do 'nervous'. And if *he* was nervous, *she* was nervous.

Was this the lead up to 'I had a great time last night but this isn't going to work as anything more than friends' chat? The reiterating 'there's no future' chat?

'What's wrong?'

'*Nothing.* Why would you think something's wrong?'

'Because I'd like to think I've got to know you pretty well and for the first time since meeting you, you're nervous. What's going on?'

'I'm not nervous.'

She cocked a brow.

'Not really, it's just...'

The smile became a grim line that had her wishing she'd left well enough alone.

'I got an email from Geoffrey during the night.'

'And?'

'It's about the gala.'

'The gala...?'

'We were waiting on the final table to confirm their list of attendees.'

'And have they?'

'Yes.'

'So that's a good thing, right?'

'Yes, in that we know where we are with the numbers and have a full house.'

'So, what's the problem?'

'One of those attendees is my ex-fiancée.'

Her mouth fell open, her heart swooping with it.

'I know I haven't—'

'Your *what*?' Her stomach was in a dancing frenzy, her shoulders inching around her ears. Had she really heard him right? He'd been *engaged*. After all his talk of never wanting such a thing, he'd… 'I don't understand. You said—'

'I know and I'm going to explain in as quick a fashion as I can because I don't want you to think I haven't mentioned her for any reason other than the truth—Zara hasn't been a part of my life for a decade and I mean that. We grew up together, same social circles. Our families earmarked us for marriage when we were young. We were engaged when I was eighteen, more a publicity stunt by my father than a real proposal of marriage. And it soon went sour when his dodgy dealings and debauched behaviour became public knowledge. Her family disowned mine, and she disowned me.'

Her heart was racing as fast as his words.

'When I told you of my friends turning their backs on me when everything went south, she was one of them. I saw no reason to differentiate her as a special case, because Zara wasn't one. I never loved her, not really. I was infatuated as a boy, yes. But love, never. So please, don't think any more on it than that.'

She was struggling to *think* on anything as she tried to fit this revelation with the man she thought she knew. Anti-love. Anti-marriage. Anti-everything she didn't want too, but now…

'If that's the case, why are you so worried about her attending now?'

'Because when I told you there were those that returned with my success…'

'She was one of them?'

'Yes.'

'And has she made any attempt to…?' Her stomach twisted.

'Rekindle our relationship?' His eyes told her before he even confirmed it. 'I would be lying if I said she hadn't.'

'I see.'

'But as her father is one of our biggest benefactors and she's his guest—'

'Why let them come at all after the way they treated you and your family?'

'If I cut everyone out who had something to say about my family back then I'd be depleting my charity's funds quite considerably. I'd rather take advantage of their very deep pockets and be the bigger person.'

So why the continued nerves, the edge to his voice, unless...

'You think she's coming to make a play for you?'

He shifted in his seat, cleared his throat. 'Possibly. Probably. Geoffrey has suggested I reconsider my lack of a plus-one...'

A plus-one? A date. Of course. Her gut gave another twist.

'You want to ask my permission to take someone with you?'

'Not just any someone, Fae.' He gave her a bemused smile. 'I want to take you.'

'Huh?'

'I want you to come to the gala with me.'

'Are you *mad*?' she blurted even as her heart rejoiced. 'What do I know about galas and fancy events?'

'They're just a great big party. All you need to do is be yourself and everyone will be as enraptured as I am, I promise.'

Enraptured? Now the room was spinning along with her head and heart.

'Are you asking me to go as your friend or as your...?' She swallowed, nerves stealing her voice.

'Considering the night we just shared, I think we're a little more than friends, don't you?'

She did, but...it didn't change who she was. How out of place she would be. Didn't he need someone sophisticated, elegant, a Sasha not a Fae? Would he have asked if Geoffrey hadn't put the idea out there?

'Fae?'

'Are you asking me because you need rescuing from this woman, or are you asking me because you want me to go with you?'

He wrapped his hand around hers. 'I don't make a habit of being backed into a corner by anyone, least of all my ex-fiancée, so believe me when I tell you, I'm asking you because I want you to come with me as my date. I don't know how much clearer I can b—'

She cut off him off with her kiss as she leapt into his lap, her heart fit to burst from her chest.

She didn't care that she was nervous, terrified, treading unknown waters. Right this second, she was all about him and the fact that he wanted to take her as his equal, his partner, his *date*!

'Is that a yes?' He broke away with a breathless laugh.

'To use your words, I don't know how much clearer I can be. Of course, it's a yes.'

She had no clue what to wear but she had Sasha's wardrobe at her disposal. Her sister was taller, more statuesque, but with some heels she'd be able to make something work.

And she had two weeks to solve that problem; right now she had a man plus a sugar fix to enjoy…

And yes, the nervous wriggle still existed but it was oh so easy to mute when he looked at her like he was doing. 'You know you're supposed to salivate over the food, Rick?'

Keeping her locked in his lap, he forked up some waffle and bacon and lifted it to her lips. 'Can't I salivate over both?'

'You're full of the best ideas.'

'And don't you forget it.'

CHAPTER TWELVE

MONDAY MORNING CAME around and they were in Rick's kitchen eating breakfast having just got back from walking the dogs along the coastal path.

He looked across the black granite breakfast bar at her wearing his grey T-shirt and felt an all-consuming rush of warmth fill his chest.

'What's that smile about?' She patted the top of her head. 'Is my hair out of control again?'

'I make no secret of the fact that I love your hair out of control.'

She gave a chuckle and bit into her toast, her body bobbing on the stool, which suggested her legs were swinging underneath. Much like the dogs' tails wagged when they were happy, she was happy. And he was glad she was happy, because he was happy too.

Exceedingly so, having received another email from Geoffrey overnight confirming a certain addition to his morning appointment…and he couldn't wait to share it with her.

'So you know I have my tailor coming at ten to make any final adjustments to my suit for the gala.'

She hummed her acknowledgement.

'Well, he's bringing a friend of his. Alanna. She runs a ladies' fashion house here in Sydney and will be bringing an array of outfits for you to choose from.'

She choked over her toast, her eyes watering as she stared back at him. 'She's *what*?'

He grinned. 'Surprise!'

'Rick, I can't afford—'

'It's a gift, Fae. I'm the one who invited you so it's only fair I get to treat you.'

She picked up her orange juice, took a sip.

'But I already have a dress.'

Of all the responses he'd imagined, this hadn't been one of them.

'You do?'

She flinched. He hadn't meant to sound so surprised but...

'I wouldn't have thought you'd—'

'I'm borrowing one of Sasha's.'

She slid off the stool, his T-shirt swamping her tiny frame as she dropped what was left of her toast in the bin.

'There's really no need to borrow one. I'd like to buy you one. Like I say, it's a gift.

'She'll bring a range of accessories too,' he hurried to add when she said nothing. 'Shoes, handbags, jewellery, you can take your pick. Whatever your heart desires.'

And now he wished he'd just stop talking because with every word, her shoulders hiked higher, her skin paled further.

'Fae?'

Her mouth twitched into a smile. The kind she'd given him the day they'd met. When he'd untangled her from the dogs' leads. Not good.

'That's sweet of you. Thank you.'

'Hey, come here.' He reached out for her wrist, pulled her into his arms, kissed her lips. 'Are we okay?'

'You've just handed me your bank card for whatever my heart desires—what woman wouldn't be happy?'

You, his gut was saying, sirens blaring in his mind telling him she was only saying what she thought he wanted to hear. Though aloud he pressed on, 'So I'll send her around to you for ten?'

She nodded, gave him a chaste kiss, then tapped her thigh for Precious.

'Come on, darl, we have a fancy fashionista to prepare for. Bet you're gonna love her.'

He winced. Was Alanna in for the cold shoulder?

And he thought they'd come so far…where had he gone wrong?

Alanna was everything Fae had feared she would be.

Beautiful. Elegant. Sophisticated. Sasha would have loved her.

Where was her sister when she really needed her?

Oh, that's right, on her honeymoon having the time of her life as she should be.

But as Alanna left her a few hours later in a cloud of expensive perfume and doubt, Fae wished her sister was here.

Better still, she wished her mum *and* her sister were here.

Which was ridiculous. She was a fully grown woman, going to an incredible event for an incredible cause with an incredible man.

So why did she feel like she was *this* close to Lone Pizza Date Gate again?

Rick would never treat her that way.

The inferiority was all within her.

Even Alanna and her team had cooed over the chosen dress and Fae had to admit, there had been something about it. When she'd taken a good enough look…if you can call a quick turn and the briefest scan 'good enough'.

But she'd been too self-conscious to truly look at herself while three stunning strangers were doing the exact same.

Though she knew the grey silk taffeta gave the gown a fairylike feel that made her think of Rick and the way he saw her. The off-the-shoulder cut and corset lifted her chest and enhanced her slender waist. The flowing fabric, delicately layered and reaching all the way to the floor, possessed a hidden slit to the thigh that only became visible when she walked. It had felt so perfect, even if she herself hadn't.

And as she eyed the dress bag containing it now, she wondered if she'd made a terrible mistake. Maybe she should have stuck to her guns. Told Rick she was happier in something of Sasha's. Anything but agreeing to this, because instead of making her feel like she would fit in, which had to be his intention, she felt ever more out…

Over the next two weeks, no matter how busy things got with work, the estate, the gala, Rick always made time for their twice-daily dog walk, and they always fell into the same bed at night.

The edginess of Fae's appointment with Alanna had passed with the day. The dress itself had appeared in its dress bag and remained under wraps ever since. He'd asked if she was happy and she'd told him she was. She hadn't offered to give him a sneak peek or asked for his opinion and he hadn't wanted to push his luck so he'd left it. Though every time he saw the bag hanging on her wardrobe, he had to fight the urge to look.

He'd seen the shoes. Tall stilettos. Silver.

That was it.

And the thought of her stepping out in a gown… He imagined it was akin to seeing one's bride for the first time on her wedding day. Hell, he'd never *seen* Fae in a dress. Or would it be a suit?

He wouldn't be surprised and would be just as in awe.

'What are you thinking about?' She lifted her head from his chest.

It was late, gone midnight, another passionate lovemaking session had been followed by another and now his hand was in her hair, toying with the playful pink strands as he lost himself to his thoughts.

'How did you know I was thinking about anything?'

'I could tell by your breathing you weren't sleeping.'

He kissed the tip of her head. 'Are you going to be okay walking both Precious and Ralph tomorrow? I wouldn't leave if I didn't have to but…'

'I am more than capable of looking after two dogs, Rick.'

'It's more the walking of two dogs I'm worried about.'

'Are you saying I'm not strong enough?'

'I'm saying, Ralph alone weighs more than you. It's a legitimate concern.'

'And in case you haven't noticed, I think Ralph listens more to me than he does to you these days.'

He chuckled. 'I can't argue with that.'

'Not if you know what's good for you…' She planted her chin on his chest to meet his eye. 'Is that really what you were thinking about?'

He couldn't lie to her, not when she was looking at him like she was, naked and trusting.

'I was wondering about your dress for the gala.' He looked to the item hanging in its cream Alanna-monogrammed bag. 'That's if it is a dress…?'

'*Yes*, it's a dress!' She dug him in the ribs. 'What do you think I am, an animal?'

'We've already established the answer to that and to be fair—' he let his teasing gaze drift back to her '—plenty of women wear dinner jackets these days. It's the height of fashion…or at least it was.'

'Well, I wouldn't know.' And there was that look again, the same unease that had come over her that morning two weeks ago when he'd first mentioned Alanna and his 'surprise'.

'You're not worried about it, are you?' He held her by the chin as she tried to duck his gaze. 'Fae?'

She hesitated, her brow furrowing.

'You really don't need to be. It'll be fun and you're going to be stunning. Whatever you wear.'

She licked her lips. 'We'll see. I have a call lined up with Sasha and Gigi tomorrow and they're going to talk me through my make-up and hair.'

He cursed. 'I should have thought. I could have booked you in with a stylist. They'd come here and do all that for you. It would have taken the pressure off. Wait, let me—'

He started to reach for his phone and she pressed him back. 'No, you don't.'

'It's no trouble. Geoffrey will get straight on it. It's what all the ladies do.'

'Not me.'

He gave a perplexed smile. She couldn't be serious. The gala was a big occasion and women always got their hair and make-up done for big occasions. Didn't they?

Surely it helped alleviate the nerves too. And she had to be seriously nervous if she was disturbing Sasha and Gigi on their honeymoon. *Especially* when her and her sister hardly had a bedrock of sisterhood—though he knew that had changed quite a bit in the past month. Their calls and messages had become more and more affectionate on both sides. Which was great to see but still...

'It's okay to treat yourself once in a while.'

'I'm serious, Rick. I'm quite capable of doing it myself... with some tips and tricks from experts like Sasha and Gigi.'

'Doesn't beat having an expert actually do it and take the pressure off. You should relax and enjoy it. Enjoy being pampered. Is it the money you're worried about, because I'm paying? Money is no object, Fae. I want you to be happy.'

He sensed the tension running through her and wished he could shut this down. Shut his own mouth down. But he was so desperate to have her relax, to have her enjoy what he was capable of giving her.

'No, it's not the money.' She rolled away and slipped out of bed. 'I *want* to have that time with Sasha, it's what *sisters* do.'

'Of course, but if you change your mind…'

'What time are you setting off in the morning?'

He frowned. 'I'll likely be gone before you wake up.'

But he didn't want to talk about leaving, not when he could feel the emotional gulf building between them now. A gulf he couldn't understand.

He wished he didn't have to go into Sydney. But he had attendees flying in from across the globe who deserved the VIP treatment of a pre-event meet and greet. Something he always ran personally to express his gratitude and that of the charity's. It was also the first time the gala had been held in Australia so the pressure was on to impress and make it one to remember.

'I'll be back around five to change for the gala. The car will be here to collect us just after six.'

'Six. Got it.'

She disappeared into the bathroom and closed the door softly behind her. He stared at it long after she was gone, feeling she might as well be in another country for the distance that had formed.

It's just nerves, he told himself.

And tomorrow, she would prove to herself that she could do it and all would be well again.

Wouldn't it?

The next day, true to his word Rick was gone early. Fae hadn't been asleep when he'd kissed her forehead goodbye though. Not fully.

The night had been a restless fit of worry.

How could she have thought to say yes to any of this? A gala! Her!

It wasn't even the dressing up and looking all *fancy*. But the people. A whole room of Rick's kind of people.

It wasn't like the bar, where her customers chose to come into her domain and she could be the person who she was. No airs and graces.

This was like going back to private school. Her father's chosen schools. Walking the halls with people way out of her league and she was sick to her stomach with it.

And for all she told herself she wasn't worried about his ex-fiancée because to use Rick's words, he'd never loved her, Fae was terrified of coming face to face with the woman. Knowing that she came from his world was enough to send her inferiority complex into overdrive.

Having Precious and Ralph to look after for the day was a good distraction but that only went so far. She was hoping that Gigi and Sasha would soothe away the rest.

Even if it was more creating the perfect mask than it was curing it.

'Fae-Fae!'

She'd set the laptop up on the dressing table in her bedroom and she waved at the two sunny lovebirds as they popped onto the screen.

'Hey, Sash, Gigi!' They looked like they were cosied up in bed, sharing one giant pillow, their heads tucked together. 'Thanks for staying up late to do this with me. You sure you don't mind?'

'Mind? We wouldn't miss this for the world.'

'Hardly the kind of romantic endeavour you envisaged for your honeymoon, hey? Having to come and rescue my image via satellite?' She flapped her hands at her shower-flushed face and towel-wrapped hair.

'But this *is* romantic. You're going on a date, Fae-Fae. Your first in how long?'

She screwed her face up, trying to remember her last proper date—one that involved going out some place nice—and came up blank. It was probably the nondate that had become meme-worthy in her teens. And that really *wasn't* the thing to be thinking on right now.

Her sister winced with her. 'Clearly too long if that face is your answer.'

'Fine. But let's just get this done in the quickest time possible.'

'We will, but first champagne!'

Fae rolled her eyes but couldn't help grinning as she lifted her own glass of ready-poured bubbles to the screen. 'Way ahead of you.'

'Great minds! Now before we make any decisions, we need to know a few details,' Sasha said as Gigi dutifully poured their drinks. 'First off location. Where is it being held?'

'Sydney Opera House.'

'Exquisite. Dress code?'

'He didn't say, though he said something about losing the dickie bow...'

'Okay, probably a dark suit, maybe a tie,' Gigi said passing a full glass to her wife.

'Thank you, darling. And lastly, but most importantly, we must see the dress. We can't choose colours without seeing the masterpiece we are to pair you with.'

'Really?'

They gave a vigorous nod, a chorus of 'Really!'

She eyed the bag like one would a trapped spider and swallowed. 'Okay.'

Setting her glass down, she wiped her palms on her robe and crossed the room.

As she unzipped the bag, her mouth quivered—a hint of

a smile. The same wistful smile that had caught at her when she'd spied the fairylike fabric on Alanna's portable rail.

'Oh, my goodness, Fae-Fae!'

'It's exquisite.'

She touched her hand to the silk. 'You approve?'

'We adore!'

She smiled as she zipped the bag back up. So far so good…

And for the next hour and a half, she did as Gigi and Sasha directed. Every colour choice and stroke of the brush, until finally, Sasha gave a resounding '*Et voilà!* You are ready for your dress, Cinderella!'

'Really, Sash?! *Cinders?*'

'Sorry, Fae-Fae, it's the bubbles going to my head. You know I don't mean anything by the reference but seriously, when he sees you…'

'Are you…*crying?*'

Fae peered closer at the screen as Sasha dabbed at her eyes. 'If your mother could see you now… You wouldn't even wear a dress to our wedding.'

Fae rolled her eyes. 'Yeah, yeah, I know.'

'Are you going to put it on now so we can see?'

'Absolutely not. I have to walk the dogs before I'll risk getting in it.'

Sasha sighed. 'Putting our babies first.'

Fae smiled. 'See, told you, you could trust me.'

'Just look at them…' Sasha was all goo-goo-eyed as she looked past Fae to the two dogs, who had appeared halfway through the makeover session and curled up together on Fae's bed. 'They're so sweet together.'

'Ralph's certainly won you around,' Fae said to her.

'Much like his owner has won *you* around,' Sasha quipped back.

She'd walked right into that one…

'You do seem very happy beneath the nerves,' Gigi commented, her observation softer than Sasha's. 'You have a lightness about you, a glow.'

Likely the same glow Rick had mentioned. Nothing to do with Bondi, and everything to do with him.

'It's true, the last month has been...' She searched for one word to sum it up and failed. 'I don't know how to describe it. He's like no one else I've ever known. He makes me feel like no one else. He's so thoughtful, and generous, and kind. He makes me laugh. And he can cook, which is a huge bonus when I can't. Don't get me wrong, he also drives me crazy at times and if he offers to pay for— *What?*'

They were sharing a look, their eyes sparkling, their lips pressed together.

'Why are you looking at each other like that?'

'You sound like...' Sasha said to Gigi.

'She does,' Gigi agreed.

'I what?'

They both looked to her.

'You sound like you're falling in love, Fae-Fae,' her sister cooed.

'Give over.'

Though wasn't her sister saying everything she already knew, had already thought, and just cemented it in her mind?

'It's been a month, sis! You can't fall in love in a month!'

Sasha's eyes widened, Gigi's too. 'Did you— She just...' She pointed at the screen, looked at Gigi, looked back at the screen and leaned in. 'Fae-Fae, did you just call me sis?'

'I—' She swallowed. 'Yeah, I guess I did.'

Sasha covered her mouth, definite tears filling her eyes now.

'Oh, jeez, don't cry on me, Sash! I won't do it again.'

Her sister was fanning her face now and Gigi was hugging her while grinning wide. 'Don't worry, she's fine, I think you just made her honeymoon.'

'Sorry, Gigi, I didn't mean to steal your thunder.'

'Steal away, I don't mind for that, not one bit.'

'Oh, Fae-Fae, I love you.'

She gave her sister a shaky smile. 'And I love you too.' And she had an awful feeling that for all she said she didn't love Rick. That she couldn't have fallen in love with him after only a month. She did. And there was nothing she could do about it.

She may not belong in the world she was about to step into. *His* world. She loved him.

The question was, could the two mix? She was about to find out.

At least with her sister's help she was as ready as she ever would be.

'And thank you for the help today, I couldn't have done it without you both.'

'Any time, *sis*. Though you should have more faith in yourself—you would have been fine without us. Wouldn't she, Gigi?'

Gigi nodded. 'And can I just say, if he doesn't fall in love with you too, he needs his head examined.'

Fae's heart flipped over. The idea of Rick falling in love with her...she gave a pitched laugh. 'We'll see.'

'Keep us posted,' Sasha said.

'I will.'

'Now go be the best-looking dog walker Bondi Beach has ever seen...'

Walking two dogs while trying to protect her hair and make-up from the sea spray was quite the challenge. Not enough to keep her mind off the nervous churn doing its best to return now that she didn't have Sasha and Gigi to distract her. But she was getting it done with her head held high...

'Hey, miss. Hey! You dropped this.'

'Huh?'

She turned to find a dark-haired guy racing up to her, his curly hair flopping about, a satchel over his shoulder and Precious's garish pink poo bag dispenser in his outstretched hand.

'Oh, wow, thank you, I didn't notice. I must have caught the clasp.'

'No worries.' He flicked his fringe back as he handed it over. 'Happens.'

He was British. English. Nothing like Rick's hoity-toity English though. More down-to-earth. Friendly too. His grin was wide and open. Though he was definitely eyeing her funny, likely wondering what on earth she was doing made up like she was from the neck up, dressed like she was from the neck down.

'Cool dogs,' he remarked.

She smiled. 'This one is my sister's. Her name's Precious. And this one is my...my...' What was Rick? How would he introduce her tonight? As his girlfriend, his partner, his other half? The idea warmed her as she said the same. 'My other half's. His name is Ralph. Say hello, guys.'

'I always fancied a Great Dane myself.'

They gave him an inquisitive sniff as he gave them an awkward pat in return. Strange. Though she supposed it was good to be wary of dogs if you didn't know them personally.

Then his eyes were back on her, just as curious. Oh, right, the make-up versus the outfit. Of course.

'I'm off out,' she said, clipping the tiny bag dispenser back on its ring. 'Hence the OTT top half.'

'Ah, right, gotcha. Going anywhere nice?'

'A gala.'

'Sounds fancy.'

She laughed. 'My sentiments exactly.'

She nipped her lip, thinking how nice it was to talk to someone so obviously on her level and how different she would feel in approximately two hours.

'You don't look too excited about it, if you don't mind me saying. Is it not really your bag?'

'My bag?'

'You know, your scene? You don't seem that into it.'

Her laugh was tighter this time. 'You could say that.'

'Looks like I'm heading your way if you fancy offloading a little. I can promise you a good ear and maybe a few laughs for distraction…?'

Now that did sound good. And perhaps the distraction of some company, practice talking to a friendly stranger, might help prepare her for the evening ahead. And he did seem nice. It would be like old times back in the bar. And perfectly safe walking along the seafront with many others around too.

'Sure, why not? I'm Fae, by the way.'

'It's a pleasure to meet you, Fae. My name's Simon…'

CHAPTER THIRTEEN

RICK ROLLED HIS head on his shoulders. It had been a long day and he was feeling it. But the night was yet young. He needed a shower and to get ready, but he wanted to see Fae first.

He'd called round to Sasha's, but she wasn't there. And Ralph wasn't back at his. He assumed she was still out on their afternoon walk so he was waiting on the front terrace, keeping lookout.

He was worried. He hated how they'd left things the night before. He wanted to clear the air, make sure—

Fae!

She appeared in the distance, Precious and Ralph trotting dutifully just ahead. But she wasn't alone. She was deep in conversation with a guy. A guy who made her laugh suddenly. Rick shifted on his feet, shook off the strange feeling trying to work its way in.

You can't be jealous of another guy for making her laugh.

No. But then the closer they got, the more the unease grew. There was something about him. Something familiar. Something...

What in the hell!

He was down the steps and out of the gate in a flash, upon them before he could draw a full breath.

'Fae!'

'Rick, you're home!' Her smile froze on her lips as her eyes met his. 'Everything okay?'

No, nothing was okay.

And when he didn't reply she turned to her companion. 'This is—'

'I know who this is.'

'You do?'

She looked from him to Simon and back again, a frown forming as the other guy took a step back. 'Lord Pennington, it's good to see you looking so well. Bondi Beach certainly suits you.'

'It certainly doesn't suit you.' Rick ignored the hand Simon proffered and took Fae by the elbow. 'Now if you don't mind, we have somewhere we need to be.'

Not that he cared if the guy minded; he was already marching Fae and the dogs back to the house.

'Rick, you're hurting me.'

He slackened his grip with a grimace, wishing for the life of him that he could be calmer, more in control, but his brain was racing. So many scenarios. So many stories.

What could she have told Simon?

The second they were inside Sasha's domain, she rounded on him. 'What the hell was that about?'

He raked an unsteady hand through his hair. Tried to remind himself that this was Fae, not some money-hungry acquaintance or an untrustworthy peer from his past—*Fae!*

'He's a reporter from the British press. He works for the *Daily Tattle.*'

She froze and he imagined that beneath the carefully applied make-up she paled. Though the make-up was a perfect mask. Quite exquisite too. The smoky eyeshadow drawing out the golden hue to her eyes…which now flared back at him. Shocked. Hurt.

She wet her lips, their glossy pink finish unaffected by the move.

'A reporter?' she whispered, clutching at her stomach.

'A reporter who you seemed pretty quick to bond with. What was it? His looks or his voice that worked in his favour?'

'Rick!'

Inside, his head was screaming at him to take it back, but his heart...his heart hurt.

She was shaking her head, her eyes wide and wounded. 'I had no idea, I swear it.'

'He was drilling you for a story, Fae.'

'But I... But he was nice. He...he...' She looked to the dogs, who were drinking at their bowls. 'He was asking about the dogs and the gala and...'

'And?'

'Us.'

'Us?'

'You.'

His gut rolled. 'What did you tell him?'

'I... I don't know. I told him that you hadn't been here long. That you were from the UK. That we'd met only recently.'

'What else?'

She started to tremble, the stress emanating off her in waves. 'I don't know. Stuff. Nothing big. He was nice and he was making me feel better about going tonight. Making me feel confident about how I looked and...and telling me that I shouldn't be nervous.'

'But what about my family and my father, the title...?'

'I don't think I mentioned any of that.' And then her frown deepened. '*Why* would I mention any of that?'

He stepped closer. 'You don't think, or you know?'

'I know I didn't.'

'Are you *sure*? Reporters are skilled at getting the information they want out of people unawares.'

She reacted as though slapped, her head flicking back. '*Yes*, he made me feel at ease. *Yes*, I enjoyed his company. I didn't suddenly become an untrustworthy gossip, Rick.'

'I got enough out of you once you got over your first impression, and you had no such qualms with him.'

'The stuff I told you was about *me*, and nobody else. It was mine to share.'

She couldn't have been any clearer or more reassuring. It was him that was jumping to conclusions. Seeing red having seen Simon. So why were his shoulders still around his ears?

'Oh, my God!'

Her exclamation drew him up short. 'What?'

'You don't trust me, do you?'

He stared at her, his little pixie with her fists on her hips, her wild pink hair tamed by a single silver clasp to one side… Breathtakingly beautiful and spitting fire.

'Rick, answer me!'

'I *want* to trust you, Fae. I do.'

'But you don't.'

'I trusted before…'

'And you were burnt. Yes, we've done that discussion to death.'

'And I'm trying…'

'You need to try a hell of a lot harder because this…this doesn't work if that trust is all one-sided.'

And then she spun away. 'Come, Precious, it's bedtime.'

'But Fae, the gala…?'

'I'll see you outside at six.'

How could she have been so foolish?

Actually, scratch that, Fae knew well enough. Rick was right. Her prejudice had risen up to bite her on the arse. She'd *assumed* Simon was a good 'un, based on his voice, his looks, his presumed similarity to her…so different to her present company.

She glanced across at Rick in the back of the swanky car that had been hired to take them to the opera house. His face was angled away, his attention on his phone as it had been for the entire journey. He *looked* busy, but was he?

Or was he just avoiding her?

She was the woman who had betrayed him by getting all cosy with the reporter. She gritted her teeth and looked to the window. When she thought back over her conversation with Simon now, the warning signs had been there. How he'd kept bringing the conversation back to her. Much like Rick had done, but in Simon's case, she hadn't questioned it; she'd gone along with it.

Thankfully, she hadn't given anything incriminating away. Well, nothing other than her relationship to Rick. And if she was honest with herself, she wasn't so sure she'd got that right anymore.

If he didn't trust her, what did they have really?

It was that doubt that stopped her from speaking up in the privacy of the backseat.

And it was that doubt that made her hesitate now as the car pulled up at their destination and the door was opened for her.

Should she just stay where she was and tell him to go without her? *Before* they stepped out in public and the whole world questioned it.

She turned to suggest as much but he'd already gone. Seat empty. His masculine scent on the air. She breathed it in and turned...

You can do this.

She stepped out, her eyes lifting to take in the Sydney Opera House, which gleamed in all its glory, the sail-shaped roofs flaunting the evening sun. She wished she could be a fraction as impressive because though she wore Rick's wealth like a cloak, his money couldn't buy what her heart truly desired and without it, she felt bare. Vulnerable. And terrified of joining all the others who were making their way inside, every one of them as elegant and sophisticated as him. Every one of them belonged here.

Rick arrived at her side, his hand gentle on her arm, and her gaze leapt to his, desperately tried to read his.

The storm had lifted, but in its place was a clear kind of torment. She wasn't sure which irked her more. And then he leaned in close, and her heart stopped.

'I'm sorry, Fae.'

'*You* are?'

He nodded.

'It's…it's okay.' She licked her lips, unnerved but grasping at the unexpected olive branch. 'I should have been more aware.'

'No.' His jaw pulsed. 'I should have warned you that he might be lurking around.'

'You *knew*?'

'Geoffrey mentioned that he might come out here looking for a scoop. I didn't think any more on it until I saw him with you and I… I jumped to conclusions. I'm sorry.'

She huffed, her smile as weak as her knees. 'You're talking to the right person when it comes to jumping to conclusions. I've learned my lesson there.'

His mouth twitched, his tormented gaze keeping her in its grip. Did he not believe her?

'I've called in a few favours. Whatever story he thinks he has, he'll struggle to find a home for it. You should warn your friends and family to be on their guard. I'm afraid your association to me makes you of interest to them now.'

She hadn't even thought…hadn't even considered…

'Is that what you were doing just now?'

'Yes. I couldn't bear it if you got hurt in the crossfire.'

Her heart swelled with his concern. 'I'll warn them.'

'Good.'

And for the first time since they had come together again

since their fight, she took a full breath and allowed herself to drink him in. The carefully groomed stubble and the swept back hair with its misbehaving strands that fell forward, framing his impassioned gaze. The dark suit that was cut to enhance his frame. The crisp white shirt, smooth against his front. And the tie that made her want to wrap her hand around it and tug him in so that she might kiss his lips. A real kiss-and-make-up session—not that she dared in such company.

He was so deeply, darkly sexy and she knew every eye, male or female, would be drawn to him tonight, whether he was commanding the room or not.

And he was her date. *Hers!*

She glanced around at the cameras that lined the entrance and the people milling about. The people who *did* belong… She tried to tell herself that she did too.

Channel Sasha!

Don't you dare, Fae-Fae, she imagined her sister saying. *You be you!*

Then came Gigi. *'If he doesn't fall in love with you, too, he needs his head examined.'*

If only.

'Fae…'

Her gaze snapped back to his. He sounded raw, hoarse… his blue eyes blazing as they dipped over her. And she realized this was the first time he'd looked at her properly too. No phone. No distractions.

'My God…'

He said no more for several seconds, *did* nothing more, until she could no longer stand it.

'Rick?'

He blinked, blinked again, his eyes returning to her face. 'You are… There are no words.'

She tilted her head, lifted the skirt out. 'Please give me *something* so that I at least know I'm on the right track.'

'If I wasn't hosting tonight, I'd be taking that track back to our car so we can go home and I can show you just how right it is. You look…ethereal. And every man and woman here tonight will struggle to take their eyes off you.'

She gave a choked laugh. 'I was thinking the same about you.'

He pulled her to him. 'They won't see me for you.'

And then he lowered his mouth to hers. 'Rick…' She pressed him back. 'There are people.'

'And?'

He gave a wolfish grin and kissed her deeply. She was vaguely aware of camera flashes going off, the murmurs of the people, and her cheeks burned, but that burn had nothing on the electrifying effect of his lips against hers.

She may not have his trust yet, but they had this. She could cling to this…take strength from this…couldn't she?

CHAPTER FOURTEEN

'Well, I'll be! I wasn't expecting to see this kind of display on my arrival.'

Rick broke away from Fae to find Geoffrey, grinning ear to ear at their side, an earpiece in, phone in hand. All set to stay on top of the event as well as Rick's life simultaneously.

Though the most important life event was clearly taking place in front of him judging by his PA's face.

'Fae, I'd like you to meet Geoffrey. Geoffrey, this is Fae Thompson, my date.'

Fae's eyes sparkled up at Rick before she turned to greet him. 'It's lovely to meet you at last. I've heard so much about you.'

'And I wish I could say the same about you, but this one keeps his cards close to his chest.'

'Geoffrey.'

The warning in Rick's tone was unmistakeable but his PA waved a nonchalant hand. 'Yes. Yes. Behave. I know. Says the man who was just seen by all and sundry sharing some extreme PDA.'

Fae stifled a giggle and even Rick smiled. 'It's my party. I can kiss who I want to.'

Geoffrey's eyes bulged. 'Oh. My. God. You really did find a life in Bondi. Wait until Kate hears this.'

'And I say again, whose PA are you?'

He wagged a finger. 'Ah-ah, you don't scare me anymore,

sir.' He sent a wink Fae's way. 'Okay, maybe he does a little, he does pay the bills after all. Now shall we get inside before your guests drink *all* the champagne…?'

Rick shook his head as Fae chuckled. Never mind Bondi going to his head, Australia had clearly done something to Geoffrey's.

'I like him. A lot,' Fae murmured as they followed Geoffrey inside.

'Something tells me he already likes you a lot too.'

Once inside, they mixed and mingled with the masses in the lead-up to his welcome speech. The Hamiltons were noticeably absent but then he wasn't surprised; Zara liked to be fashionably late and make an entrance of her entrance.

Which was all he needed…

'Are you ready for your speech, sir?' Geoffrey came up to them, a fresh glass of champagne in each hand, which he offered out. 'Most of the guests are here.'

Rick scanned the room and noticed Fae was doing the same. She'd only met half the room. Was she trying to work out which one was Zara? Should he save her the trouble and tell her she wasn't—

Ah, never mind, there was a flurry of activity at the door, the Hamiltons had just arrived and Zara was straight out in front.

'And here I was hoping she might have been taken sick last minute,' Geoffrey murmured under his breath as they watched the woman take a glass of champagne from an approaching waiter.

'Geoffrey…'

'I know, behave.'

'Is that…?'

'Zara Hamilton, indeed,' Geoffrey said to Fae, 'aka the devil reincarnate.'

* * *

Fae gazed across the room at the statuesque blonde dressed in scarlet red. And she wasn't the only one. Every eye in the room seemed to swivel her way as Fae's heart sank into her stomach.

She was everything Fae wasn't.

Older. Richer. Classier. So at ease with the attention. So at one with the elegance of the room…

And he'd been engaged to this woman? Would have married this woman? Did Fae honestly think he would ever do the same with her?

'Fae?'

'Huh?'

'I asked if you'd be okay while I do my speech.'

Get a grip, Fae. He's with you, not her. He chose you. Not her. He could have asked her. He asked you.

'Of course.' She sipped at her drink, her eyes drifting back towards Zara and struggling to see her through all the men who had now flocked to her side. If she was lucky, Australia's eligible bachelors would keep the woman suitably distracted and busy the entire night!

'I'll be back as soon as I can.'

He swept a chaste kiss against her cheek and she watched him go. Focused on him and his speech. Lost herself in a side to Rick she hadn't yet seen. He was a charming host, captivating the masses with such effortless ease. But then it made sense, he'd been born into this.

As for his obvious passion, the charity wasn't just close to his heart; it *was* his heart? The hereditary disease brought tears to her eyes now and she dabbed at the corner of her eyes, praying no one else would see.

'He's good, isn't he?' Geoffrey said as he appeared at her side, discreetly handing her a handkerchief.

She nodded.

'As are you. I never thought I'd see the day he'd smile or joke or laugh like he has since you came into his life. You've cast some kind of spell over him, Miss Thompson.'

She choked on her bubbles and the unshed tears.

'You're giving me too much credit.'

'And you're not giving yourself enough.'

Geoffrey gave her a warm smile.

'Right, that's the welcome over with,' Rick said, returning to their side.

'Not quite. You still have a few latecomers to meet, including you know who…'

Rick's smile twisted. 'I suppose I must.'

'It will be noticed if you don't.'

Rick turned to her. 'But only if you're okay with it.'

She nodded, hooking her arm in his. 'Of course.'

He covered her hand upon his arm and she lifted her chin as they followed Geoffrey through the crowd.

You've got this, she told herself. *You look the part so* feel *the part.*

Though every step, she felt the spike of her heel. Unsteady. Teetering. The eyes were turning. From Zara, to them, to Fae.

She could feel their gaze sweeping over her, assessing her. Did they know who Zara was to Rick? Were they comparing them both? Finding Fae lacking?

Her knees trembled as the slit in the gown permitted her every step and she fought the urge to draw it together, to prevent them from seeing. She tried to take a breath, but the bodice that had felt made-to-fit only hours ago now squeezed at her ribs. Her skin felt hot and clammy.

'You look stunning.'

His words brushed like a caress against her ear, triggering a tiny tremor through her middle and a smile from the depths of her despair.

'You scrub up well yourself.'

He chuckled softly and then Zara's eyes found his as she gifted him a smile for him alone, shattering the moment so completely. Her eyes drifted to Fae on his arm and something flickered across her face—pain, distaste, jealousy… Whatever the cause, her smile never wavered but her eyes said it all.

She turned to her neighbour, said something before weaving through the crowd towards them.

Geoffrey stepped forward to run the introductions, but she swatted him aside. 'Cedric, darling, it's so good to see you…' Blood-red nails clawed his upper arms as she leaned in to peck his cheek, her perfume unnecessarily cloying—or was that just the effect of her presence? Provoking Fae's inferiority complex and a jealousy she didn't want to acknowledge or feel?

'And who is this…sweet little thing?'

Sweet little thing… It made her think of Rick and his pixie penchant. But he wasn't belittling her. *She* was. Zara. And she hated the woman for tainting it now. Hated it even as she pinned a smile to her face.

'This is Fae. Fae, this is Zara. Daughter of Sir Hamilton, our prestigious benefactor.'

Was he trying to make her feel better by qualifying Zara's presence here by association with her father?

Zara gave a soft chuckle. 'My, my, Cedric, I'm a little more than that, wouldn't you say…'

Rick stiffened and Fae touched a hand to his arm, a silent communication not to worry. She had this. She hoped.

'I trust you are having a pleasant evening, Lady Zara.' She wanted to vom at the words coming out of her mouth, but she was determined to play nice and play the role expected of her.

Zara's eyes narrowed to slits and then she cackled. *Truly* cackled.

What had she said? Done even?

Her inferiority complex rose to greet the laughter head on,

and Rick might as well have been made of stone for all he was moving now.

'I'm not a *lady*, darling. My father is Sir Hamilton, my mother is called Lady Hamilton but alas, I am simply Zara. Oh, my, Cedric, you must teach her some etiquette for when you return to England. You know how cruel some people can be.'

Fae's cheeks burned deeper with every word, her gut shrivelling to the size of a walnut. If only the ground could open up and take her…

'Perhaps it's you—' Geoffrey started and Rick stepped in.

'Perhaps it is you who needs to learn some etiquette,' he said through gritted teeth. 'And do close your mouth, Zara, you wouldn't want to ruin your appetite with a predinner fly. Now if you will excuse us, we have other people to greet.'

They moved on swiftly, Geoffrey positively vibrating with glee. 'Just when I thought I couldn't love you more, sir.'

'Yes, well, maybe next year we'll reconsider having a blacklist.'

'Excellent idea.'

'I wish I'd thought to come out with that,' Fae murmured to Rick.

'I'm just sorry you had to endure it. Please forget everything she said.'

'Consider it forgotten.' The laughter though…she could still hear it ringing in her ears, just like when she was fourteen, only so much worse.

'Now allow me to introduce you to our next guests…' Geoffrey said pausing beside another group of people who stopped conversing at their arrival and started to turn. 'This is esteemed surgeon, Mr Fraser Manders. His wife, Martina. And daughters Eloise, Florence and Grace.'

With open horror, Fae stared at her father, his wife and his daughters. The other family. Her worst nightmare. And the glass in her hand fell and shattered with her heart...

Rick watched her crumple. Physically she was still standing but everything about her had shrunk. Her light, her confidence, her energy.

'Fae...?' He reached out but she shook him off as a waiter rushed up with a dustpan and brush.

'I'm so sorry,' she blurted, her eyes failing to make contact with anyone as she apologized and ran, pushing her way free of the group and then the room.

'Fae!'

She didn't stop.

'Fae!'

She kept on going, falling over her own feet, shrugging off his hand when he tried to make her pause.

'Fae!'

It wasn't until she was outside that she rounded on him, her eyes wild, chest heaving. 'How *could* you?'

'How could I what? I don't...'

And then the pieces started to fall into place, his gut lurching with them... The surgeon. The man and his family.

No, please, God, no.

'He's my father,' she whispered through quivering lips, tears filling up her eyes.

'Fae...' It was an anguished groan as he threw his hands into his hair, grasping handfuls when all he wanted was to take hold of her. 'I didn't know. I swear it! You *have* to believe me. If I had known, I *never* would have invited him.'

'Really?' A choked scoff. 'No blacklist, remember? Money's money, and he has plenty of it.'

'I wouldn't have taken *his* and put you through this. I *swear* it! You have to believe me!'

'You take Sir Hamilton's!'

'That's different. That's my past, my pain to deal with.'

'Your pain?'

'You know what I mean.'

'Do I? I don't know what to think anymore.'

'I'm so sorry, Fae.'

'Are you? You're the one who brought me here. You're the one who gave me all the money for my heart's desire and dressed me up like one of you. Made me like *her...*'

She choked on the last, openly crying now, tears streaming down her face. Mascara running. It killed him to see her in so much pain. Pain that he had caused.

'You once told me not to change for anyone or anything and this isn't me, and yet you gave me your money and told me to change.'

'I didn't. I told you to get yourself something nice for an event. I couldn't care what you wore, so long as you were happy. Hell, you could have come in your shorts and T and I would have been just as proud to show you off.'

She choked on a laugh. 'Yeah, right.'

'I'm not kidding, Fae. We would have had some funny looks, but I'd have walked in there, head held high because yours was...'

She shook her head, eyes wide and disbelieving. 'I can't do this, Rick.'

He stepped forward, softened his voice, held his hand out hoping that she'd meet him halfway. 'I know. I don't expect you to go back in there now. I wish I could go home with you. The last thing I want to do is leave you after the shock you've had but—'

'No, you don't understand. I can't do *this*! Me and you.'

His throat closed over. She couldn't be serious. 'Fae, it's been a hell of a night. Once you've had time—'

'Time isn't going to change the fact that we don't belong together.'

'You can't mean that.'

'But I do!'

'Please Fae, don't do this.'

'Don't do what? Don't end this relationship before you have a chance to end it further down the line when you realize what my father did, that I'm not good enough. Worthy enough to choose. Did you *see* them? His…his *daughters*! Did you see how perfect and beautiful they were? Did you see how they looked at me? And did you see his face? The recognition and then, the *disgust*.'

'It looked more like fear to me.'

'Whatever it was, it wasn't love.'

'Fae, please.' He took another step and she backed up, stumbling in her heels.

'Don't, Rick.' Her eyes were frenzied, desperate. He knew her head wasn't fully in the present. That right now, he wasn't sure who she was seeing, who she was fighting, him or her father, but he wanted to wrap her in his arms. Whisper sweet nothings until she calmed. Anything but this…

'Let me be there for you.'

'No. I need to go, and you have a gala to get back to. I won't ruin your night any more than I already have. Goodbye, Rick.'

And then she swept away, her farewell as final as one could be, and he watched her go. Unsure of how long he stood there for but eventually he returned to the gala in a daze.

Most people gave him the decency of space as a sympathetic Geoffrey sidled up to him, but her father had other ideas. He made a beeline straight for him as he left his baffled wife and daughters behind.

Bring it on, thought Rick. He had plenty to say to the man. Like how he could think for a second that his money could replace the love his daughter had so desperately craved and deserved all her life…?

And that's when it hit him, his epic blunder. He'd been no

better than her own father all along. Showering her with his wealth when he should have been showering her in his affection, his...*love*.

He hadn't found a life worth living because of Bondi; he'd found it because of her. Fae. His sweet little... His fists clenched as he thought of the words Zara had twisted but he was determined to reclaim them. Because Fae was his sweet little pixie goddess and she was his one true love.

And he hadn't told her.

But he would.

Just as soon as he could.

CHAPTER FIFTEEN

'HEY, DARL, COME HERE.'

Poor Precious seemed to be suffering with empathy for Fae the next morning. Not only had she sicked up her breakfast, what little she had eaten, but she was also totally uninterested in leaving the house.

After a quick Google, Fae had decided it was likely nothing to worry about, but she'd keep a close eye on her all the same. And so they had curled up on the sofa and watched the sunrise from there, Fae stroking at her fur and finding some comfort in the company. Though her mind was restless, replaying the night's events over and over.

She'd have to message Sasha and Gigi at some point. The pair would start to hound her soon for an update—that's if the gossip tabloids didn't get there first! It was one thing for Rick to try to stop Simon circulating anything, but an entire room of partygoers sharing the scene she had made...

She swallowed back the nausea, but nothing could beat back the desperate ache within her chest. She'd heard his car return in the early hours and her ears had strained for footsteps on the path, her heart pleading for him to come her way.

He hadn't. He'd done as she had asked. Let her end it.

But she'd been so jacked up on the pain of her past.

No, the pain of her past *and* her present. Both colliding in such a way that she hadn't been able to think clearly, let alone process her feelings enough to tell him what truly mattered.

That she loved him. That against the backdrop of all that glamour, the only reason it hurt so much was because she feared she couldn't be enough for him. And the idea that she would love him and that he would in turn reject that love… she hadn't been able to bear it.

Precious whimpered in her lap. 'I know, honey, I was a wuss.'

The poodle made the same sound, longer this time, lifting her head further, her tail beating against the sofa.

'What is it?'

Fae looked to the sliding doors and the steps that led down to the front gate as Precious dropped to the floor and trotted up to the glass. Rick? Was it possible?

She stood. Started to walk. Precious barked. She checked her watch. It wasn't yet seven in the morning…would he really call now?

She stared out. Nothing. No buzz of the intercom. No movement. Yet the poodle's tail still wagged.

'They've probably gone for their walk, darl.'

She stroked her head, started to turn away when Precious barked and ran through the gap she'd left open in the door…

One of you has the right idea, came her inner conscience. *Get after him and tell him the truth.*

She thought of how she'd felt when those footsteps hadn't come her way and knew she couldn't wait on him. This was on her.

Heart in throat, she grabbed Precious's lead and raced out, uncaring that she was shoeless and still in her threadbare PJs. The only sight she cared about was him.

Latching Precious onto the lead, she threw open the gate and launched forward, straight into a solid wall of muscle. Strong hands gripped her arms before she could rebound onto her butt.

'Fae!'

'Rick!'

She blinked up at him. Crumpled and creased in the suit from the gala, tie stripped, shirt unbuttoned at the collar, hair askew, eyes shadowed. 'You look like hell!'

And yet, he still looked better than any other man alive.

His mouth quirked to one side. 'I've yet to see a bed...'

'But... I heard you come home in the night.'

'I sent Geoffrey home for Ralph. I knew I couldn't come home and not come straight here. I was right. Case in point.'

He lifted his hands out and her body instantly missed the warmth of his touch as she wrapped her arms around her middle. 'But where did you stay?'

His eyes flared. 'Not with *her* if that's what you're worrying about.'

'God, no. I just meant...'

'I had Geoffrey's hotel room, but I didn't use it. I walked until the sun started to rise and then I got a cab. And now I'm here because I have to tell you what I should have told you last night.'

She swallowed. 'And what's that?'

He lifted his hand to her face, stroked his thumb along her cheek, his blue eyes searing in the golden hue of the morning sun. 'I love you, Fae. And I'm sorry I didn't just shout it after you last night, but I do.'

Laughter bubbled up within her. Delicious. Joyous. Disbelieving.

He frowned. 'What's so funny?'

'I don't believe it.'

'Well, it's the truth.'

And still she laughed, so light and so happy and...

'Not the reaction I was expecting.' He scratched the back of his head. 'No, seriously, Fae, I need you to listen to me.'

'I am listening, and that's not what I don't believe, though it is rather surreal.'

'Then what is…?'

She slipped her fingers into his hair. 'It's that you took the words right out of my mouth. That *I* should have told you the exact same thing last night. That I realized my mistake the second I got away. That of all the things I had told you, I hadn't told you the most important thing…that I love *you*.'

'You do? After everything I got wrong? Throwing money at you, thinking it was the answer to everything, your nerves about the gala, meeting Zara… I hadn't stopped to think that what you were truly lacking was me. After everything you'd told me of your father, of growing up too… I couldn't believe I'd be so thoughtless, so heartless.'

'You're not heartless, Rick, you're never heartless.'

'No? I was plenty heartless when it came to telling you how I felt. Because I don't think I realized myself how deep my feelings ran until I was forced to watch you walk away from me. Because I love you, from the bottom of my heart, I love you.'

His words seeped beneath her skin, permeating her heart and warming her through.

'I love you, too. And I'm sorry I ran from you and that I ruined your gala.'

He went to interject, but she touched a finger to his lips. 'It's my turn to explain. I just couldn't bear it, being in the same room as him, as you. Realizing I was in the same impossible situation, craving love from a man who couldn't return it.' He hesitated beneath her finger, his lashes flickering over eyes that blazed with his love. 'Only this time it was worse, because this time I not only loved that man, he was worthy of it too. Because I do love you, Rick, and you really are worthy of it.'

She slipped her finger away and kissed him softly.

'I'm so sorry you had to face him,' he murmured fervently against her lips, his arms slipping around her waist. 'If I could go back and change it…'

'You weren't to know.'

'Well, I do know now, and he knows my feelings very well. He'll be making his donations from a distance in the future.'

'What did you say to him?'

'Nothing that wasn't warranted and nothing that would cause you or your mother any harm, I promise.'

'And his family?'

'Still blissfully unaware. That's his own bed to deal with.'

She nodded. 'So he'll continue donating if you…'

'No, Fae, I would never resort to blackmail. If he wants to assume such a thing then that's down to him.'

She nodded, her stomach swimming with it all.

'But I really don't want to talk of him anymore, do you?'

'Absolutely not.'

'I'd suggest we get Ralph from Geoffrey and take them for a walk, but I could really use a shower…'

'I'm not sure a walk is on the cards. Precious is behaving a little off this morning. Though she perked up a little with your arrival…'

He looked at the fluffy white pooch who in the time they'd been talking had dropped back to lie down.

'Maybe she's missing Ralph. Tell you what, come back to mine, we'll shower there…'

'*We'll* shower?'

'Do you think I'm letting you out of my sight when I've only just got you back?'

'What about Geoffrey?'

'He'll be too relieved to see you again to pass comment.'

She laughed. 'How about we go get Ralph and then we'll shower here instead?'

'Deal.'

EPILOGUE

One month later

'DARLING, I KNOW you're smitten, but can I steal you for a second…?'

Fae could barely tear her eyes away as she sat cross-legged on the floor. She *was* smitten. Head over heels, one hundred per cent in love with seven tiny fur balls.

The last few weeks had been a blur. With Sasha's return from her honeymoon being delayed due to a freak storm in the Caribbean, there hadn't been a 'right' time to explain about Precious's condition, which had become apparent after the gala. A bit of extra googling and they'd booked her straight in with Rick's vet for confirmation.

No expense spared for Sasha's darling.

And though Fae felt immensely guilty that she hadn't told Sasha, ever more so that it had all happened on her watch, the idea of delivering the news over the phone or video call felt wrong, especially when there was nothing her sister could do to get home any faster.

She just had to hope that she took it well. Though one look at Precious nursing her babies, how could Sasha not melt on the spot?

'I can lend you an ear,' she compromised as Rick wrapped an arm around her middle and eased her to her feet.

'A man can get jealous, you know.'

She laughed as she turned into him. 'What about a dog? Look at poor Ralph—he doesn't know where to put himself.'

'I know how he feels.'

She looped her hands around his neck and kissed his pout away. 'You're not really jealous.'

'Of course not, but I do need to talk to you about something before your sister arrives. Because I have a feeling once she gets here we won't have much opportunity for talk and this is important.'

His sudden severity had her stiffening, her heart thudding in her chest. 'What's wrong?'

'Come with me.' He took her by the hand and led her into the front room.

'You're worrying me. Is it the doctor? Has something changed…?'

'No, nothing like that, not really…' He paused in the middle of the room and turned to her.

'Not really?' That was hardly reassuring. She covered her throat with her palm.

'Look I know when we got together, that kids were not on your radar and that suited me just fine. But I've watched you this past week. I've seen you with those pups, and you're so soft, Fae. So soft and loving and I don't know, the idea that you and I…' He raked a hand through his hair. 'Because of the risks.'

She stepped up to him, placed her hand over his heart as she realized where he was heading with this. 'You can't choose the heart you fall in love with, Rick, and I choose yours. I fell in love with yours.'

'But what of the future, of our children if we were to reconsider…'

A smile played about her lips. She had been thinking along the same lines. The future filling up with possibility the day she had let their love colour it pretty. 'About that… I've been meaning to talk to you too.'

'You've changed your mind?'

She nodded. 'More than just changed it. I want lots, Rick. Lots and lots. I want to love as many as I can in this one lifetime.'

His brows disappeared into his hair line as he choked out, 'Okay, now you're scaring me. I know the risk doesn't increase with each child but…'

She gave a soft laugh. 'Not quite what I was meaning… How would you feel about fostering? We have the most glorious location for any home. We have the stability. You have the means and I have the time…'

'But what about all your talk of going back to school, of counselling, or maybe even opening a bar of your own?'

'They were all ideas that centred around my past. This is about the future and what I truly want to fill it with. And that's love. Our love. And I want to give a home to kids who for whatever reason don't have that in their lives. I want to make them feel wanted and loved again. I know it'll be hard and come with challenges of its own and there'll be lessons to be learned along the way. But it's something I'd like to explore…if it's something you would like to explore too.'

His blue eyes were awash with something. She just wasn't sure what. Shock, maybe?

'Please say something.'

'I never thought I could love you more.'

She huffed out a relieved breath. 'Does that mean you'll think about it?'

'I'll do more than think about it. I'll make some calls first thing tomorrow, while you're out with your sister and Gigi.'

'Really?'

'Really.'

She reached up on tip toes, kissed him with all the gratitude and love she felt inside. Contemplated whether now was the time to ask if they could keep a puppy or two as well, but… baby steps.

'And while we're on the future,' he broke away to say, 'there's just one more thing I need to ask and then you can go back to your four-legged babies…'

'Anything!'

'In that case, Fae, my spirited pixie…'

She gasped as he dropped to one knee, the sun's rays lighting up his eyes as out of the back pocket of his jeans he lifted up a ring box.

'There will be those who say it's too soon and pass judgement on us before we can prove our worth. But I don't care, because when you know, you know, and the only judgement I care about is yours.' Then he grinned. 'Besides, they'll soon come around to what beats beneath the surface—you sure did.'

She gave a choked laugh. 'I can't believe you're managing to make a proposal about me and my prejudice!'

He shrugged. 'Isn't that what they're supposed to be about? The "you" bit, that is. So what do you say, will you do me the honour of becoming my wife?'

She grinned wide. 'Yes, Rick! Yes!' She swooped down to hug him to her, tears streaming down her cheeks. 'Of course, I'll be your wife!'

'Fae-Fae, we're home! Oh, my God!' There was a squeal, followed by another, and Fae and Rick leapt apart, eyes wide on the door to the kitchen. *'Fae!'*

Fae looked at Rick. 'Uh-oh, do you think she's found them?'

Rick looked at Fae. 'What do you think?'

They scrambled to their feet and raced into the kitchen to find Gigi and Sasha standing over Mum, proud Dad and the babies…

'Hey sis!' Fae gave a sheepish wave. 'Meet the newest additions to the family, your Great Danoodles! You always said you wanted a big family, right?'

One big *happy* family…or it would be, once her sister came down off the ceiling.

* * * * *

*If you enjoyed this story,
check out these other great reads
from Rachael Stewart*

Fake Fling with the Billionaire
Unexpected Family for the Rebel Tycoon
Reluctant Bride's Baby Bombshell
My Unexpected Christmas Wedding

All available now!

DRIVING HER IMPOSSIBLE BILLIONAIRE

ELLA HAYES

MILLS & BOON

For my dear friend Hayley, with love.

PROLOGUE

Today's Sporting News:

British Touring Car Championship driver Max Lawler Scott walked away from a horrific crash at Donnington this afternoon, clutching his left hand.

The thirty-three-year-old celebrity publicist, who achieved a podium place four times last year, refused to be stretchered off, but was clearly in pain as he withdrew from the track surrounded by officials and medics.

His sister Felicity Hewitt, anchor for News Global, later confirmed Lawler Scott's injury to be serious, saying that it might well preclude him from driving again for the rest of the year. She admitted that this would be an immense blow to the speed-loving playboy who loves to race.

Neither Lawler Scott's father, media mogul Sir Gerald Scott, nor his mother, News Global Editor Tamsin Lawler, have made any statement, but were snapped arriving separately this evening at Cromwell Hospital, where their son is being treated...

CHAPTER ONE

Three weeks later...

'HELLO, YES? WHAT?'

Tommie felt herself flinch. Hardly the warmest of welcomes. Three words, not even polite ones, barked over the intercom! The man sounded impatient, irritated, as if she was interrupting something—but that couldn't be right because this was definitely the correct address, the correct day, and she was bang on time.

Breathe...

Maybe there was a simple explanation. Maybe this wasn't *the* person, but some poor, hard-pressed minion, who didn't know she had an actual appointment—in which case all she had to do was set him straight...

She aimed a smile into the security camera, making sure to keep her gaze and tone level. 'I'm here for the interview.' And in case that wasn't enough information... 'I'm Tommie Seager.'

Short pause.

'Tommie...?

Oh. *Of course.* Here it was. The familiar note of surprise. Next would come the half-beat of recalibration while assumptions were laid to rest. Her sister Billie got it all the time too.

She widened her smile a touch. 'Yes, that's right.'

'Ah…'

Slithering off his high horse now, wasn't he? Regrouping. It was hard not to smirk, not to show just a touch of enjoyment, but it wouldn't endear her to him any—which was, after all, the whole point of coming. To make a good impression. Never mind that Prince not-so-Charming didn't seem to be similarly motivated. Still, if he was *the* person—the prospective employer—she didn't have to like him to work for him.

The intercom emitted a cough, then a little throat-clearing noise. 'Apologies, Tommie. I was…'

She held her breath. How could he be struggling when the words were so obvious? Curt. Gruff. Rude. Any of them would do.

'…distracted.'

Slippery, much?

And then his tone steadied, seeming to find its groove, public-school-polite, formal. 'Please, come in.'

A buzzer sounded, then a lock sprang in the high black gate.

She pulled in a slow breath and pushed it open.

Wow! The house was impressive. Architect-designed. Vast, but not cold, not austere. Rather, it was warmly appealing. Acres of plate glass and external lighting. A flat roof covered its two storeys, overhanging the walls by a deep margin. The walls themselves were of a polished light grey block, softened in places with narrow vertical strips of golden cedar cladding—like barcodes. The whole thing was softened further by lush, exotic planting around the perimeter and around the edges of the pale monobloc frontage. It was all very Zen. Neat. Private.

Beautiful!

She felt her eyes going to the four—yes, *four*—garage

doors. What was behind them? A sleek, gull-winged sports car? Some high-end electric fantasy? Or something classic and sedate? Probably all of the above. And none of the usual garage junk. No rusty barbecue on wheels, no rolls of old carpet that 'might come in handy one day'. No way—not in a pristine place like this.

She checked herself. Now who was the one making assumptions?

She shut the gate and set off towards the front door— all charcoal-grey and brushed steel—trying to ignore the butterflies in her stomach. Hard not to conjecture, though, when you had no actual information. That was the thing about the agency Billie worked for—Neville Cutter Services, recruitment for the rich and famous—it was all so discreet, so cloak and dagger. She'd had to sign a non-disclosure agreement just to come for this interview, and even Billie didn't know who the employer was, because names were never supplied until a candidate was accepted for a role, only details of the post being offered.

In this case, *Personal driver. Eight-month contract. Live-in. Luxury annexe accommodation.* Stapled to a *Strictly no guests, day or night* stipulation. Free run of the owner's pool and gym—although since 'erratic, unsociable hours' were promised, even at weekends, it was probably a token gesture. Days off were to be allocated on an ad hoc basis to fit with the employer's schedule. It was basically twenty-four-seven, which was why the job paid a fortune—a fortune that could change Tommie's life. *That* was why Billie had called her the moment it had landed on Neville's desk.

'It's got your name all over it, Tommie! You've got the skills. The experience. And I know you're going to say you don't want to go back to driving, but think of the money and the free accommodation—in Hampstead, no less. No more

living with Mum and Dad! And I get that it's demanding, but it's only eight months, and then you'd have the funds you need to go for it. And, yes, there's all that waiting around— but, hey...old news, right? And I'm not trying to wind you up about New York, because I know you're still livid, but you learned a lot too—so why not use it? Use the waiting around time to sketch, develop some new ideas, make over- tures to buyers. I mean the Lincoln Lawyer worked out of his car, so why not you, Tommie? Why not you?'

Launching her own fashion label from the front seat of some billionaire's luxury ride seemed a tad far-fetched— but, oh, the money...the possibilities it could deliver. As for the annexe accommodation... A place of her very own for the first time in her life. Never mind that it would only be for eight months, at least for those eight months it would be hers—all of it. A place to be herself, to breathe, think, sketch, dream... No Mum and Dad, no New York roomies, no Jamie...

She felt her chest tightening on cue. Ridiculous to *still* be feeling guilty about Jamie. It wasn't as if any of what happened was by design. She hadn't *asked* him to chat her up in the pub that night...hadn't *asked* him to ask her out, or to offer her a job three months later, driving for his fam- ily's start-up business Chauffeur Me.

She hadn't asked, but of course chauffeuring was a step up from delivery driving—more glamorous, better paid—so of course she'd accepted. Who in their right mind wouldn't have? But she'd never asked to become so involved in the business, to get caught up in the constant in-fighting—Jamie and his dad; his dad and his brother—had never asked to become chief mediator or to become the driver most fa- voured by their female celebrity clients, the one business- women felt most comfortable with. She'd never asked for those five years to slip by in a blur, never asked Jamie to propose. And she totally should have but never had asked herself why she'd said yes, moved in with him.

It had all been slow drifting—until it hadn't. Until the day she'd got the gig driving iconic fashion designer Chloe Mills for the whole of London Fashion Week. A glorious week! Talking non-stop fashion with Chloe, feeling the old fires stirring, brightening inside, confessing to Chloe-freaking-Mills, of all people, that she designed stuff too—had used to do Spitalfields Market with a friend every Saturday, selling her own creations.

Used to... Because she didn't any more.

Didn't have the time, or the focus, because of Jamie and *his* business...because she'd somehow let her dreams drift away.

It had been a sobering behind-the-wheel realisation—one that would have been bound to change things anyway. But that last morning she hadn't asked Chloe to offer her a dream job, to be her personal assistant in New York, and she hadn't asked to be faced with making that decision in that moment.

Chloe had asked *her*. And how could she have turned it down, the chance of lifetime, when mostly life had dealt her short straws?

Yes, it had meant blindsiding Jamie, hurting him, leaving him a driver short. And, no, it hadn't been her finest hour. But she hadn't planned it—any of it. Still, Jamie could content himself with the last laugh, because here she was eighteen months later, back in London with her tail between her legs, shafted, and smarting.

So much for once-in-a-lifetime chances, so-called golden opportunities!

She shook herself. But now wasn't the time to be dissing golden opportunities—not when she was staring down the barrel of another one, and not when Billie had pushed her to the top of Neville's pile to give her the jump on the other candidates. She owed it her best shot—owed Billie. And maybe chauffeuring again did feel like a backward step, but at least this time it was a means to an end. And it was infinitely better than tidying the ravaged clothes rails at Belle & Trend, for little more than minimum wage, kidding herself that she was still working in fashion.

Bottom line: Billie was right. This job had her name all over it. All she had to do was win over Mr Grumpy!

She squared herself up to the door, lifting her hand, but before she could bring it down to knock the door was opening wide, revealing a tall, fair, sickeningly familiar figure.

'Tommie?' Laser-blue eyes swept over her without a vestige of recognition, and then he broke into a slightly forced-looking smile, extending his hand for her to shake. 'Max Scott. Thanks for coming.'

She felt dryness seizing her throat, her heart seizing altogether. *No, no, no!* This could *not* be happening. Max Scott! Well, he could call himself that if he liked, but it didn't alter the fact that this was *the* Maxwell Lawler Scott, publicist to the rich and shady. Worse, he was Chloe Mills' publicist—lying, thieving Chloe Mills, who'd stolen her designs and passed them off as her own, then fired her when she'd got up the nerve to challenge her about it. Not that he was likely to know about that, since Chloe would hardly have confessed it to her publicist, of all people, but, still, he was on Chloe's team, and as such the enemy.

She found a steadying patch of breath. At least he didn't seem to recognise her. Then again, why would he? Thanks to Billie, there was nothing in her application to jog his memory. No mention of New York, no mention of her working for Chloe. Billie had said they should leave it out because it was irrelevant, and it might actually count against her—make her seem like not a serious enough candidate for a personal driver position. And it wasn't as if he'd given her more than a passing glance that long-ago night when she'd run into him—*literally*—back in her early days of working for Chloe, back when it had all still felt so exciting…

New York Fashion Week… Chloe's after-show party…

Chloe had sent her scurrying to organise more canapés, because they were going to run short. She'd said it to her in that arch way she had, implying it was *her* fault—which it absolutely hadn't been. But, as she'd quickly learned, Chloe was a highly strung control freak who insisted on signing off on everything from buttons and fabric swatches to the exact number of freaking canapés.

She'd been flying out through the door as Max had been coming in, with supermodel Saskia Riva on his arm. She'd caught him with her shoulder momentarily, and nearly died on the spot because he was so utterly drop-dead gorgeous. But before she'd been able to stammer out an apology he'd swept on as if he hadn't felt the impact—as if she'd made no impact on him at all.

And now here he was, looking at her with a perplexed and visibly narrowing gaze. Narrowing because she was still silent, rooted to the spot, instead of greeting him back, shaking his hand like a normal person, falling over herself to make a good impression.

Well, that boat had clearly sailed. His expression spoke volumes. He wasn't going to employ her, was probably wondering why the agency had sent her at all.

Her heart lurched. *Oh, God!* And that wasn't going to reflect well on the agency or on Billie, was it?

For Billie's sake—even though this was suddenly the last

job in the world she wanted—she needed to step up, show Max she was a contender, not a complete waste of his time.

Breathe, Tommie.

'Max…' She put her hand into his, shaking firmly to seem confident. 'Thanks for seeing me.' *And now smile…* 'It's very nice to meet you.'

He gave a slow nod, his lips parting slightly as if he wasn't sure what to say, and then he seemed to rally, stepping aside with a new, tight smile. 'Please, come in.'

She forced her feet to move, but a few steps in they were faltering again, along with her breath.

It was so light inside…so airy, calm and serene. Unexpected, somehow, for a renowned man about town. *A player!* She pushed the thought away. Maybe all the plants had something to do with it—large, expensive specimens, lush and green and not remotely dying, like her plants always were. Or maybe it was the acres of solid Maplewood flooring, the pale couches, and all the lovely natural textures that made the place feel so tranquil and homely…those warm accents of red earth and charcoal-black.

A soft *thunk* filled the silence. Max closing the door.

'Come on through.'

And then he was skimming past, trailing a pleasant soapy smell, leading the way towards the rear of the house, where vast windows were pulled back, letting in the balmy morning air and the dappled green of the garden beyond.

She felt her lungs releasing. Here was a second to breathe, to take him in. Dark blond hair, curling at his nape, nice shoulders…broad, muscular, shifting smoothly as he walked. He was wearing a plain black tee shirt, loose black trackies and…she heard the quiet catch of her own breath… some kind of splint on his left hand.

She stared at it. So that was why he needed a driver—

and why he was dressed like that. Pull-on, pull-off stuff was probably the best he could manage with one hand. Her heart pinched. It must be awkward as hell. And this was an eight-month contract, wasn't it? So he would be anticipating eight months of awkwardness. No wonder he wasn't exactly radiating sunshine. She wouldn't be either, in his shoes. Not that she could let herself feel sorry for him. She had one job: to spend five minutes presenting herself well, so that Billie wouldn't seem incompetent, and then she was out of here!

CHAPTER TWO

SHE WAS LOOKING him over. He could tell. He could feel
her grey-green eyes burning into his back, drilling holes
into his skull... Or maybe that was just a tension headache
coming on, because, God help him, she was even more attractive in the flesh than she'd looked on the Entryphone
camera. Heart-shaped face. Milky complexion. Sweet full
lips reddened with confident lipstick. Impeccable, too. Pro-
fessional-looking, with her efficient blonde chignon and her
crisp white shirt. Her pale grey suit was well cut, the trousers fashionably cropped above pristine black patent loaf-
ers. She was dream stuff—if you were into those sorts of
dreams—quite the package!

But what was with the attitude? That cool, vaguely bait-
ing gaze she'd greeted him with before she'd so obviously
reminded herself that she ought to smile. It wasn't the puz-
zled flash of half recognition he sometimes got from strangers; it was something else. Almost as if he'd offended her in
some way. But how? He'd only known her for two minutes
and barely opened his mouth in that time.

Unless...

He raked his teeth over his lip. Unless it was because
he'd been a tad irritable over the intercom. Initially, anyway. Not his fault! How was he to have known she was the
candidate? He'd thought she was trying to sell him some-

thing: encyclopaedias…gym membership. *Whatever!* Taking up his time when he was expecting a guy to pitch up for an interview any second.

Honest mistake!

No, Max. Not remotely honest…

Felicity's voice, in his head, reprimanding him as only a sister could. He ground his jaw. She was right, of course— as always. If he'd taken the time to read Tommie's details properly, instead of skimming them literally as the buzzer was sounding, he'd have known she was female. But no. Too busy fuming about this whole intolerable situation to spend five minutes preparing—fuming because he didn't want anyone living here—even in the guest annexe—invading his sanctuary, seeing him reduced like this, fencing with this useless hand.

He focused hard, trying to detect some sensation, but it was no good. He couldn't make his fingers feel…move. Didn't stop him trying, though, did it? Constantly. Involuntarily. Like a dog with bone. Trying to force feeling through wrecked nerves that might or might not knit themselves back together in the correct register. Months of uncertainty lay ahead, with no guarantee of being able to grip again, pick up a cup, drive—race!

And maybe Fliss was right. Maybe he *was* taking the specialist's direst warnings too much to heart instead of embracing the rosier picture, that he *might* get most of the function back, and the feeling. But he didn't want to feed his hopes only to have them dashed. Bad enough listening to the preachy voice inside his head saying he only had himself to blame, because he was the one who'd put himself in that car, on that track.

He knew the risks…took the risks. For heaven's sake, he knew accidents happened!

He pulled his lips tight. He'd just never thought that one would happen to him. Not deep down. Too welded to the myth of his own invincibility, too hooked on racing. On the strategy, the split-second decisions, the pure adrenaline rush of it. But he wasn't invincible. And now, because he wasn't, he needed a driver, must tolerate a stranger living in his personal space because he couldn't—just couldn't—spend the foreseeable future waiting for cabs to come, relinquishing his independence on top of everything else. And not only because his clients paid him a lot of money to be available round the clock, but because freedom was the air he breathed—*must* breathe.

A trade-off, then. Necessary. But he hadn't expected, wasn't prepared for Tommie Seager. Cool. Unfathomable. Threatening to send his brains south even while she was for some inexplicable reason totally freaking him out. No way could he employ her, cope with this kind of discombobulation on a daily basis. This whole thing was a bust—a waste of time. But he was stuck now…must force himself to go through the motions, at least give her the interview she'd come for.

He made for the kitchen end of the living area, then drew in a breath and turned to face her. 'I thought we could chat in here…'

Because the centre island was two and a half metres wide—the perfect amount of distance to put between them.

He motioned for her to sit. 'Can I get you something? Tea? Coffee?'

She flicked a glance at his injured hand. 'No, just water, thanks.' And then her gaze came to his, opening out a little. 'If you tell me where the glasses are, I'll get it myself…'

He felt his chest tighten. She was being considerate. But he didn't want consideration. It only made things worse, amplified his frustration, that feeling burning inside him that he wasn't fully in control any more.

He forced out a smile. 'Thanks, but it's fine. I'll get it…'

He crossed to the cupboard where he kept the glasses and took one down. Easy enough to pop it into the fridge door water dispenser and pull the lever. As for himself, he'd have coffee—not because he really wanted one, but because he wanted her to see that he could set a cup into the machine, slap in a pod and set it going. Maybe it was petty…petulant of him…but he couldn't help it. He was frustrated on more levels than he could count, and if showing her that he was perfectly capable of rustling up two simple beverages soothed something inside him then why not do it?

She was watching, at least. He could feel the weight of her gaze on his back, feel it siphoning the strength from his legs. But then suddenly the weight was lightening, lifting away.

'You have a lovely home, Max.'

He felt a small, reluctant swell of warmth. Did she mean it or was she just making small talk? Who knew? And what did it matter? The only thing that mattered was that *he* liked his home. He'd put a lot of time and thought into the design of the place, the décor and the landscaping, all to get it just so. If she genuinely liked it—great. If not—also great. But for politeness' sake he ought to say something…acknowledge the compliment.

He mustered a suitably appreciative tone. 'Thanks.'

'Have you lived here long?'

'About five years…'

He reached to extract his steaming cup from the coffee machine, felt his breath check. *Idiot!* He hadn't thought this through, had he? Two drinks meant making two separate trips—one to deliver her water and one to fetch his own coffee. He sank his teeth into his lip so hard it hurt. So much for showing her how capable he was! The only thing she was going to see now was how utterly useless—

'And do you live alone?'

What? Why was she asking him that? What did his relationship status have to do with anything? And if he told her, disclosed that he was single, would she ply him with further impertinent questions, like *Why?* Christ, as if he had the time or the remotest inclination to get into that… divulge the details of his difficult journey to this blissful state of total self-reliance—*control*—where no one could touch him, sideline him, make him feel *less*.

And maybe Fliss was right—he *was* too sensitive, had taken everything too hard growing up, building a wall around himself because of it. But what was wrong with that if he was happy? He didn't diss *her* choices, did he? He was pleased that she was all loved up with her husband Gavin, joyfully newly pregnant. But he didn't want what she wanted—wasn't up for pinning his whole happiness on someone else, giving someone else that power over him. He was fine as he was, wasn't up for having his hard-won equilibrium wrecked by heartbreak.

Because that was what always happened in the end. He'd seen it too many times, spent too many years papering over ugliness for his clients, managing the media around their various heartbreaks, infidelities or plain old foolish indiscretions, to believe that love was real, something meant to last.

The fact was, all relationships were transactional—whether the people in them realised it or not. Ultimately everyone was out to get something from the other person. Money. Status. Power. Advancement. Certainly the women who hit on him always seemed to have one eye trained on what he could do for them. And, yes, maybe that was a hazard of the job, down to the circles he moved in, but it didn't exactly swell the heart, make it skip.

So, no, he wasn't diving into that shark tank, and if by staying out of it he'd earned himself a playboy reputation, then so what? It wasn't true, but it suited his purposes... ensured that the women who approached him were primed not to expect romance or commitment. As if he had time for any of that anyway. Lawler Scott PR kept him busy enough—and now he had his brand-new venture to handle as well: motor sports news agency Alpha News. And of course motor racing was king—the absolute love of his life.

He frowned down at the still-steaming coffee cup. It was a good life, all in all. One he liked...enjoyed. He was happy running along in his groove. He liked his house, his own space, his own company—and privacy. *Especially* privacy. So whatever Tommie was angling for with her question, the only thing she was going to catch was a cold!

He drew in a breath and turned. 'I...'

But the rest wouldn't come. Because for some reason— *why?*—she was on her feet, gliding through the precious buffer zone towards him, foxing him with her perfume and her level grey-green gaze. He could feel his jaw trying to slacken, and a very inconvenient stirring sensation happening down below—which, in these track pants, might draw her attention if he didn't do something about it and fast!

He made a quick pivot, pulling out a drawer to cover himself, rooting for a spoon he didn't need. 'I do live alone, yes.'

'Ah...' She came to a graceful stop by the fridge, carefully removing the glass of water from its little shelf in the door—seemingly the thoughtful point of her mission—and then her eyes came to his, her gaze dispassionate. 'I wasn't prying...' She adjusted her grip on her glass. 'I was only asking because it must be tricky not having anyone around to help you with your hand like that...'

He felt his heart skidding off its rails. Well, wasn't she the candid one? It was refreshing—sort of. But still, he wasn't getting into this with her. All the different ways life had become tricky, the coping strategies he'd had to devise just to get by these past three weeks, such as living in pull-on clothes. No doubt she'd noticed his uber-casual attire, given that she'd put herself together so well...

For an interview. Which he was somehow, very successfully, failing to give her.

Focus, Max!

'I manage.' He set the spoon down and picked up his cup, seizing the moment. 'Shall we sit?'

She obliged, going back to her spot, positioning her glass in front of her. He parked his coffee, then himself, trying to recall what he'd read about her.

'So, you've worked as a chauffeur before?'

'Yes.' She nodded slightly. 'I was with Chauffeur Me for five years.'

A familiar crowd, highly reputable—not that he'd ever used them.

'And you enjoyed it?' Pointless question, but it sounded good...made him feel as if he was controlling the show.

'Yes.' She nodded again, then smiled as if she thought she should. 'I liked meeting different people. And it was more interesting than delivery driving.'

'Which is what you did before you became a chauffeur?'

'Yes, for three years.' A different smile touched her lips, some private amusement. 'I did like driving vans, though.'

He tried to picture her behind the wheel of some great high-top thing, screeching up to his door, swinging out with a parcel and a scanner device...

'What did you like about it?'

Her mouth straightened. 'I liked that it gave me an ency-clopaedic knowledge of London, and I liked the challenge of driving a van… Working around the limited visibility, reverse parking into tight spots and so on. It taught me how to use my mirrors well, to know my blind spots.' Her eyebrows lifted a little. 'It made me a better driver.'

Textbook answers, designed to impress. Unlike himself, she'd obviously prepared for this interview, knew which boxes to tick.

'So, I assume you've got a clean licence?'

Her gaze flared an incredulous degree. 'Of course.'

Nice one, Max!

Because he'd stipulated an unblemished licence, hadn't he? Or rather, his sister had. Fliss was the one who'd helped him get his act together with this whole hiring a driver thing, so he could 'get on with living' while his hand got on with healing. If only she'd agreed to help him with the interviewing as well, but when he'd asked her she'd just stared at him.

'It's a driver, Max! How hard can it be?'

Quite hard, as it was turning out. Because Tommie wasn't 'Tommy'. And maybe it was wrong to view her differently because she wasn't a guy, but he couldn't help it. She was beautiful, and beneath that cool, composed exterior there was clearly a warm heart beating—a kind heart—offering to get her own glass of water like that, then collecting it for herself, subtly saving him from his pathetic, self-inflicted quandary. Impossible to imagine that a girl like this didn't have a life to be living. Friends. *A lover…*

And, no, it wasn't any of his business—except that he couldn't consider anyone, male or female, who wasn't free to be at his absolute beck and call. Not that he *was* actually considering her, but if he didn't interview her thoroughly as

if he were she'd no doubt suss him out for a fake. So he had
to continue, ask her the questions the way he'd ask anyone…

He took a sip of his coffee and met her gaze. 'So, how do
you feel about the demands of the position?'

Her brow wrinkled. 'Which particular demands?'

'The hours. The living arrangements.' His temples pulsed.
'The rules…'

She pursed her lips. 'I'm fine with all of it.'

Or was she just saying she was? Filling his ears with
the music she thought he wanted to hear in order to seem
like a good candidate, to win him over? No chance of that.
But still, to make the charade seem real he couldn't not dig
deeper.

'You're fine with having to be here unless I give you
leave?'

'Yes.'

'Fine with not having any guests over? Day or night. Family. Friends…' He could feel his pores starting to prickle,
his headache striking up again. But he had to say it. '*Special* friends.'

Her eyebrows lifted. 'Are you trying to ask me if I *have*
a special friend?'

That frankness again, stripping him for parts. But it was
fine; he could be just as frank.

'No, I'm not.' And just in case she was reading between
non-existent lines… 'It's of no personal interest to me whatsoever. I'm simply trying to make my position clear. I'm
paying a lot for a driver because I realise I'm asking a lot.
And I'm asking a lot because I'm a very private person…'

Weird and slightly obsessive, Fliss would say. But if admitting it was what it took to clarify things, then so be it.

He drew in a breath. 'I have a thing about personal space,
okay?'

Something dislodged in her gaze. 'I can relate to that...'

So he wasn't the only one. He felt a valve releasing some-where. If she got it, then he could just say it, couldn't he? Not sugarcoat it.

He looked at her. 'Truth is, I don't want anyone living here at all. But circumstances have dictated otherwise, so here we are. I need to find the right person—someone I can see fitting in. And I need that person to stay...not be drawn away by personal issues or obligations. I don't want to be going through all this hiring business again.'

She nodded. 'I understand....' She looked down, toying with her glass for a moment and then her gaze lifted, clear, and direct. 'I don't have any obligations, personal or oth-erwise. My family lives in London, so if you were to offer me this position I could see them even if I only had an hour or two off. But in any case they'd know the demands of the job, so...' She gave a little a shrug and then, for an instant, her gaze opened like a window. 'I'm living at home with my parents at the moment so, as you can imagine, the live-in aspect is a quite a draw.'

Living with her parents...

Why would she be living with her parents at—what? Twenty-eight, twenty-nine years old? He felt his eyes star-ing into hers...searching. Was it the same reason she was free of obligations, why she didn't have a *special* friend? Not that she'd exactly answered that question. More deflected it. But it all pointed to a break-up of some sort—some big life-change which made her one hundred percent available, one hundred percent unlikely to leave him in the lurch. In short, it made her even more perfect for the position than she was already.

He felt a tide rising, crashing over him. Damn this inter-view! He'd meant it to be a token gesture—a quick formality before he showed her the door. But here he was, still sitting in front of her, and there she was, looking at him with that gaze of hers, somehow changing every dimension in the room and any second now she was going to notice that he was losing control of this thing…floundering. He had to shake himself, say something quickly—anything to bring this to a close.

'So…' He picked up his cup to buy a moment, and then he had it—the perfect interview-like thing to say. He allowed himself a quick sip and the briefest of smiles. 'I think I've got everything I need. Do you have anything you'd like to ask me?'

This would be the moment to get up and smile, say, *No, I'm good, thanks*, then leave. So why wasn't she doing that?
Why?
She swallowed hard. God knew. But for some infuriating reason she couldn't seem make herself move, couldn't free herself from that compelling blue gaze. And at any moment those eyes were going to narrow, and those dark straight brows were going draw in, and those beautiful lips were going to part slightly—because she was sitting here silent. So she had to think of something fast—*anything!*

And then it was there, staring her in the face. The obvious question…the one that had been burning her candle at both ends from the moment she'd noticed his splint.

'Yes, I do actually…' She pulled in a breath. 'What did you do to your hand?'

His brows lifted. 'My hand?'

He seemed taken aback, but it was a reasonable enough question. His injury was the reason he needed a driver. And it was obviously troubling him…hampering him physically, mentally, giving his pride a workout. *Geez!* Such a performance with the drinks…getting himself in a tuck—and all for what? To show her he was Cool Hand Luke, able to triumph in the face of adversity? It had been hard not to laugh, watching him, but at the same time impossible not to feel for him, so she'd had to get up and help. And he hadn't said anything, but he'd noticed, all right. Because there'd been a sweet moment of gratitude in his eyes…

Was that why she was still sitting here? Because that glimmer he'd shown her—that peek behind the mask—was tugging at all the usual strings, appealing to the good nature she'd been saddled with. That impulse she had to look for the best in people, to care about them…help them? If so, then she was crazy, and she needed to stop right now. Because that impulse always backfired so that *she* lost out…

Jamie. His dream. His business. His family. Squeezing her dreams out of the picture.

Then Chloe. Trying to help her when she had been blocked creatively. Talking inspiration with her…concepts. Showing her some of her own work, thinking it might refresh Chloe's and, yes, maybe hoping to impress her too. Hoping that Chloe might give her a chance, as she'd promised to do, a tiny slot in a show…at the front…at the end. Just a moment in the spotlight to set her dreams free… Tommie Seager Designs…

She felt her stomach hardening. Well, she'd got a spot in the show, all right. Her designs. Choe's name. No comeback. Just a shove out through the door and a ticket home.

She drew Max back into focus. And here he was. Chloe's publicist—*Chloe's guy.* Appealing as hell with his wounded blue eyes and tousled hair, appealing as hell despite his uptight demeanour and silly, masculine pride. But she couldn't let her caring nature win, let him think she was asking for any other reason than to establish how his injury might impact the business of working for him.

Should that situation arise.

She nodded, trying to keep her gaze level, trying not to hate herself for being so matter of fact. 'Yes, your hand… I mean, that's why I'm here, isn't it?'

He blinked. 'Indeed.' And then he set his cup down. 'I was in a car crash.'

'Oh, my God! Where?' As if *that* mattered. But it was out of her mouth now, attached to an all too obvious note of horrified concern.

'Donnington.'

The word spun for a beat.

'You mean, the racetrack…?'

'Yes.'

Racing one of those lovelies sequestered in the four-door garage, no doubt.

'Track day?'

He shook his head. 'No. I was racing.'

She felt her breath pause, her eyes staring into his. But he wasn't a racing driver. He was a PR guy! International city slicker, celebrity apologist, chisel-jawed escort to supermodels. Sharp-suited, sharp-witted all-round mover, shaker and schmoozer. He *wasn't* a racing driver!

Except… His gaze was serious, deadly deep, reaching in all the way to her toes, which was a very unnerving sensation.

She swallowed hard. 'You're saying you're a racing driver?'

'Not exclusively—but, yes. I race touring cars.'

'Like…saloon cars?'

He made a little impatient noise. 'Modified, race-prepared touring cars. They look like regular cars on the outside, but that's where the similarity ends.'

She bit down hard on her lip. But it was no good—she couldn't *not* ask, couldn't make herself *not* want to know. 'So, what happened?'

A shadow flitted through his gaze. 'My car was clipped by another driver at one hundred and twelve miles per hour. It flipped and rolled, and now my left hand is wrecked.'

She felt her eyes going to his splint, her traitorous heart squeezing. *What to say?* Pointless telling him he was lucky to be alive. He knew that—must have heard it a hundred times already. What was plaguing him now, moving behind his eyes, was *how* wrecked his hand was…the extent of it. And she didn't want to rub salt into his wound, even though he was the enemy, but she wanted to know—couldn't stop herself from wanting to…

'I'm sorry, Max.' She took a breath. 'What's the prognosis?'

His eyebrows flickered. 'You don't hold back, do you?'

But maybe he didn't mind. His gaze wasn't abrasive… wasn't making her think she couldn't come back at him.

'It's a natural question. You just told me your hand is wrecked. Am I supposed to ignore it…sit here silent? I think you'd think I was odd if I did.'

His eyes registered the logic, the light inside them softening momentarily. 'You have a point.' But then his features were tightening again. 'The prognosis is currently uncertain. The bones will mend, but there's some nerve damage.' He threw a disparaging glance at the offending hand. 'I can't feel anything, don't know when, or if, I ever will again.'

She felt an echo inside…recognition stirring. She knew that anxious state-of-limbo feeling. Not that it was the same, or even came close, but when she was fifteen she'd somehow contracted glandular fever. It had floored her—dragged on for weeks before her mock exams. She'd thought she would never come right again. Turned out, she'd been right. Because she never had come right…hadn't seemed to settle back into school afterwards, hadn't been able to get to grips with the work she'd missed. She'd flunked her big summer exams and kept on going, spiralling downwards.

That was until the day she'd passed her driving test. Everything had changed then. Driving had saved her—opened the world up again. Driving those vans, tearing around all day long delivering stuff, had made her feel she *was* somebody. Worthy. In control of her life. Powerful…

She looked at Max. Staring down at his cup now, his face drawn. Had he felt powerful before the crash? In control? And now fate had flipped his coin and he was having to hand control to someone else just to get about…losing his independence, his precious privacy. For a man like him, who oozed privilege from every single one of his beautiful pores—a man who'd probably never suffered a single setback in his whole charmed life—it must be devastating.

She couldn't let herself feel too sorry for him, though. He could afford the best care, the best surgeons and physios. It was grim, for sure, but not as grim as it would have been for someone ordinary like her. Still, she didn't want to seem heartless…couldn't leave without trying to gee him up a bit first.

She took a quick sip from her glass and set it down. 'I don't know anything about these things, but there must be some hope, surely?'

He drew in a breath that sounded like a sigh in the making. 'There is, but I don't want to cling to it. I need to be realistic.'

'I get that—as long as you don't let *realistic* become pessimistic.'

His eyes flashed. 'You sound like my sister.'

Which was what? A good thing or a bad thing? *Fifty-fifty.*

She drew in a breath. 'Well, she sounds like a sensible person to me.'

'She is. Irritatingly so.'

But his gaze was softening with affection. So he was fond of his sister...

Stick with it, Tommie.

'Does she live in London?'

He nodded.

A sister in London... It wasn't much to have in common, but still...

'Mine does too. Her name is Billie.'

'Billie?' The corner of his mouth twitched upwards. 'Did your parents want boys, by any chance?'

A barely-there smile, but nevertheless genuine. Transforming. *Attractive...* Not that she could let herself fall under its spell.

She slid her eyebrows up to put him down. 'Oddly enough, I've never heard that joke before.'

His eyes registered the sarcasm with a flicker. 'Sorry.' But then he was leaning forward a little, looking at her. 'There's got to be story behind your names, though?'

One he obviously wanted to hear. Did she want to tell it, though? All she'd been trying to do was lift his mood— not get into an actual flowing conversation. But then, she was the one who'd started the ball rolling, wasn't she? And he was responding, being different from how he'd been before, and—God help her—she could feel curiosity burning inside her to see more of this different Max and, even though curiosity had done for the cat—which, by the way, had had nine actual lives to her paltry one—she couldn't switch it off any more than she could button her lip and not answer. Because not answering him would be immature and just…weird!

She took a quick sip from her glass, trying not to look too engaged. 'It's not much of a story. My dad's a Billie Holiday fan—hence Billie. And my mum had an eccentric great-aunt called Thomasina—'

'So, you're Thomasina?'

He was twisting his mouth to one side, as if trying to stop himself from laughing, but it was good-natured, not cruel, and it was doing something magical to his eyes that was infuriatingly attractive and somehow infectious.

She absorbed the giggle she could feel rising into the tightest smile she could manage. 'No. I got off lightly with a modern upgrade. I'm just Tommie.'

His mouth opened, then closed again, as if he'd thought better of saying whatever it was he'd been about to say. And then he was looking down, moving his cup aside, even though it wasn't in the way.

'So, would you like to see the accommodation before you go?'

Seriously?

Was he actually *considering* her for the position?

Because he didn't seem the type to waste his time on pointless missions like showing someone the living quarters if he didn't feel they were worth his time. The thing was, she *wasn't* worth his time. She'd only been trying to present herself well for Billie's sake, and the agency's, not for his.

She blew out a slow, quiet breath. Or maybe she was getting ahead of herself—jumping to conclusions—*assuming!* After all, he wasn't exactly meeting her eye right now, was he? Nor giving her *You're the one* vibes? In fact, truth to tell, he seemed somewhat restive, unsettled. As if…

She felt her pulse slowing. So maybe this was just a formality, then—a way of moving things along because he *wasn't* interested, was trying to bring things to a polite close.

Whatever!

Bringing this to a close was perfect. A relief! She'd already stayed longer than she'd meant to, anyway. She didn't even *need* to see the accommodation, although if it was like the rest of the house it was bound to be gorgeous...

She chewed the corner of her lip. Maybe there'd be no harm in seeing it, since he was offering. No harm in showing a bit of enthusiasm to complete the whole presenting herself well charade. For Billie's sake. Obviously.

'So...?' Max shifted his cup back the other way and looked up, his gaze firm. 'Do you want to see it?'

'Sure...' She switched on a smile. 'I'd love to.'

CHAPTER THREE

'I'M SO PLEASED you found someone, Max.' His sister's voice through the speaker was warm, relieved. 'It'll make such a difference.'

'Yes, it will…'

Although Fliss was only thinking about his independence—not the difference it would make having Tommie around twenty-four-seven. That was the difference he was wrestling with…the decision that was still blinking right or wrong inside his head, even though he'd thought long and hard before making it. Even though he'd interviewed three other candidates before reaching it. Top-notch people. Qualified. Experienced. But for some reason Tommie had stuck—wouldn't let him go—so he'd gone with her.

'So, what's he like?'

He felt himself bracing. 'Well, for a start, he's a she.'

'Oh!'

Silence. Somewhat loaded. And then…

'Okay… I'll rephrase: what's *she* like?'

'Polite, professional, experienced.'

'Attractive?'

He clenched his stomach. How did his sister always manage to do this: light on the one thing that was relevant but shouldn't be? The one thing that was gnawing him to the bone? The worry that, deep down, he'd offered Tommie the job because she was gorgeous and turned him on.

He swallowed, trying to sound nonchalant. 'She's okay.'

Fliss chuckled. 'Have you any idea how transparent you are?'

His body pulsed hot. 'And have you any idea how *annoying* you are?'

'Now, now…keep your hair on. I said you're transparent, not shallow. She obviously hits the mark professionally or the agency wouldn't have sent her. If she's attractive as well, then great!' And then suddenly there was pause, and a vague kerfuffle. 'Oh, bother! Sorry, Max. Can I put you on hold for a sec? I've got another call coming in.'

'Sure…'

Situation normal! Fliss's life at the news desk was a perpetual whirl.

He got up to make a coffee, felt his angst abating a little. Whether Fliss had meant to make it or not, she did have a point. Tommie *did* tick all the professional boxes. She *was* gorgeous, of course, and got his motor running as all gorgeous women did. *That* was just biology! Pure animal impulse. But she'd also genuinely been the best candidate, had brought that bit extra to the table.

Kindliness, for one thing. Oh, he hadn't been looking for it, didn't expect—or *want*—anyone running around after him on account of his injury. But still, none of the other three had got up to fetch their own drink as Tommie had—he'd run the same the routine with them as a test. And none of them had asked him about his hand either. Which was fine, perhaps an indicator of professional discretion and detachment—absolutely on point. And yet… Tommie's directness had felt intriguing. *Refreshing!* And then, of course, none of the other three had been anything like as enthusiastic about the annexe as Tommie…

He felt a smile coming. All that studied coolness in her had given way to what had looked like pure delight when he'd taken her up. There had been joy on her face as she'd trailed her fingers lovingly over the kitchen counters and the chair-backs, and her eyes had shone like magic in the bedroom, practically popping out of her head in the bathroom. Pandering to his pride, no doubt, because he loved his home, had put so much of himself into making it perfect. But it couldn't have all been an act to win him over, because everything he'd shown her—way more than he'd intended—had got the same sparkling reaction. The pool, the gym, the cars in the garage…all bringing a glow to her face, her eyes.

What to do? She'd left an indelible impression. He'd tried so hard to shake it off, tried so hard to make himself consider the others, but the truth was they'd never stood a chance.

His phone blared with some brief, unintelligible cacophony and then Fliss was back, her voice breathless, slightly harried.

'Max, are you there?'

He raised his own voice so it would carry. 'Yes, still here.'

'So, where was I…?

He carried his coffee back to the island unit and sat down. 'You were saying how great it is that my new driver is attractive.'

'Ah, yes… So, I was going to add that attractive is all very well, but remember she's only a driver, Max—not to mention an employee. So don't go getting your back seat mixed up with your front seat.'

His pulse jumped. *Seriously?* Offering up *'only a driver'* before getting to the substantially more important fact of Tommie being his employee! Fliss was a diamond—his best friend in the world—but sometimes…just sometimes…she was far too much like his parents.

He wanted to scream, *Don't be such an insufferable snob!* But if he did it would only come back to bite him—make him sound as if he had actual designs on Tommie, which of course he didn't!

He squeezed his lids shut, trying to cool his veins. He would never cross the employer-employee divide. God help him, he'd crossed too many lines with Tommie already. Allowing himself to feel some warm, real curiosity about her, almost blurting out that he liked her name when she'd said that thing about how she'd got off lightly not being named Thomasina. Offering her the job when it was the total opposite of what he'd resolved to do sixty seconds into the interview!

That was more than enough line-crossing as far as Tommie was concerned. It was clean slate all the way from here on in. Professional distance! He was already striking a pure note, wasn't he? Starting as he meant to go on, keeping well away while she moved in—which she was currently doing, ably assisted by Isak, his gardener-handyman.

Not that he hadn't done his bit to make her feel welcome. He'd seen to getting her fridge and cupboards stocked with some basics from the deli, and he'd asked Jenny, his cleaner, to make up the bed and give the place a good going over, because the other three applicants had tramped their feet through it, hadn't they? And absolutely he would check in with her later, to give her tomorrow's itinerary, but he was going to keep it brief, polite and formal. So Fliss could take a great big hike with her unwanted and completely unwarranted advice!

He took a sip of coffee, permitting himself some sarcasm. 'Thanks for that, Fliss. I honestly don't know how I'd get by without you here to keep me on the straight and narrow. And, by the way, *she* has a name.'

Stunned silence, and then… 'Oh, God! I'm sorry, Max. I'm being an absolute cow.' She sighed heavily. 'It must be the pregnancy hormones.'

Which maybe it was—partly at least. His heart pinched. Poor Fliss. He'd sort of stolen her thunder by getting nailed on the track just as she and Gavin announced they were expecting. He felt a prick of guilt. He hadn't even asked her how she was feeling today, had he?

He made his voice gentle. 'Are you getting morning sickness?'

'Don't even get me started!'

He felt a smile coming. 'Okay, then you're forgiven on the grounds of being seriously knocked up. By the way, tell Gavin if he needs a refuge…'

'Oh, ha-ha, aren't you funny!' And then her voice was filling with a smile. 'He says I look *"glowing".'*

'Well, he would say that, wouldn't he? He's probably terrified of you!'

'Oh, Lord, now you're on a roll…' She chuckled, then drew in an audible breath. 'So, are you going to tell me her name or not?'

He felt a weird stirring in his chest. 'It's Tommie.'

'Unusual…'

'Named for a great-aunt, apparently—Thomasina.'

'I prefer Tommie.'

'She does, too.'

'Right…' Felicity was sliding into distracted mode. 'I've got stuff piling up here, so I'd better shoot. I guess I'll see you next month at the wedding?'

His ribs tightened. Cousin Lucy's wedding to Fraser Pringle. Two hundred guests. Including his parents. He pushed the thought away.

'Yep. I'll see you there.'

'Great! Take it easy, Max.'

And then she was gone.

He put a finger to his cup handle, pushing it back and forth, watching the cup twist. How were things going in the annexe? Was Tommie all moved in now? Was she comfortable? Happy?

Gah!

He got to his feet and went out onto the deck, drawing the sweet grass and honeysuckle smells into his lungs. Of course she was happy. She'd stung him for more money and was now moving into a luxury apartment equipped with all the mod cons. No earthly reason for her not to be. And no earthly reason for him to be thinking about her—not when he had more important things to think about, ducks to line up in a row for tomorrow. Wall-to-wall meetings—back to business!

He felt his focus sliding down his left arm. Back to business with this lame appendage. Attracting attention, pity, questions he couldn't answer.

He shuddered. *Nightmare!*

CHAPTER FOUR

TOMMIE GLANCED INTO the rearview mirror. Was this a dream she was having? Monday morning. Six-thirty. Maxwell Lawler Scott back there, clean-shaven, with his hair brushed and swept back off his forehead, wearing a dark jacket over a white vee-neck tee and dark *proper* trousers—which must have been a devil to get on one-handed—looking extremely handsome, every inch the hotshot billionaire, while she, Tommie, was behind the wheel, driving him to his Canary Wharf offices!

She gripped the wheel harder. No, not a dream—and so *not* the way she'd thought this would play out. Billie's fault! Okay, maybe a little bit hers too, for falling head over heels in love with the annexe.

Oh, she'd known it would be gorgeous, but she hadn't expected it to take her actual breath away, shred every last vestige of her composure. Space, light, air... The apartment was a sublime echo of the main house. And such a bedroom! All natural tones and deep-sprung comfort. Such a bathroom! All buff tiles and gleaming white porcelain.

How was it possible to keep your guard up when everything you were seeing was pure delight? When your delight seemed to be pleasing the other person? Not that pleasing Max had been her aim, and not that he'd exactly shown that he was pleased, but there'd been something intriguing going on behind his eyes. A sort of look behind the look.

He'd shown her more than the annexe, anyway, which she hadn't expected, making a few gruff remarks about the house's design and ecologically sound materials as he went. Gym. Lap pool... *Spa vibe central!* He'd said whoever got the job would be able to knock themselves out in there, since he was out of action. Then it was the garage. No rusty barbecue on wheels. No rolls of old carpet. Just three sleek sports cars and this one—this black, top-of-the-range hybrid four-by-four that smelt of its butter-soft leather interior and drove like a dream.

She just hadn't imagined that *she* would be the one driving it. Because Max had asked the agency to send three further candidates for interview after her—not that Billie was meant to have known it was Max who was asking. But stuff the non-disclosure agreement! After the interview she'd had to call her sister to let off steam, tell her that the prospective employer was Chloe Mills' damn publicist, and that she'd nearly died when he'd opened the door...

'Oh, my God—but Max Scott is gorgeous! Sex on a stick. Was he nice?'

'Not exactly. He was stiff, standoffish, and even though his hand's in a splint, because he bust it in a car crash—which is why he needs a driver—he insisted on getting me a glass of water, even though I offered to get it myself, which would have been a lot easier.'

'But that's kind of adorable...'

'No, Billie! He wasn't being adorable. It was a pride thing. He didn't want me to help him. He wanted to show off instead. It was so ridiculous, so stupid! Why not accept help?'

'Well, maybe because being helped makes him feel worse. Not independent.'

'Okay...maybe... But, see, that's still down to pride. I helped in the end—forced the issue.'

'Attagirl. How did it go, otherwise?'

'I endured, answered his questions, did my best not to show the agency up.'

'And what about the set-up? The apartment? Decent?'

'As expected, it's to die for.'

'So, if he offers you the job, you're taking it, right?'

'I can't. This is Chloe Mills' publicist, remember?'

'So you'd cut off your nose to spite your face? Not take a brilliant job with a drop-dead gorgeous man just because Chloe Mills happens to be one of his clients?'

'Drop-dead gorgeous is irrelevant, Billie! This is a job, not a dating show, you know. With professional boundaries and everything. If I was working for him, he might just as well be Quasimodo.'

'Okay, well, obviously there's that. But since he isn't, at least you'd have a nice view in the rearview mirror!'

'I'm not interested in the view.'

'Funny...that's not the vibe I'm getting.'

Billie had been barking up the wrong stupid tree. For sure, she'd felt a bit sorry for Max, with his hand cased up like that, and he had looked quite appealing, trying not to chuckle over 'Thomasina', and, yes, seeing that had made her a bit curious about him and, for heaven's sake, a girl would have to be dead on a slab not to find him attractive, but it didn't mean she was interested in Max in that way. He was from a different world socially. He was prideful, uptight *and* Chloe Mills' publicist. He was also beside the point, since she was fully focused on higher goals—in other words, herself.

It was the house, in particular the apartment, that had broken her. It had felt like home straight away—a place she could see herself in, sketching, researching, swanning around doing her own thing. *That* must have been the vibe Billie had picked up—apartment infatuation!

Neither here nor there, though. She'd written the whole thing off when Billie had told her Max was interviewing other people. But then, out of the blue, Billie had called her at work…

'Guess what? Max called Neville. You got the job! He wants you to be his driver!'

'No…'

'Yes!'

'How come?'

'Well, I'm assuming it's because he'd didn't like the other three as much as he likes you… Tommie? Are you still there…? Say something? What should Neville tell him?'

'I don't know.'

'Oh, for God's sake! You're not still stuck on the Chloe Mills thing, are you?'

'I don't know. She stole my designs, Billie, and he's on her team. And he doesn't even know I worked for her—'

'He doesn't have to! Geez, Tommie. Are you going to let Chloe Mills shaft you twice? Stop you taking a job that could set you up, give you another crack at the dream? You don't have to tell him anything…you don't even have to talk to him. All you have to do is drive his car.'

'I know, but—'

'Would more money sway you? Make the pain worth the gain?'

'No, it's not that. It's just—'

'Leave it with me. I'll tell Neville you're havering because you had a slightly higher figure in mind. He loves to negotiate up because it's more commission for him. If Max bites,

then there's your compensation for suffering the Chloe Mills connection. If he doesn't, then we regroup...'

But Max did bite. And she'd listened to Billie, got her priorities straightened back out. Max was an unfortunate fly in the ointment, but so what? The ointment was the thing. The job was still the same job she'd gone off that morning desperately hoping to get—for the money and for the blissful bonus of having her own little apartment.

She flicked the indicator, merging the vehicle into the flow of slowing traffic. So here she was, and there he was in the back, staring fixedly out of the window, with a face on him like a wet weekend. So much for Billie teasing her about how readily he had shelled out the extra money to secure her, saying how it must mean he liked her. If he did, he had a funny way of showing it.

He hadn't even come by to say hello when she'd arrived yesterday. Oh, he'd provided the lovely Isak to carry her stuff in, and the fridge had been full to the brim, stocked with expensive delicacies she wouldn't have bought for herself in a million years. And the bed had been made up, all ready for her. And the whole place had been spotless, which it had been the first time she'd seen it as well, but he'd clearly had it spruced up for her arrival. It had been a welcome of sorts—not lost on her—but he'd only shown his actual face later, seeming pleased to see her for all of three seconds before reverting to poker-up-the-jacksie mode, briefing her stiffly about today's trip to the Lawler-Scott PR and Alpha News headquarters—*'The other things I do besides wiping out in racing cars'*—and about how he didn't want or expect her to open the car door for him, or anything like that, that she was a driver *not* a chauffeur. Then he'd moved on to the cleaning and laundry arrangements—taken care of by someone called Jenny—and finally he'd given her a list of the local restaurants he had accounts with, so that she could order whatever she wanted, whenever she wanted, because *'You won't always have time to shop and cook.'*

It was all very thoughtful and efficient, but he hadn't smiled once. And this morning he'd only smiled briefly as he got in and said hello. Since then he'd barely looked at her, hadn't said a single word to her. And she could hear Billie's voice in her head, saying that as a fully paid-up privacy nut he was probably just acclimatising to having her around, and her own voice adding that it didn't matter, she should just ignore him, but for some reason she was struggling to do that.

She checked her mirrors, slid over a lane. Was it because of that Thomasina moment and all those other little glimmers? That flicker of acknowledgement—*gratitude?*—in his gaze when she'd retrieved her water from the fridge door? That hard ache behind his eyes when he'd talked about his hand? That obvious warm affection for his sister, and that indefinable but arresting *something* at the edge of his gaze as he'd been showing her around?

Had her sappy subconscious decided they were signs of a potentially likeable inner being and woven them into some sort of loose expectation that they might get on? Even though getting on with Max wasn't important?

Who knew? She just didn't want to feel it buzzing away in her brain like this, taking up space when she had more important things to think about—like getting some ideas down for a Tommie Seager summer collection. She didn't want to keep looking at him in the mirror either, but she kept doing it all the same. Moth to flame, on account of his not being Quasimodo!

He was clenching his jaw now…rhythmically. Was he irked because he wasn't the one driving. Was she grinding his gears just by being here? *In. His. Space.* Nothing she could do about that, since she couldn't make herself invisible!

She looked again. Or maybe the jaw clenching had nothing to do with her at all. It could be work related…

Her breath checked.

Going back to work-related…

She glanced at him again. Was that what it was? First day back nerves? If so, she could relate. She'd hated going back to school after her glandular fever, dreaded the looks, the attention, the questions.

'Where have you been?'

'What happened to you?'

At least when she went back she was better, though…over it. But Max wasn't, was he? It was all still hanging in the balance for him. Her heart pinched. Much harder to deal with on a personal level, never mind in front of work colleagues.

She slowed to let a car filter in from the left. Oh, and now there was that voice starting up in her head, saying that it might help him to know she understood. What was it with her and wanting to help people all the time? It never ended well! She needed to steer well clear.

She concentrated on the road ahead. The traffic was building now—probably the Limehouse contraflow effect—but the road was pretty, with trees either side, blue sky above and soft morning sunshine. She felt a tingle. The weather! Now, there was a safe subject. Everyone talked about the weather, didn't they? It would be a little something to break the ice with…lighten the air. Max might even appreciate the distraction.

She drew in a breath and smiled into the mirror. 'You've got a lovely day for your first day back.'

His body tensed, then his eyes snapped to hers. 'Seems

so. But I don't want to talk about the weather, Tommie. In fact, I don't want to talk at all. So if you could please not talk too, then I'd appreciate it.'

Seriously? Talking to her like this? Looking at her like this? Looking *away* now, back through the window, as if that was it—Tommie dismissed!

She felt a blaze reaching up under her ribs, then tears prickling, scalding her eyes. So much for good intentions. So much for trying to lighten the air. If Max was happier stewing in his own juices, grinding his own jaw to dust, then let him. At least she knew the score now. So, happy days!

She lifted her chin, breathing it all down. Made it easier, didn't it? Not talking. Not trying. Oh, and suddenly how very gratifying that Neville had put the squeeze on him for that extra fifteen percent! She'd never wanted it—had been too discombobulated about the job offer to make that plain to Billie—but she was cock-a-hoop about it now!

Money! That was the thing. Making enough to set herself up. Nothing else mattered—especially not Max Lawler Scott. She didn't need to talk to him…didn't need to be his buddy. All she had to do was drive his fricking car!

CHAPTER FIVE

MAX BLINKED. Where the hell was Tommie going? These buildings weren't familiar...and this road... This wasn't the right route!

His heart dipped. *Oh, God!* Now he was going to have to say something—look at her...brave the fall-out. And fall-out there would be, for sure, because her gaze in the mirror when he'd asked her to be quiet had solidified like cold metal. It would have turned him into a pillar of salt if he hadn't been feeling like one already, *this close* to crumbling along his edges.

Dammit! He'd intended to be curt with her, yes—to stop her in her tracks because he did *not* want to talk, engage. But he hadn't meant to be quite so obnoxious. It had just come out that way because he was in seriously bad shape: dreading walking into work, having to deal with the looks, the well-intentioned sympathy, the ignominy of not being fully himself, not being in total control. All that, while trying to fathom these very weird feelings he was getting around Tommie. Not that he'd been around her much, but it didn't seem to take much.

Take last night... He'd gone up to brief her about today, full of clean slate intentions, and she'd opened the door balancing an armful of magazines on her hip, wearing low-slung jeans and a tight white tee that skimmed her navel and left nothing to the imagination as far as the size and shape of her breasts went—small and pert—her hair swept up but coming out of its clip so that loose tendrils were grazing the side of her neck. She'd looked adorably unkempt, momentarily soft, all softly lit up, and he'd felt something stirring inside him that was like desire but different—a sort of unholy clamour in his chest. He'd wanted to take her face in his hands and kiss her…kiss her long and slow…stretching it out, sinking into it, diving deep, drowning…

Drowning! That was how it had felt, suddenly—as if he couldn't get any air into his lungs. As if he was losing control of his breathing, too—and *that* didn't even happen on the racetrack at one hundred and twelve miles per hour! He'd panicked, fenced himself off, cracked on through it.

Forget time-wasting pleasantries.

Forget smiling.

But he couldn't forget the feeling. The skew and twist of it. It had kept him awake all night, tossing and turning. Then, to crown it all, this morning he'd taken so long struggling to get these ruddy trousers on that he hadn't had time for a coffee—and he *hated* that. He needed his caffeine fix first thing otherwise it was bear, sore head…the whole nine yards. All of it together had got him out of whack, out of sorts and biting Tommie's head right off instead of just baring his teeth to protect himself, as he'd meant to.

And now, having said he didn't want to talk, having told her he didn't want her to talk either, he was going to have to engage—because God only knew where she thought she was going!

He looked at her. 'Tommie, it's *Canary Wharf* we're headed to.'

Her shoulders stiffened perceptibly, then released. 'I know that, Max, but there's roadworks through Limehouse.

You said last night you wanted to be in for seven-thirty this morning, so I assumed you'd rather I take you round them and get you in on time than get stuck in a contraflow. But if I've called it wrong, then I apologise.'

Tart tone. Strong whiff of *Sorry, not sorry.* But that was fine. If she hated him now, so much the better. It would keep her at bay…keep her eyes out of the mirror and out of his.

'No, it's fine.' He slid his gaze back through the window, hating himself for playing the role he'd cast himself in. 'You've called it right.'

Called it right because she was a professional driver. She'd have checked the road reports last night, planned this route and probably a back-up too. She was a safe pair of hands. A pair of hands he could—*should*—trust. But she was dangerous all the same…wearing her loveliness as if she didn't even know it was there, making his blood quick-march. Asking her disarming, candid questions—making it run cold.

'Do you live alone?'

'What did you do to your hand?'

'What's the prognosis?'

She'd been gearing up for another round, hadn't she? Stapling that *'first day back'* remark to a banal nicety about the weather. But he was on to her.

He shut his eyes. The kicker was that for a nanosecond he'd felt a tug…a faint desire to confide in her, tell her how much he was dreading facing his colleagues today. But she'd have pressed him then. Would have wanted to know why it was such a big deal. And he couldn't have got into that—the whole ugly labyrinth. Couldn't have told her how he couldn't bear showing weakness because he'd spent too much of his early life feeling weak, diminished, discounted. How he couldn't let anyone in because letting them in meant letting go, trusting, putting your happiness and self-esteem into someone else's hands... Someone who might be always too busy to come and watch you at the go-kart track, too self-absorbed to flick you a crumb of genuine attention. Someone who might promise to take you, watch you, praise you, love you, then renege because every other damn thing was more important. Themselves. News Global.

All their cronies. All those parties. Shrill and braying voices reverberating through the house every weekend, all weekend long, when he was growing up, taking up every bit of room, every bit of air. Journos and politicians, advisers and schemers, insiders with the latest on whichever juicy scandal was kicking off at Westminster that week. Catnip to Fliss. Purgatory to him.

It had got so that he couldn't wait to fly the nest, free himself from the noise and everything that went with it. From the pain of always being last on his parents, Tamsin and Gerald's list, pain that had curdled into resentment.

Most of it had anyway. There was still some of the pliant material there, lurking in his shadows, but he didn't give it houseroom—that sting of their disappointment in him for not joining the News Global dynasty after journalism school, as Fliss had, for going into showbiz journalism instead of becoming a 'serious' journalist, for boosting himself from there into the 'trite' world of celebrity PR.

But if Tamsin and Gerald chose to be disappointed in him for starting what was now the top celebrity PR firm in London and for launching Alpha News, for becoming independently wealthy and influential in his own right—and a respected motor racing driver to boot—then that was their problem.

Their problem, not mine!

Now, a fortune spent on therapy later, he could say those words out loud, and mean them.

He opened his eyes, surveying the unfamiliar road. Houses. A church. Shops. But therapy could only do so much. It couldn't un-weld him from this habit of self-reliance, of wanting to be in control of his space, his emotions, the terms of his relationships—everything. It couldn't make him want to let anyone in…couldn't make him not be scared of doing that.

That was what he would tell Tommie if he could—that his bark was worse than his bite, that he barked out of fear, not loathing. But Tommie was his driver. An employee. Not a friend and confidante. He liked her more than he wanted to, and he did want to kiss her, long and slow, but she was a tangle he could not afford to get himself into, even in the privacy of his own head. A head that was busy thumping right now, craving caffeine and—

Hallelujah, there's a coffee place!

He leant forward. 'Tommie, pull over, please.'

'Where?'

'As close as you can get to Roasted Joe's.'

So, Max was craving coffee, was he?

She checked the mirror, not letting her eyes stray off-piste, then flicked the indicator. Hopefully it would put him in a better mood before he made his grand entrance at work—hoping this for his colleagues' sake, obviously, not his. He could drown himself in his cup for all she cared!

She braked smoothly, pulling into the lucky space that a delivery van had just vacated right outside, then killed the engine, keeping her gaze forward.

There was a sharp click—Max's seatbelt—then silence, hanging like a dead weight.

Then… 'Would you like something?'

She felt a hot ripple beneath her skin, instant pathetic

tears burning behind her lids. How could a voice do that? Just by not being cold…just by containing the merest, tiniest sliver of something that at a distant push might be said to feel like an apology.

She swallowed hard, drawing a silent stream of air in through her nose, taking it into her lungs, willing it to even her out. She wanted to say no…wanted to say it with spite in her voice, to sting him like he'd stung her. But that would only feel good for a barbed instant, and it wouldn't achieve anything except possibly to lose her this job. And she couldn't risk that—losing the money and the gorgeous apartment that already felt like home.

She drew in another long stream of air. No. The best payback was to stay professional, keep on taking his money, and do as little as possible for it—which, of course, ruled out offering to go and get the coffee. She felt another tingle. Or rather, *coffees*—because, actually, although she didn't like driving with a hot drink in the cup holder, she might make an exception this once for the sheer unadulterated pleasure of watching him work out how he was going to carry the damn things.

It was so perfect she could weep for joy. But only inside her head. Obviously.

Poker face, Tommie…

She inclined her head towards him without looking at him. 'That would be great, thanks. Tall Americano, please. Hot milk, no sugar.'

Nice and unwieldy!

'Got it.'

And then the door sprang open, letting in a whoosh of road noise before shutting with a soft *clunk*. She held her breath, counting to ten, then allowed herself to look.

Max was standing at the counter, giving his order to a

female barista who was clearly smitten, batting her lashes at him, smiling and laughing—*gushing*—and falling over herself like a total twit. And Max was—*stop press!*—smiling back at the girl, with actual dents in his cheeks and everything. He was gripping the back of his neck now—which he had to know was a very disarming gesture, making him seem a bit shy, a smidge vulnerable...

She tore her eyes away. Oh, here she was again—tuning in to all the wrong things about him, imagining shyness, vulnerability, looking through the damn window in spite of herself, not to crow, not to gloat but—*admit it*—to see if he did actually need her help.

She sucked in her cheek, biting it hard. If only she could make herself not want to help people—but it was instinctive. It was who she was. She could rant and rail inside her head all day long, try on spite for size, but even though Max had been rude, and obnoxious, the fact was he'd been through a lot.

She felt a shudder rolling over her. She'd watched his crash online last night—watched his car flipping, rolling, five, six, seven times before ploughing to a dismembered, upside-down stop on the grass. And then the marshals and the medics had come swarming in, with the commentator describing the scene in a breathless, overawed voice, saying that the car would have taken the bulk of the impact, but for all that sounding keyed-up and anxious. And then the crowd had parted and there was Max, on his feet—white helmet, blue race suit—walking away, clutching his left hand. The commentator had been euphoric then. Max was okay. Walking away meant that he was okay.

But he wasn't. She'd seen the devastation behind his gaze when she'd asked him about the prognosis that day, had caught fear in his voice as well as bitterness.

'I can't feel anything...don't know when or if I ever will again.'

That was why she'd looked through the café window—because, no matter what had gone down between them earlier, he could only use one hand right now. And, yes, he'd probably rather die than ask her for help, but what kind of cold-hearted person would she be if she were to let him struggle?

She turned to look again, and felt her stomach spasm. He wasn't struggling, though, was he? The gushy barista was pulling the door open for him, all pink-cheeked and flirty smiling, handing him a cardboard tray with two white-lidded cups secured in its slots.

Of course.

It was the obvious solution—one a smart billionaire hotshot like Max would have seized on before he'd even got through the door. Because you didn't get to be a business success, a billionaire in your own right, independently of your estranged billionaire media mogul father—she'd looked that up too, and some other things—by not being able to solve problems, grift when you had to, make nice with a barista to get attentive service.

From the hopeful look on her face, the silly girl was clearly hoping to get his number.

Not happening!

Max would no more look at that girl than he'd look at *her.* It was all on the internet, in the public domain. He had a 'type', pedigree racehorses one and all. Models, mostly, or actresses. Usually highborn. No one ordinary.

And now he was saying his goodbyes, turning, coming back across the pavement, tray in hand.

She composed her face, unclipped her seatbelt and got out, going round to open his door. Last night he'd said not to do that, but with the best will in the world he would never manage the car door without putting the tray down on the pavement first, and no professional driver would ever make a client do such a thing, no matter how trying that client was. And she *was* a professional…did have standards. But she wasn't going to smile. This was a bare minimum gesture, nothing more. Because whatever was going on inside her, whatever thoughts she couldn't seem to keep out of her head, Max *had* been brusque earlier, and unnecessarily rude. For self-preservation, and to stop all those other thoughts sending her down the usual road to disappointment, *that* was the thought she needed to hold on to with all her might!

CHAPTER SIX

'How's it going, Max?'

He felt a little sinking sensation inside. Fliss wasn't asking him about work. She was using that sisterly tone of hers to go for his soft underbelly, using her *knowing* tone. But then, of course, she *did* know him—better than anyone. She knew he would have been struggling with himself this morning, with his various tics and demons, but surely she should also know by now that he was adept at hiding them, at controlling his own narrative.

Still, if she needed an actual run-down...

He leant back in his chair. 'It's all good, Fliss. I gathered the team together, told them that rolling my car hadn't been the most enjoyable experience but that my hand's still on the end of my arm, so it's not all bad, and that the rest is a waiting game. And then, of course, the Danny Gates thing kicked off, so it was action stations.'

'Fortuitous! Although not so much for Gates, obviously.'

'You saw it?'

She scoffed. 'Hard not to. Danny Gates and an escort! The socials are awash with it.'

He closed his eyes, trying to unsee the images. Danny Gates, until now a dream client, the nation's most popular kids' TV presenter, caught with his trousers down and a large-breasted woman in his hands. At various angles... none of them flattering.

'You did a nice quick mop up job on it, though, Max. Excellent admission and apology statement, and very smart to remind the nation that he's single, so there's no infidelity rap, and only twenty-two, so he should be forgiven for being an idiot. And that in spite of being *only* twenty-two, he's raised millions for children's charities.'

'Thanks, but it's standard procedure: admission, apology, then pile on the positivity. It won't save him his job.'

'No, but it'll save his career—which is what you're aiming for, right?'

'That's the hope. It's about the long game now.'

'So, what's next for Gates? A stint on *I'm a Jungle Star*?'

He felt his lips twitching. 'Ideally. Swallowing a mouthful of wriggling grubs seems to be a modern-day act of redemption—especially if it's followed by some tearful remorse for past wrongdoings by the campfire. His star will be shining again in no time. Then it'll be *Baking Blitz* or *Ballroom Blitz*—one of the primetime blitzes, anyway. I've already talked to his agent.'

Fliss chuckled. 'Sounds like you're all over it.'

'I'm paid to be all over it.'

'Don't be disingenuous, Max, it doesn't suit you. You don't need the money. You do it because you love it. And I'm not even going to start on *why* you love it…'

'Ouch, Fliss! You wouldn't be taunting me about my control issues, by any chance, would you?'

She laughed, but then her voice was softening, edging into seriousness. 'If not me, then who, Max? Who else is ever going to call you out?'

Who else would he ever let close enough to call him out? That was what she meant.

He felt a knot tightening in his chest. She was badgering him yet again with the same old chestnut—his refusal to let anyone in, open himself up to love. As if love was the answer to everything. As if just because she could do it— *was* doing it—sharing her life with Gavin, having a family, he should be doing it too. But they weren't the same. She had a natural resilience, had sailed through their childhood unscathed, whereas he'd had to cultivate his…grow it in sour earth. Different legacy. Different attitude. Couldn't she get that, leave it alone? Leave *him* alone to simply be who he was?

'I don't need calling out, Fliss. I know what I am.'

'Do you, though?'

His body flashed hot. What was that supposed to mean? Not that he had any intention of asking her.

'I don't want to talk about this, Fliss.'

'You never do.'

'So why aren't you getting the message, then?'

'Nice!'

Grit and hurt in her voice. He felt the knot in his chest break.

'I'm sorry, Fliss, I didn't—'

'Forget it. I've got another call coming in. Have a nice rest of the day, Max!'

And then she was gone.

He clenched his jaw hard.

Good going, Max!

Upsetting Tommie. Upsetting Fliss.

He slammed his phone down and got to his feet, pacing the room. But how was he supposed to react? Why was everyone always trying to help him? Swamp him with help he didn't want, hadn't asked for, didn't need? Couldn't they see he was fine as he was? What was this need Fliss had to 'fix' him? He'd done the therapy…got himself fixed as far as he needed to, wanted to.

As for Tommie… Flicking him glances from the second he'd got into the car, trying to—what? Break him down? All she'd achieved was to wind him up more, force him to keep his gaze averted. Oh, but she'd kept on looking over, hadn't she? He'd felt her eyes on his face over and over again. The tingle of her, the goddamn tug of her, messing up his messed-up head even more. But this was what no one got: even as he was stewing in that back seat, indulging in some private self-pity—what *should* have been private self-pity anyway!—he'd known exactly how he was going to present himself when he pushed through the doors of these offices…known exactly what he was going to say. Because that was his talent. Controlling the narrative for his clients, and especially for himself.

He stopped pacing and turned to the expanse of London that filled the vast plate glass window of his office. Couldn't seem to control it around Tommie, though, could he? Offering to get her a coffee, hoping she'd read amends into it—and this after deciding that if she hated him it was for the best. Then flirting—yes, *flirting*—with that barista, hoping against hope—*why?*—that Tommie would be looking, noticing, feeling jealous. Which was insane. *Insane!* His driver. His employee. So far off limits it wasn't true. Not any kind of situation he wanted to get himself into. Oh, but there he'd been… Out of control, unable to stop himself, employing every disarming trick he could think of, making a total goof of himself, making that poor girl blush and simper, think that—

He screwed his eyes shut, grinding his teeth. Out of character. Not him at all. Some other Max. An alien being. He drew in a deep breath, reconnecting with the view. Luckily Tommie had missed the whole excruciating performance—which he knew because he'd checked a few times, and every time she'd been in the same pose, staring ahead, obviously still ticked off with him for jumping down her throat in spite of his peace offering—tall Americano, hot milk, no sugar.

She'd been on the pavement, opening his door for him, when he got back with it, saving him some awkwardness, but she'd taken it with the scantest 'thanks', not even popping the spout on the cup, just wedging it into the cup holder untouched as she slipped behind the wheel again. If that was a message, he'd got it. And it was absolutely the perfect outcome. Short shrift suited him down to the ground. Nothing to snag himself on, or to tug at the strings that had kept him awake all night. He was good now…back in control…

Golden!

CHAPTER SEVEN

'So, Danny Gates, huh…?'

Tommie felt her forehead wrinkling. 'What?'

'Oh, come on…' Billie's voice was cajoling. 'I *know* you've signed an NDA, but I'm dying to know: did Max tell you anything? I'm not asking for specifics, I just want to know: *was* there more?'

She put Billie on speaker, so she could plump her pillow and snuggle back. 'I don't even know what you're talking about.'

'Really?'

'Yes! *Really*.'

'Cripes! You're telling me you didn't see the pictures? Danny Gates, caught *in flagrante* with an escort. The media's been buzzing. And Max is Gates' publicist. He put out a statement…' Billie made a little impatient noise. 'And this has all somehow gone right over your head?'

'Well, obviously…'

And not surprisingly, since she was steering well clear of her computer and the internet search app on her phone. Too tempting to look up Max facts—like the fact that his sister was Felicity Hewitt, anchor for News Global. Too tempting to trawl through pictures of him, handsome and smiling, at red carpet events, at the racetrack, at Wimbledon… Not that she would tell Billie her guilty secret. It was bad enough living with it herself, trying to make sense of it. As for Max filling her in on anything about his work… It might as well be his tongue in a splint, not his hand.

'So Max didn't mention it?'

'Why would he? I've told you before: he's the strong, silent type.'

'You mean still…?' Billie sounded incredulous. 'But it's been a week now. Isn't he loosening up a bit? Are you guys not—?'

'No, we're not friends. And before you ask, yes, I'm fine with that. He's easy on the eye, but in every other respect he's difficult. And I don't care for what he does…oiling the wheels for the likes of Chloe Mills, covering up for Danny Gates.'

'The statement wasn't trying to cover anything up, Miss Know-it-All. It was actually an apology.'

'Yeah, right. I'll bet "error of judgement" was part of the script. It's what they always say when these people do bad stuff.'

'Geez, Tommie, when did you get to be so prissy? Gates had consensual sex with someone, that's all. He didn't ask to be filmed doing it. He's actually the victim here. Max was trying to limit the damage—which in my book makes him quite noble.'

'There's nothing "noble" about it, Billie! He doesn't do it for free! hang on—' Her phone was vibrating with an incoming call.

Max!

'Sit tight, Billie, he's calling…' She inhaled and switched calls. 'Hello Max.'

'Hi, Tommie. I need to go out. Can you be ready in ten minutes, please?'

Seriously? Just when she was all tucked up in bed. Then again, this was what he was paying her for, wasn't it? To be at his beck and call.

She dialled up her professional tone. 'Of course. Where are we going?'

'The Dorchester. I'll see you out front.'

'Okay.' She switched back to Billie. 'We seem to be going to the Dorchester. He wants me outside with the car in ten minutes.'

'Ooh!' Billie's tone turned to honey. 'What's our boy going off to do in a luxury hotel at this time of night?'

Tommie felt a lurch inside. 'Don't know, don't care. But I've now got nine minutes, forty-five seconds to be in place.'

'Go, then! You can tell me all about it tomorrow.'

'NDA, Billie… NDA. Bye.'

Thirty seconds later she was getting dressed. Fresh white shirt. Tailored grisaille cropped trousers. Pointless, really, since it was dark and no one was going to see her. But she had standards. Hair—quick twist up into its chignon. Face—quick once-over in the bathroom, lipstick…

She met her own eyes in the mirror. Did Max have standards though? Was Billie, right? Was he really going out to…?

She felt a sudden throb between her temples, a sick stirring in her stomach. How could he do that? Let himself be that guy? And why was she letting it bother her?

She pulled in a breath.

Whatever, whatever, whatever!

It didn't matter what Max did, day or night. His body, his choice. And was it really such a surprise? He had a playboy reputation, after all, and there was usually no smoke without fire. And he wasn't in a relationship…didn't want anyone living in his house, cramping his style, didn't want to *share* himself with anyone. He was selfish like that. He was also a hot, successful, single, virile billionaire player. It totally stacked up that he would do this kind of thing!

She rammed her feet into her shoes and went to stuff her sketchbook into her bag. Might as well use the booty call waiting time to work on some designs, try and distract herself from...

Oh, God! Maybe it did stack up, but didn't Max know he was better than this? Couldn't he see that he was selling himself short? *Gah!*

And there she went again, crediting him with way more than he deserved because, whatever she'd said to Billie, she *wanted* to see the good..., believe it was there in him. Glimmers getting into her eyes again, that beat of silence in the car that had felt like regret. That *'Would you like something?'* that had felt like an apology. And if he had been trying to apologise, then that pointed to some sensitivity in him, some good stuff, so why not share that good stuff with someone? Have a real relationship...something warm and tender, deep and joyful? If only she could talk some sense into him...make him see—

Stop!

She snatched up her bag, heading for the stairs, taking them fast. What the hell was she *on*? She couldn't talk to him. This was Max!

Into the garage now, past the gleaming row of cars to the four-by-four. She zapped the remote and got in. She'd paved that road with all her good intentions before, hadn't she? Just to lighten the air in the car, lighten him, and she'd got her head on a plate for her trouble. So, time to take a breath, take inventory.

Yes, Max had bought her a coffee to apologise—*perhaps*—but he hadn't *actually* apologised. And, whatever smidgeon of regret he might have been feeling when he'd offered to get it, it couldn't have been weighing on him that heavily, since ten seconds later he'd been in full spate, flirting with that bloody barista! And maybe he *hadn't* been rude to her again this week, but he hadn't made any effort to engage either. He'd just issued his polite back seat instructions: 'Kensington Mews, please, Tommie.' Or, 'Staverley Gardens, please, Tommie—physio appointment.' As if she even needed to know that... And, yes, she'd felt her heart going out to him because he'd looked rather downcast when he came out, but still, he was being attended to by a top post-operative specialist physio—she'd hopped out to read the brass plate by the door while he was inside—so he was luckier than most. And, downcast or not, he'd had a whole week to ask her how she was finding the apartment, ask her about anything, but he hadn't.

She triggered the garage door, watching it rise, then eased the car out.

Good pep talk, Tommie!

So many reasons not to care a fig about Max. Let him get on with it. His body. His choice. His life. Nothing to do with her. All she had to do was belt up and drive!

Max slid in, pulled his door shut. 'I'm sorry it's so late.'

He wasn't waiving his quiet in the car policy, or anything, but he couldn't *not* apologise for dragging Tommie out at getting on for eleven-thirty at night—not after upsetting her on her first day like that. For sure that unfortunate little episode had kept them suspended in a polite manageable silence which suited him down to the ground, and kept all those weird drowning-type feelings at bay, and for sure he was paying her extremely well for doing exactly this kind of thing. But still, given that he wasn't exactly overjoyed about traipsing out to the Dorchester at this time of night himself, odds were she was feeling the same.

'It's fine.'

Her eyes flicked him hard in the mirror and then she was easing the car through the gates and they were off, turning out onto the road, picking up speed.

Saying 'It's fine' but her tone implied the opposite—and her demeanour.

He tapped his fingers on the seat. He didn't want to encourage conversation, and maybe it didn't matter that she didn't know *why* he was heading off to the Dorchester since he didn't usually tell her why they were going anywhere. Although for some reason he *had* told her he was going to the physio…maybe because they'd spoken about his hand at the interview, so it had felt all right to mention it. *Whatever!* But it *was* late, and she *did* seem ruffled, so maybe he should bend a bit…offer up some sort of explanation, some context. Brief, of course.

He looked into the mirror. 'This sometimes happens… Something blows up that needs a quick response. The socials never sleep.'

Her body stilled momentarily and then her eyes came to his. 'So this is a PR situation kind of thing?'

'Yes…' And that was as far as he was going.

He turned his gaze through the window to show her he was done. The rest was his business…his problem to sort out.

A frantic Christy Blume, furious because rival supermodel Luna Sanchez had just put out on social media that, at an event they'd both attended earlier, she'd overheard Christy saying that Crème de Zeus, the luxury American skincare brand Christy was ambassador for, was 'no better than the cheaper brands', and that it was the same stuff in superior packaging!

A case of the usual drill. Off to the Dorchester—his go-to neutral but suitably luxurious buffer space—to meet

Christy, her manager and her legal bods, to pull a damage limitation PR response together before morning alarm clocks started going off Stateside and Christy found herself dropped.

He rolled his head back against the rest, closed his eyes. What a week!

Upsetting Tommie on her first morning…upsetting Fliss the same afternoon. Then Danny Gates had upset the whole damn applecart with that escort. And then Paul, his new physio, had upset *him* at their very first session by stressing *degrees* of recovery over *speed* of recovery. Not that he'd been getting his hopes up about his hand, or anything, but somehow hearing all that slow, cautionary talk, the same stuff the surgeon had said weeks ago, had knocked the wind out of his sails, brought back the grim reality that he might never fully recover, never race again.

And now there was this Christy Blume situation!

He sighed and looked out through the window. At least Tommie wasn't coming back at him, trying to talk. She seemed to have cottoned on to his signals, decided he wasn't worth her trouble.

Oh, God! If only she knew he was shamming, playing a role—and not because he didn't want to talk to her, but because he did. *That* was the problem. *That* was the cat scattering his pigeons. How was he supposed to control this? This feeling of wanting to know her—know her properly—and be known by her in return. It was new…disconcerting, inciting bizarre behaviour like flirting with baristas. And he didn't want to be feeling these things, period, never mind feeling them about Tommie. She was his driver, for goodness' sake, his employee.

Oh, but for some reason he couldn't stop his mind from replaying that moment at her door, the day she moved in—

couldn't stop himself wanting to relive the rapture. Time slowing to a crawl, his eyes taking in all her little nesting touches: photo frames set out neatly on the shelves, a blue throw folded and draped over the arm of the sofa, piles of magazines neatly arranged on the coffee table, taking in *her*—the slow, breathless rise and fall of her body, magazines stacked on her hip, her warm, pleased gaze reaching right inside him, that sweet golden skew of her hair, that soft cling of her tee shirt. That sudden, rushing, desperate urge to take her face in his hands and slow kiss her mouth, pour himself into her to the last hopeless drop—

'Max…?'

Tommie! In a somehow stationary car! Twisting round to look at him, her face golden in the lights of the hotel entrance.

'Do you know how long you'll be?'

How were they here already? And was it his imagination, or was her gaze a little gentler than it had been of late?

He shook himself, shrugging the thought away. 'That's the million-dollar question, I'm afraid. Lots of voices in the room and all that. Could be a couple of hours. You can give the keys to the valet.'

Her eyebrows flicked up. 'The valet?'

'Of course…'

His heart paused. Or maybe it wasn't obvious to her at all. And he'd never even thought to mention it, had he? Because he wasn't used to having to explain this stuff to anyone—let alone to a female driver who obviously needed to be given extra consideration as far as night-time safety went.

Must do better, Max!

He refocused. 'I'm sorry if that wasn't clear. For future reference, whenever we go out late at night, if there's valet parking, we'll always use it. And if there isn't…'

What then?

He licked his lips quickly. 'If there isn't, I'll walk with you from wherever we park so you're not walking alone. And late at night, wherever I am, you must always come inside to wait—okay?'

'Okay.' Little smile. 'Thank you.'

'You don't have to thank me. It's…' He bit down on his tongue. He'd been going to say *common courtesy*, but since he hadn't exactly been a model of courtesy that first day, common or otherwise, it wouldn't cut any ice.

Move on!

He signalled to the doorman to come and open his door, then looked at her again. 'I have a tab here, so whatever you want food-wise, drink-wise, knock yourself out.'

'Thank you.'

God help him, her gaze was opening into his, tugging him into the vortex again.

Time to bail…get himself out of this car and up to Room 452!

Tommie turned her face into the pillow. What was that soft clinking noise? Familiar… Metallic… And what was that aroma? She tried to concentrate on it. It smelt…almost like…

Coffee!

Her eyelids sprang open. Cups. Saucers. Cafetière. Set out on the low table. And Max, at an odd angle, regarding her from the opposite sofa.

Sofa?

She glanced at her pillow.

Oh, God!

Not a pillow but a cushion—the cushion she'd pulled under her head as she'd felt her eyes drooping. This was still somehow the same night…still the Dorchester Hotel!

His eyebrows lifted. 'You're awake.'

She felt a fire blazing up under her ribs and scrambled upright, thrusting her half-open sketchbook back into her bag, raking at her hair with her hands.

Had he been watching her for long? Had he seen her sketchbook? What must she look like? What must he be thinking?

He gestured to the cups as if he wasn't thinking anything at all. 'Have some coffee.' And then he was leaning forward, pulling one of the cups over to his side of the table, lifting it to his lips. 'It'll set you up for the drive back.'

Gah! Which was only bringing back every excruciating second of the drive here, trying—*failing*—not to think about what he was heading out for, only to find she was wrong, only to then wonder if he was saying it was a PR thing to cover up the *actual* thing that he was doing which was the thing Billie had said—*hating* herself for wondering about it, for letting it churn her up inside when it absolutely didn't matter. When Max was *nothing* to her, could never be anything to her, when she was supposed to be focused on herself and all her higher goals.

Only to find then, after all that stupid, incomprehensible anguish, that Max had been telling the truth. Easy to see in the proper light of the hotel entrance that his face wasn't the face of a man anticipating a happy frolic between the sheets but that he was here for the reason he'd given: work! And then he'd made his little speech about valet parking, and keeping her safe, with a sort of wounded protective look in his eyes, and she'd heard Billie's voice ringing loud in her ears about Max being 'noble' and it had suddenly felt as if it might possibly be slightly true.

And now here he was, with coffee *nobly* poured for her, when he probably just wanted to get home and crash. Because he looked done in, didn't he? Shadowy under the eyes and along his jaw, where new growth was coming in. He was in just his dark vee neck sweater now, sleeves pushed up a bit, jacket slung over the back of the sofa, and maybe it was the low light in the room, but he looked softer, sort of hazy and careworn. Maddeningly appealing.

Her heart lurched. Which was the last thing she should be letting herself think when he was sitting right here in front of her and might see it on her face. The thing was surely to be *not* sitting here in front of him in this dim lounge, with these empty sofas all around, and the silence pressing in at whatever ungodly hour of the morning this was. The thing was surely to be moving, sitting safely behind the wheel with him safely in the back, and the sooner the better.

She dug out a smile. 'I appreciate the coffee, Max, but I'm wide awake now. I don't need it.' She put her hand on her bag to seem ready to rise. 'We can just go.'

'What? And risk you falling asleep at the wheel?' He made a little scoffing noise. 'No, thanks.'

'I *won't* fall asleep!' Couldn't he see that she was firing on all cylinders? Maybe if she plundered the well of her own crippling embarrassment... 'I had a nap.'

The corner of his mouth twitched. 'Even so, I think you should drink it...fuel up. It's pretty good coffee.'

As if to demonstrate, he took a sip. And then he was setting his cup down, pulling out his phone, parking it on his knee. His eyes glanced up. 'Excuse me a sec...' And then he was tapping at his screen, scrolling.

Was he playing power games to make her drink the coffee because he really thought she might fall asleep at the wheel? *As if!* Or was he genuinely checking something important on his phone?

Whatever! She tipped some milk into the other cup and

sat back with it, sipping. Point to him: it *was* excellent. She felt a stir in her chest. And the view wasn't bad either. Max, hair awry from the hand he'd just pushed through it, deeply engrossed in whatever he was reading on his screen. Rubbing his thumb over his lower lip now…slow strokes.

She felt her eyes staring, a curl of heat unwinding inside her. It was wrong to be looking…watching. But how not to watch when she could feel every thumb-stroke, when the fantasy of it was giving her delicious up-and-down ripples inside. That mouth of his…those lips. So perfect. His nose was perfect too. Straight, not too thin, not too broad. As for those cheekbones, and those thick lashes, and those dark straight brows, and the way his hair was falling forward over his forehead….

Gorgeous!

Her heart pulsed.

But what was he on the inside? *Who* was he?

Another pulse.

And why was she even asking herself that? Just because at this particular moment he was choosing *not* to be his usual shade of sullen! *Geez!* Why did it take so little to throw her backwards? Get her looking for the good in him? Whatever he was—good, bad or indifferent—it didn't matter. The only thing that mattered was that he was her meal ticket. Her boss…

Her breath caught. Her very handsome boss. Who was somehow suddenly looking right at her, raising his very nice eyebrows.

'Okay?'

She felt warmth flooding into her cheeks, her throat turning to parchment. 'Mm-hmm.'

'How's the coffee?'

She sipped some quickly, so her voice would work. 'It's fine, thanks. Good.'

He nodded. 'Good.' He ran a tongue across his lip. 'The coffee's always good here. Special Colombian roast, or something.'

And then his hand was going to the back of his neck, giving him that open, vulnerable, appealing look he'd had with the gushy barista.

'There's more in the pot if you want.'

'No, I'm good…'

Seriously? How many times could two people say 'good' in the space of ten seconds? Stilted, much?

She felt a rise in her chest. And was it any wonder? From her side at least. Because what was his actual script here? Was he genuinely trying to be friendly, making an effort?

Earlier, in the car, telling her *why* they were coming here, when aside from mentioning his physio appointment he'd never once supplied a reason for going anywhere before, apologising for the lateness, apologising for not explaining about the valet parking, then setting out what they would do in future when they had to go out late at night. Ordering this coffee for her, wanting her to drink it, and now he was sitting there—possibly against his own inclination, because he must be tired, possibly using his phone as a delaying tactic—while she did drink it.

To what end? Safety? Hers? His? Trying to show he was a good employer? It was quite the sea change, but why? What did it mean?

And now she was feeling like the proverbial cat on a hot tin roof, tongue-tied and wary in case—if she picked up the baton, made conversation back—she inadvertently pushed the Max button. Not that he looked wound tight right now… not like he had that first day…

Her stomach roiled.

Oh, to hell with it!

All this tiptoeing around not being herself was exhausting! He was a big boy. If he didn't want to talk, then let him say so. But she was going to jolly well pick up the baton. Because for one thing he was holding it out—albeit at half-mast—and for another, for good or ill, right or wrong, she wanted to know more about him, about who he was. If only to stop herself wondering about it…if only for a bit of peace.

She took a quick sip from her cup and smiled. 'So, how did it go with your PR situation? Did you save the day?'

His eyes filled with a momentary reluctance, but then he was releasing his neck, bringing his hand back down to his phone. 'I was just having a look.'

'And…?'

His lips set. 'The statement's getting some traction on the socials.'

Keeping going, Tommie…

'So, was it, like, a real emergency situation?'

He let out a short, wry laugh. 'What constitutes an emergency in PR terms wouldn't register on the scale of real emergencies—but if you count a damaging, unfounded rumour going viral, threatening a client's reputation and potentially a significant portion of her livelihood, then, yes, this was one.'

Such a grounded perspective on emergencies! Keeping his client's name private, but fully answering her question. She felt a warm swell of admiration, felt it rising into her eyes. He was good at this… Her heart squeezed. Oh, but he did look tired…probably wanted to get going. He was bending to his phone again now, which was maybe to make her feel that she didn't have to rush with her coffee, or maybe it was just that he wanted to look at his phone. Either way, it was beyond late.

She drained her cup and set it down. 'That's me done, so we can go. You can carry on with that in the car...'

His scrolling finger stilled, his whole frame stiffening. 'No, I can't.' And then he looked up, his gaze flat as glass. 'The phone slips off my knee.'

Her heart seized. *Idiot, Tommie!* How hadn't she put two and two together? Max never took out his phone in the car unless he was answering a call. *How* hadn't she noticed? All these things he was having to contend with—simple, everyday things she took for granted.

She looked at him, pressing her gaze into his so he'd know how terrible she felt. 'I'm sorry, Max, I didn't think. I was only thinking about how tired you look, that I should be taking you home...'

'It's fine—don't worry about it.' He looked down, closing his screen. 'We're both tired, so let's just get going.'

And then he was pocketing his phone, lifting his jacket, getting to his feet all in one swift moment, moving beyond the little two-sofas-and-a-coffee-table combo into the wider room.

Standing apart. Distancing himself.

She felt her heart sinking. Was this another sea change? A switch back? Or just tiredness at the end of a long day?

She reached for her bag and got up. Just when things had been feeling easier, more level... And, no, it shouldn't matter how level things were, because all she had to do was drive his car, keep taking his money and push forward with her plans, keep her eye on the prize. But for some reason, right at this moment, it did matter. Very much.

CHAPTER EIGHT

MAX DREW UP with a start. *What the...?*

Tommie! Sitting in Reception, legs crossed, sunglasses perched, absorbed in *Vogue* magazine as if this were a hotel lobby instead of a *private* physiotherapy practice. As if he wasn't a *private* patient attending a *private* appointment. As if he didn't want—*need*—a few *private* moments after his appointment to process and regroup...a few moments *not* to be burning at the end of her eternally questing gaze!

He reversed a few paces, leant back against the wall.

For pity's sake!

Was this his reward for trying to be the same with her as he was with his other employees? All he'd been trying to do with that coffee at the Dorchester last week was make amends for not briefing her properly about the night-time parking arrangements, for not even thinking about all the nuts and bolts of that stuff because of this constant ridiculous tailspin she had him in, this clamour that had him reverse parking into himself all the time, instead of dealing with practicalities.

That meeting with Christy Blume et al... Half his mind on the job, half on Tommie, on how he needed to get his act together around her, treat her like he did everyone else. Be a better boss, a better human. In other words, normal Max.

Coffee because she was out for the count...because he'd

have done the same for any member of his staff, done it for Fliss. And, yes, watching her sleeping hadn't exactly been a hardship—because when did he ever get the chance to really look at her, enjoy the sweet sight of her? The neat arch of her eyebrows, the delicate line of her nose. And those lips… full, slightly parted in sleep. She'd looked loose-limbed, every contour soft, her hands, fingers, losing their grip on a half-open sketchbook. Pencil lines. Too dim in the room to see detail. Then she'd woken up, treated him to some quite amusing conniptions…

It had been fine. He'd had it all under control. For sure, he'd had to get out his phone, to show her he wasn't heading anywhere until she'd drunk the coffee, until she'd properly come back to herself and was fit to drive. And, yes, he had almost got too absorbed in checking the socials to see how the PR statement was tracking. But he'd pulled himself back to the moment, had a stab at conversation.

Catnip to Tommie, of course. Predictably, she'd started with her questions, her gaze opening out, and that had started the tailspin feeling. But he'd kept his cool, powered on through. And then she'd said that thing about how he could use his phone in the car, and it had felt like a lightning strike in his chest because that was another thing he couldn't do because of his hand. The worst thing, though, was the way she'd looked at him then, reaching right in with her gaze. As if she cared…could feel his pain and frustration. And he'd felt fear rushing into his head, grabbing hold of his mind, shouting, *No, no, no.* He didn't *want* anyone feeling sorry for him, especially her. He didn't want anyone seeing the fragile tips of him, seeing the pain, because that stuff was private, his alone. He was no one's sideshow.

He'd called time quickly, gone to chat to the night manager to level himself out while the car was being brought round. And maybe Tommie had read his mood, seen that he needed his own space, because she hadn't said much on the way home. And these past few days she'd been keeping to her corner…except for her eyes, that grey-green gaze. Always there whenever he looked up, trying to peel him open.

He ground his teeth. And now it wasn't only her eyes but herself—here where she had no business being, here at exactly the wrong moment, when Paul had just rained—*no*, poured a fricking deluge—on his parade.

'Sorry, Max. The twinge in your palm is just that. It isn't a sign that the nerves higher up are repairing themselves. You've got to be patient, buddy. On the bright side, your bones are almost healed, so we can put you in a less cumbersome splint, air those fingertips…'

He looked at his hand. As if air made any difference! As if being able to see his fingertips made any difference. He couldn't feel them, make them move. He was still at base camp, and the last thing he needed—the very *last* thing he could cope with right now, when he was feeling this low, this frustrated, when he was patently *not* in control of this thing—was Tommie up in his face. God help him, he didn't *want* to upset her, but he couldn't make himself not feel furious. He couldn't have her waltzing in here like this—he just couldn't. She needed to know, to be told in no uncertain terms that she was not to come in here. Ever!

He drew in a breath and pushed away from the wall, striding back out into Reception. He sensed her gaze lifting, but he couldn't bring himself to look at her. He just kept walking, through the doors, through the lobby, and then he was at the main door, seizing the handle, yanking it open, stepping outside.

'Max?' She was a step behind, looking at him with wide, searching eyes. 'Are you okay?'

His heart kicked. Could those eyes really not see what was happening here? How she was pushing him to the brink, making him this person he didn't want to be? Chaotic. Emotional. Unable to hold back. Struggling to keep his voice level.

'No, I'm not okay, Tommie! Why did you come inside?'

She recoiled a little, frowning. 'To wait for you, of course...'

'You haven't happened to notice that it's a *private* clinic? Haven't processed that I was attending a *private* appointment!'

Her features drew in. 'But I wasn't *in* the appointment room, Max! I was *in* Reception.'

Seriously? Emphasising the word to him? Arguing semantics? Was she trying to make him crosser than he was already?

'I'm not asking you to state the obvious. I'm asking you *why* you were in Reception, where you had no business being, instead of in the car, where you should have been!'

Her eyes flashed. 'And asking rudely, it must be said!' And then her gaze flattened. 'Maybe you should look around you, Max, ask *yourself* the question. *Why wasn't Tommie waiting in the car?*' She jerked her head towards the street behind him, indicating where he should look. 'Go on—see if you can work it out.'

Glinting gaze...triumphant.

He felt his stomach tightening, dread circling. Why did it seem that he was about to be bested, humbled?

He swallowed hard and turned. Curved street. Railings. Communal garden. Two phone engineers bent over a junction box with a spaghetti of wires hanging out of it. Van alongside, doors open... *Oh, God.* In more or less the same place as—

Her voice wrenched him back, cutting the thought out from under him.

'Those guys asked me if I'd mind moving so they could get their van close to the box. And, believe it not, this being London, it wasn't that easy to find another parking space. I managed, of course, but it's streets away. I thought of texting you, to let you know, but then I thought about what you said the other night about your phone and your hand…'

The glint in her eyes faded for a second then relit, setting shame alight inside him.

'I thought that if you didn't know the street you'd struggle to use the maps app on your phone, so I came back to collect you. And maybe you'd have rather I sat down on the doorstep to wait, but I'm sorry, Max…' Her eyes were glistening now, driving in the knife, twisting it hard. 'Even for what you're paying me, I'm not sitting on any bloody doorstep!'

Words…ringing…reverberating. The sudden, awful dead weight of himself.

'I'd never ask you to sit—'

He bit down on his tongue hard. So *not* the thing to lead with! His heart pulsed. What the hell was wrong with him? And what was he doing, dithering about like this? From the look of her, she was *this* close to walking away—and he couldn't let that happen, couldn't lose her. Not this kind, thoughtful, professional, beautiful woman who'd come back for him when it was the last thing he deserved.

He pulled in a breath. 'I'm sorry, Tommie. I was out of order.'

Her mouth twisted. 'Not only that…'

Holding him at the pointed end of her gaze.

His heart pinched. 'And I was rude, yes…'

Her eyes confirmed that he'd hit the mark. Would his apology hit the mark too? Buy him forgiveness?

He shifted his stance. 'I'm sorry I was rude to you. I—'

Didn't have a leg to stand on was the honest truth, because the problem was all his, wasn't it? Perpetually seeing The Inquisition in her eyes when it was—could only be—simple kindness, routine concern. Kicking off, pushing back against it, because accepting kindness and concern felt like an admission of weakness, an admission that he wasn't in control, that he was fragile and vulnerable, that he might actually need somebody.

He knew his triggers. Fliss had told him a million times what they were, and therapy had filled in the blanks. It was just that he wasn't used to *being* triggered. That was the difference with Tommie. The perplexing, agonising push and pull of her—sorting it out in his mind, separating the purely physical, sexual tug of her from the other, scarier one. That tingling, alien impulse to confide in her, trust her, dive into her ocean. A bad impulse. *Wrong!* Because she was his employee—his employee who was looking at him now, waiting for him to explain himself, maybe waiting to make a 'stay or go' decision on the basis of what came out of his mouth.

His heart swung. It had to be the truth. Not the whole private messy truth of himself, but everything else… He drew in a breath. 'I'm not trying to justify anything, because I can't. I was rude, out of order, and I'm sorry…really sorry, Tommie. I have some things to say though, if you'd please hear me out…'

She folded her arms, holding his gaze, and then suddenly something gave way in her eyes. 'Okay. We should probably walk and talk, though, since it's about twenty miles to the car.'

His heart lifted. Not words she'd be saying if she was about to quit on him. He felt a smile trying to come and held it in.

'Good idea.'

'Right.' She dropped her shades, adjusted her tote, and then she was off.

He fell in, matching his stride to hers. 'So…this isn't meant to be an excuse, but it's context, okay?'

'Okay.'

'The thing is my session back there didn't go so well.'

She glanced over. 'I'm sorry.'

'Don't be. It's my own fault. Remember at the interview how I said I didn't want to get my hopes up with this hand? That I needed to be realistic?'

'Yes! And I said you shouldn't let realistic become pessimistic.'

Verbatim!

'Well, seems I'm not much good at being either. I felt a twinge in my palm yesterday, and I went from nought to full-speed optimism in the space of a second. I thought Paul—he's my physio—would be full of happy news, but seemingly a twinge is just that, doesn't mean a thing. And then he gave me The Talk—you know… *"Be patient, these things take time."* And then it was the hopeful stuff. *"You're young, fit, your chances are good."* Then came the usual warnings about *"no guarantees"*, and about how I need to take one day at a time. Basically the same stuff the surgeon said weeks ago. What it amounts to is that I've made no progress at all since the crash. And I'm not trying to make you feel bad, but after I'd seen Paul I just needed a bit of time…you know, to get over myself, pull myself together.'

'Oh, God, and instead I was there!' She stopped suddenly, pushing up her shades, filling his eyes with her gaze. 'I'm so sorry. I didn't even think—'

'Would you please stop apologising? This is me, trying to give you some context so you understand, but it doesn't alter the fact that I *shouldn't* have lost it, and I *shouldn't* have spoken to you like that. *None* of this is your fault, Tommie. You didn't know. It's not like I briefed you on the whole wait-in-the-car-because-this-injury-is-testing-every-scrap-of-my-patience thing.'

She blinked. 'Well, no, but I *did* wait in the car last time, so you probably assumed I'd do the same again.'

Cutting him some slack, being kind…

Her gaze cleared. 'Probably the thing to focus on is that I know *now* that you need some space after your session. So, if anything like this happens again here's what we'll do: I'll text you, right?'

He felt his head nodding. 'Okay.'

'Then, when you're finished, you can text me back, or call, and I'll come for you.' She scrunched up her face. 'I don't know why I didn't think of that this time, actually.' And then she was shrugging her shoulders, rolling her eyes at herself, looking completely adorable. 'Epic fail.'

Just 'epic' would do. His heart squeezed. Did she have the slightest notion of how lovely she was? It didn't seem like it—not like the women he dated. Their beauty seemed to float apart from the rest of them, exist as a separate layer of awareness. Whereas Tommie was complete…everything zipped into her skin. Loveliness, openness, kindness, thoughtfulness. No wonder he was in a whirl. His breath checked. A silent, staring, mesmerised whirl.

He shook himself. 'Hardly a fail. In any case, I think that gong already belongs to me.'

Her eyes smiled, registering his quip. 'Don't be too hard on yourself, Max.' And then she was dropping her shades, turning to walk. 'It must be tough for you. Very frustrating.'

'It is…' He felt a beat of hesitation. He didn't want to regale her with his woes, but if he'd forced himself to brave the swirl of her gaze from the get-go, laid a few things out about what he was dealing with, trying to cope with, it might have saved them both some grief. In any case, he was enjoying this...talking to her. Why not talk more? Hell, it might even do him some good to get this stuff off his chest.

He looked over at her. 'You never think, until it happens to you, how an injury can make it hard to do the simplest things. Every damn thing becomes an exercise, a problem to solve. Everything takes longer: showering, getting dressed. And some things you just can't do—like buttoning a shirt, lacing a shoe. As for opening a packet...don't get me started. And no disrespect, because I'm lucky to have such an excellent driver in you—' just so she would know he was grateful to her, sorry to his bones for being so obnoxious, and that he didn't take her for granted '—but I miss driving my own car. Miss racing. It would still be frustrating, even if I had an end date, but I don't. So there's that as well. No progress. No end in sight.'

'You've got a different splint on, though...'

Which sort of felt like a prompt.

He raised his arm to show her. 'That's because my bones are nearly healed. Apparently, this is enough protection now.'

She took it in. 'It's less cumbersome, anyway, and if your bones are getting there I'd call that progress.'

'It doesn't make any difference if I can't *feel* anything.' He dropped his arm back to his side, allowing himself a bit of petulance. 'I'm still on the bottom rung, going nowhere.'

Her sunglasses glinted. 'Oh, look, see—there you go. You've got your pessimism back!'

'Very funny.'

She flashed a grin. 'You're welcome.' And then she was

looking ahead again. 'At least you can see your fingertips now...*touch* them. You could try massaging them.'

'To what end?'

She shrugged. 'I don't know... It sort of feels like something that would help. Has Paul given you any instructions?'

'Not yet. If my bones are a hundred percent next session he's going to take me through some "active assisted" exercises.'

'Well, maybe when you start doing those you'll feel a difference.' She chewed her lip for a moment and then she pushed up her shades again, looking over. 'In the meantime, remember I'm right here if you need help with anything...' She broke into a smile. 'I'm a dab hand at opening packets and strong-arming lids off jars.'

His heart clenched. Lovely Tommie. Touching him to the core with her kindness. But he could feel resistance stiffening in his chest...could feel that fear reaching up into his mind again.

He looked ahead, fighting to keep his tone neutral. 'You're not my nurse, Tommie.'

Little pause.

'I wasn't offering to be your nurse.'

And now it was a main road, and the pedestrian crossing, traffic whooshing left and right, moments of glinting chrome and scrolling reflections.

Tommie pressed the button to cross and then she was turning, looking at him, her gaze soft and serious. 'I watched your crash online, Max, and I know it was horrific. Whatever you feel about it, and whatever you feel about your injury—anger, frustration, misery—it's okay to feel those things. But it's also okay to accept help sometimes. Whatever you think, it isn't a sign of weakness.'

'I never said it was.' For some reason, the only thing he

could think of to say. And then something else crashed in, taking him by surprise. 'Thanks, Tommie.'

She broke into a sudden smile, her eyes filling with warm, lovely light. 'You're welcome.'

And then she was turning back to the road, adjusting her bag on her shoulder as if she hadn't just blinded him, taken his breath away.

'Right, only another ten miles to go.'

CHAPTER NINE

SUCH A LOVELY AFTERNOON! Blue sky. White clouds. Reflecting in the glass of the high-rise buildings all around. Faceted blocks of bright sky against a backdrop of even more sky. And somewhere inside the biggest block, behind one of those vast glass panes, was Max, busy doing his PR thing while she, Tommie, was busy not concentrating on the one-shoulder ruffled blouse she was supposed to be sketching!

She forced her eyes back to the page, drew a line with her pencil. *Gah!* Not right! The whole damn design was off. She flipped back a page. Same thing. *Wrong!* She flipped again. Also wrong!

Flip, flip, flip.

Wrong, wrong, wrong!

She flung the pencil down and reached for her cup. All wrong. Three hours sitting here on this café terrace and the only progress she'd made was through two tall soda and limes and a pot of tea!

She felt her eyes drifting upwards again to Max's glass tower. *Max!* He was the problem. Nothing new there. But he'd become a worse problem since last week's showdown, because sorting everything out afterwards had changed things. The lie of the land... Her heart squeezed. The way *her* land lay in relation to his...

She sipped her tea, cradling the cup in her hands. The

problem was that it was impossible not to like the Max who'd emerged from the ashes after she'd well and truly put him in his place. And it was especially hard not to like—and not to keep remembering—the way his eyes had softened all the way into hers when he'd said, 'Thanks, Tommie' at that crossing. Genuine warmth there…gratitude, honesty, openness. It had felt as if all the glimmers she'd ever seen in him had come together in that moment and fused themselves into one brilliant light so she could see him—*really* see him.

She put her cup down. That was the moment she kept coming back to—the one that wouldn't leave her alone. She couldn't stop those fierce little claws in her mind scratching at it, wondering what it meant, what it could mean—that he could look at her like *that*, make her feel so…so drawn, torn, flipped and rolled. *Crashed!* And now—even though she wasn't looking for a relationship with anyone, when she was set on her own goals—she couldn't seem to stop her imagination from running off all the time into an alternative Max and Tommie universe.

No wonder there was no imagination left to put into her designs. No wonder she couldn't sketch anything right.

She picked up the pencil, flipped to a new page. It was annoying. *Distracting!* She didn't want to be wasting time and energy on pointless thoughts and stupid fantasies. Max Lawler Scott was not, and never would be, interested in her. Not in *that* way. She was a train driver's daughter from South London with an accent to match and not even two half-decent exam grades to rub together! She wasn't putting herself down, or anything, because she had big plans, big dreams. But facts were facts. Max was silver spoon, and she wasn't.

She drew a fresh line, then another, drawing a bodice.

In any case, Max wasn't the relationship type. He wasn't even interested in his thoroughbred women, was he? If he'd been the settling down type, wanted that kind of thing, he'd have been with someone by now...married, maybe. But he wasn't.

She drew another line.

It was sad in a way...a shame. Because even though he seemed to be quite messed up, and proud, not to mention touchy as hell, underneath it all he was a good guy...had good qualities.

She shortened her pencil strokes, drawing a frill.

For one thing he wasn't too proud to climb down, admit fault, apologise. And he had a lovely wry sense of humour that he didn't seem to mind turning on himself.

'I think that gong already belongs to me.'

She liked that kind of quip, the neat way he put things. It was right up her street, brought the smile out in her, because it was her sense of humour too.

She felt a smile coming. These past few days it was what they'd been falling into more and more. Quips and teases. Back and forth banter. It was fun. Irresistible! Her stomach swooped. But it was muddying the waters. And she'd tried reminding herself that Max represented the rich and shady, but she couldn't seem to make that mud stick any more, since what little he'd told her about what he did always seemed to involve helping people...saving them from themselves. And she'd tried reminding herself that Max was Chloe Mills' publicist. But all that did was stoke the guilt inside her because he didn't know she'd worked for Chloe, didn't know she was keeping it from him. It hadn't seemed important before, hadn't bothered her when he'd been shut off, staring out of the window, communicating in monosyllables, but now—

'Hey!'

What the...?

'Max!'

Here! How? *Why?*

Because he never did this—came down to the commercial levels where the cafés and shops were. He always texted to say he was leaving the office, so she'd be back at the car, ready to go, when he emerged from the lift. But now he was pulling out the opposite chair, sitting himself down, amusement playing through his gaze.

'You look shocked, Tommie.'

What did he expect, blindsiding her like this? Sketchbook open. Secret dreams on show.

She drew in a breath. Admission...deflection. The gospel according to Max. The publicist's way of handling awkward situations. Well, this here was the mother of all awkward situations, so...

'Of course I'm shocked. You coming down here is a very random act.' She smiled into his eyes, using the moment to close her sketchbook and draw it close. 'Not that it isn't delightful to see you.' Now the pencil. Casual little pick-up. 'So, what brings you to the Netherworld?'

The corner of his mouth ticked up and then he was glancing out at the dock, lifting his gaze to the sky, looking around. 'It's a nice day. I've been trapped inside, looking at it through the window.' His eyes came back. 'I just fancied a bit of fresh air, and you said earlier that you often come to this place, so I thought I'd have a walk, see if you were here.' He gave a little shrug. 'Come and find *you* for a change.'

God help her, those blue eyes, that face, that hair lifting a little in the rippling breeze. Too gorgeous, too distracting.

Time to cut loose.

She smiled. 'Well, you've found me now, so shall we

go?' She put her hand on the sketch book, ready to slide it into her bag.

'Not so fast...' His eyes darted to it, then came back. 'I've seen you with that book before and I promise I won't be offended if you tell me to mind my own business, but I have to tell you, I'm curious...' A keen light stole into his gaze. 'Before you not so subtly closed it, I saw what looked like a terrific design sketch for a blouse?'

She felt her breath stilling. He *liked* her design? Thought it was 'terrific' even though it was all wrong?

So unexpected. So nice. Making her heart glow.

But she couldn't talk fashion with Max. Couldn't talk about her big, shiny dream. Because what if it somehow jogged his memory about that moment at Chloe's party? Brought everything crashing down? That critical omission, that little bit of dishonesty? Maybe her fessing up about New York was on the cards at some point, but she couldn't do it now—not when they'd only just found a rhythm, when things were good, pleasant between them. If he pushed her on this, all she could do was take what he'd seen and spin it into something tiny and insignificant...something that was happily also true.

She took a quick sip of tea and smiled. 'Thank you, but really, it's nothing.'

'It didn't look like nothing.' His hand gestured to the book. 'Can I see?'

Her stomach tightened. If she dug her heels in it would only make him all the more curious. Better to fold, downplay it, be casual about it.

'Sure...' She handed it over, opening it up for him.

He scanned the page. 'I like this...' And then he was flicking through, page after page. 'These are good, Tommie!'

Way to make her blush!

And then he was looking up, forehead wrinkling. 'What are they for?'

Honest face, Tommie.

She shrugged. 'They're for me. I make some of my own clothes.' And as luck would have it… She glanced down. 'Like this top I'm wearing.'

His gaze dipped for a long, tingling second, taking it in, then came back all warm. 'Very nice. I like that black contrast trim around the neck…the way it sets off the white…'

Her pulse pinged with joy. 'That's *exactly* the detail I changed from the mass market version they were selling in the boutiques!' The man had an eye—got it totally! She felt a smile breaking, the fire stirring inside her. 'That's why I design stuff. Why I sew. So much fashion fails for want of the right detail, or the right finish. And so much of it is shoddy. Clothes should fit well, flatter, last, but so much of what's out there doesn't tick any of those boxes. It seems like it's made for landfill, when that's the exact opposite of what we should be doing with our clothes. It drives me insane!'

He smiled. 'I'm getting that…'

Nodding, gazing into her eyes, then *at* her eyes it felt like, taking her in, all her bare surfaces, making heat curl and pulse low down in her belly like it did at the Dorchester that night when she was watching his thumb, his lips, his lovely, lovely mouth.

And then suddenly he blinked and looked down, closing the book carefully. 'Thanks for showing me this.' He offered it back across the table with a nod. 'I'm impressed.'

'Thanks, but like I said, it's nothing…'

Unlike the messy way he'd just made her feel. Could he see it in her eyes? On her face? His face was composed, every plane in place, as if the moment had never happened—as if he hadn't just set those claws off again, scratching in her mind.

His eyebrows flashed. 'We should go.' And then he was getting up, looking down into the glinting water of the dock. 'I've got to stop off in Belgravia on the way back, but it shouldn't be for long.'

'Okay.'

She slid the sketch book into her bag. Talking about Belgravia but not saying who he was seeing, or why. Completely normal Max behaviour! Looking about him now, looking controlled, calm, completely normal. Whereas she... She took a breath and got up. Had she imagined that moment somehow? Read more into that look than was really in it? Her stomach pulsed. She must have...

And now that she was on her feet he was turning, heading for the exit, attracting furtive looks from the women seated at the other tables. She set off, following, trying not to notice the lovely way his hair curled at his nape or the confident flow of his stride.

She must have. Must have. Must have!

And she had to stop her imagination doing this—sliding over lines, causing mayhem. Because it was pointless, and not even anything she wanted—to get caught up, become embroiled in any kind of relationship. Especially one with her gorgeous, impossible boss. What she *wanted* was to put herself on the fashion map, make something of herself, feel the satisfaction inside that she'd achieved something in spite of the knockbacks, feel that she was truly as good as everyone else.

She straightened, quickening her pace, inhaling deep into her lungs. *That* was the thought those little claws needed to sink themselves into. Tommie Seager was going to make it, prevail, show the world just what she was made of!

CHAPTER TEN

'YOU SAID YOU needed some—'

Tommie's eyes quickly registered his naked upper half, then attached themselves, somewhat firmly, to the shirt he was dangling from his finger.

He felt a dip in his chest. She was uncomfortable, but what could he do? Last-minute decision. He couldn't wear his usual sweater-jacket combo to Lucy and Fraser's wedding, especially now that he was *sans* splint. Without that explanatory prop he'd likely come over as casual, disrespectful or lazy—and, given that this wedding was already set to be hell on a stick, why make it even worse for himself by committing a wardrobe *faux pas*?

And if Tommie was feeling uncomfortable, then it was worse for him, not being able to attend to himself, having to ask for help. Worse still that he was going to have to endure her at close quarters when she was looking even more gorgeous than usual today, in those neat black cropped trousers and that white sleeveless mock turtleneck top that showed off her smooth lovely arms. It was going to stretch his self-control in the downstairs department to the limits of endurance.

But what choice did he have but to push through? Try to make it as painless as possible for both of them?

'I'm sorry, Tommie.' He smiled to put her at her ease. 'I wouldn't be asking if—'

'Don't be sorry. It's fine…' She smiled quickly, then plucked the shirt off his finger, opening it out, lifting it high in front her face. 'I said I'd help you if you needed me to, and you can't do this yourself. Turn round.'

Sounding brisk, exactly like…

He felt a real smile rising and turned, poking his right arm into its sleeve, then the left. Then he turned back round again. 'You've got a bit of a nursey tone about you today.'

'Sorry about that.' Eyes down, she was pulling the two halves of his shirt together, doing a button in the middle. 'Just trying to get the job done.'

Focusing so hard on it that she hadn't got the reference. He wouldn't have minded, except that he was poking fun at himself here, trying to lighten her up.

'Tommie?'

Her eyes flicked up. 'Yes?'

'I was joking…' He raised his eyebrows. 'Remember how I said I didn't want a nurse?'

Recognition flickered in her gaze.

He tried a smile. 'I was trying to make this feel a little less awkward…'

'Ah…' She drew in a little breath. 'Sorry. I was preoccupied. I suppose I was thinking that since you never even came back to me on packets and jar lids, asking me to help with *this* must be a heavy deal for you, so you'd want me to crack on…get it over with.'

His heart squeezed. Thinking of him, of course. Maybe of herself a bit too. Because this wasn't 'packets and jar lids', was it? This was above and beyond.

Probably the best thing he could actually do was just let her get on with it.

'You're right. On both counts.' He lifted his chin, looking ahead. 'Feel free to crack on.'

Except that cracking on meant enduring this torture of movement. Air moving, churning up delicious little wafts of her perfume. Fingers moving, tugging the shirt fabric against his skin. It didn't take much to set his blood alight around Tommie. Christ, just watching her face, all that lovely animation when she'd been talking about fashion at Canary Wharf last week, had sucked him in, got him losing himself in her gaze, feeling heat pooling in places it had no business pooling, and all that with zero touching involved!

And now her hands were moving lower, pulling the shirt away from his body and towards hers.

Oh, God!

Was it because she could sense what her touch was doing to him down there? He clenched his jaw. He needed a distraction fast…a sexual buzz-killer. Oh! And what better subject could there be…?

He exhaled. 'I don't even know why I'm putting us both through this. It's not as if I *want* to go to this bloody wedding.'

Her fingers stilled. 'Why don't you want to go?' And then she was bringing her hands up to his chest, doing up a button, making the fabric tickle and tease, catch at his nipples. 'Don't you like your cousin?'

Focus, Max.

He shook his head. 'Yes…no, it's not that. Lucy's absolutely lovely. And, Fraser, her intended…he's decent. It's just that—'

What?

What was he doing? He couldn't tell Tommie about Tamsin and Gerald, about the way he didn't like being around them. Because then she'd ask him why, and he couldn't dig into all the whys with her. She was his driver, seemingly his dresser now too, *not* his therapist. His heart shifted. But that was the other tug of her, wasn't it? That incomprehensible *something* about her that made him *want* to talk to her, tell her stuff he'd never told anyone.

Such a relief, in the end, offloading to her about his hand, and it was a relief being able to talk about it every day, about every twinge, every little tingle, to get it off his chest, get her measured but always upbeat take on it.

But Tamsin and Gerald were a whole other can of worms. Talking about them, even to Tommie, would only rile him up, and riled up was not how he wanted to arrive at the wedding. Odds were he'd be leaving that way, so why start early? He bit his lip. But now he'd left 'It's just that' hanging, hadn't he? He needed to scoop it up, press it flat, leave nothing for Tommie to seize on.

He pushed out a sigh, going for a weary, slightly bored tone. 'It's just family stuff, you know—foibles and irritations.'

'Right...' She was at his top button now, hesitating, glancing up. 'Can you lift your chin so I can—?'

'Of course.'

He obliged, looking up at the ceiling, trying to block out the warm sensation of her fingers against his throat. But then suddenly they stilled.

'Didn't you say yesterday there were two hundred people going?'

'Yep.'

Her fingers carried on. 'Well, with that many people milling about, couldn't you, like, hide?'

Great minds!

'That's exactly my plan—find a quiet corner...' Unless

Lucy had put him on a table with Tamsin, Gerald, Fliss and Gavin, in which case he was doomed.

'So you'll be fine, then…' Tommie stepped back, taking in his shirt front with her eyes. 'Right, you're done.'

If only…

'Not quite, I'm afraid.' He lifted his hands, flapping the cuffs. 'I need my cufflinks.'

'Oh, of course.' Her gaze flitted off. 'Where are they?'

'On the side table, there. With my tie.'

'Okay.' She made a pivot and went over, hanging the tie around her neck, bending to the box to free the cufflinks.

He followed, folding his left cuff as he went, to speed things up.

But then suddenly she was spinning round, head down, clearly unaware that he was there, and before he could move she was ploughing into him, breasts against his chest, hair in his face, in a soft, lovely explosion.

'Sorry. Oh, God, sorry!'

Pulling away, blushing, but it was *his* fault—unequivo-cally!

'No, *I'm* sorry, Tommie. I was coming to you…trying to be helpful.'

'But I should have been looking where I was going!'

This whole crazy situation!

He looked at her, offered up a shrug. 'Maybe it doesn't matter.'

Her eyes held his for a long, tantalising beat, then soft-ened with a smile. 'Maybe you're right. Shall we just do the cufflinks?'

'Okay.' He held out his left hand. 'You'll note I've folded the cuff, ready for you…'

She paused. 'Being helpful again?'

He felt a smile spreading into his cheeks. 'It's the least I can do.'

She chuckled softly. 'Okay, well, the other thing you can do is please hold still. Because this is fiddly.'

And then she was pinching his cuff together, sliding the cufflink in, giving it a twist.

'You're doing great...' He swapped hands. 'I'm very grateful, you know.'

Her eyes glanced up, twinkling. 'So you should be.' Folding his cuff, fitting the second cufflink. 'This is over and above, you know.'

His heart paused. Which called for something in return, didn't it? A thought to come back to.

'I'm aware, but thanks for the reminder.'

She stepped back, raising her eyes to his with a smile that had a touch of relief about it.

'Just the tie now. Windsor knot?'

'You read my mind.'

She grinned. 'Well, it's the best one, according to my grandad, so I figured that was the one you'd want.' But then she frowned. 'The only thing is, I can only do it on myself. So I'll do it three-quarters on me, then adjust it on you.'

'Whatever works. I'm in your capable hands.'

Hands that were lining up the tie now, expertly looping and threading. Hands that at any second would be around his neck from an up-close position, her body right there, her smell and her shimmering warmth putting him through the mill again.

And now she was stepping in, a flicker affecting her gaze. 'I need to stand your collar up...'

'Okay.' He straightened, lifting his chin, trying to hold his body away.

Last push, Max.

Hands, working his collar upright, fingers catching his hair at the back, shooting tingles through him. Moving round now, little brushes to his neck, jaw, briefly his cheek. He bore down. Could she hear his heart thundering? Feel the heat pulsing through him? Oh, and now she was lifting the tie over her own head, encircling him in her lovely smell, placing it over his head. Her face so close. Her lips slightly parted in concentration.

Torture!

Tugging, adjusting, her hands at his throat again. Top button…then reaching to the back of his neck again, pressing close, that little shower of her perfume, folding the collar down, working it round, eyes focused on the job, then moving back to the knot. One last adjustment and then she was melting back, a little breathless, a little blush in her cheeks.

'You're all done.'

Done for, more like—not that he could let it show.

'Thanks so much, Tommie.' He smiled, feeling the knot, which was spot on. 'You're a superstar.'

Her eyes lit with a tease. 'Too right, I am.' And then she was moving back a little. 'What time do you want to leave?

Now would be perfect, to steal a march on the weekend traffic, but he needed a moment to catch his breath—and from the look of her, Tommie did too.

He pushed his hair back. 'I've got a couple of things to do before we go, so shall we say thirty minutes?'

'Great!' She seized the door handle, pulling the door open. 'I'll have the car outside for then.'

And then she was gone, leaving warm traces of her perfume behind her.

CHAPTER ELEVEN

TOMMIE FELT HER breath catching. 'Oh, my goodness, Max, this place...'

'Nice, isn't it.'

Nice?

She looked at him in the mirror. 'It isn't "nice"—it's blooming Pemberley; it's Mr Darcy and Elizabeth Bennet and Jane Austen!'

Three storeys of vast pale stone house, with a grand pillared entrance, immaculate lawns and terraces all around and wooded parkland beyond. Most likely there'd be a lake somewhere.

She slowed the car down so she could look properly, fill her whole gaze with it. Because if she did that, filled her senses to the brim, maybe it would push out Max and that whole shirt-buttoning business...

'Hey, Tommie, could you pop down a sec please...help me with something?'

No warning about what that 'something' was. He'd just opened the door and stepped back, parading his abs and his pecs and all those other muscles she didn't know the names of, dangling his shirt from his finger as if that explained everything. Which it had. And then it had been a case of girding herself, coping with that clean, fresh smell of him and that up-close heat radiating from him, coping with that crackling charge that had seemed to be there, skewing her senses and her hand-eye co-ordination, buttons slipping, fingers slipping. Oh, and then colliding with him like that! Coming up against that wall of chest and cotton and delicious heat. Cufflinks... Collar... Fingers trying, failing, not to catch his hair, his hot neck and his smooth, tense jaw. But it hadn't only been the sensory overload, it had been the looks, their little exchanges, that sense of...

And that sacred half-hour afterwards hadn't stopped her mind from swirling, and the drive here hadn't stopped it either. Because even though Max had been mostly quiet, preoccupied—undoubtedly with those so-called family *'foibles and irritations'*—which she knew from the internet were weightier than that—he was nevertheless right there on the back seat, looking impeccably, impossibly handsome, tugging at her senses like a great big bloody magnet.

Maybe getting out into all this space, walking in the grounds, communing with the trees in those woods, breathing in the bright green air, filling her senses with other distractions, would help her tamp these feelings down, stop her mind's eye seeing that tantalising, compelling light in his gaze and reading all the wrong things into it. Not only reading those things into it but, God help her, wanting them to be real, wanting *him*, wanting to know him, get close to him, *be* close to him, be someone to him, *something* to him...

She blinked, refocusing, turning the car onto the sweeping frontage, and then felt her eyes blinking again, a different focus arriving. Oh, what kind of fool was she, wanting 'real' with Max, feeding herself minuscule doses of a Max and Tommie reality, imagining that it could happen?

This was the reality check right here—all of this. This grand house, these lovely grounds, these sleek cars pulling up, these people getting out of them. Privileged people. Rich. Entitled. This was Max's world, wasn't it? He came from this. Not from this specific house, but from one like it—one that was nothing like the South London semi she'd grown up in, with neighbours, and barking dogs, and youths wheeling prams with the free papers in, shoving them through the door, half in, half out, making a draught whistle through the hall.

She braked, easing the car to a stop.

Different world.

'Right...' Max's belt unclicked and then he was leaning forward, so close, pointing through the windscreen, his cuff-link catching the light. 'So, just follow those other cars to the western side of the house and park there. They want the front of the house left clear—for photos, presumably.'

Of course they did—a grand façade like that. She could imagine the photos already... Lucy in flowing silk and an heirloom veil, Fraser in tails and pin-striped trews, the pillars of the family pile rising in the background.

Different world.

Not hers. Not one she could ever belong to. That was the reality.

'Tommie...?'

She shook herself. 'Got it.'

'When you've parked, go round to the back. I believe they've made a sitting room available for suppliers and drivers and so on. You'll be catered for too, obviously...' He smiled. 'It'll likely be a version of the wedding breakfast, so pretty decent.'

'Sounds good.'

And then his smile faded a little. 'Thanks again for helping me out with the garb.'

There it was, that look behind the look again...messing with her senses, her imagination.

She turned away to cut free. 'You're welcome...'

And then her heart stopped dead.

Jamie! Booted and suited. Opening the rear door of his beloved luxury sedan for a stunning-looking woman in a fuchsia suit and black heels.

She felt her eyes staring, her lungs slowly crimping. Jamie… Here… Right where she was. *Oh, God!* And if he was here, she couldn't be. Not after all the pain she'd caused him. She'd only see it in his eyes again—the hurt, maybe loathing, or maybe some little gloating joy because she'd failed. Not that he'd ever been that kind of man, but she might have turned him into one, mightn't she? Ruined him for love…for trust.

Whatever!

She couldn't bear it. Couldn't be—

'Tommie, are you okay?' Max was peering at her, concern etched on his face. 'You look like you've seen a ghost.'

Her heart lunged. *What to say?* Then again, if she was upfront about it then at least he would get why she wanted to leave, hopefully sanction it.

She drew in a breath and looked at him. 'That's because I sort of have.' She jerked her head in Jamie's direction. 'See that chauffeur over there, with the woman in pink?'

Max's gaze arrowed through the windscreen and back 'Yes, I see him.'

'Well, he's my ex.'

'Your ex?' There was that look again, searching, then softening. 'I'm guessing it didn't end well?'

She felt a twist inside. All over his face that he thought Jamie was the one who'd hurt *her*—but she couldn't get into that with him now…not when Jamie was only feet away, might look up at any second and see her.

She swallowed hard. 'No, it didn't. So, if it's all right with you, I'll go into the village or something…wait there. I'm sorry, but I just can't be here if he is.'

'Of course…' Nodding, frowning a bit. 'Whatever you want…' And then he was moving back, reaching for the door. 'Mind, I want to leave straight after Lucy and Fraser have danced their first dance, so be back here for seven-thirty sharp, okay? Right in this spot. Not a second later.'

Her heart squeezed. Because he didn't want to be here either, did he? Both of them, exactly where they didn't want to be.

She smiled to bolster him. 'Seven-thirty sharp. I'll be here. I promise.'

Max reached for the pillar, steadying himself. That last drink had probably been one drink too many. Or maybe it was those last two. *Two too many!* For crying out loud, though, listening to Gerald issuing forth from the next table, giving it his 'man of the people' routine—listening because Gerald's booming voice made it impossible *not* to listen—was enough to drive anyone to drink…make them want to numb their ears!

He straightened, trying to focus on the cars out front. *There!* Tommie was waiting exactly where he'd asked her to wait. He felt a stir in his chest. At least *she* was reliable. At least he could count on *her*. Not like dear cousin Lucy. When he'd hugged her after the ceremony, she'd whispered to him that she'd put him with Fliss and Gavin, on a separate table from Tamsin and Gerald. What she hadn't said was that their two tables were right next to each other!

He looked at the steps, lining himself up to descend.

Or maybe it hadn't been Lucy's doing but Fliss, sticking her oar in at the hen do, saying to Luce that *she* wanted to be close enough to chat to Mum and Dad even if he didn't. Maybe Lucy had simply been trying to compromise, try-ing to make them all happy *Whatever!* The upshot had been misery. For him, anyway.

He launched himself down the steps, and then somehow the car was gliding up, idling right in front of him. He reached for the rear door handle then pulled his hand away. No... *No, no, no, no, no!* He was sick of riding in the back, of seeing the headrest every time he looked ahead... sick of always having to raise his voice slightly every time he wanted to talk to Tommie. How could two people have a flowing conversation like that?

Enough!

He wasn't a back seat person. Never had been.

He seized the passenger door handle, yanked it open and got in.

'Oh!' Tommie drew back a little. 'You're in the front!'

'Yes, I am.' His heart paused. Was he making her uncomfortable? Too damn fogged to have even considered it. He licked his lips quickly. 'You don't mind, do you?'

She shook her head. 'No, of course not. It's your car. You can sit where you like.'

'I think that was my thinking too...' He pulled at the seatbelt, getting it on the second attempt. 'But I'm sorry if I've shocked you.'

'No need to be sorry...'

Her gaze was taking him in piece by piece, it felt like, as she waited for him to click the belt into place—which he managed on the first attempt, thankfully. And then she was easing the car forward, making the gravel pop.

'Also, I'm not "shocked".' Her eyes glanced over. 'You surprised me, that's all.'

'I don't see how...' He tugged at his tie so he could get to his top shirt button. At least he could *undo* it unaided. 'I'm a driver, Tommie, not a passenger. I hate sitting in the back and that's the truth. I want to look ahead, see the road, see what's coming...' He rolled his head back against the rest. 'I like to know what's coming...'

Such as knowing where he was sitting at the wedding breakfast. If he'd known what was in store, he could have sneaked in ahead and swapped some name cards around, put himself on the kids' table with the crayons and the bubbles and the easy-to-eat food.

He looked at Tommie. 'I like to know the script.'

She smiled. 'I get that about you.' And then her gaze turned ahead. 'So, how was the wedding?'

What to say?

'It was a nice ceremony.'

'What I meant was, how did the hiding thing work out?'

That frankness again.

'Not as well as your hiding thing worked out, I imagine.'

Her features tightened slightly. 'Yes, well, I was in a position to leave—you weren't.' And then, as if she could sense that he was thinking of asking her about it, she swept on. 'So, I'm assuming, if it didn't work out well, that means you were found...?'

He let his eyes close. 'Not so much *found* as hoodwinked.'

'By?'

'My cousin. She put me on a table that was right next to—' His pulse jumped. What was he doing? Blabbing! Too fogged to remember that Tommie didn't know his story— that he couldn't talk about this...that he never talked about this with anyone...hadn't since his therapy days.

'Right next to who?'

She was pursuing it, of course.

'No one.' He forced his eyelids to open, looked over. 'Forget it. It doesn't matter.'

She scrunched her face up. 'Are you sure about that?'

Cryptic look…sliding her eyebrows up. Like Fliss with that whole *Do-you-really-know-yourself?* angle.

'What do you mean?'

She sighed. 'You've been drinking, Max, and I might be wrong, but it seems to me that that's got more to do with this thing you say *"doesn't matter"* than it has with the happy occasion of Lucy's wedding…'

They were coming to the estate road's end now, pulling up at the junction with the main road. Tommie shifted the car into neutral and then she was turning, looking at him.

'I get that you're a private person, and you can tell me it's none of my business if you like, but I can't help wondering what's going on with you…'

Wondering. Which was really just another way of asking him the question. Looking at him with that warm, open gaze of hers, full of concern, kindness, setting those strings tugging. He bit down on his lip. Did he really want to get into all this with her, though? Churn up all the chaff? Then again, it was already churning away inside him, wasn't it? Courtesy of today. And it wouldn't stop until he was miles away from this place—until he'd shoved it all back into its box again. So what difference would it make, talking about it? Other than that it might actually feel good to get it off his chest…help him put it back in that box all the quicker.

He looked into her eyes, felt warmth kindling. And it wasn't as if he didn't like talking to Tommie…didn't enjoy hearing her candid take on things. She'd been supportive about his hand, hadn't she? Listened to his fears and frustrations…helped him with his damn shirt earlier. So why not trust her with this? Talk to her about this? *Why not?* Just to kill time on the road…just to release the valve…

He drew in a breath and looked at her. 'What's going on with me is that I don't like my parents, Tommie. I don't like being around them. But I couldn't avoid it today—especially after Lucy put me on that table...'

Holding her gaze. That look behind the look again—just when she'd talked herself round, got her head together, decided that there couldn't be anything real happening between them. Just when she'd resolved to see him as a friend only, care about him as a friend only. And now, this...this deep, stirring look... this moment that was feeling pivotal, somehow.

Whatever it meant, she couldn't let it slide by.

'So, when you say you don't like them, does that mean you don't see them? Don't talk to them?'

His gaze flickered. 'That's right.'

Her heart dipped. So all that stuff online was true. *Unimaginable*... Not a moment to stay in, though. Better to be moving on, moving on and talking.

She checked the road, put the car into 'drive' and pulled out. 'I'm so sorry, Max.'

'Don't be.' Shaking his head. 'It is what it is.'

'But how did it get to *be* like that?'

Silence. And then... 'Fundamental differences, I suppose, right from when I was a kid.' His eyes glanced over. 'You know who my parents *are*, right?'

'Yes. They're News Global.'

He scoffed. 'Very well put! They are, indeed, *one hundred percent* News Global, and always have been.'

Emphasising the percentage as if... 'You're saying they didn't—'

'Have time for us?' Bitterness in his voice now...sliding along its edge. 'That's exactly what I'm saying. Here's the big scoop on Tamsin and Gerald, Tommie. They were bad parents. Busy all the time. Self-absorbed. No time for anything but work when I was growing up—oh, except for the parties. Every weekend the hordes would descend and fill our very big house—media friends, political cronies—carrying on until the wee small hours.'

His eyes flashed.

'Want to know why I'm obsessive about my privacy? Why I love my home, my own space, a bit of fricking peace? Because I grew up in Bedlam, that's why! Even after Fliss and I started as weekday boarders at school, when all we had were weekends to see them, it carried on—crowded house, no time, lots of excuses. I hated it. *Loathed* it!'

What to say? Then again, it seemed that maybe he didn't need her to say anything. He seemed to be on a roll of his own, just unspooling.

'I wanted normal parents…wanted not to live in a perpetual madhouse. I wanted some one-on-one time, some attention. Not because I was a brat, but just because I was their kid. I wanted Dad to come to the karting track with me, watch me, see how good I was.'

'And he didn't?'

'Oh, he promised to, but nine times of out ten he'd renege…' He turned away, looking through the passenger window, his voice flat. 'And when he did actually come he'd be on his phone the whole time, so it was like he was only half there.

Her heart crimped. Not like her dad, then… When his shifts had allowed, he'd used to come watch her and Billie at their ballet class, never once dropping his gaze, never once not brimming with pride even though they had four left feet between them. And Gerald Scott hadn't even put his phone down long enough to watch his son doing the thing he loved. She felt tears welling up from her chest. How must that have made Max feel? Surely even less important than he'd felt already.

So much for a so-called privilege.

So much for the silver spoon!

She swallowed hard. 'So, you hold it against them?'

'Too right I do. But I haven't got to the kicker yet. After all the time they didn't give me growing up, fast forward a few years and they're up in arms because I'm not falling over myself to join News Global, like Fliss did.'

Fliss... What was her take on things?

She checked the road behind them, then glanced over. 'So Fliss was okay with it all? Didn't mind the way things were when you were growing up?'

'Oh, she'd get hacked off sometimes on my account, because I was her little brother and she knew it was hard for me, but she was all right with it herself.' He sighed. 'She's more like them than I am. She used to like all the craziness...listening to the heated political debates—especially as she got older. She was always going to join NG.'

'But you wanted to tick them off, so you didn't?'

Another scoff. 'I think a jury would pardon me if I'd set off with that intention, but it wasn't like that. I trained as a journalist, after all, following the family tradition. I just didn't have it in me to do the nepotistic thing—jump straight into a plum job at NG. I wanted to earn my stripes honestly, you know. So I went to Focus News instead...moved through the various departments until I landed up on the showbiz desk. And it was like...*bazinga!* It felt right. I was good at it. Good at getting celebs to trust me...good at getting exclusives. I didn't want to move on. I came into my own, I suppose, found my spotlight...'

A spotlight he'd never found at home...

He was rubbing his injured fingers now, talking on, more relaxed suddenly.

'The rest was circumstantial. I got to know a lot of showbiz people, had a lot of contacts. It was a no-brainer to move into celebrity PR...run my own show. Gerald and Tamsin took the huff, of course, called it "trite" and "pointless", went on and on at me about what a disappointment I was to them because I wasn't a hard-hitting political journalist at News Global. That's when I bowed out...called time on the whole filial relationship.'

He let out a sad-sounding sigh.

'There's only so much a soul can take, you know, and I'd had enough. I did some therapy, got some perspective on Tamsin and Gerald—and on myself.' His gaze flickered over, attached to a pale smile. 'I've got it under control now. I love what I do—love looking after my celebs and misfits. And, not to be crass about it, I've made a lot of money out of it...built my own castle. If Tamsin and Gerald can't compute, can't see any merit in it, then that's their problem, not mine.'

Her heart dipped for him. 'Except that being around them drives you to drink...'

He chortled. 'Oh, don't read too much into that. I was just trying to numb my ears because Gerald's very loud voice was spouting the usual rubbish and I couldn't remove myself. You know, the man actually *believes* he's a socialist! Ask him the name of his own cleaner, I say, then you'll find out how much a "man of the people" Gerald Scott is... Because I guarantee you, Tommie, he wouldn't have a clue.'

Whereas Max *did* know the names of all his people, didn't he? And everyone else's. He greeted hotel doormen by name...all the staff. Everywhere they went he knew names, acknowledged people. Her heart pinched. Was it because he'd felt unacknowledged growing up? Didn't want to make anyone else feel like that?

She touched the indicator, slowing to turn onto the motorway slip road. So much to take in, and so much more to Max than she'd ever imagined—all of it good. Billie had been right about him all along, hadn't she? Max *was* noble. But he was so much more than that. He was principled, decent, honest and...

Her heart pulsed. Looking across at her with an irresistible smile hanging on his lips.

'Have I achieved the impossible and stunned Tommie Seager into actual silence?'

She felt her own lips curving up. 'No. I'm just taking it in, that's all.'

'Are you shocked?'

'A bit.' She filtered the car into the flow of traffic, then looked over. 'Mostly I'm just glad that you told me.'

His gaze softened. 'I'm glad too...' And then he was looking down, massaging his injured fingers again. 'I don't usually...'

Struggling for words now, but that was fine.

She focused ahead. 'I know you don't—but it's good to talk, right?'

'Yeah.' He nodded, and then suddenly he was looking up again, a new smile on his lips. 'But it's your turn now...' He angled himself towards her. 'Tell me about your family... all the Seager secrets.'

Dancing eyes. Sadly, soon to be disappointed.

'I've already fessed up my only family secret—at the interview.'

'What secret?'

'Great-Aunt Thomasina, of course—my almost namesake.'

'That's your biggest family secret?'

She felt a giggle coming. 'Tragic, isn't it?'

He smiled. 'No, it's actually quite heartening.' And then

he was lolling his head back against the rest, fixing her with a slanting downward gaze. 'You've got to give me something, though. What about if you tell me about your dad, since I told you about Gerald.'

Happy ground!

'Okay, well...my dad's called Ian, and he's a train driver.'

'Seriously?' Staring at her. 'Did he ever take you to work? Did you ever get to sit up front while he was driving?'

She felt warmth reaching up into her chest. He was genuinely excited. He wasn't trying to be cute or pretending to be impressed, this billionaire son of a billionaire, this honey of a man who hadn't taken the express route to a glittering career at News Global, who'd wanted to earn his stripes honestly.

She felt her heart softening, flowing out to him. Dad would like him, for sure. Not as much as she did, though. No one could like Max more than she did at this moment.

'He took us into the cab, yes—but not when he was driving, because it was against the rules. He'd let us sit up on the seat and *pretend* we were driving, though.' She felt a memory loosening, a chuckle coming. 'He pulled a blinder once. I was on the seat, pushing buttons, pretending I was driving, and the train beside us started to move...'

'Which made you think *you* were the one moving...' Max was laughing, already there.

'Exactly! But Dad was like, "What have you done, Tommie? Don't tell me you touched the red button? Because that's the *Non-stop to Birmingham* button." And I was like, totally panicking, because Dad's looking at me with this worried face he can put on, reeling me in... Because I *had* touched the red button—which he jolly well knew!'

Max chucked softly. 'You adore him, don't you?'

'I do...' She felt unexpected tears welling. She was so

lucky to have her dad—a feeling Max had probably never experienced with Gerald.

She swallowed hard. 'He's always been there for me...' Encouraging her to go to New York, siding with her dreams. But no more than Mum—Mum who'd had a dream and followed it. They were both eternally in her camp, believing in her, and it meant the world. She smiled. 'Both Mum and Dad have.'

'So, tell me about your mum.'

Her heart went soft. 'She's Sally. She used to be a classroom assistant, but she always fancied running a little café. Three years ago she went for it—took a lease on a small, local place with a friend. So now she spends her days making tea and bacon rolls.'

'Are you actually *trying* to make me jealous?' Max was staring over, chuckling again. 'A train driver dad *and* a mum who makes bacon rolls!' Shaking his head. 'Geez, I do love a good bacon roll!'

How were they talking about bacon rolls now...of all things? Such ordinary stuff, making everything feel looser, easier, warmer. Making it feel like they were becoming friends—proper friends. Making a smile rise inside her...

She looked over. 'Define "good" for me, please. Just so I know we're on the same page.'

He laughed. 'Okay. Well, first, it has to be a morning roll—one of those slightly chewy ones, floury on top. Well buttered. Nice bacon, obviously. And it's got to be brown sauce, not ketchup. What about you?'

She felt a warm beat inside. 'Strangely enough, we're one hundred percent compatible in the bacon roll department. Although I would add that I like my bacon very, very crispy.'

'Oh, God, yes...' There was longing in his voice. 'I mean, I'll eat it any which way, but *that's* the ultimate.' And then he was sagging into his seat a little. 'We shouldn't have started talking about this because now I want one.'

'Even after the wedding breakfast?'

'*Especially* after the wedding breakfast, since I barely touched it. I tend to lose my appetite when Dad's issuing forth. I resorted to wine instead—which is why you're breathing in my fumes.' His finger tapped his knee for a moment, and then his gaze was sliding over. 'Look, I know it's been a long day, but I don't suppose you'd consider going back via your mum's café...?'

'No point. They close at five.'

'Oh.'

Disappointed tone. Tugging her heart out. Putting an idea into her head.

Because he could hardly make one for himself, could he? Getting bacon out of a packet was a challenge at the best of times, even with two good hands. And he could do with something to mop up the alcohol. And how bad would she feel if she didn't even offer?

She looked over again. 'Look, if you want, we could stop to buy the stuff and I'll make one for you.'

'Seriously?' Staring at her, smiling. 'You'd do that for me?'

That, and so much more, for some reason. And maybe she'd need to think about that later, but right now making him smile like this, making him this happy, was the only thing in the world she wanted to do.

She nodded. 'Yes, I would.'

'Wow!' He leaned back in his seat. 'I'm sure I don't deserve it, but thank you, Tommie...' And then he was smiling again, looking over. 'Which means *yes*, by the way. I'm totally taking you up on your offer!'

CHAPTER TWELVE

'THIS IS AMAZING, MAX!' Tommie was beaming over, sunglasses glinting, her hair lifting in the breeze. 'I can't believe you're letting me drive this.'

Neither could he. He never let anyone drive his sports cars. But what could he do? The idea had hijacked his brain, as the garage door was rolling up, that if he was going to Thruxton race circuit he ought to be going in something racier than the four-by-four, and that Tommie would get a happy kick out of driving something with real guts for a change.

Not that the second thought should have been a factor, but it was. Somehow… Quite an important one. Probably because ever since Lucy's wedding—ever since all that business with his shirt, and letting his drunken tongue wag on about Tamsin and Gerald, and especially after all that business with the bacon roll… Tommie in his kitchen grilling and buttering, mimicking the way her mum chatted to customers in the café, making him laugh until his sides ached, looking after him, making him feel cared for—he'd felt the desire to give back, to do something nice for her in return so she'd feel the same way…all warm in the heart area, a little bit indulged.

He felt a smile coming. Letting her drive one of his precious babies was just the start—not that she would ever know. Because he wasn't going to tell her, or make anything of it…the car…this whole day… This was all strictly between him and himself.

He let his smile break back at her. 'It needs a good run, that's all…doesn't like being holed up in the garage.' He glanced behind and ahead, to check the road. *Nice and clear.* 'Speaking of which—you could put your foot down a bit.'

She shook her head firmly. 'I'm not breaking the speed limit.'

He squinted at the speedometer. 'I'm not asking you to break it…just get a bit closer to it. The overtaking lane's clear. You could get past this van, have a bit fun in the process…'

'You want me to overtake the van?'

Smiling over, a little bit mischievous.

'Yes! I'm bored with looking at its boring white tailgate!'

'You *really* want me to overtake the van?'

She was giving him the side-eye now, sinking her teeth into her lip.

He felt a tingle, his pulse moving up. Maybe it was because he was looking at her lovely mouth, or maybe it was because she was toying with him, both of which were a bit of a turn-on.

Focus, Max!

'For the hundredth time, yes! If I'm condemned to getting my kicks vicariously then you're "it", since you're the one behind the wheel.'

'Righto.'

She looked ahead, and then suddenly the engine was roaring and they were taking off hard and fast into the overtaking lane, hammering past the van and the next three vehicles, before sliding smoothly back into the centre lane.

And then she looked over, her lips curving like a cat in a post-cream situation. 'Happy now?'

He felt a fresh smile breaking, warmth and admiration surging under his ribs. 'Oh, yes…' *More than she'd ever know.* Just to be riding shotgun beside her, looking at her lovely face, her lovely smile… 'You totally nailed it.'

'I did, didn't I?' She turned her gaze ahead, jutting her chin out. 'I can't have you thinking I don't have it in me.'

His chest tightened a fraction. There was something about her tone, the set of her features. A little edge there…some competitive fire going on, maybe. Or some defensiveness. Some tender spot, anyway… It felt like a *handle-with-care* moment.

He made his voice gentle. 'I would never think that.'

'Good.' She smiled, her face turning back into Tommie's again.

Oh, and why did that make him feel better? That she was herself again. That she was past whatever that little moment had been. Why did it matter the *way* it mattered…in this deep way, in this foxing, discombobulating way?

His heart pulsed. *Oh, God!* What was happening here? It was one thing to be noticing the physical stuff—her smile, the tantalising rise of her breasts in that faded khaki tee she had on—another to be feeling these other confusing things.

His heart pulsed again. And there was a whole day ahead of them now, wasn't there? All planned out. Not for himself, but for *her*, to give back…

Thruxton… Fourth stage of the British Touring Car Championships. Pretty much the last place on earth he wanted to be himself since he couldn't race, couldn't join in, when simply being there was going to put him at risk of being recognised by fans who might ask him questions about his hand which he couldn't, didn't want to answer. But it was the only place he could think of to give her a day out—to thank her for all her kindness—a relaxed, fun day that wouldn't seem like more than it was, or—God forbid—inappropriate. Which of course it wasn't. Absolutely not! Because Tommie was his employee, his driver, nothing more!

He fixed his gaze ahead, heart drumming. It must have all stacked up in his mind at some point.

Touring car racing because it was exciting, his 'thing'—which made it easy to pretend that he wanted to go and watch, even though he couldn't race himself. VIP terrace—a surprise he was holding up his sleeve—because he wanted her to get the best possible view, which he could pretend was because *he* wanted the best possible view. Casual clothes for both of them because it was a casual day, going around together for the same reason, and because Tommie didn't know anything about touring car racing and was bound to have questions he could answer.

But that thing just then—that jut of her chin, that tone—and then that coming back into herself…all of it was making him feel…stirred, curious. More curious than usual. Curious on a different, deeper level than usual. He wanted to know what was behind that little shift in her mood—wanted to ask, tap into that seam, open it right up.

But what hook did he have to grasp at other than this feeling inside himself? It was like when he'd seen her ex… that chauffeur guy. He'd wanted to know about him too, but she'd given him nothing—nothing to pick up and run with. Which made revisiting it impossible—not without coming over as plain nosy, anyway.

So different from their 'Tamsin and Gerald' conversation. When she'd asked *him* what was going on it had felt almost like a continuation, since he'd already alluded to not wanting to go to the wedding because of 'family' stuff when she'd been helping him with his shirt. And then they'd had that little 'hiding' dialogue going on too—and, most particularly, since he'd more or less poured himself into the car blabbing about Lucy hoodwinking him with the table plan... *That* had called for some sort of explanation!

But these feelings...these curiosities springing up with no place to go...were making him feel dizzy, blurry. Out of his depth. Because what were they, actually? What did they mean? That he was getting attached to Tommie in the wrong way? That he was crossing a line?

He hadn't exactly gone back to sitting in the back seat, had he? He was the Robin to her Batman now, and he liked sitting up front, liked talking to her. Not getting into anything deep, but talking all the same, both of them, about music and movies, and about houseplants, of all things— how he managed to keep his alive and thriving when it seemed Tommie's always died. And about the new twinges in his middle finger that Paul had been reservedly positive about. Talking all the time...

He felt a tingle, his heartbeat steadying. Oh, but then maybe *that* was it! Both the problem and the answer. Tommie was his driver, his employee, but she was also a *friend* now too—the person he spent more one-on-one time with than anyone else. His heart pulsed. *Of course!* That was why he was tuning in to these little shifts of her mood, why he wanted to know what lay behind them. Because he was getting to know her better day by day. Because he liked her... *cared* about her.

As. A. Friend.

He looked over, felt warmth flooding into his chest. That face... Almost more familiar to him now than his own. The curve of her cheek, the smooth plane of her forehead, that tiny freckle just below her ear. *Just a friend*. And these swirling feelings...just curiosity about a friend—about the parts of her he didn't know. Natural, surely. Normal, for pity's sake! Nothing to be scared of. And definitely *not* inappropriate!

'Hey…' Catching him staring, blushing a bit. 'What are you so busy thinking about?'

If only she knew… Or maybe it was better she didn't. He pulled in a slow breath. The main thing was he'd thought himself back out of the rabbit hole, could feel his mood lightening, could almost see the sky brightening.

He flicked a glance ahead. 'I was just thinking that we should get past this very boring SUV…'

'Ah!' A slow smile spread into her cheeks and then she was turning her gaze ahead, adjusting her grip on the wheel. 'Okay… Well, you're the boss, so I suppose I'm duty-bound to do what you say…'

CHAPTER THIRTEEN

'YOU DID GOOD, TOMMIE...' Max was standing by the open passenger door, stretching, and then he pushed up his sunglasses and smiled. 'You handled the car beautifully.'

Her heart gave. *So gorgeous!* And so adorable...surprising her with this car this morning...trusting her to drive it. Not only that but trusting her—*encouraging* her—to give it some proper welly. And now he was twinkling at her, looking heavenly in his jeans and faded red tee, his hair ruffling in the breeze, and she was supposed to...what...? *Not* feel this ten-ton truckload of confusion?

No normal day at the office, this! Not from the clothes she was wearing to the plan, which was to watch the racing together. *Together!* As if she wasn't just his driver. And, yes, maybe since Lucy's wedding it had been feeling more and more as if they were actual friends, with Max always sitting in front now, wherever they went, but still... Aside from making him that bacon roll—oh, and doing up his shirt—there had always been that critical separation before. Max going into his office...she to her usual Canary Wharf haunts to sketch and research; in the evenings Max going to his dinners and events, she to wait in a back room or a coffee lounge or something. But now it was just the two of them. No safety barrier. No script. Although she could actually do with one—could do with saying something instead of just standing here, gawping and tingling...

She smiled back. 'Thanks. Although, full disclosure, now that we've arrived, I confess I was terrified of crashing it the whole time.'

'No, you weren't.' He was shaking his head. 'Or if you were, then you shouldn't have been. You were really good—and I *am* actually qualified to judge, by the way, so no arguing.' He let out a soft chuckle. 'I figure you've got a bit of competitive steel inside you, Tommie Seager.'

He could see that in her? Amazing, given that for all her brave talk to Billie, and the endless pep talks she gave herself, she could only catch that fire, that zeal inside herself in rare moments these days.

It had been there in the early days with Chloe, all right—when she'd thought she was on her way. Before that, it must have been there in her Spitalfields Market days, sharing a stall with Henry, selling the clothes they'd made…upcycled, reconfigured. Henry liked tweed, had created hotchpotch pants, waistcoats, jaunty caps. She'd been into Bohemian glitz: satin, silk, taffeta… That silent gauntlet going down every Saturday, that little flame igniting inside: whose designs would rock the most…who could sell the most…?

'Hey…' Max was looking at her, his expression worried. 'Did I say something wrong?'

Bless his heart…

'No, of course not…'

In fact, maybe he'd actually said the perfect thing—given her the perfect way to come a little bit clean with him about who she was inside. Which was what she wanted to do—had been wanting to do for a while now. Because holding on to it all didn't feel right any more now that they were sort of friends—now that Max had opened up to her about his family and his hand, and about how he kept his plants so green and healthy! But she wasn't opening up in return, was she? Not really. And keeping her inner workings to herself had felt fine at the start—more or less essential on the fashion design front—but it wasn't feeling fine any more. And the thing was, Max of all people wouldn't be fazed that she wanted to be more than a driver, would he? He had multiple strings to his own bow, after all—PR, motor racing, a motor sports news agency... He'd most likely applaud her for wanting more. And wasn't she desperate to tell him about Chloe Mills? Shuck off that weight? Not that she was quite up to that yet, but this could be a way in, a way to set to the wheels in motion...at least put them on a more even footing.

She drew in a breath. 'It's just what you said about me being competitive. It reminded me that I actually am—used to be, anyway...'

His gaze narrowed slightly. 'Well, they always say, use it or lose it.' And then he was shutting his door, looking over with a soft smile. 'If you want to talk about it, we've got a bit of a walk to the stands.'

Not pushing. Being gentle. No wonder his clients trusted him. She did.

Looking at him, on the other hand, was far too distracting.

She zapped the locks and set off walking. 'You've very kind, Max.'

'No more than you.' He was falling in beside her, pulling his sunglasses back over his eyes. 'I mean, you listened to me banging on about my tragic privileged childhood. If you want to offload to me now, go for it.'

She dropped her own shades. 'It's not really offloading, as such, it's more that I want to enlighten you—about me.'

'Intriguing...' He smiled then chuckled. 'I'm all ears now—ready and waiting to be *enlightened*.'

That smile...that lightness of touch... He was making it easy to be light in turn, easy to begin...

'Okay, well… So, in spite of my recent *outstanding* performance in your sports car, and my previous jobs, it might surprise you to know that I didn't set out to be a professional driver. It's what I do, but it isn't where my heart is.'

'Hold up.' Max stopped walking, pushed up his sunglasses. 'This isn't some roundabout way of telling me you're quitting, is it?'

What?

'No!'

How could he be even thinking that? And looking at her as if she'd just told him she'd run over his cat—not that he had one.

She pushed up her own shades so he could see her eyes, see she was serious. 'I'm not going anywhere.'

'But you want to?'

'Well, yes—'

'But you just said—'

For the love of God!

'Stop, please!'

So much for being a good listener!

She put a hand up to stay him before he interjected again. 'Look, you're getting the wrong end of the stick. I'm not saying I don't want to be working for you. I'm saying that driving wasn't my first career choice.'

Was he getting it now? The agitation in his eyes seemed to be abating at least. Safe to breathe again, to lower her hand.

'Driving's just where I ended up, okay? What I'm doing for now—*happily*, FYI…' Just in case he was thinking of jumping at shadows again. 'But there's an endgame, more to me than driving…'

Her heart wavered. Or was she deluding herself? It was all very well Billie saying that if Chloe had stolen her ideas then her ideas must have been worth stealing, but for all the sketching she'd been doing these past few weeks she hadn't nailed anything definitive yet. Then again, that was the creative life, wasn't it? Constant self-doubt. It came with the territory—like the possibility of crashing being part of motor racing. No glory without risk.

Her heart stood up. And she wanted glory, didn't she? Some full-fat Technicolor glory to put back what the glandular fever had cost her, what getting sidetracked into Jamie's life and business had cost her…what Chloe Mills had stolen from her. Surging up again now, igniting inside her. That vital spark. The other Tommie. The *real* Tommie.

She looked at him. 'I love fashion, Max. I'm passionate about it. And those sketches you saw…' *Just say it, Tommie!* '… I downplayed them…said they were for me because you caught me unawares and I was embarrassed. But they're not for me. The truth is, I'm trying to put a collection together to show some buyers. I want to be a fashion designer. Always have. That's my big dream.'

His mouth opened, then shut again. 'Wow!'

Looking at her, his gaze busy with comings and goings—interest, admiration, fascination—and then suddenly he smiled, costing her a breath.

'Well, if those sketches are anything to go by, I'd say you're halfway there already.'

She felt a surge in her chest…hot, grateful tears welling behind her eyes. 'You think so?'

'Yes!' He was nodding now, his gaze all warm. 'I said so at the time, didn't I? You've got an eye, Tommie, a real talent.'

'Thank you.' She swallowed hard. 'That means a lot.'

'And thank *you* for saying that it does.' And then suddenly, as if he was thinking she might need a moment to gather herself, he was dropping his shades, motioning for her to walk on. 'We should get going if we want to catch the first race—walking and talking, mind, because I want to know more.'

More... Exactly what she wanted to give him, just for the sheer joy of sharing...of letting him in the way he'd let her in.

'Okay.' She smiled, walking on. 'What do you want to know?'

'Well, for one thing, why didn't you study fashion design? I mean, if it's what you've always wanted to do...?'

Her heart pinched. Thank goodness for walking and looking ahead, for the distraction of the grandstand and all the people on the move, streaming towards the pedestrian tunnel.

'It's because I got glandular fever when I was fifteen— just before my mock exams.'

'Geez, I'm sorry...' Max was frowning. 'Someone at my school got that. It was rough; they were off for quite a while...'

At least he knew the score.

'So was I. The whole thing knocked me for a loop. I couldn't seem to make up the ground afterwards...couldn't fit back in. Partly because of friend group stuff that left me feeling pushed out, on top of everything else. The upshot was that I didn't get good enough grades to go to college. And I couldn't face resits. I got it into my head that I wouldn't do any better next time around...that I just wasn't good enough.'

'For goodness' sake, Tommie! And your teachers didn't tell you otherwise? Or your parents?'

Her heart pinched again. 'Only all the time...'

Dad switching off the telly *'Come on, Tommie, let's have a chat...'*

Mum, coming in armed with a box of her favourite chocolate eclairs, putting the kettle on. *'Resits wouldn't be that tough, Tom. I mean, you've done the work already; it'd just be revising...'*

She shook herself. 'I didn't listen, though. I was a teenager!'

His sunglasses flashed. 'You were difficult?'

'Not intentionally. I was just really down on school... down on myself, I suppose. Passing my driving test was the gamechanger. It gave me a boost—opened some doors. As soon as I could I got a job delivery driving, and it was great...'

'I remember.' He smiled over. 'It gave you an encyclopaedic knowledge of London, made you a better driver, et cetera.'

Those careful lines she'd fed him during the interview. She felt her lips curving up. 'You were paying attention.'

He laughed. 'I always pay attention, Tommie.'

Her heart skipped. Maybe this wasn't a normal day, but what could be better than this? Walking along in the sunshine with Max, talking to him, letting him in more, letting herself off the leash. As long as she didn't go too far...

'So...' He was looking over again. 'Are you about to tell me you loved delivery driving so much that you put fashion design on ice?'

'No. It was actually the opposite. What I didn't say in the interview was that the *best* thing about delivery driving was the money. Mum and Dad wouldn't take anything off me for living at home, so I had money to buy fabric and trimmings and charity shop clothes. I'd take the clothes apart, mix them up, create quirky one-off dresses and skirts. Then I met this guy, Henry Pugh, at Spitalfields Market. He was doing similar stuff to me, but with tweed. I showed him some of my creations, and next thing he's asking me if I want to share stall space with him. I did that for a couple of years. Delivery driving… Sewing at night… Spitalfields Market at weekends…'

'Collapsing in a heap on Sunday afternoons?'

'Spot on.'

'I'm impressed, Tommie. Seriously. It takes lot of drive to work at something that hard.'

'Maybe so… But it never felt hard because I loved doing it…learning little sewing tricks, going at my own pace, trying things out. It was magic. Creating…seeing how people loved my stuff.'

'So you were selling? Doing okay out of it?'

So many questions!

'I wasn't about to float on Wall Street, or anything, but I did okay. I had a following, sold enough to cover my share of the stall and make a bit extra.'

He nodded, then suddenly stopped walking—which meant she had to stop too. 'So what happened?' He levered up his shades with a finger. 'What took your eye off the ball?'

She felt her insides curling up. That would be Jamie, and everything that went with him. And she didn't want to talk about him…relive it all. But Jamie was the key to Chauffeur Me, and Chauffeur Me was the key to Choe Mills. And, no, she wasn't crossing the Chloe Mills' bridge today, but she had to at least step onto it—*make* herself step onto it for Max's sake, so he'd be primed for the truth when she could get up the nerve to tell it.

'Tommie?'

He was stepping in now, with gentle concern in his eyes. As if she deserved it.

She swallowed hard. 'What happened was I met Jamie—that chauffeur who was there at Lucy's wedding…'

* * *

Pain in her gaze…just like at the wedding. *Why?* What had happened? He wanted to ask…wanted to know everything. But maybe she didn't want to talk about this. For sure, she'd started the ball rolling—opening up, letting him in—and he liked it, being taken into her confidence. But this could be the moment to rein back.

He glanced ahead. The tunnel was coming up anyway, which was no place for a heart-to-heart. It was the perfect breathing space, though—one she could make longer if she wanted to…indefinite, even. Because on the other side were the pits, the paddock, the cars, the crowds and the fumes and the noise. Timely distractions if she wanted to use them. It was up to her, and whatever she decided he'd respect it.

He pulled his shades back down, motioning for her to walk. 'How about you hold on to that thought while we go through here?'

Her eyes flashed gratitude. 'Good idea.' And then she was turning to walk again.

He fell in beside her, both of them slowing because the people in front were going at a plodding pace.

Into the tunnel now. Gloomy because of his sunglasses. But he wasn't taking them off. He didn't mind being recognised when he was in the pits with his team, because the people who stopped to talk to him there would be motor racing fans, more interested in the car and the engine than in him as an individual, but he didn't want to be recognised here—not with Tommie in tow, not when they were halfway through a thing.

He shot her glance. She was looking ahead. Face closed. Was she thinking about that Jamie guy or about him? His stomach dipped. Hopefully she wasn't replaying the moment when he'd jumped with his two left feet to absolutely the wrong conclusion about why she was telling him that there was more to her than just driving. How had his freaked out, idiot brain converted *that* into an imminent intention to resign? Thank goodness she hadn't made anything of it. But it was a litmus test, wasn't it? For him. For how much he couldn't bear to lose her as his driver now.

His heart pulsed. As a friend…

Not worth dwelling on, though, since she wasn't quitting, and since they were emerging into the sunshine now, heading up the incline. And now the pits were opening out in front of them—all the rows of giant team trucks with their workshops and canopies and mechanics, banners blazing brightly with sponsor logos, speakers blaring out the endless commentator chit-chat, and that smell in the air of fuel and fried onions. And everywhere, people.

Tommie stopped dead. 'Oh, wow!'

His heart filled. Nothing closed about her face now. Now she had it all going on—eyes shining, sweet lips curving into a wide, irresistible smile.

'This is amazing. Look at those huge truck things!'

'Team vehicles.'

'With workshops?'

'You need a workshop. And a team of mechanics.'

Wide eyes came to his. 'Do you have all this stuff?'

He felt a smile breaking. 'Of course. I wouldn't get very far without it.'

She was gazing around again. 'I just never considered the scale of it…what's involved. I mean, look at it all…' She was practically squeaking now. 'Oh—and look! There's the track!'

He looked, felt her excitement throwing switches inside him, making his veins buzz as if it were his first time here too. Suddenly it wasn't even bothering him that he was here to spectate and not race. It was simply good to be here, with her, in the sunshine.

He smiled. 'Yes, indeed. Fastest track in the UK.'

Her gaze swung back, full of teasing light. 'I think you might have said that already—along with how the circuit follows the line of the old Thruxton airfield perimeter road that used to be here, and how it's "a true driver's track".'

All that history…all the facts he'd spouted out to help fill the time when they'd hit that slow patch of traffic. All credit to her that she hadn't tuned out. He felt a smile coming, loosening in his cheeks. Too irresistible not to run with this, tease her back…

'Okay, then, clever clogs. What's the fastest time recorded on this track?' He slid his eyebrows up. 'Bonus point if you can tell me who the driver was.'

She laughed. 'That's easy! Fifty-seven point six seconds, and the driver was Damon Hill.'

'What was his average speed?'

'One hundred and forty-seven miles per hour.'

'You were paying attention.'

Her eyes lit with palpable glee. 'I always pay attention, Max.'

Using his own line back at him.

Tilting her head over, teasing him.

His heart squeezed. God, she was lovely. But focusing on that was only going tangle him up. Better to keep the banter flying.

He tilted his own head, giving her a look. 'Very droll.'

She grinned. 'What can I say? You bring it out in me.'

As she was bringing it out in *him*: this urge to play—*flirt*. And it was wrong, inappropriate, but he couldn't seem to stop now…couldn't make himself care enough to want to stop.

'Okay, so here's a toughie. What's the exact length of the track?'

Her eyes closed for a long thinking moment, then opened triumphantly. 'Two point four.'

No flies on her! He couldn't hold back a smile. 'I'm officially impressed.'

She laughed. 'You should be—although don't get the idea that I hang on your every word. That hybrid stuff went right over my head. All those rules about hybrid deployment: how much, and when.'

'It's a bit of a tangle, to be fair...'

Like the one he was losing himself in right now, just looking at her, at the way the sun was kissing her face, playing with her hair. What he'd give to be that sun...

'So...' She smiled, then seemed to notice she was holding her sunglasses instead of wearing them. 'What's the plan? Where do we go now?'

He shook himself. Movement. Going. That was the thing—and not to be staring at that mesmerising hollow between her breasts. And, of course, there was the whole business of where they were going...

He felt a smile coming, let it fill his cheeks as she slid her shades on and looked up. 'Oh, I've got a place in mind... somewhere with a decent view.'

Max hunkered forward. 'Rory's still leading...'

She pushed her sunglasses up. 'How can you see?'

Because even though she was leaning over the rail, same as he was, staring hard at that place where the cars always surged into view, she couldn't see anything yet.

He grinned. 'X-ray vision, I guess.' And then his hand touched her arm. 'Look, here they come...'

She felt a rise in her chest. *There!* Now she could see

them, swarming like angry bees, sounding like them too, with a sound she could feel in her body, reverberating, pushing a thrill up through her, crushing the living breath out of her. There was Rory Bates! Orange car. Leading. Max's chief rival, apparently, and the one to beat. But there was a new car hanging on his bumper now. Blue. Not the green one that had been tailing him before. And then suddenly—somehow—the blue one was surging forward, right below them, cutting through, taking Rory on the inside, going hard, fast, pulling ahead—only just, but doing it. *Doing it!* Poaching the lead.

'Whoa!' Max rocked back off the rail, shaking his head, his expression incredulous. 'Did you see that?'

As if she could have missed it, from here of all places!

She straightened, aiming a smile into his dark lenses. 'Of course I did. Because of the—' she scratched quotes in the air '—"decent view"! Understatement of the century!'

His cheeks creased. 'Are you going to get over it any time soon?'

She felt warmth rippling inside her. Unlikely. Four races in and she was still nowhere near getting over it. How *could* she get over that moment when he'd led her up here and through the glass doors? VIP viewing terrace, no less. Such a view! Starting grid to the left…the corner called Allard right below. A *'fast fourth gear'* corner, he'd said, that delivered thrills every lap—like the one that had just happened.

Never mind that it had taken her eye off the ball just as she'd been about to get back to telling him about Jamie and Chauffeur Me, about how she'd lost her grip on her fashion dreams. That could wait. At this moment she was here on the VIP terrace at Thruxton with gorgeous Max Scott, and she didn't *want* to get over it, or downplay it, especially when it seemed—*felt*—as if he'd organised it just for her.

She shook her head. 'I've no plans to, no.'

He laughed, looking pleased. 'Well, I'm glad you're getting a buzz out of it.' And then he was turning to rest his forearms on the rail again, looking back up the track. 'Geez, I'll bet Rory's spitting feathers. Cillian deployed hybrid at exactly the right moment, and Rory's got none left. This close to the end, it could cost him the win...'

Hybrid again!

She slotted herself back in beside him. 'How do you know he's got none left?'

'I know how he operates, that's how.'

She felt a dip inside. Did he have a handle on her too? Know how *she* was operating? Could he feel her eyes sliding over the smooth curve of his biceps every time his head was turned? Could he feel the weight of her gaze on his nice forearms? She didn't want to keep looking, torturing herself with impossible thoughts about how those arms would feel around her, but she couldn't help it. Because he was tantalisingly close, radiating delicious heat, smelling clean, irresistibly fresh. Hard enough keeping her senses straight without having to keep her eyes in line too.

Her heart pulsed. And on top of all that here were the cars again. Sound. Fury. Vibrating in her chest. Building and building. Louder. Closer. She could feel her heart rising, drumming in her throat.

Max bent lower. 'Here they come...'

She leaned out, craning to see. *There!* Blue car. Orange. Green. Fencing. Dodging. Vying for the lead. And then, out of nowhere, a mighty weight jolted her from behind, ramming her hard into the rail.

She felt a sharp pain in her ribs, a cry hurtling up her throat and out. 'Ow!'

'Hey!' Max was up in a flash, squaring up to the man who had shoved her. 'What the hell are you doing?'

'I was trying to see—'

'By ploughing into my friend?'

The man's chin lifted. 'It was an accident.' His eyes came to hers briefly then returned to Max. 'I'm sorry, okay?' He gave a dismissive shrug. 'I didn't mean any harm.'

Max shifted stance. 'Maybe so, but you seem to have caused some.' And then he looked over, shades glinting. 'Are you okay, Tommie?'

That would be a resounding *no*—and not because of the shove either, but because of what *Max* was doing. Facing off against this guy for her, not letting it go, waiting for her to give the word—which she must, *now*, before the air got too thick to breathe.

'Yes. I'm fine.' She smiled to seem light. 'It was an accident.'

'You're not hurt?' His jaw tightened visibly. 'Because it sounded to me like you were.'

Spot on—but if she admitted it, what then? Pistols at dawn?

She shook her head. 'I got a fright, that's all.'

He stared at her for a moment, as if he wasn't sure whether to believe her or not, and then he turned back to the man. 'Lucky for you she's okay.'

Seriously? Of all the things to say. What would he do if the guy rallied? Came back at him with, *Or what, big shot?* She scanned the faces of the onlookers. All very well Max being protective, but if some wag got a notion to pull out a phone and film the three of them then he could find himself at the centre of his very own PR disaster.

Not on her account—no way!

'Look, I really *am* fine.' She stepped in close to him,

lowering her voice. 'And you *really* need to drop it now. People. Are. Watching.'

His voice came back, low and gritty. 'If you're hurt, and this guy needs a talking-to, then I don't care who's watching.'

Way to melt her heart... But irrelevant! What *was* relevant was that if the guy decided to start talking with his fists, Max was going to be in serious trouble with only one fist to fight back with. This had to end now.

She squeezed his shoulder, making her tone sharp so he'd listen. 'Well, *I* do. So, please, let it go.'

Short pause. Then... 'Okay. If it's what you want.' He exhaled audibly, then turned back to the man. 'Seems we're good.'

'Good...' The man stepped back, clearly relieved in spite of his earlier bullishness. He half lifted a hand. 'Sorry again.' And then he was melting away, disappearing.

She felt her limbs loosening. One problem eliminated! Now there were just the few curious onlookers left. Motor racing fans—which meant Max stood a chance of being recognised. And maybe he was finally waking up to that too, because suddenly he leaned in.

'Come on.'

And then, before she could catch her breath, his arm was going around her shoulders and he was propelling her through the doors, into the hospitality suite and onwards, towards the stairs, talking in her ear.

'I'm so sorry, Tommie. I didn't mean to cause a scene—but, seriously, that guy. What a fricking impertinent jerk!'

'Exactly! He's the jerk. So there's no need for *you* to be apologising.'

'But you're missing the end of the race now...'

'That's still because of *him*, not you...'

Not that it was important anyway. Because what race finale in the world could compare to walking with Max like this? The delicious weight of his arm around her shoulders, this gorgeous closeness, the warm, deep smell of him. Such a feeling! She didn't want it to end, let alone be the one to end it, but she had to. Because he was beating himself up and she wasn't having that.

She drew back and faced him, felt his arm falling away. 'Look, you did a good thing, sticking up for me like that…'

He pushed up his shades. 'But I annoyed you too, didn't I?'

What?

'No! Not at all.'

His brow pleated. 'But you *sounded* annoyed.'

'I was trying to make you *listen*, that's all. People were watching us. I thought you might be recognised—which you clearly don't want since you've hardly taken your shades off since we got here.'

His lips set. 'Oh.'

How was he doing this? Tugging her heart out, but at the same time making a smile come?

She looked into his eyes. 'For the record, I thought you were very gallant. In fact, for a moment there, you made me feel like quite the damsel in distress.'

The corner of his mouth ticked up. 'And that's a good thing?'

Feeling cared about? Protected? What wasn't to love about that? Her heart pulsed. But Max wasn't her knight in shining armour, was he? He was her boss. Even if, at this moment, it didn't quite feel like it. But she had to remember it, hold it in her head—who they were, what they were. Because this day was already confusing enough.

She shrugged to seem casual. 'Well, it's not a bad thing.'

'Okay…' His smile broke through for a beat, but then it was fading again. 'I need to know, though, Tom—truthfully now—are you hurt?'

Her heart gave. Shortening her name the way Mum and Dad did, the way Billie did. It felt sweet, affectionate, but she couldn't focus on that, not now, not when he was looking at her like this, with concern in his eyes, and that filament of steel too. And maybe he caught her noticing it, because he went on quickly.

'Don't worry, I'm not thinking of going after the guy or anything. I was just thinking that there are medics here, so if you want someone to check you out, we can do that.'

Her heart gave again. He was still looking after her, making her pulse skip and flutter, ramping up her confusion.

She shook her head to reset. 'No, I'm fine—honestly. A medic's only going to tell me what I know already: that I've copped a bruise…' Maybe if they got going, walked on again, this weirdness would disappear. She licked her lips, felt a tingle. 'Actually, what I could really do with is a cup of tea.'

His eyebrows flickered. 'Well, that can be arranged.' And then suddenly his whole face brightened with a smile. 'We could grab a bacon roll to go with it, if you like, sit up on a bank somewhere…'

That face. That smile. And a bacon roll, too.

Oh, hell! Maybe this day *was* confusing, and utterly discombobulating, but at the same time what wasn't there to love about it? What wasn't there to smile about? Maybe she needed to stop thinking so much and just take it, enjoy it, moment by moment.

She reached up to pull her shades back down, letting a smile come…unwind all the way. 'I think *that* sounds like a most excellent idea!'

CHAPTER FOURTEEN

'THAT WASN'T BAD…' Tommie was wiping her fingers, reaching for her tea. 'Not bad at all.'

He held in a smile. 'Well, it could hardly miss the mark, could it? Since you told the guy exactly how you wanted it.'

'I didn't *tell* him.' Her eyes lifted, twinkling. 'I made a couple of requests, that's all.'

'Oh, yeah…?'

How could he possibly resist doing an impression of the mesmerising spectacle that had been Tommie, ordering a bacon roll…?

He parked his hands on an imaginary counter, tilting his chin up, trying to smile the way she did. '"Could you butter the roll *right* to the edges, please? Top and bottom. Because I don't like dry bits of roll. And I like very crispy bacon. And when I say *very* I mean—"' he batted his eyelashes, because even though she hadn't done that, she might as well have done '"—*very*. And, please, if you don't mind, I'll do the brown sauce myself. Because I don't want too much, but equally I don't want not enough."'

She let out a satisfying chuckle. 'Very funny—although your mockney accent could do with some work.' And then she was pushing her hair back, smiling into his eyes. 'I was very polite, though, wasn't I?'

'You were. Although—heads up—you had the guy eating out of your hand anyway...'

His heart clopped. As he was. Right now. Eating out of her hand, drinking her in, losing himself in the sweet sight of her.

Not good!

He picked up his cup to cut himself loose, break her spell. No good getting lost, no good losing control. See what had almost happened on that terrace? Coming *this* close to decking that oaf! And maybe the jerk hadn't meant any harm—maybe he really *had* bumped into Tommie accidentally—but he wouldn't know, would he? Too busy losing his rag at red mist central!

He took a long, slow sip of tea. What was happening to him? He wasn't aggressive. Wasn't a fighter. For crying out loud, he was known for being cool and calm in a crisis, for being *in control*. But up there, God help him, even though he'd never hit anyone in his life, he'd wanted to—no matter who was watching. Because that guy had hurt Tommie, ruined the end of the race for her, and he hadn't looked nearly sorry enough!

He sipped again, shooting her a quick look. She was watching the Minis now, on their warm-up lap. Face rapt. Eyes following. Lips slightly parted. *So lovely.*

His heart squeezed. Was that why she cut so deep with him? Brought out this protectiveness in him? Or was it the loveliness inside her—that warmth, that kindness, that honesty—that had him fighting for her honour?

He felt a smile starting. Or was it that she was funny... made him laugh, feel light inside?

He looked again, letting his gaze linger. Probably it was all of those things. Everything she was, inside and out. A good driver. A good person. A good friend... A friend with dreams in her heart. A friend who had been thwarted by glandular fever, knocked back. A friend with talent, fire in her belly. A friend worth fighting for, sticking up for—

Her gaze flickered suddenly, finding his. 'All right?'

His heart lurched. A friend who was also gorgeous and got his motor running every time she looked at him. A friend he wanted to slow kiss. A friend he wanted to touch, undress, feel against his body, skin to skin.

Could she see it in his eyes? Sense it? Had she felt it, sensed it in him, when she was helping him with his shirt? Had she felt it back there, when he'd put his arm around her shoulders? Felt how much he liked being that close to her, feeling her warmth beating into his skin, her soft perfume filling his lungs. Had she felt…sensed…how desperately he didn't want that moment to end? And if she'd sensed all that, what did she feel about it? What did she think, feel, about him?

He shook himself. As if it even mattered. It was just a stupid fantasy. Impossible! Where was this even coming from? Outer space? Because these were definitely alien thoughts.

Meanwhile, she was still looking over, waiting for him to reply.

He smiled. 'I'm great, thanks. How about you?' He lifted his cup, sipping again. 'Is the tea measuring up? Putting you to rights after your encounter with Oaf Man?'

She laughed. 'It's okay. Not as good as Mum's, but it's hitting the spot.'

As she was with him.

Gah!

He had to get himself off this beat. Tommie was attractive—so what? It wasn't news, was it? She'd been every bit as attractive on day one. For pity's sake, it was the first damn thing he'd noticed about her. Nothing was different.

She hadn't changed. Look at her. Same eyes, same cheek-bones, same sweet lips—

'Max...?'

'Yes.' He blinked. 'Sorry...what?'

'Truthfully, now, are you okay?'

She was frowning, reaching in with that grey-green gaze of hers.

His heart pulsed. Could she see what was running through his head? His heart pulsed again. Then again, how could she? For sure, he'd stood up for her on the terrace, put his arm around her to walk her away, but those things totally stacked up with what had gone down. As for the attraction thing... He'd been coping with it, hiding it, from the start— hadn't he? Just because these thoughts were jumping around inside his head, it didn't mean they were showing on his face. He was a past master at hiding his feelings, after all.

He inhaled slowly. No, this flurry was all in his own head. He was probably just feeling it more today because they were here, in this strange situation. That had to be the difference he was feeling. Sitting here on this bank with her, instead of the two of them sitting strapped into seats. Being out in the real world with her, in the open air, in a non-specifically work situation. And, of course, he was the one who'd told her she should dress casually, so it was his fault she was in those faded jeans that hugged her rear in all the right intoxicating places, and that vee-neck tee that kept leading his eyes astray.

All this was, was a heightened version of normal. It was nothing he couldn't handle...control. He was fine—could say so with his hand on his heart.

He sipped his tea, then looked her square in the eye. 'Yes. I'm a hundred percent.' But out of sheer curiosity he had to know... 'Why do you ask?'

She gave a little shrug. 'I don't know… You seem distracted.' And then she was putting her cup down, hugging her knees to her chest. 'I was just wondering if you're really okay with being here today, given that you're not racing…'

There was that empathy in her. Oh, and that gaze. Turning him over. But if he didn't nip this in the bud right now she might pursue him, and he couldn't risk stumbling into the real reason he'd come today since she was it.

Not a mess he could afford to get himself into!

Better to deflect, put the focus back on her…

He knocked back his tea and parked his cup. 'I'd be lying if I said I wasn't bummed out not to be racing today, but I'm not dwelling on it. I wasn't thinking about that…'

And now, switch…

He met her gaze, feeling his own softening. 'Maybe I looked distracted because I was thinking about you…about what you were telling me earlier about your dream of getting into fashion design…'

Here was something he could help her with if she'd let him, something he *wanted* to help her with, because she deserved a boost, a leg up—not only because she was his friend, but because she was a real talent.

He smiled into her eyes. 'I was thinking that you never finished your story…'

That was what he'd been thinking? All those comings and goings in his eyes had been over her big dream? Then again, this *was* Max. He'd been all ears earlier. Full of questions and kindly admiration. He wouldn't have forgotten that she'd never finished. And she hadn't either. She *wanted* to get back to it…edge closer to the infernal rock in her chest that was Chloe Mills. Not that she wanted to talk about Jamie any more now than she had earlier, but it was a good that

Max had brought it up—because if not now, when? When would she get the opportunity again to be sitting face to face with him, looking into his eyes like this, with nothing between them but grass and air?

His gaze broke suddenly. 'Look, it's okay…' He shifted a little, massaging his injured hand. 'I got the feeling earlier that it was possibly a tricky subject, so if you don't want to talk about it—'

'No. It's fine.' She smiled so he'd believe her. 'I totally meant to get back to it—and I *do* want to talk about it…' Even if it was a tricky, and painful. Because there was never any gain without pain, was there? She pulled in a breath and looked at him. 'So, I was delivery driving, designing clothes, selling them and all that, and then one night in the pub I met Jamie.'

Max's gaze narrowed by an infinitesimal degree.

Perhaps 'met' wasn't conveying it properly…

She licked her lips. 'What I mean is, I met him one night and started going out with him. He was five years older than me—twenty-six—and his family were starting their own chauffeur business…'

Max raised his eyebrows. 'Chauffeur Me, by any chance?'

'Yes.'

'And he asked you to drive for them?'

'Yes. A few months after it got going. He thought having a female driver on board would help the business, and we were together, so…you know. It seemed like a no-brainer. Also it was easier work…more money.'

'But it took you away from fashion design?'

Max looked vaguely annoyed, vaguely protective—like he had at the wedding, when she'd said to him that she couldn't stay because Jamie was there. Drawing the wrong conclusions. And she'd let him draw them because it had suited her purpose. But she was the devil of this piece—not Jamie. She had to own it now, trust Max with it—because he'd trusted her, hadn't he? Filled her in on his whole family dynamic? And, yes, maybe he'd felt a little bit obliged to, because of what he'd said when she was helping him with his shirt, and because of being slightly the worse for wear when he'd got back to the car after the wedding, but it had also felt as if he *wanted* to confide in her. And she *wanted* to confide in him too, let him in.

In any case, it was all context for why she'd jumped ship and gone to work for his client Chloe Mills. All relevant.

She let her knees go, flopping them out to buy a moment, then met his gaze. 'Not immediately, but over time, yes. I got sucked into the business...' She could almost feel some internal valve releasing, thoughts and words clamouring. 'It wasn't just Jamie's business, like I said. It was a family concern. His dad. His brother Simon. And his mum, Myra, did the admin, all the books...'

Mug of tea on the go, office heater sweating it out because Myra felt the cold...

'They were grafters...thick as thieves. But in spite of that—or maybe because of it—there was a lot of drama, a lot of arguments. I tried not to get involved, but it was impossible. Jamie would come in fuming, asking me to talk to his dad about whatever it was, or to have a word with Simon, and I didn't have it in me to refuse. It got so that between the driving and the placating I didn't have much time for creating.'

Max's brows drew in, eyes all stormy. 'And Jamie was all right with that?'

'Jamie was focused on the business, that's all. And I didn't mean it to happen, but I got to be the same. I hated the family rows, but I liked it that I was pivotal in sorting them out—liked it that I was popular with the clients, especially the female celebs. After everything that had happened at school—getting glandular fever, flunking my exams—driving glamorous people around all day made me feel important…special…like I actually counted. And I liked that feeling. Who knows? Maybe I let it go to my head. Whatever! The upshot was I stopped designing, stopped sewing, stopped doing the market with Henry. But it wasn't Jamie's fault.' Her heart pinched. 'It was mine. I was the one who got distracted, sucked in…'

And now here it was, finally… The dark drop…the dragging ache.

'All of it was my fault, Max. Getting involved, getting engaged…'

His eyes widened. 'You were *engaged* to Jamie?'

'Yes.'

'And then he called it off? Dumped you?'

Way to turn to the guilt screw…make her eyes prickle hot. But of course he was bound to assume…

'No. It was *me*. I called it off.'

His gaze checked, then softened, reaching into hers. 'God, I'm so sorry, Tom.' Using that affectionate pet name again. And then he was looking down, massaging his fingers—to give her some space, probably. 'At least you realised it wasn't right *before* you tied the knot.'

'True…'

Her heart twisted. Never mind the *way* she'd realised—the speed of it, the way she'd knocked Jamie for six. Never mind that she still couldn't quite sweat the guilt out.

'You know…' Max looked up suddenly, his gaze a little hesitant, but warm, keen, brightening by the second. 'I've been thinking… I could help you get into fashion. I mean, you've got the talent, and I've got the clout…some really good contacts…'

No! Her heart pulsed. She needed to nip this dangerous bud off right now.

She shook her head, making her voice firm. 'It's very sweet of you, but I don't *want* help. Not from you, not from anyone. I want to make it on my own, get there by myself.' Was he registering, taking it in? She felt a sudden tingle of inspiration and pressed her gaze harder into his. 'It's important to me—like earning your stripes was important to you…'

He nodded slightly. 'I get that, but still… Just hear me out, would you?'

Oh, no.

'The thing is, Tom, I represent someone who I think would be right up your street. She might be good for some advice…a little mentoring, perhaps, maybe even an internship…'

Please, God, no…

'You'll have heard of her, no doubt.' He broke into a generous smile. 'Chloe Mills?'

No, no, no…

She could feel her heart choking, tears springing up, stinging her eyes. Damn him and his kindness! This wasn't the way she'd wanted to tell him. First part, Jamie—all that. Then *later*—not now…not today, of all days, when he'd trusted her with his fancy car, taken her onto the VIP terrace, stood up for her against that guy, bringing all the heroics—on a different day, she'd have got to the Chloe Mills part. Eased him in gently.

But now? Now she was coming apart at the seams. And he was seeing it, leaning forward.

'Tommie? What on earth's the matter?'

Kindness in his gaze, concern, making it worse, making her tears spill over, so what else was left but to say it all, confess, get it over with?

She wiped her eyes, forcing them to meet his. 'What's wrong is that I haven't just heard of her, Max. I know her.'

He drew back sharply, eyes narrowing. 'What?'

He was shocked, of course, but not as shocked as hē was going to be…

She swallowed hard. 'I worked for her in New York.'

'You *worked* for her?' Staring at her now, his mouth opening then closing again, as if couldn't find any more words. And then his gaze was clearing, cooling, hardening. 'And you knew—have known all this time—that I represent her?'

'Yes…' Her heart turned over. 'I saw you once at one of Chloe's parties.'

He let out a short, incredulous breath. 'And you didn't think to mention any of this?'

There was pain in his voice, in his eyes. Loud. Pulsing. Pounding her to pieces.

'For Christ's sake, Tommie. I had you down as one of the good guys. I had you down as honest!'

Her blood surged. 'I am!'

'Not from where I'm sitting.' Shaking his head now. 'Nothing about this in your details! Not a peep. Why the hell not? Kind of relevant, isn't it?'

'Yes, but I didn't know that till *you* opened the door! The agency is so cloak and dagger, so discreet, that even Billie—who works there and put me up for this job—didn't know that *you* were the prospective employer.'

His gaze flickered…conceding, maybe. It was a half-beat to breathe anyway, slow herself down.

'I wasn't trying to pull the wool over your eyes. Not in a scheming way. It was just the job paid so well, and Billie thought the money would help me set myself up, because things with Chloe didn't work out—which is a whole other story, and the reason I'm back in London.'

Another flicker, that felt like a release, somehow.

'Billie was only trying to help. She said no one would consider me for a long-term driving gig if they thought I wasn't a committed professional driver. She said we should leave my time in New York out—that it didn't matter, wasn't relevant. But then you opened the door and suddenly it was *very* relevant. But I couldn't say anything. I decided all I could do was try to seem like a good candidate, so that the agency wouldn't look bad for sending me, then leave as soon as possible. because I didn't *want* to be in this position... didn't *want* this weight pressing down on me.'

He looked away momentarily, as if he was replaying something in his mind, and then his eyes snapped back. 'So, if your plan was to leave as soon as possible—if you didn't want this lie weighing on you—why did you take the job?'

Her heart crimped. Would he believe her if she told him? Or just think she was trying to soften him up? *Whatever!* No more lies. Not to him. And especially not to herself.

She drew in a breath. 'I took the job because I liked you.'

His eyebrows lifted by a derisory degree. 'And the money?'

Seriously?

'Of course. That too! It's the whole point of work, isn't it? But I can tell you I'd have passed it up in a heartbeat if you'd been intolerable...'

He scoffed. 'So I take it, then, that I passed muster?'

Sarky! But was that a spark behind his eyes? Something was glowing there anyway...warmer, brighter, softening the air, making it seem all right to breathe, carry on.

'Yes, at the interview anyway. I confess I had a few

doubts after that…but here we are. And you shouldn't be offended because any job is two-way traffic.' She levelled her gaze into his, to press the point. 'I mean, you wouldn't have offered *me* the job if I hadn't fitted your brief, would you?'

His gaze turned inwards for a beat. 'No…'

'So it was the same for me. I liked you, and the set-up, and the money. And…'

'And what?'

He was looking at her—listening with his whole body, it seemed. Her heart quivered. Would his silly pride hate this?

She swallowed carefully. 'And… Well, the truth is, I thought I could help you with stuff. *Be* of help, I mean.'

His gaze faltered, and then suddenly it broke and he was Max again—a little subdued, but himself nevertheless. 'Well, you have helped me. And I'm grateful—indebted, really…' Then his brows drew in. 'But about Chloe—'

'Oh, Max…' She felt her heart dipping, rising, spilling over. 'I *wanted* to tell you so much—have wanted to for weeks. But I couldn't think how to. It's why I jumped on that thing you said this morning about me being competitive. I thought it would be a way to open up a conversation about fashion design…thought if I could just start telling you, take you some of the way, then later, when the time was right, I could get to Chloe, tell you everything…'

Truth in her eyes…brimming, welling. *Undeniable!* It was doing its work, tugging at those strings, realigning every errant pole inside him, every shredded fibre of his being, back to her north.

His heart dipped. But she *had* shredded him, hadn't she? Let him down with this news. Caused him pain. And even though her explanation stacked up, made sense, he could still feel that initial hurt throbbing inside, and it felt exactly

the same as it had used to when Gerald let him down—
said he'd come and watch him at the karting track and then
hadn't because something else cropped up. And that was a
warning, wasn't it? *Timely!* That believing in someone too
much, trusting them too much, was a risk, came with consequences. Extra consequences where Tommie was concerned. Because for some reason—probably because she
was gorgeous—he was susceptible, vulnerable around her.
So he needed to be on his guard, stay level, keep some ob-
jective distance.

He pulled in a breath. 'How about you tell me everything now.'

'Of course.' She blinked, wiping her face, and then she
was looking up again, meeting his gaze. 'I met Chloe a
couple of years ago. She booked Chauffeur Me for London
Fashion Week. I was her driver.'

Stacked up...

A smile ghosted over her lips. 'I was thrilled, obviously.
Back then she was my favourite designer.'

But not any more, if the clouds in her eyes were anything to go by.

'Anyway...' She tossed her hair back as if to clear her
head. 'Chloe was nervous about the show she was putting
on, and I thought if I chatted to her it might take her mind
off it. So I got going—not fangirling her, or anything, but
talking about fashion. And she engaged...chatted back. And
I was, like, in seventh heaven, talking fashion with Chloe-
fricking-Mills. It was unreal...'

The memory was lighting her up even now. But then she
was frowning again.

'It shook me up, Max. Reminded me that fashion was
what I loved. What I wanted to do. What I *had* been doing
before I got sidetracked. A few hours with her were all it

took. I *loved* talking to her, *being* with her, being part of her *whirl*. I loved getting her to her meetings on time when she was running late—which she nearly always was. Loved carrying her bags and samples into the hotel for her; getting her favourite chai latté for her, so it was there waiting when she got in the car...'

Being *Tommie*, in other words. Being her warm, nurturing self—which Chloe would have liked, of course.

She swallowed. 'Anyway, you'll have worked out already that she offered me a job—as her personal assistant.'

He felt the penny dropping. 'So you split with Jamie and went to New York?'

'Yes.' Her eyes filmed over briefly. 'Jamie was devastated, but I couldn't pass up the chance. Chloe said she'd mentor me...help me. She said she'd pull some strings, rush a work visa through for me. I was touching down in New York three weeks later, all set to live the dream...'

Which hadn't worked out in the end.

He made his tone gentle. 'So, what happened?'

Her gaze flickered, then steadied. 'What happened was that Chloe was different in New York to how she'd been in London. Always too busy to talk to me—except to bark out demands. She didn't mentor me, like she'd promised, didn't let me into her design process at all. I spent most of my time running errands...' She bit her lip, clearly wrestling with something, and then met his eye. 'In fact...full disclosure...that party I saw you at... I did more than see you. I bumped your shoulder.'

'What?'

'Chloe was stressing over the canapés, thinking we were running short. She sent me to organise some more with the kitchen. I was running out through the door just as you were coming in with Saskia—'

'Saskia Riva!'

That jolt. A flash of blonde. Fleeting apology. *English accent!* Buried all this time, until this very moment.

He looked at her. 'That was *you*?'

She gave a little shrug. 'Yes.'

And now she was here, sitting with him on the bank at Thruxton.

Unbelievable!

He refocused. 'So what happened with Chloe?'

'Okay…' Little breath. 'Fast forward a year. Chloe was struggling with a collection she was working on. I think her husband was up to no good with some other woman and it was affecting her creativity. I felt for her, in spite of everything, and I wanted to help, to get back a bit of what I'd had with her in London. So one night I hung on after everyone else had left and went in to see her. I talked to her a bit, then I showed her some of my sketches, chatted about my ideas.' Her gaze opened out. 'I'll admit it wasn't completely selfless. I wanted her to see what I could do…show her I was credible…'

He felt a cold weight sinking inside. 'She shot you down, didn't she?'

'No, but she wasn't blown away either. That's the vibe she put out, anyway.' She pressed her lips together and then her gaze hardened. 'But here's the funny thing: she got going on her collection after that, and what she came up with looked remarkably similar to what I'd shown her.'

He lost a breath. 'You're telling me she stole your designs?'

'Stole…used…was inspired by. It's all rather grey.'

His heart missed a beat. It couldn't be true. Not Chloe! She'd always been straight as a die. A little fragile, for sure, but solid, creatively speaking. Then again, her husband *was* playing away. Everyone knew it. And Chloe was crazy about him. If she'd been blocked, desperate, taking that depression medication she'd joked about in the past, mixing it with booze, she just might have been tempted to…

He drew Tommie back into focus, felt his heart missing again. And those eyes weren't welling up for nothing, those beautiful grey-green eyes weren't lying.

He swallowed hard. 'Did you challenge her?'

She nodded. 'Yes—when I plucked up the courage.' Her mouth twisted. 'I got a one-way ticket home for my trouble.'

He felt himself staring at her, his heart pinching. The unfairness of it! Sacked for trying to help, for trying to hold Chloe to a promise she'd made. All that after putting her dreams aside once already to help Jamie. Yes, to help Jamie, because whatever she said about it being her fault, it had all started with her trying to help, trying to do good.

He gritted his teeth. He was going to give Chloe a piece of his mind. As for Tommie…

How could he not reach for her hand, wrap it in his. 'I'm so sorry she treated you that way.'

'Don't be.' She shook her head. 'It's not your fault. You didn't raise her. You're just her PR guy.'

'That's under review…'

'No, please…' Squeezing his hand, beseeching him with her eyes. 'It's over. I don't want revenge, I don't want you to axe her—not for me.' And then her features were softening. 'I mean, it's not as if I didn't get anything good out of it. Chloe let me down, but she made me remember what I am, who I want to be.' Her gaze lit suddenly, as if by a sunbeam. 'Nothing's going to stop me now. I'm back on track. So, you know…silver linings and all that.'

His heart squeezed. *Tommie.* Always seeing the good. He

looked into her eyes. 'You're something else—you know that?'

Her gaze flickered, then opened out all the way into his. 'Am I forgiven, though?'

His heart caught. 'Oh, Tom…'

Way to slay him…finish him off. And maybe it was inappropriate, risky, every shade of wrong and unwise, but at this moment he couldn't make himself care.

He freed his hand from hers and put it to her cheek, so she'd know he was feeling every word he was saying. 'Yes, you're forgiven. Oh, God, yes. A million times over.'

Tears rose in her eyes. 'That's a lot of times.'

But she was smiling, leaning into his touch, and she wouldn't be doing that if she didn't *like* his touch, would she? Wouldn't be looking at him like this, with this warm glow in her gaze, if she didn't want, didn't feel…

His heart pulsed. 'Oh, Tommie…'

And maybe this was unwise too, but he couldn't stop himself from moving, leaning in all the way, putting his lips to hers, letting them find the place. *Yes…* He felt his eyes closing, his spirit settling. Right here. Just like this. Warmth, softness, moving in sync now. Slow kissing, achingly slow, drawing up delicious heat. Oh, he could feel himself stirring now, rising and falling at the same time. Top lip. Bottom lip. The ache inside. This was exactly how he'd imagined it. Kissing her slow, teasing himself, teasing her, stretching it out. Taking her full mouth now. And she was right there with him, kissing him back, her lips so warm and perfect, moulding to his as if they'd been designed for him.

Yes…

Tongues now, tentative strokes.

Yes… Yes…

He could feel his whole focus arrowing into sensation.

Softness. Warmth. The sour-sweet taste of her mouth. The grain of her tongue. He was going blind, spiralling away, could feel desire pumping, running through him like molten lead, making him properly hard, making his heart drum, fit to explode. Kissing had never felt like this before. Nowhere near. Never as tender, never as deep, never as connected.

Like drowning.

Yes...

Sublime drowning.

Yes...

And he wanted more, didn't want it to ever stop.

His heart faltered.

But it must. It must. Because this wasn't the place, was it?

He slid his hand back to her cheek, then broke away softly. 'We need to stop, Tom...'

'Why...?' Her eyes flickered, then opened, all hazy, and then her hands were coming up, taking hold of his face. 'I don't want to stop, Max.'

He felt his heart surging. That face. Those hazy eyes. *So beautiful*. Wanting him back.

He moved in, kissing her quickly. 'I don't want to stop either, but look where we are.'

'So what we do?'

Looking at his eyes, then into them.

His stomach tightened. This would be the moment to put the brakes on. This would be the moment to remember that she was his driver.

His heart caught. Oh, but he didn't want to remember it. Didn't want to do the sensible thing. Because this unsensible thing they'd got going on—whatever it was—was feeling so good, so right, and he didn't want it to end. He wanted more. All of it. All of her.

His heart pulsed.

And she wanted him too. Oh, God, yes, she did. He'd felt it in her kiss, could see it in her eyes right now. Desire and something else that was giving him tingles. And he wanted to know how it would feel to make love with her, how it would feel to make *connected* love. Because he'd never felt this kind of connection with anyone before. How could he make himself not want to go the whole way now he'd had a sublime taste?

He moved in again, brushing his lips over hers, feeling that tingle running through him. 'I think we should go home, Tom. Would you please drive us home?'

She let out a little sigh and then her lips curved against his, smiling. 'Yes, I will.'

CHAPTER FIFTEEN

TOMMIE JOLTED AWAKE. Strange ceiling. Strange slate-blue walls. Strange bedroom.

Max's!

She turned her head. No Max, though. Just that odd noise. Muffled. Drilling. Insistent.

Phone!

She sat up quickly, looking around. *There!* On the floor. Her jeans. She swung out of bed to scoop them up, freeing the phone from a back pocket, squinting at the screen.

Billie.

She drew in a breath and swiped right, trying not to sound as if she'd just been leaping about in a strange bedroom. 'Hey.'

'So, what's going on?'

Her heart paused. Billie's tone had something of the tapping foot about it.

'Nothing…' She got back into bed, clawing the duvet up and around herself. 'Why?'

'So that wasn't you in those pictures, kissing a certain Maxwell Lawler Scott at Thruxton yesterday?'

What?

'What are you talking about? What pictures?'

'I've just sent them. But you don't need to see them to answer the question. Was it you kissing your boss? Or was it some other blonde who looks exactly like you?'

Her stomach lurched. 'Just, hang on will you…'

She swiped at her screen, heart pounding.

She and Max on the terrace, looking towards the finish line… The two of them with the shover guy, looking for all the world as if they were having a friendly conversation… And one…no, two…*no*, three pictures of…

She felt her head trying to swim. A private moment. Invaded. Their precious first kiss. That warm, deep, slow, tender, perfect kiss that had blurred the lines between right and wrong, wise and unwise. That kiss that had landed her in this bed with the most beautiful, loving, giving, passionate man in the world. And now it was out there for the world to see…

Her pulse arced. *Oh, God!* Did Max know about these pictures? And where the hell was he? In the pool? In the gym, doing planks and those one-handed press-ups? In his office, doing business?

'Tommie?'

She swallowed hard. 'I'm here.'

'So…?'

No point denying it.

'Yes. It's me in the pictures.'

'Wow!' Little pause. 'I mean, obviously I *knew* it was you. And I know you and Max have been getting on better and everything, but I didn't realise you were getting on as well as *that*!'

'We haven't been… Not like that. But we talked a lot yesterday, and I ended up telling him about Chloe and about everything that happened in New York. Which was hard, and emotional, but such a relief, and then afterwards the kiss just sort of happened…'

That look in his eyes, then him leaning in, coming closer, making her heart rush and tingle, and then…oh, that sublime first touch of his lips. Warm, like home, feeling so right, so *meant*...

She shook herself. 'I just can't believe that some seedy bloody paparazzo managed to catch us!'

'Oh, Tom...' Billie sighed. 'If it helps, I only recognised you because I know you so well, and know you're working for Max, but I don't think anyone else would. I mean, for one thing, in the kissing ones your face is mostly hidden by Max's hand. And in the one where you're watching the race you've got your shades on. And in the other one it's just your back and your hair.'

Good old Billie, trying to help as always.

'Thanks, but I'm not that bothered about being recognised. It's more the thought that someone was creeping around us like that. It was a special moment.'

Billie drew in an audible breath. 'So, are you guys...? Are you in love with him?'

Her heart stilled. Was she? That wave...crashing in the instant he'd said she was forgiven for keeping Chloe a secret...that look in his eyes and that other look behind it... the emotion in his voice...his hand coming to her cheek... All those simmering feelings inside her...all the tingles... all the tugs and pulls...old ones, new ones... Freeing themselves in that moment, surfacing, taking shape...

And that shape was...

She felt her heart agreeing, tears welling, a smile coming. 'Yes. Yes, I am...' That dear, dear face. Those eyes. That smile. 'He's everything, Billie. Kind, and noble—just like you said. And he's warm and funny and—'

'Sexy...?'

Her stomach dipped. 'Yes, that as well...'

Driving back, leaning over to blow her mind with a kiss at every red light, caressing her nape, sometimes her thigh, sliding his hand all the way up, just short of… Making her body howl for contact, release. Then it had been the two of them barrelling through the door, kissing, touching, shedding clothes all the way up the stairs. Oh, and then the joy of his body, the firm crush and heat of him, that sublime first thrust, both of them ready, greedy, giving in, unravelling, crying out, exploding. Round one…

Round two had been a slow dance, achingly tender. Every kiss, every touch, perfection. Hands and mouths exploring. That deep light in his eyes that looked like love, felt like love, as he moved inside her, that put a sob in her chest, tears in her eyes, then in his.

Round three—under the shower in his wet room. Bodies sliding together, wet hands. Sliding down to take him in her mouth. Then her hands on the wall, his body behind her, water raining down, steam rising. Mind-blowing. Sexy as—

'Are you in his bed right now?'

She glanced down at the snowy expanse of duvet. She could lie—but why? This was Billie, her best friend in the world as well as her sister. And she wasn't ashamed. She *was* in love with Max—had given herself to him in love. And he was in love with her too. For sure, he hadn't said it, but then neither had she. But he'd made love to her like he meant it, and she'd definitely made love to him that way, feeling it inside her.

'I am…yes.'

Billie's breath hitched. 'He isn't *there* with you right now, is he?'

Seriously?

'No! Would I be sitting here talking to you about him if he was?'

She looked at the empty doorway, then at the room, taking in what she'd barely registered last night. Vast windows framing a view of sun-dappled treetops. Pale overstuffed sofa. Long mahogany chest. Acres of bed…acres of snowy linen. Her heart tugged. Too many acres without Max here. Where was he? Disappearing like this didn't seem in keeping with last night…with the way he'd loved her.

'Listen, Billie, I should go. I don't actually know where Max is right now, or if he's seen these pictures, but he definitely needs to know about them.'

'Okay.' Billie's voice dipped. 'Neville's coming through the door now, anyway, so I need to look busy. Catch you later.'

'Bye…'

She lowered her phone, turned it over in her hands. So why wasn't she jumping up now to go and find Max, tell him about the pictures? Why were there suddenly dark thoughts creeping in? Thoughts like, Max wasn't the love and commitment type, the relationship type. Thoughts like, if Max loved her, why had he disappeared before she'd even woke up? Why wasn't he here to hold her, kiss her, tell her they were a couple now? Why wasn't he here to talk about how things were going to be from now on, how they were going to manage this thing?

Her stomach clenched. Thoughts that hadn't even crossed her mind until now… The living reality of a Max and Tommie universe. Planet Silver Spoon orbiting Planet South London. And her job! Was she still his driver? She didn't want to stop driving him—didn't want to stop being paid for doing it either, because she needed the money to set herself up. And about that… Max had talked about helping her get into fashion, about clout and contacts… Would he pursue that now? And if he did…

She bit her lip. How would it actually feel, being helped

by her billionaire lover? Her chest went tight. How would it make her look to the world?

She hugged her knees. Less credible, for sure. Like a little vanity offshoot of Lawler Scott Inc. maybe—not that there really was such a thing, but taking any help at all from Max wouldn't feel as good as making it on her own, would it? On just her own talent, grit and determination, blazing her own trail, having that satisfaction. And even if she did cut her own honest path, would the world always think that Max had had a hand in it somewhere along the line? Would she be seen as a hanger-on, an opportunist?

So much to sort out. And he wasn't here to help her do it, put her mind at ease.

She pulled in a breath. *Enough!* She didn't want to be chasing after him—didn't want to seem pathetic and needy, as if she was begging for little scraps from his table. But there it was—they had things to talk about and she couldn't just sit here twiddling her thumbs. She needed to find the rest of her clothes, then find him…talk to him!

CHAPTER SIXTEEN

'COME ON, MAX. Who is she?' Fliss was trying again, honeying her tone now. 'Don't be so mean. Here I am, pregnant, feeling fat and about a sexy as a double decker bus, and you're kissing some "mystery blonde" at Thruxton. Please share...permit me a little vicarious delight.'

God preserve him from Fliss's vicarious delight! Especially when the walls were closing in around him faster than he could push them back.

First light... Tommie... Lying asleep beside him in the bed he'd never shared with anyone, looking like an angel with her halo of blonde hair and her sweet, peaceful expression. Dreaming of the sublime night they'd just spent, perhaps, the love they'd made. Tender love. Warm. *Connected!*

His heart turned over. Exactly what he'd wanted, wasn't it? To experience real connection, the deep ecstasy of it, the drowning feelings, the never wanting to stop feelings...feelings so powerful that he'd felt his stupid eyes welling, a sob trying to break out of him every time he'd climaxed. Oh, and how peaceful had he felt afterwards? Lying wrapped around her, breathing her in, caressing all her sweet dips and curves, drifting away...

But looking at her first thing, at her lovely face and the soft splay of her hair, he'd felt all that peace shattering, splintering into blind panic. Because he didn't do sharing.

Not his bed. His personal space. His life. And definitely, definitely *not* his heart. Because feeling the way he'd felt making love to her—whatever that all-consuming feeling had been, whatever name you gave it—could only end in pain. And he couldn't put himself in that position...make himself that vulnerable.

Not after years of Tamsin and Gerald. Feeling stung by their neglect and then by their disappointment in him. That was what he was in for with Tommie if he got in any deeper, got to need her. One day he'd need her and she wouldn't be there. She'd be too busy, too absorbed in her big dream—a dream that, quite rightfully, after everything she'd been through, she didn't want anything or anyone to get in the way of.

And what about his tics and demons? He was fine if he could control the script, the narrative, but he couldn't with Tommie. Experience had shown him that already. And what was he without control? Susceptible, lost, exposed, all ragged around his edges. And maybe that version of himself wouldn't be good enough for Tommie. Maybe he'd fail her, disappoint her, get in her way like Jamie and Jamie's family had, end up hurting her in the long run...

All of it, churning away inside him—how was he going to manage this situation?—and then he'd heard his phone vibrating in the hallway, where it must have fallen last night.

Fliss. Breaking the good news that, on top of everything else, he and Tommie had been caught on camera by some fricking low-life paparazzo!

He flicked through the images again. Himself and Tommie on the VIP terrace, sunglasses glinting, looking towards the grid. Another shot with the shover, happily suggesting conversation rather than aggression, and mostly featuring Tommie's delectable rear and the blonde tumble of her hair. And then the kicker—proving that the photographer had been stalking them—the kissing pictures. Several long lens shots, deeply intimate—which was why Fliss was on his case.

Max—her locked-down, emotional fortress of a baby brother—had been caught in the wild, demonstrating finally that he was human after all. But if she thought for one second that he was going to give her rope to hang him with, she had another think coming!

He switched his phone from speaker and got up, putting it to his ear, because all this haranguing was too much to take sitting down. 'Look, I've told you already. She's no one. Not important.'

'I'm sorry, Max, I'm not buying it. I mean, at the risk of sounding icky, you look like a romantic movie hero in those pictures. The way you're cupping her cheek... There's a serious vibe going on.'

A vibe and so much more... But he wouldn't yield. *Couldn't!*

He set his jaw. 'There *isn't* a vibe! It was just a stupid kiss, okay? A second's worth. No! Less. A two hundred and fiftieth of a second's worth. It didn't mean anything. The girl was just a casual date.'

'I don't *believe* you.'

Annoying sing-song voice.

His blood pulsed.

'For God's sake, Fliss. This is me you're talking to. You know I don't do relationships!'

She let out a provoking laugh. 'Are you sure? I mean, sorry to point out the obvious, but look at the evidence... You're Mr Total Privacy. You don't *believe* in public displays of affection! You've never been photographed kissing anyone. None of the models you go out with. Not even on the cheek. No one. *Ever!* Yet there you are at Thruxton, with tens of thousands of people around you, kissing a girl like you mean it. Why not just give it up and tell me?'

His heart crimped. Because how could he tell her? If he told her that the girl was Tommie she'd give him the back-seat, front-seat lecture. If he went further, and told her that Tommie was upstairs asleep in his bed right now because of that kiss—because he'd spent the two-hour drive back, which could have been a cooling off period, fondling her neck and her thigh, kissing her at every red light, keeping the flame going not deliberately, but because he couldn't control himself around her, so that by the time they'd got back there had been no way to dowse it except to take things all the way… Well, God knew what she'd say to that. Except that he was an idiot, and cruel to have started something he couldn't finish…

'Who she is, is going to come out anyway, now that those pictures are circulating, Max. Someone's going to recognise her…put it out there. Is that the way you want me to find out?'

At least he was on firm ground here.

He crossed to the window, running his eyes over the garden. 'Nothing's going to "come out", Fliss. I'm of *minor* interest to *some* motor racing fans and of absolutely no interest to anyone else. As for the "mystery blonde"—no one's going to recognise her from those pictures.' His heart tugged. 'My hand's obscuring most of her face. Besides, she's a total unknown. There are no leads on her to follow, and I'm certainly keeping it that way…'

Except that this was Fliss, his friend in need, his ally, his sister. He ought to give her something, at least soften his voice a bit, and his demeanour, so he didn't seem so overreactive. If nothing else, it would lend credibility to the lies he was telling, maybe stall her, at least for the moment.

'Look, I'm not being mean. It's just that there really *is* nothing to all this—no story to tell.'

Fliss scoffed. 'That's the story you're sticking to?'

'Yes.' His heart twisted. 'Because it's the truth.'

The truth! No story to tell!

Tommie felt her knees trying to give, her heart trying to crack. How could Max be saying these things? Saying them so matter-of-factly? She screwed her eyes shut, bearing down, but it was too much hurt to hold in, too much devastation, too much rage. To think she'd come to find him to talk to him about the two of them. The future. To think she'd actually thought there could be one.

She pushed away from the wall and stepped into the room. 'So, I'm "no one" am I, Max? "Not important"? A "casual date"?'

He spun round, as well he might, his face blanching, phone hand dropping to his side. 'Tom!'

'Don't you *dare* call me that!'

Tears stung her eyes. Yesterday he'd used the little pet name. Sweet then. Charming. Not now.

'Tommie... I...' He was shaking his head, blinking. 'You've seen the pictures? I...'

Gasping like a bloody fish. Of course he was, caught dissing her six ways to Sunday. But it was fine. She had plenty to say.

'Yes, I've seen them.' She folded her arms to quell the trembling inside, jerking her head towards the phone in his hand. 'I suggest you actually end that call before your sister finds out who I am. You can tell her you've got to go. Got a little *meaningless* business to attend to.'

Shaking his head. 'Don't…' And then he was lifting his phone into view, cancelling the call with an obvious press of his thumb, his face grey. 'I'm so, so sorry.'

Her body flashed hot. 'What for? For kissing me? Having *sex* with me…?'

That hit the mark. Flinching all along his jaw. Good to know she could inflict a bit of pain—if that was actually what it was.

'Or are you just sorry you got found out? Were overheard?'

Another flinch, then a step towards her, a placating hand. 'You're angry… I get it.'

'Well, that's something, at least!'

His shoulders sagged. 'Please, Tommie…' His gaze was wet now, glistening, pleading. 'What I said to Fliss…' Another step. 'It's…' He gave a little shrug. 'I have to be careful…'

'Why?'

His eyes flashed. 'Because she's got this notion in her head that my lifestyle isn't normal—that's why! That I'm missing out by not being with someone. She's aways going on at me to settle down…do the happy families thing like she is. If I'd told her one single thing about you she'd have jumped on it…made a great big fricking thing out of it!'

Her heart plummeted. 'And it isn't "a great big fricking thing" to you?'

Silence. He was looking at her. Just standing there. Looking. Staring.

She felt her head trying to swim, her knees trying to give. 'Yesterday you told me I was "something else". Yesterday you kissed me like it mattered. Last night…' Her heart tore. She couldn't let herself think about that… She swallowed hard. 'And today you're telling your sister that our kiss was nothing, that you don't *do* relationships, and you're telling me that you said that stuff to her so she wouldn't make too much of us, but what I'm not getting from all of this is what *you* think, Max…'

His mouth opened, then closed again.

Which was maybe the answer. But why? How to understand…to even begin to? Oh, and how to stop these tears from prickling, scalding her eyes? How to stop this ache from tearing through her, this frustration from burning a hole in her chest.

'For crying out loud, Max, say something! I just want the truth. What was last night to you? A meaningless roll in the hay? Because it didn't feel like that for me. And maybe I was reading you wrong, but I just…'

How to stand this pain…stay standing upright?

She wiped her eyes. 'I just need to know.'

His throat rolled and then he was breaking her gaze, looking down. 'It wasn't meaningless, Tommie.'

But he wasn't looking at her, was he? And he wasn't coming forward. Wasn't taking her in his arms, kissing her, soothing her, saying it was going to be all right.

One last stupid question to ask…

'So what *is* the story, Max?'

His chest rose on a breath and then he was looking up again, his gaze level. 'The story is that you're my driver. I shouldn't have kissed you…shouldn't have…' He ran a tongue over his lip. 'I crossed a line I shouldn't have. and I'm truly, deeply sorry. It was a mistake.'

She felt her heart cracking from side to side, fresh hot tears welling, spilling. A mistake! He was writing off last night—all the love they'd made, shared, all that sublime, joyful connection—as a bloody *mistake*!

His hand came up, reaching out. 'We can put it behind us…'

Her pulse jumped. 'Seriously?' She swiped at her eyes. 'You actually think I can go on working for you now? After this?' *Unbelievable!* 'What planet do you think you're living on, Max?'

His mouth opened, but whatever he was going to say next she didn't want to know—couldn't bear to hear.

She held up her palm to stay him, forcing her legs to move before they buckled out from under her. 'Not another word, Max. I'm going to grab my things now and then I'm leaving. Don't bother coming to see me off.'

CHAPTER SEVENTEEN

Three days later...

'OH, I'M SORRY, MAX.' Jenny stopped, half in, half out, her cleaning bucket dangling in her hand. 'I didn't realise you were in here.'

No reason why she should have. He wasn't in the habit of loitering in the guest annexe like an aimless cloud, was he? The thing to remember was that he didn't have to explain himself.

He smiled. 'It's fine.' He nodded to the bucket. 'Don't bother cleaning in here for now, okay?'

Her features drew in. 'When you say, "for now", you mean—?'

'Until I instruct you otherwise.'

She nodded, flicking a bewildered glance around the room. 'Okay...' And then she was reversing out, closing the door behind her. She probably thought he was mad.

He turned, heading into the bedroom. Maybe he was—or well on the way to being so anyway. Haunting the annexe like this, clinging to remnants...

He sank down onto the bed, pulling out the pillow that smelt the most of Tommie and wrapping his arms around it, pushing his face into it to breathe her in.

What to do? How to come back from this? How to stop this hard, relentless ache inside him? How to stop missing her, feeling lonely without her? He'd felt a lot of things in his life, but never lonely. He liked solitude, peace and quiet, liked his own company. But he was miserable company for himself now…couldn't stop replaying that awful scene…

Tommie's stricken face. Her beautiful eyes hurt, angry, uncomprehending. And he'd just stood there like a robot, struggling to think of a single damn thing to say—a single thing to say that would make sense to her, that wouldn't tie him in impossible knots. Because he hadn't had time to think anything through, had he? To prepare a response, get a script together.

One minute he'd been waking up, feeling the panic rushing in. The next he'd had Fliss on the phone about the paparazzi photos, putting him through the inquisition. And then Tommie had appeared, blindsiding him with her fury and her pain. He'd gone into defence mode, failed her, handled the whole thing appallingly. And now she was gone, and he was sick inside…empty and aching.

But what the hell was he supposed to do about it? He couldn't make amends, rock up at her door without a script, a plan—without something to offer her. Something other than his own stupid self-pity and loneliness. But what else could he offer her? What else was there? Because he was still the same old mess inside…still scared.

He tossed the pillow away and got up, drifting back through to the sitting room. No photos in frames now, no blankets draped, no magazines stacked. He dropped down onto the sofa, rolling his head back. Neville Cutter had called him earlier about a replacement driver, but he didn't want a replacement—didn't want anyone living in this annexe but Tommie.

Oh, God! If only letting her go meant *actually* letting her go. Dispensing with her. Being free of her. But it didn't. She was in his head twenty-four-seven, under his skin and, yes, in his heart too. Somehow. Deep in. Like a thorn…hurting like one, throbbing away day and night. So she might as well still be here, mightn't she? He might as well have just dived in, taken a chance on them, given it a go, for all the inner peace he wasn't achieving. Then at least she'd have still been here, reminding him to do his active assisted exercises, brightening his day with her smile and her teasing… But also kissing him the way she had, holding him, loving him, making him feel alive to his bones, blissfully out of control…

Out. Of. Control.

He felt a tingle. Was that the key? To embrace *not* being in control? Embrace *not* knowing the script? It wasn't much to give her, but if he went to her and fessed up that he was terrified of being in a relationship, of failing, of not being what she needed, terrified of being rejected, hurt, sidelined, told her that that was why he'd let her walk away, would it cut any ice with her? Would she understand? Forgive him? Come back?

He felt his pulse picking up, resolve winding through him. Even if she didn't, at least she'd know the truth of him—the whole naked truth—and she deserved that. He could give her that.

He tilted his head, catching a glimpse of white under the opposite sofa.

Paper?

He dropped to the floor, reaching to get it. Yes. Paper. A sketch, of course. A stunning one-shoulder evening dress with a long, draping cape. Little arrows and annotations written in neat script. *Red crepe, silk/rayon*. And next to the cape a note: *Detachable?* More notes down the side. *Zip length options. Buttons. Lining. Trim*. All of it meticulous and so utterly, completely Tommie.

He rocked back on his heels. She'd definitely want to have this sketch back in her hands, wouldn't she? He felt a tingle. Which could be the perfect icebreaker… That was if he could track her down.

He got to his feet. But that should be easy enough. Neville Cutter would never disclose Tommie's parents' address to him, which was absolutely as it should be, but Billie worked for Neville's agency, didn't she? No doubt Tommie had painted him black to her sister, but if he could convince Billie that his intentions were one hundred percent honourable she'd surely take pity on him…help him out. As long as she thought that Tommie would *want* to see him, that was…

CHAPTER EIGHTEEN

TOMMIE FOLDED HER arms over her face to block out the light, the room, to stop her eyes from seeing anything. But she couldn't block out Max…couldn't stop seeing his shut-down face with all that emotion banked up behind it, couldn't stop hearing him saying 'It was a mistake.'

Lying to her.

Because what else could it have been but a lie?

A kiss couldn't lie! The way he'd kissed her, touched her, held her, loved her… None of it could have been a lie. What had happened between them hadn't been a mistake. Maybe it hadn't been wise, because he was her boss, she his employee. Maybe they should have put the brakes on, talked about what they were getting themselves into before they'd got themselves into it. But a mistake? No. Never. She couldn't make herself believe it, nor make herself believe that he did either.

But he hadn't stopped her leaving. And, as she'd asked, he hadn't come to see her off. He'd paid the full contract fee into her bank account, though…

She lowered her arms and sat up, staring at the fireplace. How to even feel about that? Billie's take on it was that Max was trying to make amends, making sure she wasn't out of pocket because of his 'indiscretion', and that she deserved the money, should crack on with honing her designs, getting her sample collection together. But it wasn't that simple. For one thing, it felt wrong taking money she hadn't earned, and for another, she could barely even get up off this sofa, never mind get going again with her collection.

She pulled in a breath. Maybe a walk would help. Ah… except she couldn't go anywhere—not until the courier came with her mum's package. She sighed out the breath she'd just pulled in. Why hadn't Mum just had the package delivered to the café, like she always did? Then again, Mum had probably assumed it wouldn't be much of an inconvenience to her, since she'd barely moved off this sofa since she'd got here.

She reached up, tousling her hair, then raking it back into place. *Geez!* She needed to get a grip…pull herself together. She had a life to live, a plan, stuff to get on with. Her heart swung. Oh, but how to do that with all these torn edges inside her? When this thing with Max didn't feel resolved? When he was all she could think about? When she was missing him—his kiss, his body, even though both of those things were so new?

Her heart caught. So unfair. They'd only just been getting started…only—

And there was the doorbell chiming…

The courier!

She got up and went to the door, fiddling with the locks because they were stiff. Just a good old yank and—

'Hello, Tommie.'

Her heart stood still.

Max! Here! *How?*

She felt her lips trying to move, to frame words, but nothing would come.

And then his hand was lifting, attached to a sheet of paper.

'I brought you this. I found it under one of the sofas in the annexe.' His eyes glanced at it then came back to hers. 'It's a really good sketch, so I thought you'd want it.'

She found a patch of breath. 'You came all this way to—?'

'No…' Shaking his head. 'It's not why I came.' He swallowed. 'I came to ask you if we could please talk? If you'd please let me talk to you, explain…' Blue eyes, reaching in, beseeching her. 'Please, Tommie…'

What to say?

How to even speak when her throat was filling with tears like this? When her heart was skipping with irrational hope and love in spite of everything.

In. Spite. Of. Everything.

'How did you know where I was?'

'Billie gave me the address.'

Which meant he must have convinced Billie. And Mum too. That courier story had clearly been a ruse to keep her here. Because Mum *always* had packages delivered to the café, didn't she? And if Max had convinced them—if they were part of this—then it must mean they trusted him… trusted him with her, and thought she'd want to hear whatever it was he had to say.

Her heart pulsed. And she did—so much.

She looked at him. 'Okay, we can talk.'

Relief ghosted over his features, and tingled through her too…all warm, as if they were already—

She pushed the thought away, stepping aside to make room for him. 'Come in. The sitting room's on the left.'

He brushed past, so close, filling her nostrils with his warm, deep smell, tugging at her senses. She wanted to reach out, pull him closer, but instead she drew in a deep breath and followed him, walking right into the soft full beam of his gaze.

'It's so good to see you...' The soft beam rippled. 'I've missed you...'

He was turning her heart over, drawing tears up from the well in her chest.

'I missed you too.'

He shifted a little on his feet. 'I can't even begin to tell you how sorry I am for what went down the other day...' His gaze flickered. 'I handled it really badly.'

'You did...'

He nodded a little, as if to himself, and then his eyes locked on hers. 'I've been trying to think of a way to explain my behaviour, and then I realised I'd never be able to explain it without giving up this obsession I have...this ingrained habit I have of needing to control my own narrative all the time.'

She felt her brow wrinkling. 'Which means what, exactly?'

He sighed. 'It means I've spent most of my life striving to hide what I'm feeling...who I am inside.' His lips pressed together. 'I've done therapy, Tom, so I know it's a reaction to my parents. I don't let anyone in past a certain point. Not anyone who can hurt me at heart level, make me feel the way *they* made me feel. Sidelined, unworthy, unimportant... I built myself a shell, learned self-reliance. I convinced myself that being alone was the best way to live, because that way I could control what happened to me...' He ran a tongue over his lip. 'And then you came along, and cracked my shell wide open.'

Her heart pulsed. 'I did...?'

'Oh, yes.' He let out a short, wry laugh. 'From the moment you walked through the door I didn't know which box to put you in...how to deal with my feelings around you. So I was rude, distant. I pushed you away for the very reason that I wanted to get close to you. And then I did get closer to you…let you in bit by bit. And with every bit I let you in, I wanted to let you in more. You know why I wanted to go to Thruxton! Because it was the only place I could think of to go with you that wouldn't seem obvious…wouldn't seem like a date. But that's what it was. I wanted to spend time with you, Tom, give you a day out to thank you for all your kindness to me. A day out not in the car, not as boss and driver, but just as us…as people. And then you told me about Chloe, what she'd done, and I felt so…' His eyes flashed. 'So sick for you, so furious with her—and there you were, asking me if you were forgiven, and it tore the heart right out of me. I wanted to show you how *much* you were forgiven, how *much* I care for you, and that's why I kissed you. That's why I made love to you—*love*, Tommie—like I've never felt it before…'

There were tears in his eyes now, making her own well, and then he was stepping in close, taking hold of her hand, his gaze deep and full.

'It wasn't meaningless. It was the opposite. It meant *everything*, Tommie. But when I woke up it all came crashing down on me…the magnitude of what I was feeling for you. And suddenly I was scared—scared witless. Scared of the next step—of a relationship, sharing, not being in control. And before I could even get my head halfway around that Fliss was on the phone about the photos, badgering me about you, saying how into you I looked, how I looked like I was in love with you. And I kicked back hard—because it was just making the terror inside me worse. And then you walked in, upset, angry, and I couldn't find the words, couldn't explain. So I let you go. But, see, the thing is, I *can't* let you go—because I love you, and I want us to try. But you need to know the truth, so you can decide.

You need to know that I want you, but I'm terrified of what that means. I'm scared I'll hurt you, or that you'll hurt me. I'm scared of failing you, of not being what you want. I'm scared of needing you—'

'Stop, Max, please, draw a breath...'

Because this was crazy! Crazy wonderful, but crazy all the same. She freed her hand from his, putting both of her hands to his face, loading her gaze with all the love she was feeling inside.

'I don't care how scared you are, or how scared I am, because I love you. And if you love me too, then that's all we need to know. Love will see us through. I believe that from the bottom of my heart.'

'You love me? Really?'

He was looking at her, with that other look behind his eyes, tearing her to pieces.

'How can you ask me that?' She felt her heart surging, love flowing through her and out of her. 'You must know, Max. Must have felt it.' She stroked his face, filling his gaze with hers so he'd know it for sure. 'I love you.' His gaze opened out...all warm, drawing a smile up though her and tears too. 'I. Love. You. Now, are you going to kiss me, or what?'

His face split, turning his handsomeness into a million shards of brilliant light. 'Oh, yes—and *how* I'm going to kiss you, Tommie.'

And then his lips were on hers, soft, and warm, and it felt like two planets colliding, exploding in her heart. Which was to say the best damn feeling in the universe...

EPILOGUE

Six months later...

'AND NOW HERE she is...' The compère's rich voice was building, milking the moment as only those guys could. 'Meet our New Voice in Style winning designer, Tommie Seager!'

And then there she was. *His* Tommie. His beautiful, brilliant, talented, stubborn-as-a-mule Tommie. Exploding from the wings with her models, running down the catwalk, laughing, blushing, looking so damn perfect, so damn happy.

Fliss leaned in, squeezing his hand. 'She looks stunning, Max.'

He felt tears stinging his eyes, his heart surging with love and pride. Of course she did. She was in one of her own designs, of course—the scarlet one-shoulder cape dress that had lived as a sketch beneath a sofa in the annexe once. The jewel in the crown of her collection.

And now she was stepping up to the microphone, her hand shielding her eyes from the lights. His heart skipped. She was looking for him, exactly as she'd said she would. He raised his left hand a little and she saw him, stilled his breath with her answering smile.

'Thank you, everyone.'

Her gaze slid away, moving over the crowd, and then she

was stepping back a little in that shy way she had, blushing again, collecting herself. And then she was at the microphone again, smiling.

'I can barely believe that I'm here today, but I can tell you it feels really, really good.'

A *'Wahoo!'* went up from Billie, sitting a few seats further along the row, followed by a ripple of applause.

Tommie chuckled, the infectious, throaty sound of it echoing around the room, and then she was off again. 'It's been a bit of a journey, and I have a few people to thank, so please, bear with me.' Her chin lifted. 'First, thanks to Deeks & Sanders, Fashion Retailer of the Year, for running the New Voice in Style competition, and for giving me such a fabulous team to work with. And thanks, as well, to my gorgeous models—Melissa, Jody, Babette, Himari and Bokamoso—for rocking the life out of my designs on that catwalk just now.'

More applause went up, with a few more whoops from Billie's end of the row.

Tommie let the room settle, then carried on. 'Breaking into fashion as a designer is tough, so getting the chance to pitch a collection to such a forward-thinking and generous retailer was an outstanding opportunity. So again, Deeks & Sanders, I thank you from the bottom of my heart.'

More applause.

She blinked, then smiled again. 'Next, I want to thank my family…' Her eyes travelled to their row, glistening. 'Mum, Dad, Billie…you've always been there for me with your love and support.' Her eyes flicked to his. 'Not everyone is as lucky as I am, so I want you to know I don't take you for granted. Thank you for being you.' Her voice wavered. 'I love you.'

Applause broke out again and she stepped back for a moment, wiping her eyes, and then she was at the microphone again, giving a little chuckle, holding up a tissue.

'I'm going to hang on to this, because I'm going to need it for this next one.' And then her eyes arrowed to his, locking on. 'Max, what can I say? Except that I'm sorry for almost not listening to you about entering this competition...'

He felt happy tears welling again, the memory flying in.

'You should look at this, Tom. Your designs would totally hit the mark for Deeks & Sanders.'

'I'm not entering. You're connected to it.'

'I'm not "connected" to it! I represent Melissa Kane, that's all.'

'But she's the face of the whole thing—the ambassador for the collection. How's it going to look if I enter? And if I did happen to win, everyone would think you pulled strings.'

'I don't see how they'd think that, since Melissa has no say in the judging and I have absolutely no clout or influence whatsoever with D&S.'

'Even so...there's a connection through you. I want to make it on my own, Max.'

'I respect that, but it's completely irrelevant in this instance. If you enter and win, that'd be all down to you and your talent. Nothing to do with me. All I'm doing is flagging up the competition because it's an opportunity. Stop being so infernally stubborn.'

She dabbed at her eyes, then smiled into his. 'You were right, and I was wrong.' She drew in a shaky breath. 'Anyway, I just want to say, in front of all these people, that you're the light of my life, the love of my life...' Her voice dipped low then, thick with emotion. 'I love you so freaking much, Max Scott.'

And didn't he know it? Every second of every day. She was the best risk he'd ever taken. A keeper.

He felt his focus sliding to the neat bulk of the ring box in his pocket. A moment for later. On the rooftop, with champagne on ice and the glittering London night stretching all around them. All planned.

But for now…

He touched his left hand to his chest, mouthing words back to her, feeling them to the very depths of his soul. *I love you too. With all my heart.*

* * * * *

*If you enjoyed this story,
check out these other great reads
from Ella Hayes*

Bound by Their Lisbon Legacy
One Night on the French Riviera
Barcelona Fling with a Secret Prince
Their Surprise Safari Reunion

Available now!

MILLS & BOON®

Coming next month

SECRET FLING WITH THE KING
Susan Meier

'You're not a prince.'

'One better,' Mateo said, studying her eyes. 'I'm your king.'

The way he said it was possessive and primal enough to send a zing of electricity through Jessica. Struggling with the urge to lean into him, she didn't know what she thought she was doing, moving around a ballroom floor as if she was dancing. 'There's no music.'

He laughed. 'Okay.' He began to sing the music of the *Blue Danube Waltz*. 'Da Da Da Da Da...Da Da, Da Da.'

Their slight moves became the wide swirling motions of a waltz.

And it felt wonderful. Before she could stop herself, she wished for a full skirt to bell out when they twirled. She wished for real music and the noise of a crowd celebrating in this wonderful room.

He reached the end of the song and when his humming stopped, he stopped dancing. She caught his gaze. Expecting to see laughter there, she smiled. But he didn't.

His dark eyes searched hers. A shower of tingles rained through her. Her chest tightened.

Continue reading

SECRET FLING WITH THE KING
Susan Meier

Available next month
millsandboon.co.uk

COMING SOON!

We really hope you enjoyed reading this book.
If you're looking for more romance
be sure to head to the shops when
new books are available on

Thursday 27th March

To see which titles are coming soon, please visit
millsandboon.co.uk/nextmonth

LET'S TALK
Romance

For exclusive extracts, competitions and special offers, find us online:

f MillsandBoon

X @MillsandBoon

⊙ @MillsandBoonUK

♪ @MillsandBoonUK

Get in touch on 01413 063 232

Afterglow Books is a trend-led, trope-filled list of books with diverse, authentic and relatable characters, a wide array of voices and representations, plus real world trials and tribulations. Featuring all the tropes you could possibly want (think small-town settings, fake relationships, grumpy vs sunshine, enemies to lovers) and all with a generous dose of spice in every story.

♪ @millsandboonuk
◙ @millsandboonuk
afterglowbooks.co.uk

#AfterglowBooks

For all the latest book news, exclusive content and giveaways scan the QR code below to sign up to the Afterglow newsletter:

SCAN ME

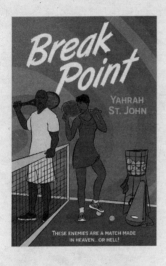
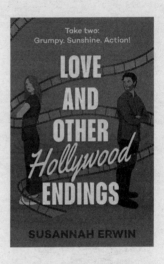
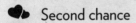
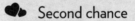
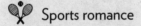
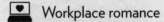
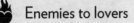
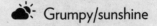

FOUR BRAND NEW BOOKS FROM
MILLS & BOON MODERN

The same great stories you love, a stylish new look!

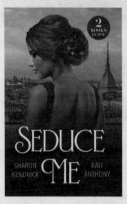

OUT NOW

Eight Modern stories published every month, find them all at:

millsandboon.co.uk

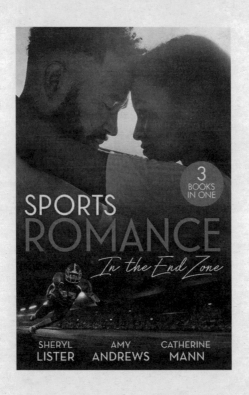